THE FLOWER IN THE SAND

GREGG E. BERNSTEIN

Table of Contents

Chapter One

A dry summer wind had finally begun to stir, mercifully escorting the flannel blanket of smog out of town and making the world safe for human respiration again. 1956 was a real bad year for smog in LA, and July was one of its worst offenders. It was too hot to do anything but sit there in my creaky swivel chair and gasp, though I suppose I was doing my lungs no favors by fostering that orphaned cigarette I'd dug out of the blackness of my desk drawer, the crumpled survivor of a long-forgotten pack of Camels. My head hurt and I was tired because of those lousy nightmares I'd been having. I get mouthy and impatient with clients—especially the crackpots—when I'm in a foul mood like this, and I know it's bad for business, but headaches every day and nightmares every night can do that to a guy. I rocked back, put my feet up on the desk and read the words backwards that the lettering guy had charged twenty-five bucks to paint on the frosted glass of my office door:

COLE DUNBAR, PRIVATE INVESTIGATIONS

It didn't really matter whether you read it forwards or backwards; no clients were coming in either way. Probably because it was too hot for *them* to do anything but gasp, either. And probably too hot to murder, blackmail, commit adultery, run away from home or skip bail, which left me out of work and wondering where my next chili dog was coming from. I mean, I *am* a private investigator, but if I got any more private, I'd be joining that smog on the next strong gust out of town.

I glared down at the phone and pleaded: "C'mon, Granite 5-6666, and earn that ten dollars the phone company is leaching from my bloodstream every month just so you can bring me some business."

Ring! Ring!

God, I love a phone that listens!

I picked up the receiver.

"Dunbar Private Investigations."

A woman's voice said, "Dunbar? It's not what you think."

"You mean you *don't* have Adolf Hitler trapped in your garage?"

"That's not funny, and neither is the reason I'm calling you."

"Then tell me the real reason, so we can *both* know it's not funny."

"I should hang up on you."

"You could, but that would defeat the purpose of the call."

"You've already done that." Her voice was throaty, with a faint whiff of finishing school; definitely not the run-of-my-office type.

I sat up a little straighter. "Sorry. Can I have another chance? It's hot, and I guess I'm a little out of practice being nice to people."

"Well, all right, but mind your manners from here on out."

I pictured my empty wallet. "Consider them minded."

"Well, as I tried to say before, this is probably not the kind of thing you're used to dealing with."

"Okay."

"And it's going to be hard for me to tell you about it."

I nodded to the receiver.

"I didn't say become a mute, Mr. Dunbar; just mind your manners."

"Okay. Uh, I mean, please go on, madam."

"Miss."

"Please go on, Miss . . . Miss . . . uh . . . ?"

"Just 'Miss' is enough."

"They say a Miss is as good as a mile."

"I liked you better as a mute."

"Check." There's no pleasing some people.

She said, "Where can we meet so we can discuss this matter in private?"

"Sounds pretty hush-hush."

"I asked you a question, Mr. Dunbar."

"Okay then, how about Pink's, tomorrow at three?"

"Really, Mr. Dunbar, I hardly think a hot dog joint is the appropriate place to discuss private business matters."

"All right then, you suggest a place." *As long as I'm not treating.*

"The Tam O'Shanter, at three, then."

"I'll be there, Miss Blank."

She barked, "Très drôle," and slammed the phone down so hard it made my headache sit up and howl again.

Was it something I said? Like I mentioned before, she was probably right about my manners. But aside from my bad mood, I just wasn't used to dealing with the carriage trade; my clientele usually skewed more toward the angry wives of philandering longshoremen. Well, I'd once had a brain with a year of college night school stuffed into it; I'd just have to dust off my courtly mien and learn to use a pickle fork again.

The next day I dug through my things until I found my most presentable tweed sport coat and a blue knit tie that, like me, had barely survived the war. I glanced in the mirror and gave myself a stern lecture about leaving the jokes and the smart remarks at home. I hoped the lecture would take, because I couldn't afford to muff this one.

I headed north on Highland then hooked a right on Franklin. Once I hit Los Feliz it was a straight shot all the way. I pulled into the parking lot and got my first look at the Tam O'Shanter. The place was kitted out as an *auld* Scottish country tavern, with half-timbered wood and whitewashed walls. I pulled open the front door and stepped inside. It looked like a good place to sign the Magna Carta: dark-beamed ceilings, dim chandelier lighting and criss-cross Tudor windows above red leather booths.

A man in earsplitting plaid presided at the front desk.

"May I help you?"

"Yeah, I'm with uh . . ."

"Oh, you're the gentleman Miss Smythe told me to watch out for. Right this way." He led me back to a dark corner table, where a gorgeous young brunette sat being admired by her martini.

She stood up and offered her hand. "Hello, Mr. Dunbar."

I doffed my hat, took her hand and gave it a quick little shake. "Nice to meet you, Miss Smythe."

"Monique, please. And how do you know my last name?"

I sat down across from her and gestured to the maître d', still standing there. "The uh, greeter, was kind enough to mention it."

The guy glared at me. "We usually say maître d'."

"Okay then, we'll split the difference: how about greeter d'?"

He slapped down two menus and flounced off in a tartan huff.

The lady shook her head. "Really, Mr. Dunbar, you must do something about your attitude."

I nodded. "Call me Cole, and a drink might help tame the wild beast." I looked around. "Where'd you get yours?"

"The maître d' knows me; it's my usual order."

A waitress came up to us. "What would you folks like?"

Monique said, "I'll have my usual tossed salad, no radish, with a glass of Burgundy."

"And you, sir?"

I cased the menu. "Let's see, bring me the Tam O'Shanter spaghetti and meatballs. And how about a beer?"

"Lucky Lager, Acme or Eastside?"

"Better make it a Lucky." I glanced at Miss Smythe. "And bring it right away, please; I may need some luck."

The waitress left, and Monique looked at me. "Sounds like you have a good appetite."

I smiled. "I never have breakfast, so I'm eating for two." Now I was close enough to see the strain on her face, a lot of it. And brittleness. It was time to quit fooling around. "So, can we get down to it? What is it that's upsetting you?"

She twisted the red cloth napkin back and forth in her hand. "There are certain things I need you for, Mr. Dunbar."

I nodded. "Good, but that doesn't tell me much. Could you be a little more specific please? Is it a crime, man trouble . . . ?"

Suddenly she flung the napkin down on the table. "I'm sorry, I just don't think this is going to work!" She shot to her feet, grabbed her things and half-ran out of the place.

The waitress arrived, having just seen Monique rush past her. She looked confused. "Here's your beer, sir. Is there, um, anything else I can do?"

It was time to do a little private investigating. "Is the lady usually, you know, this high-strung?"

The waitress shook her head. "Oh no, sir. If anything, cool as a cucumber." Her hands went to her mouth. "Hope it's okay to say that."

I nodded. "Your secret's safe with me." Maybe if I hurried, I could still catch Monique in the lot. I stood and said, "Just bring me the bill, please."

It took most of what I could dig out of my wallet and pockets, but I paid the tab and a good tip and hustled out to the parking lot, grieving my lost meal. Oh well, the Scottish aren't noted for their spaghetti and meatballs anyway.

I hoped to find Monique sitting in one of the parked cars, maybe reconsidering that hasty exit of hers. I checked out every car in the lot but rolled snake-eyes. Whatever vehicle Monique had driven here in, it was long gone now, taking my fee with it.

Now what? Stupidly, I hadn't gotten her phone number or address in that first phone conversation, so all I had to go on now was a name. I stood there with the sun doing a mean cha-cha on my ever-present headache and knew I'd have to go back into the restaurant and talk to that damn maître d' again, after the lip I'd given him at our table. But a job is a job, even though my empty pockets reminded me that I was well in arrears on this one already, and as of now the job was just a three-letter word.

Sure enough, the guy stood there at the front desk sneering at me, clearly blaming me for Monique's dramatic departure.

I approached him, hat literally in hand. "I'm sorry sir, but could I ask you a couple of questions about Miss Smythe?"

He smirked. "Tell you what: you ask 'em, then I'll tell you where you can stick 'em."

Humble does it. "Sorry, I guess I deserved that. Look, I have no idea what caused her to run out of here, but I'd really appreciate it if you could be a sport and tell me anything about how to locate her: address, phone number, or . . ."

He was still smirking. "Sorry sir, I'm just the greeter here. What would *I* know?"

Okay, he was one of those one-burned-bridge-to-a customer types, and I wasn't going to get anywhere here.

I said, "Thanks so much for your consideration," and walked back out into the dazzling smog. Oh well, I was supposed to be a professional at locating missing persons, wasn't I?

"Sir. Oh sir?"

I turned around. The waitress was standing there, looking behind her nervously to see if the maître d' was watching. She was a little bit of a thing and pretty, kind of a pocket edition Maureen O'Hara; but then a little bit of Maureen O'Hara goes a long way. Unlike the clown at the front desk, her red hair, white skin and long legs really put a Scottish burr on that tartan kilt she was wearing.

"I . . ." She looked behind her again. "Well, my name's Marie. I was your waitress?"

I nodded. "Sure, go on."

"I know where Miss Smythe lives."

I smiled. "Now we're getting somewhere. Hang on, I'll get my pencil."

She shook her head. "Oh no, I don't know the exact address or anything, but I'm sure you'll be able to find it, easy; she lives in a mansion in San Marino."

I nodded. "Hubba hubba. Big bucks, huh?"

She nodded, then looked behind her again. "Sorry, gotta get back to work before they dock me. Good luck!"

"Thanks, kid."

She took a few steps back toward the Tam, then turned back. "And my name's not kid: it's Marie . . . Marie O'Malley."

I smiled and tossed her a salute. "Thanks, Marie O'Malley." I made a mental note to give her an 'A' in spunk.

At first I was determined to get on my white horse (well, my white '49 Ford convertible, anyway) and speed off to track Monique down at home, but the longer I thought about it, the less sense it made; a runaway client is a lost client. And besides, the timing of a woman's crisis doesn't always coincide with her willingness to take action on it. So I shed a silent tear for my lost fee and pointed the car west toward the office again, thoughts crowding my head as I headed down La Brea and stopped off for a chili dog at Pink's, my favorite eating spot in town—along with The Pantry, of course.

My brain was spinning: first off, why had she called me, a low-rent bottom-feeder, when a rich girl from San Marino could afford the elite of the investigation business? Could be she wanted to keep whatever it was on the down-low, away from the prying eyes of her family and their crowd. And as for her running out of the Tam O'Shanter like that, it certainly couldn't have been from what happened at the table; as far as I knew, I'd actually kept my mouth shut this time. It must have been something that was preying on her mind already, but then once it really came down to acting on it, it became too much to face. Professional experience told me it was probably shame, fear, or a toxic brew of both.

I polished off the chili dog, told Helen, the counter woman, to put it on my tab and drove to the office with the sun searing my eyes and the smog burning my lungs. I pulled into the office lot, tossed the keys to George, the parking attendant, then hustled into the building. Considering that I didn't have a contract and hadn't been paid a cent, this case was sure taking up a lot of my time.

I rode the elevator up to four and trudged down the hallway to my office, my damp shirt sticking to me like glue. I needed a shower and a cold drink like a yowling cat needs a quickie at midnight. I opened the outer door and froze.

There sat Monique Smythe, cool, as they say, as a cucumber.

She batted her big eyes. "What took you?"

I shook my head, with a fast-building case of the mads. "Oh, nothing much; just a frantic search for one Monique Smythe, this girl who shot out of a restaurant like she had fire ants in her girdle and was never seen again. And just how the hell did you get *in* here?"

"The manager."

"But he's not supposed to . . . "

She cocked her hips. "Maybe I asked him to help me with those fire ants."

I conceded the point. "Okay, okay. So what are you doing here?"

She smiled sweetly. "Well, how are we going to do business if we don't make any arrangements? I mean, isn't there supposed to be a contract or something? Maybe even an exchange of a little money?"

I shooed her into my private office, grumbling. "I should say so, and maybe even a little extra compensation for what the party of the first part has already been put through."

She opened her red leather purse and wiggled her fingers at me absent-mindedly. "Of course, of course. Just how much do you feel all your pain and suffering has been worth so far, Mr. Dunbar?" She reached into the purse and pulled out a stack of bills that looked to me like a lifetime supply of chili dogs. She held the bills out to me, waggling them around. All that was missing was "Roll over!" and "Beg!"

I sat down in my swivel chair and began swiveling. "Look, Miss Smythe, it isn't just a matter of throwing money at this. If I'm going to get involved in this thing, I need you to level with me, about all of it."

She was still holding the money out to me like a doggie treat. I finally walked over there on my hind legs and peeled off a twenty, then double-dipped for a ten. "The twenty's because you stiffed me for the tab at the Tam O'Shanter. The ten's for the way that dim bulb at the front desk treated me."

She laughed airily. "It's always money with you people."

"Well, some of us little folk have to pay the bills with our daily toil. If I take the case, I get fifty dollars a day and expenses. But first I want to ask you one question."

"Go ahead, Mr. Dunbar, since you seem to enjoy your little games so much."

"Okay then, why me? I mean, you could have hired Harry Astrow, Ralph Birnbaum or any of the other leading lights of the profession. Why come slumming to me?"

Still trying to be lofty, she said, "Maybe because . . ." but only made it that far before tears began coursing down her cheeks.

"Look Miss, there's something you're not telling me here, and I'm not taking the job until I find out what it is."

It took her two false starts to say, "I'm not trying to be difficult or mysterious, I promise you. It's just that . . ."

She looked down and the waterworks started again.

I took the opportunity to filch a fistful of aspirins from my desk drawer and chased them with a paper cup of water from the dispenser. Then I lit a Camel and blew the smoke out slowly. "I've got all the time in the world."

I sounded tough, but there was something inside her, something soft and gooey, that was getting to me. Like me, she wasn't as tough as she pretended to be. I walked over to her and sank a hand into her soft shoulder. "Look, whatever it is, I'm sure we can figure it out together, but I have to know what I'm dealing with here."

My touch seemed to shift something. "Cole, I can't tell you everything right now. Believe me, I would if I could, but . . ."

I threw my hands up in the air. "But east is east and west is west, and brillig and the slithy tove. Good Christ, I can't do this until you're ready to do it. I don't make a move without some information—*all* of it, to be precise."

The room was like an oven. I went over and put the laboring fan on High just to show the hot air who's boss.

"You could use some air conditioning in here," she said with another toss of her head.

"Sure," I said, "and a solid-gold liquor cabinet, with a houseboy to serve us ancient Napoleon brandy."

She cooed, "Do I sense some class resentment?"

The phone rang. I stabbed at it. "Hello? Today? Just a moment." I covered the receiver and looked over at Monique. "Look, Smitty, I've got a live one on the line, who has no trouble telling me she wants me to follow her no-good, cheating husband and catch him in the act. Now, do I work for her or you?"

She held the money out to me again. "Oh Mr. Dunbar, I'll pay you, but I just can't . . ."

I turned my back on her and uncovered the receiver. "Yes, ma'am, I'm on the job. Can you make it down to my office in a half hour to sign a contract and pay my retainer? Fine, see you then." I hung up the receiver and turned around.

Monique was gone.

*   *   *

The days went by with no word from La Smythe. I didn't try to track her down. I didn't even ask around. I worked my cases by day and at night sat home drinking beer and watching the fights and ballgames on TV, and the late movies when I couldn't sleep, which was always. Once I called up a friendly gal from my past just to keep in practice—one who didn't care as much as I didn't. I went bowling a couple of times and even shot some pool, like in the old days. But mostly I tried to forget about Monique Smythe, the belle of San Marino. Hell, I had no business thinking about her in the first place; she was not only way out of my league personally and professionally, but I knew those fluttering violet eyes and that helpless manner could only spell trouble for a guy like me.

God only knows what kind of a mess a rich girl like that could get herself into—probably a lot more than a small-timer like me could bail her out of. And to get involved personally? Whew, that was just begging for it. No, I told myself, just stick to the Trixies and Angelas on *this* side of the tracks. Besides, how could a guy like me support a society girl like that anyway? Take some bullshit sinecure in Daddy's company and be a flunky for hire all my life?

No thank you, in spades. The truth was, I would never be enough for a girl like that. But there was still that something in her, that soft something, that wouldn't let me go.

Well, if my yen got too bad I could always run off and become a monk. But then those robes they wear are too hot for LA. Besides, it's hard to get a decent chili dog in a monastery.

*   *   *

Meanwhile, life in the peeper racket went on like always: deadbeat husbands, welshing debtors who lammed to Tijuana, insurance claims that smelled to high heaven, senile grandfathers who wandered off, and teenage girls who got knocked up by their Spanish teachers. I practice my trade way down in the dirty grooves of the city, where the rats and the roaches live and the decent people don't go. So I kept busy and told myself that I was well shed of Monique Smythe, trying to convince myself that it was sheer coincidence when I jerked like a marionette every time the office phone rang.

Chapter Two

Like a lot of PIs and ex-cops, I often worked security at sporting events to bring in a little extra scratch, and that Thursday night it was the Lauro Salas/Billy Evans fight, the main event at the Olympic Auditorium. On the drive down to South Grand the girls on the car radio were crooning, *Mister Sandman, bring me a dream*. Hell, the only thing Mister Sandman was bringing me was nightmares. It was getting to the point where I was almost afraid to go to sleep, knowing the chances were I'd be waking up in a cold sweat, trying to wipe images of flying body parts out of my eyes, like the guy at the gas station does with your windshield; if only a squeegee and a rag could do the job on brains.

But at the Olympic you had to keep your wits about you. Things could get pretty heated during a big fight, especially when a big Latin draw like Salas was in the ring.

The air was already buzzing as I watched guys in the long ticket lines demonstrating fancy lefts and shadow uppercuts to each other, as if they'd won all Salas' fights for him. Salas, who had taken the lightweight title from Jimmy Carter right here at the Olympic in '52, always drew a packed house because he was the pet of all the Mexican fans. But he was heavily favored tonight, so it was doubtful things would get out of hand as they sometimes did when a Mexican fighter lost a big one.

I spied Joe Antonio, an old buddy from my days on the police force who was moonlighting on security that night like me. He was casting a cop's wary eye on stands already filling up with beered-up, flag-waving Latinos. After we greeted each other he grunted, "Think they'll tear the place up?"

I shook my head. "Naw, don't think so. Salas'll probably finish this tomato can off quick, then we'll collect our pay and go home to a good night's sleep." Of course, the last part of that statement was just a joke in my case.

I was right about the fight at least. Salas dominated from the first bell, finally knocking Evans down and out in the seventh, which catapulted the crowd into a frenzy of joy and national pride, as people strutted the aisles yelling, "Viva Mexico!" waving those red, white and green flags with the eagle and serpent in the middle. There was even a guy dressed up like an Aztec warrior who strutted the aisles, waving lighted sparklers in the air.

Then I saw two fat drunks start their own heavyweight fight on the concrete steps just above me. As I ran to break it up, someone tossed a big cup of beer at my head and scored a bullseye. I didn't pay it any attention at the time, as I had my hands full separating the two struggling Mexicans, each one of whom tagged me good at least once as the three of us wrestled around together on the floor. It was only after I'd separated the two *vatos locos* and noticed people pulling away from me that I realized the extra-large cup that hit me had been loaded with pee. Son of a bitch! Unfortunately, no one does security for the security people.

I went upstairs where Aileen Eaton, the dragon lady of the Olympic, paid me off, averting her head in disgust as she held the money out to me with one tentative hand and said, "Go get yourself a shower, pretty boy."

In the parking lot I bent down and picked up some discarded fight programs from the asphalt to stuff between my clothes and the car seats. The fetid reek of urine that clung to me only ripened in the muggy air. As soon as I got in the Ford, I rolled down all the windows and gunned it. The night wind helped a little.

Finally home, I dived into a nice hot shower, then held a frozen steak against my aching jaw and tried to forget the whole night. Usually I would have wanted a couple of cold ones from the icebox, but I'd had enough beer, or reasonable facsimiles thereof, for one night, so I settled for a Camel and a big water glass of Thriftimart Bourbon.

That night I had a real pipperoo of a nightmare again, starring Okinawa of course. It was even accurate, right down to the stink of the mud and the ghastly faces of the dead. And like Okinawa, it seemed endless. I finally jerked awake around four thirty, breathing heavy, my head swimming with unwanted houseguests. I stumbled to my feet and tossed my soaked skivvies into the hamper, then put on a fresh pair and hoped for at least a couple hours of honest sleep before the new day smacked me in the face. I finally willed myself back to sleep and didn't wake up till late morning, still feeling like my brain was packed with coarse-ground sand.

*   *   *

It was time to see Doc Grimes again. He was a local psychiatrist I knew from the war, whom I'd been seeing since my "combat fatigue" returned, whenever we could match up his cancelations with my erratic schedule. He'd been out of town recently on some kind of research trip, but I was pretty sure he was back now.

I dialed his office and got his secretary.

"Hi Katy, it's Cole Dunbar. How're you fixed for times?"

"Hang on, I'll check." I waited a minute or so. "Looks like we've got an opening today at four and, let's see, next Tuesday, anytime from two to five."

"I'll take the Tuesday at two."

"Got it. You're on the book."

"Keep your seams straight."

"Gee, you're such a romantic."

Maybe you're wondering what the deal is about my seeing a psychiatrist. Well, Dr. James Grimes wasn't always a psychiatrist, and I wasn't always a private eye. The short form is that I was an eighteen-year-old Marine on Okinawa toward the end of the war. The constant bombardment by artillery and the neverending demands for impossible assaults on enemy positions, plus the rain, the mud and the stench of death were enough to drive anyone crazy, but when a mortar landed right in front of my best friend Danny Trueluck and changed him from a human being into chunks of airborne meat seasoned with a fine red mist, they tell me I started screaming and wouldn't stop. Someone yelled "Corpsman!" and I ended up being dragged out of there by a guy I only knew as Doc.

By the time they hauled me off in my semi-delirious state, I barely even remembered landing on Okinawa; what I didn't know till much later was how hard Okinawa had landed on *me*, planting its own battle flag of hurt and pain deep in my soul.

Later, on the hospital ship Mercy, I found out the corpsman's name was James Grimes. He eventually got me set up stateside at Long Beach Naval Hospital, where they helped me put the pieces back together, or at least good enough to set me free on an unsuspecting public again. Later I looked up Doc Grimes to thank him, and we kept in touch after the war as I became a cop and he became a doctor, then a psychiatrist.

So I guess it was only natural for me to seek him out a few months ago, when reality began skidding sideways on me again and I started having the old nightmares. I'm not one to ask for help, and I would have felt like a sissy admitting I had "combat fatigue" to anyone who hadn't been there, but with Jim I knew he'd understand. Danny Trueluck always joked that his last name would keep him safe, and I guess I half-believed that it would ... until it didn't. Soldiers and anyone else who goes into danger for a living tend to believe in things like signs, lucky charms and omens. But after Danny was hit, I didn't believe in luck anymore; I only believed in things I could see, hear or touch—and not even most of them. The moral of losing Danny slapped me in the face the instant he died: Don't get close to anyone again. Don't let anyone in.

But Doc? Well, I was at least willing to let him take a crack at me.

Oh, and one more thing about Doc Grimes: he wasn't one of those Freudian stiffs who never reveal anything about themselves, so that when you ask, "What do you think about that, Doc?" they say, "Hmm, so you're wondering what I'm thinking; what's that like for you?" Believe me, I saw plenty of doctors like that in the VA hospital. Nope, Doc Grimes was a regular guy; we could talk frankly about anything I brought up, man to man, and even Marine to Marine. I never imagined myself needing a head doctor again after all those years, but lately it seemed like my mind was going AWOL whenever it damn well felt like it; the crazy mood swings and the instant rages weren't very good for business, nor did they exactly dazzle the ladies. But that last part was okay with me because lately my idea of the good life was kind of like FDR's Four Freedoms, except that mine were: freedom from needing other people; freedom from being controlled by other people; freedom from being observed by other people; and freedom from having to promise things I couldn't deliver to people. Especially women.

I only hoped I could make it through the weekend to our Tuesday appointment.

Speaking of my mind, I still thought about Monique Smythe once in a while. All right then, more than once in a while. But I kept shoving her into the back of my mind.

If only she'd stay put.

The next afternoon I popped some more aspirin and drove myself down to the office. If my headache got any bigger, I was gonna have to ask it to sit in the back seat. The heat outside was terrible and the smog wasn't far behind it.

But if I expected the office to be any better, I was sadly mistaken. I sat there for awhile cursing my feeble office fan and praying for clients who could write their names without making an X. Sure, I could have worked on a few of the crummy cases still stuck in my backlog: following husbands to ratty hotels where they met up with willing, mousy girls who actually believed the eternal bedsheet fables about men leaving their wives, and checking on suspicious business partners whose bank accounts had no right to show a sudden bulge of ten thousand dollars. But somehow in this heat I just couldn't summon the oomph to make my body move. Besides, it could wait; cheating husbands, willing mice and light-fingered business partners would always be there. I wanted something different, something interesting, something worthy.

The phone rang. I reached down and scooped up the receiver.

"Dunbar Investigations."

"Dunbar?"

"Yeah."

"Every mile you stay away from Monique Smythe is another day you get to live. Got it?"

The voice was a raspy growl, like Broderick Crawford on that new cop show, *Highway Patrol.* Only meaner. Well, at least the guy had the right voice for this kind of work; I was glad he'd found his metier in life.

Unfortunately, he'd also found my weak spot: a fierce dislike for being told what I can and can't do. I snapped, "And I'd suggest the same formula back to you, only now it's about *you* staying away from *me*, Bonzo."

He growled. "Did you hear me? I mean it!"

"Get the wax out of your ears, big boy, and you'll live a lot longer. I can even suggest a good ear, nose and throat man if you're new in town."

"Keep it up and you won't even *have* a throat."

"Better hang up, because this is a toll call."

"No, it ain't."

"Sure it is, because I just *toll* you to fuck off!"

I slammed down the receiver.

Scare-boy goons like that didn't bother me. At least not much. What concerned me more was why he was so hot and bothered about my being in contact with Monique Smythe, when I hadn't been within an incorporated city of her for weeks. Unless she'd told someone that I . . .

Dammit. Now, whether I liked it or not, I had to get in touch with her and find out if—and if, then why—she'd set me up as a clay pigeon. I grabbed the Pasadena phone book from the pile on top of the file cabinet and paged to the esses. Let's see, Samuels, Saul, Smith, Smythe . . . here it was: Monique L. Smythe. I dialed the number and it rang once, twice. . .

"Hello?"

There was that cool voice again. It still got to me. "Monique?"

"Uh, yessss . . ."

"You know it's me, don't you?"

"Well, let's just say this call isn't a complete surprise."

"And why would that be?"

"Because . . . well, I guess I've been a naughty girl."

Shit, it *was* her doing. "How so? And try and be specific for once in your life, since *my* life is now on the line."

"I told . . . somebody, that you were working for me, protecting me." She paused. "But don't worry, I told them you're just my bodyguard, not a detective or anything." She paused again. "Well, I had to scare them with *something*, didn't I?"

I sighed. "So you set me up as the target in a shooting gallery without either telling me, *or* paying me?"

"You make it sound so bad."

19

"Be my guest: make it sound *good.*"

"Sorry, I guess it was pretty underhanded."

"And inconsiderate too; don't forget inconsiderate."

"Yes, and inconsiderate too."

Apologies were nice, but none of this was helping get my head off the chopping block, or my bank account out of the red, either.

Finally, she said, "So what do we do now?"

"Well, since there's probably no way they'd ever believe you if you just said, 'Sorry fellas, I take it back; I made up the whole thing about Dunbar,' there's really no choice now but to hire me legitimately and . . ."

"And . . . and tell you everything?"

"There *is* a God!"

"That's not fair, Mr. Dunbar. I assure you, the man who called you wasn't joking, and neither are the men behind him."

"As in who? And why? I assure you too, Miss Dunbar, I'm not joking either, especially now. You've involved me in this mess up to my neck, and you owe me an explanation, a detailed explanation, beginning right now!"

"I . . . I can't talk right now, not here. Meet me at the Tam O'Shanter tomorrow at one, and I'll tell you everything that you . . . well, that you need to know."

"No! Dammit Monique, not just what I need to know: everything, period!"

"All right, all right. Goodnight . . . Cole."

We hung up.

Why was she still so determined to keep information from me? Was it self-incriminating? Embarrassing? Illegal? Was she protecting someone else? Or was it that what I didn't know, I couldn't blab? Or maybe use against her? I just didn't know, and I hate not knowing; maybe that's why I became a PI in the first place, to find some answers.

What I did know, dammit, is that I liked it when she called me Cole. I liked it too much. And that scared me silly, because in my racket, liking anything more than fifty-bucks-worth a day is just plain stupid.

Chapter Three

The smug maître d' at the Tam O'Shanter was there at his post again when I walked in, giving me a smile that could flash-freeze the sun.

He gestured to the rear and led the way. "Right this way, Mr. Dumbarton."

"It's Dunbar."

"Sorry, Mr. Dunn."

Maître d's are always good with names, so I knew the guy was just putting the needle to me. But it was okay; I'd see to it that he was left out of my will.

"Well hello, Cole. How nice to see you again."

Monique stood up like a little gentleman when I arrived and waved me to the seat opposite her. This time I got right down to ordering my drink: "Johnny Walker, rocks, please." Then I fluttered my fingers at the maître d' like Monique had done to me and said, "You may go now."

The guy's face turned Royal Stewart red and he stomped off.

Monique picked up her martini. "Your manners apparently haven't improved much since our last meeting."

"Sorry, Smitty, I guess I forgot I was supposed to be working on 'em; there isn't much call for that sort of thing in my set."

She nodded, eyeing my beat-up leather jacket. "I can easily believe that. And don't call me Smitty!"

Maureen O'Hara Junior brought my drink. "You folks ready to order?" She shot me an appraising look that didn't come out of *Better Homes and Gardens*. I appreciated it.

Monique made a show of looking at the menu, then said, "My usual salad, Miss."

I added, "And could you add a dash of truth serum to her dressing, please?"

Monique shot me a glare. The waitress caught it and had to hold the menu in front of her dimpled grin.

I said, "I believe I'll have another go at that Tam O'Shanter spaghetti and meatballs. But please hold the garlic bread; I may be doing some close work later." I winked at the waitress as she took my menu. Her green eyes twinkled back at me.

Monique saw it all and didn't like it much.

Then the waitress couldn't resist stirring the pot a little. "Will you be wanting your usual beer with that, sir?"

Before I could answer, Monique barked, "Beat it!" The girl took off.

I held up a finger. "Nah-ah-ah, where are *your* manners now, Miss Smythe?"

She tossed down the rest of her martini and snapped, "Do you want to do some business or not, Dunbar?"

I snapped right back, at least as impatient as she was. "It's about time, don't you think? Say what you have to say, already."

She held up her empty glass and twirled it at a passing waiter, then began. "All right then, here it is, in high fidelity." She opened her mouth, then stopped. "Hold on. Are things between us confidential, as far as you talking to anybody else about it?"

I nodded. "They are once I'm hired by you: contract, retainer and all."

She put her hand on mine and murmured, "We won't have to go all the way to your office for that, will we?"

I barked, "Yes, we will," enjoying myself immensely.

She shot to her feet. "Fine, then let's go there now and make it official."

She started gathering her things to leave but I grabbed her arm. "Not so fast there. I ordered a meal, and this time, I'm eating every last meatball."

She had a nice arm.

Turns out it's true, there's a good reason the Scottish aren't noted for their spaghetti and meatballs. But making Monique pick up the tab eased the pain a little.

By three we were sitting in my office, finished with all the paperwork. She had agreed readily to my fee of fifty dollars a day plus expenses, and I had a hundred-dollar retainer in hand. I leaned back in my chair and said, "Okay, Miss Smythe, shoot."

"Monique, please."

"First I hear your story; then we'll see what your name is."

"All right then, it all began about four years ago. You may not have suspected this, but we weren't always wealthy. Daddy was doing moderately well in the accounting business he'd been running for twenty years or so, but we weren't really rich or anything." She turned to me. "You see, Daddy has, or at least had, a tendency to drink a bit too much, so what easily could have been a big business, competing with the national firms, was just limited to the LA area."

I nodded. "Yeah, I'm getting the picture." I was also getting the picture that she hadn't been too satisfied with Daddy just being a big deal in LA.

"He rented office space in a big, six-story office building on Wilshire from two wealthy investors who'd owned the building for years."

I nodded again. "Go on."

"Well, one day they came into my father's office and asked him if he wanted to buy the building from them." She looked at me. "I know, you're thinking that makes no sense. Father did too, at first, but they explained to him that for reasons they couldn't discuss, they had to cash out of the property within days, so they were offering it to him at a remarkably low price, if he could close on the deal immediately with a title company of their choice, and not tell anyone about it. It had to be immediate, and absolutely confidential."

This wasn't making much sense, but I nodded for her to continue.

"When Daddy asked how much they wanted for it, they said seventy-five thousand dollars."

I shook my head. "Seventy-five thousand bucks for a big office building like that, right on Wilshire?"

She nodded. "Yes, seventy-five thousand. And what's more, when Daddy scrambled to liquidate all his assets and told them that sixty thousand was all he could raise right away in cash, they said they'd take fifteen thousand of it back in a personal note, due and payable in four years, at two percent interest."

I said, "But who owned the paper on the building, the original mortgage?"

"The two of them owned it free and clear, so it was entirely up to them to decide how much they wanted for it, as well as all the financing details." She paused. "So what could Daddy say but yes? He figured if they were crazy enough to sell it to him for a song, that was their problem. So three days later, they went down to the title company and sold him a six-story office building, as is, for seventy-five thousand dollars, on the terms I've just described."

I was still shaking my head. "Hmm, that's what any competent attorney would call 'lack of reasonable consideration in the conveyance.'" I crooked my finger at her and said, "Okay, now read me the last chapter," expecting to hear about roofs, termites, fault-lines, foundations and other delights.

"So father took title, had inspections—which turned up virtually clear—and insured it in his name for its real value, which was several hundred thousand. He figured with the rents alone, he'd be set for life."

"And then?"

"Two days later, the whole building burned to the ground."

I said, "Arson? Gotta be."

She shook her head. "But who would stand to benefit? The old owners had been paid off and were out of the picture, and Daddy had all the earning power of renting out space in a desirable building for the rest of his life, and *my* life, so why would *he* burn it down? And as far as arson goes, the police arson squad, the fire department and the insurance investigators who swarmed over the whole building all concluded that it was a legitimate fire, maybe caused by faulty wiring. Just . . . " she shrugged, " . . . one of those freakish things."

"And the insurance company just paid out the claim with a smile?"

She shook her head again. "Oh my goodness no. They put Daddy through the wringer for months and months. They even tried to record our phone calls and had surveillance men following father's every move. They finally offered to pay him half of the covered amount immediately, no questions asked, in return for their dropping the investigation and the harassment. By that time, a couple of years had gone by, and Daddy was hitting the bottle pretty hard again from all the stress he was under. And believe me, we could really have used that money. But father held on, and finally they had to pay him off, in full." She paused. "By the time we got the settlement, Daddy was too beaten down to even think of rebuilding, so he just put all the insurance money in the bank, sold the lot for a hundred thousand, and retired."

I cocked my head at her. "You said the old owners were gone. But what about your father's paying off that fifteen thousand mortgage? It should be due right about now."

"At the time of the sale, they said they'd be in touch with him later to set up the payoff."

I said, "But then they vanished, never to be heard from again, leaving fifteen thousand bucks on the table?"

She nodded. "To my knowledge, no one has ever seen them again. At least no one in LA."

I lit a cigarette and took a big drag. "Okay then, it's a wonderful fairy story and all's well that ends well." I looked at her. "Is that right?"

"Well no, not exactly. This is where it gets hard."

"Hard to deal with, or hard to tell me?"

"Both." She fixed me with a matched set of spectacular violet eyes and gestured to my Camels. "Lend me one of those things, would you?"

I flipped one out of the pack. She caught it. "Light?"

I leaned close and lit her with mine, trying to ignore her perfume. "I take it this is where Broderick Crawford comes in?"

She frowned. "Who?"

"The guy with the gravel voice and the refined manners, who called and threatened my life if I continued consorting with you."

She hung her head. "Yes, he's been threatening me, too."

"About what?"

"Like I said, this is where it gets hard."

"Look Miss Smythe, I don't take money for nothing. I only get *hired* when things get hard, so will you please quit shillyshallying and get down to it already?"

She looked at me again. "You're absolutely sure all this is confidential?"

I sighed. "Look, we've been all through this before: you tell me things, and I don't tell them to anyone else—that's the way it works. Now, can we finally do some business here?"

She hung her head. "Okay then, I'm being blackmailed."

"By Broderick?"

She shook her head. "No, he's just muscle for rent. Probably doesn't even know what it's all about."

"Well, he's running neck-and-neck with me then."

She was close to tears. "Please be patient, Cole, I'm getting there. They . . . they say they have proof that Daddy set the fire, or at least hired the arsonist who did the job."

I held out my hands. "But if he didn't . . ."

She shook her head. "The truth doesn't matter. Can't you see that? The police department and the insurance people ended up with egg on their face after all their investigations; they're both just licking their chops to pin it on Daddy—they have been for years. They'd go for some phonied-up evidence like a shot, if it was half-plausible. That's why I dare not go to the police for help." She drew a lungful of smoke. "Especially since the circumstances of father's purchase of the property were so . . ."

"Hinky?"

"Yes, if you must use slang."

"So, what are they demanding?"

"It's been five hundred a month for the past six months or so. But now that they know I'm scared, it's escalating. Their latest demand is a thousand a month. But I'm sure that's just small change for them; they're working up to the big score. That's why I . . ."

"Why you called me?"

"Yes. But there's more to it than that."

"You mean Hitler really *is* in your garage?"

"Please be serious about this, Mr. Dunbar. The rest of it is that father is not well, not since all the stress of dealing with the police and the insurance investigators—plus, you know, his drinking. A few months ago I had to put him in a . . ."

"Rest home?"

"If you want to call it that, yes." She looked up at me, pleading. "And if . . ."

"And if he were to be embroiled in any more trouble, such as a jail term stemming from phonied-up evidence, it would just kill him?"

She nodded quietly. "They've also indicated in no uncertain terms that even if their phony evidence scheme doesn't work, they'll see to it that Daddy doesn't last very long."

Now I had to do a part of my job I truly hated. I took a big drag on my cigarette and dived in. "Look, Miss Smythe, has it ever occurred to you that maybe your father actually *did* have something to do with that fire?"

She turned white. "Oh no! No, father could never do a thing like that! Absolutely not. How could you even imply such a thing?"

"Look, this is no fun for me either, but I have to look at it from all angles. And while we're on the subject, what exactly is it that you want me to do for you?"

"I want you to get these horrible bloodsuckers off my back, and off father's back. Oh, it's not just about the money, not for me. But this rest home, as you call it, is expensive, and it's important to me that father have the best of care for as long as he needs it. You see, he's all I have. He raised me alone after mother died when I was ten, and he means the world to me."

I said, "Is that why he drank?"

"You mean mother's death? Yes, that's how it started. He loved her very much, and he never really got over losing her. So I had to become . . ."

"The woman in his life? His nursemaid?"

She shrugged. "Yes, I suppose so, since you seem to have a knack for putting things in the harshest light."

"Okay, so let me put it even more bluntly: they're bleeding you for money, the money you need to keep Daddy in proper care, and you feel it's only a matter of time before they grab for the big bankroll and destroy whatever quality of life is left for him. And you want me to get them off your back so you can finally relax and get sloshed at the Tam O'Shanter in peace." I looked at her. "Am I close?"

"Mister Dunbar, has anyone ever told you that you're a . . ."

"Several times, and in more colorful language than you could. But I'm still asking; did I paint the basic picture?"

She nodded in resignation.

"And is there more that you haven't told me yet?"

She shook her head. "No, that's it, the whole story, except . . ."

"Except what? Let's have it, already."

She seemed to struggle for a moment. Then, with a defeated look, she said, "Except they said that if I went to anyone for help, they'd harm that person and . . . and maybe me, too." She started crying again. "You see, that's why I was so reluctant to talk to you or engage your services in this thing; I didn't want anyone to get hurt."

I nodded. "I appreciate your concern, but you can't let these goons push you around like that."

She was still crying. And what it did to those big violet eyes made me understand why poets embarrass themselves by writing sappy stuff like "limpid pools."

She gathered herself and went on. "Maybe I'm not as brave as you are, Mr. Dunbar. You're used to danger; I'm not." She put her hand on my arm and drew closer to me. "And maybe I need your moral support as much as your professional help. I'm scared for myself, scared for Daddy, and now, scared for you too."

I squeezed her hand. "Okay then Monique, I'll be your private investigator *and* your moral support too, if that's what you need."

"Oh it is, Cole. Thank you."

Her swooning routine, fake or not, found its mark, but I wasn't being paid for romance. If I was going to be any help to her, practically *or* emotionally, we needed to get down to business. I took a deep breath. "All right then, do you have any idea how I can go about accomplishing what you're asking me to do?"

"Mister Dunbar, that's why I'm hiring *you*! I wouldn't have the slightest idea how to handle the kind of animals who'd do such things to innocent people!"

I nodded. "Just checking. Like I said, I have to look at this thing from all angles, and a smart private investigator takes ideas wherever he can get 'em."

Now I could see the fine lines of strain and exhaustion beneath her washed-out makeup. I said, "Just one more question: how much time do you think we have?"

She turned her head at me. "I'm not quite sure what you mean."

"Have they given any hint about when they're going to lower the boom?"

She licked her lips. "Oh, I see. Well, I just paid the first thousand yesterday, so I assume at this point they're like a lion that's just been fed. But God only knows what people like that are capable of, or when."

I nodded. "You keep saying, 'these people' and 'them'. Are you saying you have no idea who they are? Couldn't it just be the original owners, coming back for what they considered the real value of the property?"

She shrugged. "Cole, anything's possible. I have no way of knowing. There must be all sorts of people who try to prey on the wealthy."

"Do you have any personal knowledge of the original owners?"

Her head went back with an impatient sigh. "Cole, you're the detective; try and remember that! I was barely twenty when that transaction happened; to me, they're just two names on a sheet of paper from one of Daddy's old business deals."

I nodded. "Okay then, here's the plan: from here on out, please be very careful what you say about me, or the case, to other people. And that includes your friends, too. If there's anything important you need to tell me, you can always leave a confidential message with my answering service; they're very trustworthy. Right now, we're just flying blind. In fact, we can't even be sure the insurance company, or even some rogue cops, aren't involved in this thing."

Her eyes went wide. "Oh my God, you actually think . . ."

"I don't know, but I do know that good people sometimes go bad when there's lots of money on the table, Miss Smythe. Not to mention that cops get pretty mad when they grab for a collar and end up with a handful of nothing. And insurance companies aren't exactly thrilled when they think they've been taken for a very expensive sleigh ride, or even when they *haven't* been taken for a ride but have to shell out big bucks. So I repeat, don't mention me to anyone, since we don't know who we can trust." I stubbed out my cigarette. "Now, where do you make the payoff each month?"

"I mail it to a post office box, in cash. A different one each month. Always out of town. They tell me where, just before I send it."

"So you've never seen anyone in person?"

"No."

"Okay now, just go home and go about your life normally, at least as much as possible. I'll be in touch as soon as I know anything. Now, they already suspect that you might have hired me. If they ask you, just say you thought about it but were too frightened to go ahead with it. And if anyone asks me, I'll deny that you're a client of course, as I would in any case. But if they get wind that I'm snooping around, and that you're not alone in this anymore, they might panic and start to get . . ."

She blanched. "Hinky?"

"Yes, hinky. So just sit tight and make sure and let me know if anything unusual happens." I sighed. "Okay then, I guess that's about it for now." I paused. "I assume you know this investigation may take quite a while and end up costing you a fair amount of money; from the looks of it these people aren't kidding, and they've probably covered their tracks pretty well."

She nodded. "I understand that, Mr. Dunbar. The most important thing to me is seeing to it that Daddy lives out his life as comfortably as possible."

"Okay then, I'm on the case."

She slung her purse strap over her shoulder and headed out, then turned back at the doorway. "Oh, and one more thing, Cole."

"Yes?"

"My name's Monique to you, not Miss Smythe." She opened the door, then turned back again and smiled. "You can even call me Smitty, if you simply must." She tossed her head like Rita Hayworth and added, "Just don't overdo it."

She certainly knew how to put the period on a sentence. I threw her a confident smile out of duty, but my insides knew there was nothing to grin about. The whole thing smelled to high heaven, and to be perfectly honest, I felt like both the girl and the case were out of my league.

Unlike most of the standard, penny ante stuff I worked on every day, the whole Smythe case really came down to one thing: what the hell was really going on here? Like pin the tail on the donkey, I was working blindfolded, and these donkeys probably had a few pins of their own. I'm not proud; I knew I was playing over my head this time and the whole thing might just end up being another big cup of pee in the face.

So instead of wasting my time and my client's money unnecessarily, I decided the smartest way to start untangling a rat's nest is to go see a master rat.

I needed a meeting with Bert Fawcett, the uncrowned king of the LA confidence racket.

But even before that, I needed to see Doc Grimes to get my head straight, or at least straighter.

Chapter Four

The next day at two on the dot I showed up at Doc Grimes' building on Washington Boulevard and took the elevator up to his office. Katy gave me a nod and I settled in with my old friend, a tattered edition of *The New Yorker* from September, 1950.

Finally Jim came out with a look of concern on his face. He gestured to me and said, "C'mon in and let's see what's going on with you, champ."

I went in and sat on the recliner while Doc took a seat in his leather chair. He looked me over carefully before saying, "Okay, out with it."

I said, "Out with what?"

He smiled; we had played this little game so many times before. He said, "I think you know what. Now don't make me beg, Mac."

That familiar Marine talk finally made me smile too. "Sorry Doc, I'm not trying to be a jerk. But whenever you ask me what's going on with me, why do I always have the immediate urge to say, 'Don't worry, I'm fine.'?"

He thought a minute then said, "Hmm, sounds to me like you don't want to be a bother."

That hit bingo somewhere inside me. "So what's wrong with not wanting to be a bother? Isn't that just basic consideration?"

Jim shrugged. "Look, you're here to let me help you, man. It's not a bother, just a pain in the ass when you won't tell me what's really happening in that sealed vault of yours."

He was right, of course, which I knew well from being on the other end of the interrogation game with Monique. I took a breath and finally managed to say, "Okay then, for a minute there, I might have felt kind of sad. That's all."

"Sad? How?"

"I don't know what you mean; how many kinds of sad are there?"

He laughed. "No, that's not what I'm talking about. I mean, take me inside the sadness. What is it like? Where do you feel it? And tell me anything else that comes up when you allow yourself to feel it."

I was blank.

We sat there in silence until Jim said, "What's going on right now?"

"It's kind of hard to say; it's almost like there's a war going on inside, and each side cancels the other out."

"You mean a war about whether to let yourself feel the sadness or not?"

"Yeah, I guess that's one way to put it. It's like one part of me wants to push it away because . . ."

"Because what?"

I was blank again.

"Cole, go on, please."

"Hell, I'm trying. But I keep going blank." I paused. "Jesus, give me a minute, willya?"

He held up his hands. "No problem. I'm not trying to pressure you, just encourage you."

"Well, it feels like pressure when you do that."

"Okay, I'll shut up then, and let you decompress for a while."

That helped a little. I made a couple of vain attempts, then said, "Okay, look; it's like I'm trying to watch a stage play, but this black curtain keeps coming down to block the action."

Jim just nodded. "Stay with it."

I finally settled down a little and tried to "go inside" as he had demanded, er requested, er suggested. But I came up with something else instead. "You know, I think part of this is that it's hard for me to, you know, switch gears in here." I looked up at him to see if it registered.

He nodded slowly. "You mean switch gears from the tough guy Marine to the sensitive guy in therapy?"

I nodded back. "Yeah, I guess so, but maybe the tough guy detective, too. There's something about not believing anybody that . . ."

"You mean the cynicism and the shell you developed from the war carried over easily into the world of a cop or a private investigator, but it doesn't work so well in here?"

I considered that for a moment. "Yeah, I never really thought of it that way, but I think you might have something there."

He nodded. "I would imagine the defenses inside you that are in charge of the black curtain are saying they went to a hell of a lot of trouble to make that curtain, so now they're not very interested in helping us tear it down. Especially when you have to go back out into the tough world of a PI."

That brought on another wave of sadness, but before I could capture it, it went away and I stayed maddeningly blank for the rest of the session. I blamed myself for wasting my money and both of our time while I just sat there like a lump.

Finally Jim said, "Are you back yet?"

I shrugged. "Not really. It seems like once I go away like that . . ."

He smiled. "Guess we'll have to work on resilience, too."

Resilience? It was all Greek to me.

At the end of the hour, Jim left me with this: "Consider the proposition that there might be more than one way of being tough; putting up a black curtain is only one."

I nodded agreeably just to be polite, but I had no idea what he was talking about.

I got up to leave. When I reached the door, Doc said, "You know, wounds can be dressed, broken limbs can be set, but when you lose your faith in things . . . you can't find that at the missing persons bureau."

*   *   *

After the session I made a beeline for Pink's. The chili dog I ordered seemed to satisfy something deep down inside that had been stirred up by the session. But I knew it was just a quick fix, and the emptiness would return again and again like Monique's blackmailer.

I looked at my watch; I had an important appointment at four with Bert Fawcett—a friend, and, to be honest, even a mentor of sorts. Bert was a very unique guy, a con artist extraordinaire and savvy businessman, albeit usually on the shady side of the law. I thought of him as the Meyer Lansky of the LA underworld, a criminal savant who was the brains behind a lot of the smart money, a guy who said, "I only take from those who deserve it." Having been a cop, I couldn't agree with him there, of course, but if it was possible for anyone to be a master criminal and still a decent human being, Bert Fawcett was the guy.

I pulled into a parking space on Ventura Boulevard in front of a row of those sparkly white, three-story stucco boxes that housed legions of lawyers, accountants and other legitimate enterprises. I remembered from the old days that it was right down the street from the Tail O' the Cock, a bar where all of us cops used to congregate at night after we pulled shifts in that part of the Valley.

Bert's office was on the top floor of one of those stucco boxes, fronting Ventura Boulevard. In the elevator I pushed three and went up, wondering what I was really here for. I walked down the hall until I came to the fancy lettering on the door: "Argyle Investments."

I recognized Norma, his secretary, from my old days on the force when I sometimes came to Bert for leads, wearing my cop uniform. "Cole Dunbar to see Mr. Argyle, please."

She looked up and grinned. "A little out of character, aren't you, Mr. Dunbar? You used to play for the blue team, as I recall."

I returned her smile. "In business for myself nowadays, and sometimes exigency makes strange bedfellows."

That earned me an appreciative nod for vocabulary. "I'll tell him you're here."

As I sat there waiting on the chic, off-white Naugahyde couch, thoughts of my session with Doc kept sidetracking my mind: what the hell did he mean about there being different ways of being a tough guy?

"Hi, Cole, c'mon in."

Bert was tall, lean and dapper, a handsome middle-aged fox with thick, wavy white hair, piercing blue eyes, a perennial tan and the kind of face that you would trust all the way to the bank, where he would pat you on the shoulder with one hand while depleting your account with the other, all while making you thank him for it. If con artists are the aristocrats of the criminal world, then Bert Fawcett was the king of kings.

"So what brings you down to my humble digs?" he said in his best honey baritone, guiding me into a plush, oak-paneled office that was cool and comfortable. Bert Fawcett had *real* air conditioning.

I settled into a chair that did everything but bring you a cup of coffee and said, "Well see, I'm on this case."

He smiled. "Whew, I guess that oughta cover your office rent for at least *this* month."

I gave him a wry look and went on. "So, here's the thing: number one, I can't tell if I'm being set up or not; and number two, even if I'm not, I don't know which way to move without stepping in dog shit."

He pulled two Cuban cigars from the humidor on his desk and held one out to me.

I shook my head. "No thanks, I'll stick to my humble Camels."

He lit up one of the cigars, puffed on it till it glowed, then regarded it at arm's length as he rolled it between his fingers. "Well, I already know a couple of things right away. One, something's 'off' about the whole deal, or you wouldn't even be here. And two, there's a woman involved."

I shook my head incredulously. "Dammit, now how could you know that?"

He leaned way back in his chair. "That's why you're here, isn't it, because I know things? So let's skip the ABCs and get to the heart of the matter. Now tell me all the details as you know them, so I won't have to keep amazing you with my little tricks."

In fifteen minutes, I'd filled him in on everything I knew about the Smythe case.

The phone rang. Bert held up a finger to me and took the call. He said, "Uh huh" twice, then "Yeah, good work," and hung up. Then he turned back to me and said, "So in essence here's what we have: a girl comes to you and tells you a tale about her father being offered a fabulous deal on an office building years ago. He does the deal, then shortly afterwards the place burns down. It looks like arson, but to everyone's surprise, it apparently isn't. After years of wrangling, the insurance company finally pays off, but by this time Daddy is too worn out to rebuild, so he pockets the insurance money, sells the lot and retires. But by now his health and nerves are shot, so he needs to be put into a fancy rest home, which the loving daughter gladly pays for. But now some anonymous individual or gang is blackmailing her with threats of shoving Daddy into a frame for arson, whether he did it or not. It scares her, so she pays 'em off, but now they want more, and she's sure that soon they're gonna want the whole ball of wax. So she comes to you and begs you to intervene in some way to get them off her back so she and Daddy can live happily ever after on the payoff money." He thought for a moment, then added, "Oh, and you'd also prefer to live out the rest of *your* natural life without it being prematurely foreshortened."

I started to say something, but he held up his hand and went on. "And you're coming here hoping I can tell you what the hell is really going on, so you'll know what to do next."

I nodded, throwing him a silent salute. Strangely enough, I felt better just knowing that Bert Fawcett had all the information.

He closed his eyes as he took another thoughtful puff on his cigar, then looked at me. "So the first things you need to find out are: Was there really a building? Was there really a sale? Is there really a Daddy? Is he really sick? Who is this girl, really? Does she or Daddy have a criminal background? Is she really being blackmailed?" He looked over at me. "But of course, I assume you covered all those preliminaries before coming to see me, right?"

I shook my head, feeling like a complete idiot. "Jeez, you make it all sound so simple. And no, I haven't done any of those things yet."

He frowned. "Why not? You know your business as well as I know mine; why come to me for advice at this early stage?"

I licked my lips. "I just didn't want to . . ."

He smiled. "Fuck it up?"

I nodded.

Now he was grinning. "Aha, so *that's* where the girl comes in!"

"What's that supposed to mean?"

He smiled again. "I think you know what it means."

"Well, I admit I don't want to fuck it up, but the reason I came to you was to save myself a whole lot of shoe leather. I figured maybe you could put the word out on the underworld grapevine and find out who might be behind this thing. After all, I could waste months chasing down false leads."

Bert finally nodded his assent, though he still had that knowing grin on his face. "All right kid, I'll see what I can find out for you. But I still think this dame has thrown you for a loop."

I nodded back. "I guess we can agree to disagree on that one."

He smiled, obviously unconvinced. "So noted. Call me in a couple of days and we'll see if I can scare up anything. Now, you'll have to excuse me son; I have some other affairs to attend to."

I shook his hand, thanked him again and left.

I cruised down Ventura and hooked a right on Laurel Canyon to take the scenic route up and over the hills. I needed time to think. Was he right about the girl? No, I didn't think so, not really. Hell, even a cop would start at the top on this case, if he knew a Bert Fawcett, with all his ties to the underworld. Besides, I had my hands full just doing my job on this one; complicating it with some crazy fantasy romance would only mix everything up. After the long hot drive downtown, I headed down Spring Street to the old Hall of Records building; at least that would give me a good excuse to treat myself to a nice dinner later at The Pantry—for my money, the best steakhouse in town.

I spent the rest of the day digging through musty old archives and dealing with civil servants who were as surly as the weather was hot. But by the time the dust cleared late that afternoon I had a much better idea what I was really dealing with. Yes, the sale was for real: the building had indeed been sold to a Mr. Matthew J. Smythe for seventy-five thousand dollars on the date and terms Monique described. The title docs also netted me the names of the sellers, who, if I was lucky, might eventually be the key to this whole damn thing. Hmm, Lionel Swopes and Arnold Hagemayer. Could be aliases of course. I'd have my cop friend Dick Hartwick run 'em through criminal records and see.

Of course, Johnny Rogers and Ernie Finnegan, the police detectives who were in charge of the Smythe case four years ago, would already have done all this in their original investigation, but who knows what their game really was, or even what kind of departmental pressures they were under at the time. Cops have a lot of advantages over PIs, including a whole army of bureaucrats and technicians at their disposal, plus access to all the official records. But they work on many cases at once and are always subject to the shifting tides of politics and public pressure. A police detective can be pulled off a case at any time for various reasons and told to focus on something else. So one advantage a PI has is time to poke around at will, subject only to his client's wallet and interest in the case. Another advantage a PI has is that what he does is private, not subject to public scrutiny or politics. In other words, as a PI scurries from rathole to rathole, he can get away with a lot more than a cop, as long as he's careful and doesn't embarrass anyone. Especially himself.

When I finished up downtown, I phoned Dick Hartwick at home and gave him the names. Then I added, "Oh, and you'd better run a couple of other ones too: Matthew J. Smythe and Monique L. Smythe." I spelled the last name.

He grunted, "Monique, huh? That the girl?"

"Yeah."

After a long, uncomfortable silence, he said he'd get back to me on it the next day. He also asked me to dinner at his place that night, but I said sorry, I had to pass for now, too much going on.

He said, "There's never too much going on to see good friends."

I rubbed the pain in my forehead. "There's just, you know, a lot happening, that I have to deal with before . . ."

"Before what, buddy? Friends aren't for before and after; they're for during."

"Sorry, gotta go." I hung up quick, before the black curtain came all the way down.

I topped off the day by treating myself to a late dinner at The Pantry. It's been open twenty-four hours a day since the Twenties, and there's always a line outside, but that night I got seated in a quick twenty minutes. The waiters all knew me from my old days on the force after the war, and they brought my "usual" without having to ask me: a medium T-bone and cole slaw, with some of that crusty French bread and butter on the side. After the good meal I felt almost human—that is, for a walk-around nut job with chronic headaches and combat fatigue who was in psychiatric treatment for God knows what.

*   *   *

I spent the next day at a public library out in the Valley, just to avoid my usual turf, in case I was being watched. No, not reading great literature, but poring over all the local phone directories for the names of the sellers, who both gave phony addresses on the title documents, as it turns out. No dice. When I went out to the Sirloin Burger for lunch and checked with my service, there was a message that Dick called. I called him back and he said he hadn't turned up any criminal record on Swopes or Hagemayer. Not a thing, not even a traffic ticket, at least under those names.

I drew a deep breath. "And the Smythes?"

"Nothin' on them either." He paused. "But I did a little more digging and found a defunct DBA filing for a Lionel Swopes, for what it's worth: Superior Real Properties."

I thanked him and hung up quick, before he could lecture me on friendship again. Then I hit the phone directories some more, even doubling back to check on that Superior listing. No luck. Finally, on a wild hunch, I asked the librarian to snag a Las Vegas book for me. To my surprise, Superior Real Properties was listed as a business, with a Vegas address. Of course, Superior was probably a common business name; it could be mere coincidence.

I went out into the smoggy blast furnace that passes for weather in the Valley and found a phone booth next to the parking lot of a liquor store. I got a long-distance operator and gave her what I had on Superior. She rang it and told me, "Sorry sir, that number's been disconnected."

I said, "Yeah honey, I'm sorry too."

But I wasn't done. Someone had leased that office space to Superior, and I was going to find out who. I went back to the library and checked the Vegas book for all the big commercial leasing outfits, writing down the numbers of several likely candidates. I went back out to the blazing hot phone booth and started with the first one. I got a no. Then I got smart and asked the next ones which leasing agents they thought might have serviced that address, or at least that general area. The fourth guy said, "I'm not sure, but you might try Irv Epstein at Right Way. They handle a lot of the small stuff down that way." He gave me the number.

I was running out of coins, so I went into the liquor store, where an old man with a heavy mop of unruly gray hair was standing at the counter, studying his leathery hands like there was going to be a pop quiz on the creases.

"Hey, Old Timer, could you give me some change for the phone, please?"

He looked up and gave me the squint-eye. "Private dick, ain't ya?"

"Why do you say that?"

"They're always comin' in here, askin' for change. First, they go to the library, then they spend a lot of time talkin' on the phone." He rubbed his stubbly beard. "Now why do they do that?"

I smiled. "Well, they get information from the books at the library. Then, they try to call the people they found in the books."

"Why not just go see the person from the book then? Why talk on the phone?"

"Well, for one thing, the person in the book might not want to see them; they might be a criminal or something."

"Then why call 'em at all? Better to stay away!"

I shrugged. "You're probably right, but it's my job to find them, whether they want it or not."

That seemed to satisfy him. "How much you want?"

I got change for two ones and got ready to leave.

The man pointed his thumb back toward the cooler box in the rear. "How 'bout a soda before you go—on the house? Calling is thirsty work on a hot day like this."

I figured the old guy just wanted some company. Look how simple it can be: the old man knew what he wanted, and, unlike me, he could just ask for it without feeling a thousand unnameable "unconscious conflicts," as Doc Grimes called them. I nodded. "Sure Pops, give me a Squirt." I laid down a quarter. "But I'd feel better paying for it."

He shoved the coin back at me. "Naw, you'll need the change for your calls. You just wait, I'll be right back."

Why couldn't my work involve dealing with people like this? Regular people, steady people? Did I deliberately choose a life among the lowlifes and the dregs? Is that where I thought I belonged?

Christ, I was even starting to think like one of those goddam Freudians! I wasn't sure all this therapy was doing me any good.

"Here you go, mister." The old man handed me an open Squirt and I clinked it with his Coke and tipped the bottle up, savoring the cool lemony fizz. He seemed so normal, so nice, as we stood there and drank together, sharing a moment in time without the need for words. After a while he looked behind him and said, "Better hurry up. I'm only watching the counter for my son, and he'll be mad if he catches me giving anything away!"

I mock-hurried out of the place, smiling, as I remembered the red-headed waitress looking behind her in that same way, worrying about being seen, being caught. Are we all living in fear of the man coming up behind us?

I got the long-distance operator, gave her the number, deposited a lot of coins and took another swig of cold soda.

"One moment, sir."

As I mopped my forehead with my handkerchief, I heard a man's voice somewhere on the phone line say, "Hello?" then the Operator said, "I have your party, sir; go ahead."

I said, "Hello? Is this Irv Epstein?"

"Epstein? Naw, he's out showin' units till five. Who's this?"

"I was just wondering: do you people manage the property at 3233 Loving Lane, by any chance?"

"Yeah, we got those units. What of it?"

"I was just wondering if you happen to remember a fellow named Lionel Swopes. It would have been four, maybe five years ago?"

"Five years ago? What the hell? No, I only been here a year myself. Naw, you gotta wait for old man Epstein. If anyone'd know, he would. That suit ya?"

"Sure, I appreciate your time. I'll call back later. Thanks."

I finished the soda and dialed Bert Fawcett's office.

"Cole Dunbar for Mr. Fawcett."

"Just a moment, Mr. Dunbar."

I crossed my fingers out of habit, even though after Danny I didn't believe in luck anymore.

"Hiya, Cole. Guess you're wonderin' what the boys turned up?"

"I sure am."

"Sorry kid, but if there's any information out there on who's workin' that squeeze, it's locked up tighter than a drum. Nobody knows a thing." He paused. "Could mean it's a freelancer, an amateur tryin' to shoot the moon on a one-off. Hard to tell, but I doubt it's any of the big boys; they would've just grabbed Daddy right off, scared the kid half out of her mind and have done with it. Sorry. But we'll keep checking." Then he added, "Oh, one thing more; this Swopes guy? Rumor has it he was apparently a big plunger."

"On what?"

"Cards, dice, dames, ponies, you name it."

Hmm, maybe my Vegas hunch hadn't been so wild after all. "Any line on where he might be?"

"Nope, fell off the earth years ago, not a word since." He paused. "How's about your end?"

"So far about the same as yours. The deal actually happened as advertised. No criminal record on the names the sellers gave, or the Smythes. I got an old DBA filing in Vegas that I'm running down now with a guy, but it'll probably amount to nothing. So now I talk to the insurance man and maybe the cops who worked the case, and keep tracking down the sellers. But for now, bupkus."

"Buck up, kid, somethin' has to turn up."

"Maybe I was right the first time and I'm not good enough to crack this one."

"I told you to knock off that kinda talk, Cole. There's a long way to go on this one. Patience: that's the ticket now. Listen, they wouldn't have threatened you if they weren't scared of you, right?"

I smiled. "Sure, petrified." We hung up. *Yeah, they're all running scared of big bad me: the butcher, the baker and the money-demand-maker.*

It was too late to get anything more done that day, so I swung by the Bob's Big Boy on Riverside for some burgers and fries to go, and headed on home. I should have called Vegas again to talk to Epstein, but I was more tired and hungry than ambitious, so once I got home I just wolfed the burgers, chased them with a couple of beers and called it a day. Of course, calling it a day didn't account for the nightmares; I could never be sure what was going to happen once I closed my eyes. I didn't even think of it as going to sleep anymore; it was more like turning the keys over to the demons on the night shift.

I tried to ease my way into the night by reading a little of John Fante, one of the classic writers of Depression era LA, which to me was always the real LA. Fante was my mother's favorite writer. She used to read me his works at night, even when I was in high school, about the only time I ever felt remotely close to her. I turned to a dog-eared page and read her favorite passage out loud:

Los Angeles, give me some of you! Come to me the way I came to you, my feet over your streets, you pretty town I loved you so much, you sad flower in the sand, you pretty town!

It brought fat, painful tears to my eyes. Was it the beauty of Fante's words, the fast-fading memories of what passed for love from a distant mother, or the paltry solace I found in the fact that it was actually possible for that woman to think something in this world was good enough for her?

I was lucky that night and got a few hours of decent sleep. Maybe my failure to get anywhere with the case had satisfied the demons for the moment, so they took the night off to haunt someone else.

The next morning I opened an Eastside, lit a Camel and hoped for the best as I dialed the Vegas number.

"Right Way Management."

"Is this Irv Epstein?"

"You said it, kiddo."

"You lease the property at 3233 Loving Lane?"

"Right you are, buckaroo."

This character didn't sound promising. "Do you recall a company called Superior Real Properties, maybe around four, five years ago, that occupied that space? Or maybe a fellow named Lionel Swopes?"

"Say, who *are* you anyway?"

A PI gets that all the time, and I had a whole raft of answers at the ready. "My name is Jamison Jennings, a lawyer for a distant aunt of his, and I may have some good financial news for him."

"Well, he could probably use some, and so could I."

"Meaning?"

"Meaning he skipped out owing me more than two grand, Mister Jennings."

"Any chance you have a forwarding address? A phone number?"

"Listen, if I had any of that, I woulda had his ass served long ago, wouldn't I of?"

"Any chance you might have overheard, or read, anything that might give me a clue as to his whereabouts? There could even be a little something in it for you, Mr. Epstein."

"How little of a something are we talking about?"

"How big of a clue are we talking about, buckaroo?"

"Ah hell, I might as well just tell ya: the day before he moved out, I heard him on the phone talkin' about some big deal he had on. Of course, he's the kind that's always talkin' about big deals, y'unnerstan', but he sounded pretty excited about this one. I think he mentioned Mexico."

"Mexico's a big place."

"So is my empty pocket; a twenty might give it a little company."

"You got it."

"On the other hand, I really don't want to make any trouble for . . ."

"Forty."

"Ensenada."

"Any identifying characteristics, for another twenty?"

"Well, now that you mention it, he did walk with a bit of a limp. And he favored them flashy suits, too."

"Which side?"

"Which side what?"

"The limp; which side?"

"Uh let me think: the left. That help you any?"

"It helps me exactly sixty-dollars-worth, Mr. Epstein. The money will be on its way to you this afternoon."

"Yippie-aye-oh, we should do this more often."

I hung up.

Would Monique be willing to finance a quick trip to Ensenada, even though it might just turn out to be a wild goose chase? I knew other PIs who regularly frightened wealthy clients into springing for out-of-town investigations based on bogus clues and "sightings" the PIs had just made up. Of course it so happened that these trips were always to Tahoe or Vegas, never Akron or Des Moines. But I wasn't one of those guys. On the other hand, if my talks with the insurance guy and the cops turned out to be a bust, I didn't have much to go on besides Ensenada at the moment.

I dialed Monique.

"Hello?"

Oh God, there was that sultry voice again, turning my heart to egg foo yung. What was it about that softness under the hardness that got to me? "Hi Monique, can we talk a second?"

"Uh, sure, though I was just on my way out. Is it important?"

"Could be."

"Okay, so what is it then?"

"I may have tracked down one of the sellers to Ensenada. But of course, it's a long drive down there, so . . ."

"May?"

"What?"

"You said you *may* have tracked down one of the sellers."

"That's right, I can't be sure. But listen, at least it's a lead."

"And you want me to pay you to drive down to Ensenada?"

"To do my job; yes, that is correct."

"I'll have to think about that."

"Okay then, you think about it and let my answering service know as soon as possible. I'd like to start by day after tomorrow, if I'm going, so please let me know by tonight."

"And you really think this trip might be of some value?"

"Yes Miss Smythe; at the rate of your paying out a thousand dollars a month now, and maybe everything you own later, I'd say yes, it may be of some value."

"No need to get snotty. I have to leave now."

"By tonight, Miss Smythe."

Click.

That afternoon in my office I tried to call the insurance investigator, who turned out be a guy named Roderick Pettibone of Provident Union. He was out in the field, but his secretary promised to tell him I wanted to discuss a case, urgently. When she asked which case, I said, "The Smythe case; I believe there was some suspicion of arson?"

She said, "Oh yes, Mr. Dunbar, you can bet your . . . I mean, I'm positive Mr. Pettibone will be most anxious to speak to you. I'll give him the message."

LAPD detective Johnny Rogers, whom everyone called Buck, was not so eager to talk to me, especially since the arson angle on the Smythe case had been a big embarrassment to the Department in general, and to him personally. When I identified myself on the phone he said, "Why the hell you diggin' around in that old shit pile again, Dunbar?"

I said, "There have been some extortion demands."

"What, on the Smythe kid and her father?" He gave a snort of laughter. "What the fuck, they probably set the fire anyway! Let 'em pay!"

"Look Buck, can't I at least come down and talk to you about it? I'm just trying to look at this thing from all angles."

"Sure, and your angle is to keep sniffing around enough to fill your empty datebook with billable hours. Don't think I don't know your racket."

"Just think about it, okay? Maybe you could come up with something that helps me make these goons go away."

"Yeah, come to think of it," he cackled, "I heard the daughter grew up into a real looker. Got her claws into ya good, has she, kid?"

Men with dirty minds aren't exactly my cup of tea, but I had to play ball if I wanted to get anywhere. "No, that has nothing to do with it. I'm just trying to do my job here."

"Fine, it'll be a waste of my time, but meet me at the Tail O' the Cock on Ventura around nine tonight."

"Kinda far off your beat, isn't it?"

"I happen to live in the Valley, shit-for-brains, and please keep your opinions to yourself."

"Rightyo then, nine o'clock it is."

My fee was now feeling like fifty bucks a day and all the abuse I could eat. Fortunately, I had an appointment with Doc Grimes that afternoon; maybe it would help gird my loins for combat with Buck Rogers.

Chapter Five

I had two other cases I was just wrapping up at the time; if I was going to make that trip to Baja I had to try and make both clients happy before I hit the road. One was a bail bond-jumper on an armed robbery beef whom I'd tracked down hiding out at his ex-girlfriend's house in Tarzana. The other was Betty Greer, yet another rebellious teenage girl who'd gone missing after some friends saw her walking with some tall, older guy on Van Nuys Boulevard.

I called Monk Farrell, the bondsman who hired me on the armed robbery jumper, and gave him the dope on the Tarzana shack-up, and the name of the operative I'd hired to bring the guy in. He said my favorite words: "Good work; if it pans out, I'll put your check in the mail right away." One down. Then there was the Greer case. From the description of the "tall, older guy" I had a pretty good idea who had taken Betty Greer: Dexter Broadhurst, a recruiter for one of Mickey Cohen's entry-level prostitution rings, who had a habit of nabbing lost, pretty girls off the streets of the Valley. I remembered he used to hang out in Wally's Corner Pocket, a poolroom out in Panorama City.

I dialed.

"Wally's."

"Is Dex Broadhurst there?"

"Who wants to know?"

"The guy who's gonna get him a nice long stretch for pandering if he's not there, even if I have to frame him for it."

"Uh, lemme check a minute."

"You do that."

I waited.

"Yeah, who's this?"

"Hello Dexter, it's Cole Dunbar."

"Ah shit. What the hell do *you* want?"

"Betty Greer, pronto, and I'm not fuckin' around, either."

"Who's Betty What's-her-name?"

"The girl who's gonna put you in stir if she's not back at her parents' house by six o'clock tonight."

Silence.

"Did you hear me?"

"Yeah, yeah. So wait up, are you saying . . ."

"I'm saying you deliver her to her parents' doorstep tonight, safe and sound, and we forget the whole thing. But if not, I call Vice and you're going down, even if I have to hire ten chippies to lie in court."

He sighed. "Yeah, you'd do that, too."

"You bet your skinny little ass I would."

I heard another sigh. "Okay, deal; what's that address again?"

I gave it to him.

I called the Greers to give them the good news. Told them to be sure and leave a message with my service as soon as Betty came back. There was a lot of crying, a lot of gratitude. What they did with their wild girl after she'd seen Paree was their business.

Ensenada, here I come.

Provided Monique agreed to foot the bill.

*　　　*　　　*

Doc Grimes was looking concerned again when I walked into his office for our five o'clock. "C'mon in, Cole, you're, uh, looking a little better than last time."

"Wonder of wonders, I actually got a decent night's sleep last night."

"Good. What did you do before you went to be bed?"

That wasn't something I felt comfortable talking about. "Oh, just a little reading."

"Reading? What kind of reading?"

"Just a passage in a book."

He sat there looking at me.

I said, "Shoot, I didn't plan on talking about *that*."

"I'm sure you didn't," he said in that maddeningly calm voice, "but it would help me if you would."

I was getting annoyed. "Help *you*? Who's paying for help here, you or me? And besides, how do you know it's important?"

"I just want to know what I need to know, and I have a strange suspicion that I need to know what you were reading last night."

"Even if it upsets me?"

"Yes, even if it upsets you—maybe *especially* if it upsets you."

"Okay then, it was a passage from a book by John Fante."

"Who's John Fante?"

"See, you don't know everything!" Okay, I was being a jerk now, and I knew it.

Doc smiled. "Well, I'm glad we got that out of the way. Now can you tell me who he is?"

"He's a writer, an LA writer, a writer about LA, who should be a lot more famous than he is. He wrote this book, *Ask the Dust*, that my mother kind of idealized." Then, thinking it wouldn't kill me to be fair to her for once, I added, "Hell, maybe she idealized him for good reason; the guy could write."

"And how do *you* know about him?"

Shit, here we go again. "My mother was a writer, a screenwriter, and like I say, Fante was one of her idols . . . sort of a role model, I guess. She always said he ended up feeling unacknowledged, just like her. I hear the guy's even been reduced to scratching out screenplays now, just for the money. She used to read to me at night from lots of writers: Proust, Dickens, Lewis Carroll, Virginia Woolf, Saroyan, Dos Passos. But most of all, Fante."

"And what was the passage you were reading last night?"

"Nothing. Just this thing about LA."

"C'mon Cole, you gotta do a little better than that."

Jesus, why was I being so stingy with information? Why did everything feel so private? "Okay, okay, it's about when he first came to LA, and how he felt about it. She used to . . . like I say, she used to read to me from Fante at bedtime. Her idea of a bedtime story, I guess."

"Oh? And was that meaningful to you?"

I was getting annoyed again. "Look, do we really have to get into all this ancient history? What does it have to do with my nightmares? Or my headaches? Or the war?"

He said, "There are different kinds of wars, and they leave different kinds of wounds. Right now, we're talking about you and your mother, and I have a feeling that she had her own kind of artillery that could hurt just as bad."

Now I could feel tears burning my eyes. I didn't know why and I didn't really *care* why. But for once the black curtain didn't come down, and for that at least I was grateful.

Doc said, "Talk to me about the pain, how you're feeling it right now."

I tried to dig deep, but only came up with this: "I suppose it has to do with my mother."

"And what about her?"

Jesus, thinking about all this was stripping the gears in my brain. But finally I managed to say, "It's hard to have somebody matter that much to you, when you . . ."

"Don't matter that much to them?"

Now the tears were rolling down my cheeks, though I still didn't really know why. I told myself, what's the big deal? You have the kind of mother you have, right? But that doesn't have to affect the rest of your life, does it? Why was I being such a baby about things that happened so long ago?

Doc said, "You're very hurt and you're very sad, but you really don't know why, do you?"

I said, "Look, in life you just have to deal with things. You're dealt the hand you're dealt, and you can't piss and moan about it the rest of your life."

"But you've never pissed and moaned about it at *all*. Maybe it's time to start—at least in a safe place like this."

"It just feels so embarrassing to have all these emotions."

"Is that how she made you feel?"

"Who?" Part of me was still playing dumb.

"Your mother."

"That lady was one tough broad."

"I can see that you're proud of her for that. Is that what we should all aspire to be? Tough?"

"Are you going to start that stuff about being tough again? What else is there? You have to survive in this world." I paused. "You can't compromise."

"Where'd you get that phrase?"

"You can't compromise? That's something my mother said every day of her life."

"And how did that work out for her?"

"Well, I don't know . . . I guess she had a very hard life."

"Hard in what way?"

"Her husband, my father, left her; she had very limited professional success . . ."

"And you think that was all just bad luck?"

I bristled. "She was an amazing woman!"

"I'm not questioning that. But isn't it fair to ask what effect having such strict beliefs about compromise had on the course of her life?"

"Maybe. I mean, I guess so. I mean, maybe."

At that point the black curtain slammed down and I was blanked out for most of the rest of the session.

Finally, Jim pointed to the clock. "We're out of time for today, but there's a lot for you to think about in the next week or so." He fixed me with that excruciatingly compassionate ray-beam of his. "You know Cole, here's the way it works: life moves on, and you have to move on with it. But to move on, you have to face reality."

I groaned. "Hell Doc, that sounds too easy, too glib to be real; life isn't a fortune cookie."

He just gave me that Buddha look again and shook his head.

I left, frustrated and even angry that we'd wasted all that time on my mother when what I really needed to talk about was my meeting with Buck Rogers.

*   *   *

I got back to my office around six thirty and dialed the answering service. Sabrina told me there were three messages: Miss Smythe called to okay the trip; the Greers reported that they got their girl back, relatively intact; and a Mr. Pettibone called, suggesting a meeting at his office at two the next day. She said he sounded eager.

Good, that only left Buck Rogers tonight and Pettibone tomorrow before I hit the road. For some reason I felt for the first time like I was making progress on the Smythe case. Maybe it was just the anticipation of getting out of town; sometimes movement, any movement, feels good. But the more I thought about Buck Rogers' reaction to my call, the more I realized he was still steaming about not being able to crack the Smythe case himself, if there *was* a Smythe case. And that meant I had to be careful with him; if I ever did come close to figuring out the truth and tipped him to it, he was just the type to swoop in and claim the credit for himself, or even sabotage me, if the truth made him look bad.

I went to a local diner and gnawed on a gristly steak—the kind that fights back—then returned to the office to finish up all my paperwork so I could take off the next day. A little after eight I went down to the lot and got in my car, then swung down Coldwater Canyon to the Valley, with the tough steak and the anticipation of Buck Rogers' nasty attitude fighting for control of my stomach all the way. I made a left on Ventura and pulled up in front of the Tail O' the Cock. I stood at the front door for a moment gathering myself, then pulled it open and walked in.

Buck Rogers was sitting there at the other end of the bar, looking like a side of beef in a very bad mood. Suddenly it hit me that I shouldn't have told him about the extortion demands; now he'll just say it's a job for the police, giving him a chance to bully his way in, crack the case and come up smelling like a rose. Well, it was too late now—sometimes you just play it where it lays.

As soon as he saw me, he wiped the anger from his face. "Hiya, kid, what ya drinkin'?"

I shook his big mitt and looked at the bartender. "Johnny Walker, rocks."

Why was he being so friendly all of a sudden? Probably because he was only here to sound me out for his own purposes.

Buck banged his shot glass down on the counter. "Do it again, Nick." Then he turned to me. "So, what have you turned up so far, kid?"

His voice was thick and furry; he obviously had a pretty good snootful going already.

"To tell you the truth, nothing much. That's why I wanted to talk to you. I'm stumped."

He gave a fat man's belly laugh that sounded fake to me. "So were we back then, kid. The whole thing made no sense at all. I mean, who sells a building for a song, then disappears? And who buys a valuable building for a song, then burns the whole thing to the ground a couple of months later?" He shook his head. "It doesn't fit any pattern I know of, or any other cop either."

He eyed me carefully for a reaction. I kept my face expressionless and said, "So tell me about the arson angle."

He took a big gulp of his drink and shook his head again. "Nothin', that's what. Our own fire guys came up dry, and so did the insurance dick. All we ever heard was, 'Possibly a minor electrical issue' and that was that." He finished his drink and banged the glass down again for a refill, adding, "That's it; that's all she wrote, Jackson." He was slurring his words now. "God damnedest thing I ever seen. If someone's dirty, they sure pulled it off slicker 'n snot."

Now I'd see how far I could push him. "Say, you wouldn't know how I can get in touch with Ernie Finnegan, would you?"

His body gave an involuntary jerk, but he kept his eyes glued to the bar. "Ernie? No, I wouldn't. Haven't seen Ernie in a long while." He finally turned and focused his bleary eyes on me. "You know, Finny got a pretty bum deal from the Department." I could see anger behind his eyes.

"Oh? And why is that?"

He shook his head and I knew he didn't want to say any more. "Ahh, he got set up." He waved his hand dismissively. "The usual political horseshit."

I decided to live dangerously. "Say, that was right after the Smythe case, wasn't it?"

His body twitched again, and I could see him breathing faster. "Kid, don't push it. Now, I told you what I know, and that's all you're gonna get." The fun and games were over; now there was menace in every word. "So if you're smart, you'll go home now like a good boy and mind your manners."

That was the second time someone in this case had told me to mind my manners. There was a lot more I wanted to ask him, but I didn't feel like taking a beating at the moment. It was time for a tactical retreat. I slid a ten across the bar and said, "Okay Buck, whatever you say. Thanks for your time."

He grunted without even looking up.

As I left, I heard him bang his glass down again.

By the time I drove back over the hills and ran up the steps to my apartment off Highland, I was over being intimidated by Buck Rogers' anger and beginning to wonder why he hadn't pumped me more about my work on the Smythe case; after all, the whole thing had made him look pretty bad in the Department. I turned the key and opened the door.

That's when the world went black.

Chapter Six

I was used to waking up with a headache, but this one was on the wrong side of my head, and when I reached my hand up to rub it, it came back a bloody mess. Then I realized I wasn't in bed at all, but sprawled out on the living room floor. I know it sounds crazy, but the first thing that ran through my mind was, "Hey Doc, look at me: I found another way to be a tough guy!" Then when I tried to stand, I got dizzy and fell back down. Whoever did it to me was long gone, and I didn't think I needed a hospital, so I just slithered to the kitchen on my stomach and got myself a beer.

Then I passed out again.

Several hours later I was sitting at the kitchen table chasing four aspirin with a second can of Eastside and wondering what, or if, all this had to do with Buck Rogers. I looked at the clock on the stove: five in the morning. It was too early to start making calls. There was nothing to do but go back to bed and try to sleep it off. I dragged myself to the bathroom and fixed my head up the best I could, then shucked off my shirt and pants and slid under the covers. Just before I nodded off, I noticed a folded note set out on the nightstand. I opened it and forced myself to stay awake long enough to read:

I told you to lay off. Now it gets serious. This is only the beginning.

The letters were deliberately scrawled in childish printing.

Then I fell into a writhing cauldron of nightmares:

Business as usual.

By the time I came to, it was broad daylight and my whole body ached. Jesus, what all had they done to me? The nightstand clock said one. Christ, I had a two o'clock with Roderick Pettibone! I stood up unsteadily and weaved my way to the bathroom, trying not to look at the mess in the mirror. I started to clean up my head wound again, then figured I'd better take a hot shower first and wash away what could be washed away, then patch up whatever was left over. By the time I was in front of the mirror I could stand without listing to port or starboard—a major triumph. I swabbed the wound with Merthiolate, then gauzed it up and taped it down. With my hat on I wouldn't look any worse than the average post-op brain surgery patient.

I drove East on Sunset to the Provident Union building, found a parking spot on Vermont and made the meter happy with some of the nickels I always kept in the Ford's ashtray.

"Investigations, please?" I said to the girl at the front desk.

She gave my head a funny look and said, "That would be on four, sir."

I made my wobbly way to the elevator bank and pressed the call button. When it came, I told the operator my floor and tried not to upchuck from the motion.

"Mr. Dunbar to see Mr. Pettibone."

The secretary eyed the bandages balefully, then said, "Go right in, sir; he's expecting you."

Yeah, I'll bet he was. Except he wasn't being beaten up for being interested in the case all these years later.

Roderick Pettibone looked exactly like a Roderick Pettibone: tall and gaunt, probably in his late sixties, with what looked to have been gray hair, badly dyed to an indeterminate brassy hue, and a bulbous nose that spoke of many an open container.

Pettibone stood up, looking happy to see me. "Welcome, Mr. Dunbar. Have a seat."

I did so.

"So, you have some news for me on the Smythe case?" He had what sounded like the moldy remains of a British accent.

I cleared my throat. "Actually, I was hoping you might have some news for *me* on the Smythe case."

Now he didn't look so happy to see me. "But I was led to believe . . ."

"Sorry, all I told your girl was that I wanted to discuss the case with you— especially the arson angle."

For a moment there I thought he was going to cry. But he finally pulled himself together and said, "But what is your involvement in the whole affair, then?"

"I'm a private investigator, hired by Miss Smythe to explore certain . . . demands . . . that have been made on her." I paused, trying to look mysterious. "I can't really say much more than that at the moment."

Now he looked happier. "Oho, so there *is* skullduggery afoot, then?"

I took off my hat and pointed to the bandages. "Yes, and the duggery was performed on *my* skull."

He gasped, and I went on. "But somebody beating a tattoo on my brain may have nothing to do with the original circumstances. I'm still in the dark here."

He shrugged. "But if the Smythes have nothing to hide, then . . ."

"Nefarious people can make it *look* like the Smythes have something to hide, Mr. Pettibone. We both know, for example, that both Provident and the police would like nothing more than to pin arson, or strong suspicion of arson, on somebody—anybody."

"Are you implying that Provident would ever be a party to . . ."

I held up my hands. "No, no, of course not, sir; perish the thought." I needed to get what I could from this old bag of bones before he had the vapors.

"Is there anything, anything at all, that you can tell me about your initial investigation that would give me a leg up here? Maybe details about the fire? Questions you had about the results of the investigation? Other interested parties that were hanging around?"

He thought a moment, but only shook his head sadly.

I decided to push it. "The behavior of the police officers?"

His hand went to his face. "The police officers? Well I can tell you they were discourteous—*most* discourteous. There was a heavy-set gentleman, a Mr. Rogers, and another one as well, a loathsome specimen whose name escapes me at the moment."

"Could it have been Finnegan?"

"Finnegan! Yes indeed, that is he! He persisted in calling me Ronny, and even Petty, regardless of the fact that I repeatedly told him my name was Roderick Pettibone. I even spelled it for him!"

I shook my head. "In Finnegan's case, spelling wouldn't have helped much. Was there anything else about them, other than the fact that they were rude to you?"

His hand went to his face again. "Come to think of it, they didn't seem very interested in the case once all the investigations showed no evidence of criminal intentionality. I had the feeling they were out for what the police call a 'collar,' and if one didn't seem to be in the offing, well then why waste further time or effort on the thing?"

I stood. "Thank you very much, Mr. Pettibone, I truly appreciate your time. And if I turn up anything that might be of interest to you or your company, I'll be sure and let you know."

"And I'd appreciate that, Mr. Dunbar." His hand went down to one of his desk drawers and came up with a bottle of Pinch. He nodded to it. "Could I interest you, perhaps? It's my luncheon hour, Mr. Dunbar."

I shook my head. "I do indulge in the odd drop now and again, but I'm really more of a beer man."

He raised an eyebrow that said, "typical colonist," then stood and offered a liver-spotted hand. "Well, it's been a privilege, Mr. Dunbar, and I hope we can do one another some good in future." He pointed to my bandaged head. "And is that sort of thing a typical part of your professional activities as well?"

I nodded. "Sometimes it is, I'm afraid."

He shuddered. "Well, to each his own, I suppose."

So, Rogers had been a bust and now Pettibone too. But what did it mean that I got beat up right after talking to Buck Rogers? I drove up Sunset, pulled into the office lot and tossed the keys to George. If the beating meant things were heating up on the Smythe extortion, were they pressuring Monique too? I unlocked my office, then sat down and dialed the service. I had two messages, neither of which related to the Smythe case. Then I called Monique.

"Hello?"

"Hi, Smitty."

"I thought you were en route to Mexico."

"I will be tomorrow. I had some loose ends to tie up. I'm just wondering, have you had any contact from the blackmailers lately?"

"No. I paid them off last month, and the next payment isn't due for another two weeks. Why?"

"Well, someone with extremely hard hands paid me a little visit last night."

"Oh no, are you okay?"

It was the first time she'd ever showed any concern for me; not that it mattered to me, of course. I said, "I am now, but my head had a pretty rough night of it. And they left a love note on my nightstand too, telling me to lay off or else."

She said, "What do you think we should do?"

"Probably nothing, for now. I'm going to be down south for a while anyway, so hopefully they'll think they scared me off and I blew town. But it could mean they're working up to something. I just wanted to make sure you weren't being bothered, before I left."

"Thank you Cole, I truly appreciate that. Will you please call and check in on me during your trip? I uh . . . I need your strength."

"Of course, Monique. But you should probably be careful while I'm gone. You know, not too many wild parties . . . or three a.m. walks alone."

"I get the message. And don't worry, I'm rarely alone, especially at three a.m."

Ouch, that hurt, and I think she knew it.

The next morning, I packed my suitcase for a week in sunny old Mexico. I called the service and told Hattie I'd be gone for awhile but that I'd try and check in along the way. Then I called to let Katy know we'd have to hold off on my meetings with Doc Grimes until I returned. When I did get back I fully intended to check further on Rogers and Finnegan—especially Finnegan. I remembered him from the old days, a tall, pasty-faced drink of water who definitely wasn't drinking water; the guy was a weak link if I'd ever seen one. And I didn't believe for a minute that Rogers had no idea of his whereabouts either; for a dirty ex-cop like Finnegan, probably in need of money, a scam like the Smythe squeeze could be right up his alley.

I headed south on the Hollywood Freeway. It felt good to be on the road. To tell the truth, it felt wonderful not having to account to anyone for a while too. Doc Grimes once told me the sessions would be working away inside me even when we weren't meeting, but it was delicious to be a truant from maturity for a week or so and only be responsible for staying in my lane and keeping the old ragtop pointed south. I turned on the radio. It was the Four Aces singing, *Love is a Many-Splendored Thing*. I rolled down my window and sang along at the top of my lungs:

Love is a many-splendored thing. It's the April rose that only grows in the early spring . . .

A guy in the next car looked at me funny and I laughed out loud for the first time in forever. But *was* love a many-splendored thing? From where I sat, the Four Aces were delusional. For me, love had always been a faraway star, just the foreplay to heartache. I knew I was crazy to still be thinking of Monique Smythe. She was a client and nothing more, I told myself, but myself knew I was lying. I knew I could never be good enough for a girl like that, or her fast, rich crowd and the way they lived. For a society girl like that, I'd have to give up my whole way of life as a stray dog and an outsider; she sure as hell wasn't going to join me at the pool hall, the bowling alley or the fights. But still I wanted her, thought about her, imagined being with her. That throaty purr, saying, "I need you." It was almost like catnip, a drug. What would Doc Grimes have to say about that?

*   *   *

Sometime after five I pulled off the freeway at San Diego and decided to stop there for the night. I'd treat myself to dinner and a movie, just like a guy on a real vacation. The dinner at a seafood place was great, but unfortunately the only movie playing nearby was *Murder is My Beat*. I tried my best to sit through it, even inviting a Coke and some popcorn to join me, but it was hopeless, because I'd already seen the "coming attractions": last year, I'd been hired by Allied Artists to escort the film's co-star, Barbara Payton, and get her to the movie's Hollywood premiere on time. Barbara had a well-earned reputation around town as a "bad girl," and she sure did nothing to disprove it while I was on duty. I had to battle with the half-drunk, belligerent bottle-blonde all the way there. She insisted on stopping off at several bars along the way, and was quite willing to duke it out with me to get her way. And to top it all off, just as she left the car, the little wildcat turned around and belted me, hard. It made it pretty tough to believe in her as a desirable damsel in distress in the movie. If love was a many-splendored thing, Barbara Payton was one splendor I could do without. But I guess men need to idealize women. Is that what I was doing with Monique? Seeing her through eyes distorted by . . . by what? A mother who never had a kind word for anyone, whom I was never good enough for? Was my obsession with Monique just a rehash of my childhood drama of unreachable love?

Christ, I came here for a nice night off, and here I was peppering myself with unanswerable questions about unreachable love.

I decided to take a nice leisurely walk back to the hotel, and eventually my steps took me to Third and Broadway, the "Neon Row" of sailors' bars during the war, which we Marines called slop chutes, where Danny and I spent many a liberty from Camp Pendleton chasing girls and drinking beer. The streets looked a lot different now, but as I sauntered along I remembered one crazy night when Danny and I got roaring drunk at a whole series of dives on Broadway that we'd gotten into with fake IDs we bought from a guy the drill instructor told us about. Afterwards we sat and watched a girlie show at the Hollywood Theatre.

Still on our feet the next morning, we wandered down to Horton Plaza and ended up meeting a couple of cute girls around our age who were waiting for a bus after getting off the graveyard shift at Consolidated. Danny always went for blondes, so I took the perky brunette, which suited me just fine. Turned out they were from out of town too, so we all spent the next day seeing the sights, from Balboa Park to Cabrillo Monument, and ended up watching a slow, romantic sunset from the Point Loma Lighthouse. By the end of the day, Danny and I both thought we were in love, but that's what wartime does to a young kid. As it turned out, we never saw the girls again, so that day was just another dream to stow away in our seabags.

Danny: what a guy he was, and what a friend.

Almost to the hotel, I bought a six-pack at a liquor store, then walked back to my room and let myself in. Couldn't hurt to call the answering service, even if it was supposed to be a night off. I dialed.

"Answer World, Stella speaking."

"Hi, Stella, it's Cole Dunbar. Got anything for me?"

"Let's see. Yes, there is one here. It says, 'You did the right thing by getting out of town. Play it smart and keep your nose clean.'"

I took a deep breath. "Any name?"

"Yeah, it just says, 'Your nighttime visitor.'"

"Thanks, Stella."

"Oh wait, there's one more here."

"From who?"

"It says, 'Marie, the waitress.'"

I pictured the petite redhead from the Tam O'Shanter. "Okay, so what's the message?"

"It just says, 'Call me at Dunkirk 5-4222, after ten any night. I might have some information for you.'"

I excavated a pencil from the stray popcorn in my coat pocket and put it to work. "Dunkirk 5-4222. Got it. Thanks, Stella."

"Good night, Mr. Dunbar."

So whoever was watching me *did* think I left town for a little vacation as a result of the beating and the note. Good, maybe that bought me, and Monique too, a few days of peace and quiet. But if Lionel Swopes really was behind this whole thing and residing in Ensenada, shouldn't they be frightened that I was heading his way? And if Buck Rogers was behind it, would he have been dumb enough to have someone maul me right after I met with him? Hell, there were just too many ifs to wrap my head around. I turned on the TV, opened a beer and watched a couple of mediocre middleweights bounce each other around the ring for a while. Then my head started hurting again, so I turned off the TV, killed the lights and hit the sack. But the ifs, ands and buts kept spinning around in my head like a top, and finally I fell into a twisted dream where a large cast of characters was dancing grotesquely around a burning building, their faces hideously backlit by the licking flames: Ernie Finnegan, Lionel Swopes, my mother, Doc Grimes, Danny Trueluck, Monique, Buck Rogers. The fire and the frenzied dancing went on and on until I jerked awake and doused the flames with three quick beers. Finally, I passed out.

I woke up the next morning in a cold sweat, disoriented. My head and body ached like I'd just gone fifteen rounds with Rocky Marciano.

I guess I forgot: when you go on vacation, you bring yourself along.

*   *   *

After I tossed down a couple of eggs with toast and bacon at a diner, things looked a little better. Maybe today would be the day that old vacation spirit finally hit me.

I headed south again. The scenery went by in a blur until I reached an interminable traffic jam at the border, as the agents checked each car through. After an hour of stop and go I headed south from Tijuana and the road next to the ocean finally opened up pretty good. I put the top down and took my sweet time until in a couple of hours I hit Ensenada. I checked into a tiny room at the La Fiesta Hotel that featured one rattan chair, a miniscule desk, a ratty, overstuffed couch and a bed that must have been left over from the Montezuma Administration. When I lay down on it I almost sank to the floor; if the poor thing ever did have any springs, they were but a distant memory.

I headed downstairs and walked down the street until I found a place called Bar Fortuna. I sat there in the darkness and ordered a beer, trying to look like a gringo who had more than twenty bucks to his name and wasn't just killing time between blows to the head.

"You like me?"

I spun around on the stool and faced a woman who was pushing sixty in age and two hundred in weight.

"I like you fine, honey, but I have other things on my mind at the moment."

She laid a plump hand on my knee. "Why? You got a girlfriend?"

I nodded. "Yeah, I got a girlfriend." I closed my eyes and tried to visualize Monique putting her hand on my knee, but the picture curdled like bad milk.

The woman wouldn't give up. "Then where is she?"

That brought me back to reality. "Who?"

"Your girlfriend, estupido. If you got one, where is she?"

"She's, uh, back at the hotel."

"If she leave you alone like this, why not to be with me for a little while?"

"Because I have other things to do."

"What other things?"

"Look lady, I don't have to sit here and account to you for my every goddam move. Now let me drink in peace, would you?"

"Don't get mad, mister. I was just asking."

"Well, all right then, why don't you move on to your next . . . lucky guy and we'll both part amigos, okay?"

She gave my knee one last squeeze and said, "Okay, mister, I move on." She shuffled off tiredly to her next rendezvous with amor and I went back to my drink.

After a while I paid up and hit the sidewalk again, thinking as I walked: if this Swopes guy was still around, my guess was he was probably holed up in some cheap hotel, laying low. At least I had to start with the hotels. Then I could work my way down, or up, as the case may be. I was within walking distance of three of the other main places where a gringo might put up in town. I asked at every front desk for Swopes and Superior Properties. Nothing. An American with a limp on the left side and maybe flashy duds? Nada. Arnold Hagemayer? Zig, zag, zilch.

The next day I started in on anything that might be related to real estate: agents, management companies, title companies. No dice. Next stop, the police. They didn't quite seem to understand—or care—what I was up to, and once they did, they either didn't know anything, were protecting the guy, or holding out for a payoff.

After I'd given up for the day, I went back to my room and opened the door. Sitting there on the bed was a grinning Mexican roughly the size of a Buick. Before I could turn and run, he leaped up and got me in a bear hug. I felt things cracking inside me. Somehow I managed to wrestle free and put everything I had into a sucker punch to his gut that would have dropped a rhino. He just laughed, then drew back a huge fist and launched a left to my jaw they must have felt in Acapulco.

That's the last thing I remember, but the guy must have been awful busy after I blacked out because when I came to a couple hours later there wasn't a square inch of my body that wasnt bleeding, broken, swollen, or black and blue. Whoever hired that giant sure got a man who loved his work. I managed to struggle to my feet and looked for a note. Sure enough, there it was, propped up on the bathroom sink like before, with printing that looked childlike, but this time not intentionally:

If you done stop stickin you big nose into other people busness, you going to loose it. Laset chance!

Hmm, very poetic: it had economy, metaphor and even a certain orthographic élan.

It also told me I was onto something—something big enough for the bad guys to hire a local goon to put my lights out, which was pretty ironic, because as far as I knew I hadn't found out a damn thing. But I was in no condition to celebrate at the moment; my head was pounding like a bass drum, my ribs tortured me with every ragged breath and the blood I was pissing told me the guy had used my internal organs for batting practice and hit a lot of home runs. I had to get some medical help before I passed out again. I staggered down the stairs. The man at the front desk told me where I could find a doctor, near and cheap. I stumbled down the street to the address he gave me and limped down a long flight of narrow, uneven stairs to a dank basement where an old, unshaven geezer sat playing chess against himself. He had a satisfied smile on his face; he must have been winning.

He looked up with concern. "What you desire, señor?"

I said, "I desire to breathe again without wanting to die," and passed out.

When I came to, I was lying on a cot adorned with a filthy sheet. The old man probed my torso with a series of horrifying jabs while singing, *Hey there, you with the stars in your eyes* to himself the whole time. If he was trying to make a joke with the song, the humor escaped me. Then he taped my ribs, cleaned up the open wounds, wrote out a prescription for pain pills and said I was lucky, it was nothing a week or so in bed wouldn't cure.

When I turned to leave, he asked, "Why they hit you like this?"

"I was somewhere they didn't want me to be."

"So stay out of places they don't want you, señor."

"It's my job to go into places where they don't want me."

He mulled that over for a moment and said, "Then change jobs." He waved his hands. "No charge."

Why did I feel like I'd had this conversation before?

The old guy had a point. I always seemed to be in places where someone didn't want me, starting with my mother's home, then Okinawa, the police force and now Ensenada. Oh, and maybe Monique Smythe's bed, too. Was it just the places I chose, or was it that I didn't belong anywhere?

I filled the prescription and gorged on the fat morphine pills as I staggered back to La Fiesta. Standing there at the front entrance was a Mexican ragamuffin with big brown eyes and long, uncut hair, who always seemed to be hanging around, cadging coins off passersby.

I knelt down. "Hey kid, come over here a minute."

At the sight of me he cringed. I didn't blame him; I must have looked like a flunkout from a flophouse.

I crooked my finger. "It's all right, kid. I got a job for you."

That did it. He came over to me, making sure to keep his hands in his pockets, probably protecting the few measly pesetas he'd already collected.

"How'd you like to make yourself six fat pesos a day, kid?"

He nodded enthusiastically.

"All you have to do is come up to my room at noon and six every day and take the money I give you down to the Bar Fortuna and buy my meals, then bring 'em up to me." I paused. "Think you can be trusted to do that?"

"Sí, señor, Pedro do you one fine job."

I ruffled his hair and handed him six pesos. "Here's an advance on your salary, Pete." I winked. "Now don't blow it all on women and liquor."

He shook his head. "Oh no, sir, for positive I don't."

"Good boy. I'm in room eight."

"Ocho, yes sir. I be there tomorrow at noon."

That night I intended to call Marie back, but instead I passed out and slept like a baby—well, let's say a drugged baby in a world of pain.

*   *   *

The next seven days were an endless maze of morphine and beer, as I tried my best not to move or breathe. I slipped in and out of consciousness, and when I was awake my head was spinning, my bleary vision stippled with distorted ghosts and monsters that threatened me, like in the psycho ward of the VA Hospital after the war. Pedro was as good as his word, bringing tacos and beans on a tray for lunch that first day. But when he saw what I was going through he wouldn't leave me, pulling the rattan chair over next to my bed and watching over me day and night like a mother hen, only leaving twice a day to bring me food and a quart bottle of Tecate for every meal. He held my hand when I had the hallucinations and wiped my face when I had the cold sweats. And every time I awoke from the next fever dream, those big brown eyes were right there, full of compassion and understanding. I offered him extra money, but he waved it away, acting insulted. I'd never felt cared for like that before.

By the seventh day I was starting to feel like a human being again, and I could move without bones cracking or blood spurting. As soon as I was up and about, Pedro started looking sad.

"Hey, what's the matter, mi pequeño?"

He gave a disconsolate shrug. "If you moving around, I out of job, señor." He looked down at the floor. "And I no see you no more."

"Sorry kid, I'd like to help you, but after all, I got work to do."

"What kind work, señor?"

"Detective work, kid," I said, pulling my pants on gingerly. "You wouldn't understand."

He looked confused for a moment, then his face brightened. "You look for man, sí? I hear you talk at front desk."

"You got big ears, Pete. But yeah, I look for man all right."

"Maybe I help you!"

"Pedro, my friend, how could you possibly help me find a man that I, a professional finder, have been after for quite a while already?"

"You come with me, por favor?" He started to walk, beckoning me to follow him.

Well, I had nothing to lose, so I followed him to a trash-strewn alleyway back of town where a group of about twenty kids, all of them street urchins like him, were playing soccer with an old, balled-up newspaper.

At first the kids scattered in fear, just as Pedro had done that first time. Then Pedro stood there and announced, "Mis amigos, esta Señor Dunbar. He look for a man."

A tall kid with a twist in his smile stepped up. "What man?"

It was my turn. "A Señor Lionel Swopes. He walks with a limp," I demonstrated, "and wears flashy clothes . . . uh . . ." I looked at Pedro.

"Ropa llamativa," he said proudly to the assembled kids, as he struck a hilarious pose like a clothes model.

The tall kid said, "And what we get, you find him?"

I said, "Fifty pesos to the one who helps me."

Pedro translated, to a loud chorus of *aieeeee!*

I said, "Gracias," and most of the kids went back to their soccer game as I walked away. Pedro followed me, saying, "See, I help you!"

"I hope you're right, kid." I counted out three pesos. "Now run along and I'll see you tomorrow, okay?"

Pedro drifted back toward the alley again, dejected to be losing his exalted association with the tall American jefe, and I went back to bed, chagrined at being reduced to using the Ensenada Irregulars as my key informants.

That night it finally hit me that in my pain-fogged daze I'd forgotten to call Marie back. I went down to the front desk and got a handful of coins, then went into the fly-blown phone booth in the dingy lobby, pushed the accordion door closed and dialed the operator.

"Operador."

"Yes, I'd like to call a Los Angeles number."

"Sí señor; numero, por favor?"

"Dunkirk 5-4222."

"Momentito."

I paid the toll she asked, and waited.

After an interminable succession of clicks and whirs she rang through and I heard a woman's voice. "Hello?"

"Hello Marie? This is Cole Dunbar. You had some information for me?"

"Yes." She paused. "I thought you weren't going to call."

"Sorry, someone beat the tar outta me, and it was a week before I could make it out of bed."

"Oh, I'm so sorry. Are you hurt badly?"

"No, not too bad, but having a pretty girl ask makes it feel better already."

There was another pause. "I didn't think you noticed."

"I noticed. Now, can you tell me what this new information is?"

"Okay, that Smythe girl of yours has met with a tall, thin, creepy-looking guy here at the Tam several times in the last couple of weeks. They sit together like a couple of witches and talk in whispers."

"Love in bloom?"

"No sirree. It's nothing like that."

"How do you know?"

"I'm a woman, I've been a waitress for years and I'm a grad student in chemistry at UCLA. Will that do?"

"It'll do. I may have to revise my opinion of you."

"We were talking about Miss Smythe."

"Oh yeah. So you think they're up to something? Maybe no good?"

"That's how it feels from here. There's just something sinister about the guy, like he's missing the part that gives a girl flowers on Valentine's Day."

"Can you give me a description of this fellow?"

"Sure. I'd say he's at least six three, gawky, not much meat on the bone, has wiry, bristly hair like Uriah Heep and real weird, dark eyes, like you want to take a bath after he looks at you."

"Ever hear a name?"

"Not clearly, but once I overheard Smythe call him something that had maybe three or four syllables."

"Son of a bitch?"

She giggled. "No."

"Could it have been Hagemayer?"

"Hmm, no, I don't think so."

"Does he have a car?"

"Oh shoot, I never checked."

"Don't worry, but if he's ever in again, see if you can grab a plate number and maybe a make and model."

"All cars look alike to me."

"Well, all girls don't, and you're due for a nice thank-you dinner after I get back. And not at the Tam, either."

She laughed. "Thanks for that, at least."

"Marie, you've been a big help. I truly appreciate it."

"My pleasure."

For a second there I thought I heard heavy breathing.

It might have been mine.

We hung up.

For the moment, Monique's stock had gone down, Marie's way up. But Monique was my client, so I owed her my loyalty unless and until the "charges" were proved. Not that there actually *were* any charges, mind you, other than suspicion of consorting with a creepy beanpole and misdemeanor whispering in the back booth of the Tam O'Shanter.

The next day was another in a string of long, hot ones. I dutifully visited the local newspaper office, which was basically a hole in the wall, and asked everyone I could waylay if they'd ever heard of a Mr. Swopes with a limp and maybe a bright tie, or a Mr. Hagemayer, no description. No one had, or at least no one who was willing to talk. Finally, I got back to La Fiesta around one, flopped on my bed and dozed off in the sizzling afternoon heat, finally understanding the custom of siesta.

Was that a knock on the door? I checked the bedside clock: three fifteen.

Then I heard it again: three small taps, like someone who was afraid of being overheard. Fearing another round of demolition derby with the Mexican Buick, I grabbed the table lamp before cracking the door open. A boy stood there, an emaciated little guy I recognized as one of the Irregulars. "Yes? What can I do for you?"

"I come in, señor?"

"Sure, kid, but I don't have any money for you. Or a job either."

He looked upset. "But you say money for find man."

"Oh, that? Sure, I'll pay money if you can give me any infor . . ."

"You come." He gestured out the door, looking around like he was afraid for his life.

"What . . . *now*?"

"Sí, ahora."

In my condition, I had no patience for a wild goose chase led by some back-alley waif, but my own methods had struck out, so when we got out to the street and the kid pointed to my Ford, which he apparently already knew, I dutifully got in and started it up.

He gestured me straight ahead, and I drove down the main street, then turned east at his direction. Soon we were about a mile past the town limits. "You sure you know what you're doin', kid?"

He nodded emphatically and made the straight-ahead signal again. "Sí, dos kilómetros mas."

When we came to a dirt road on the left, he signaled me to turn onto it, then made the straight-ahead signal again.

Just when I started wondering if this whole thing might just be a setup for my next beating, he said, "Alto!"

To me it looked like the middle of nowhere, but the kid hopped out and gestured me to follow him down a meandering footpath choked with weeds.

About a hundred yards in he stopped and pointed to a cleared, sandy area off to the side of the pathway. "Ahi."

I walked over and sure enough there was a rectangle about five by seven in the sand, with a raised area running lengthwise along it.

I looked at the kid. "Señor Lionel Swopes aqui?"

He nodded vigorously, then started looking around again in fear.

"How do you know?"

"I hear men talk, maybe two, three years before, about they kill him, then put him in ground here. They no see me." He looked terrified and said, "You give me money now?" He held out his hand. It was trembling.

I counted out the money, then handed it to him. He jammed it down into his pocket without even looking at it and said, "We go now."

I knelt down and held out a ten-dollar bill. "What men?"

He backed away from me, shaking his head, eyes wide with terror, then turned and started running back to the car. For a moment I thought I'd never seen fear like that on anyone's face before. Then I remembered Okinawa. Suddenly I bent over and was sick to my stomach. It must have been a delayed reaction to seeing that crude grave; the last ones I'd seen like it were on the islands.

The case had taken a big step forward, beyond the crimes of possible arson and extortion. Now it was murder. And you don't murder people for nothing.

I got control of myself and walked back to the car, where the kid was sitting in the passenger seat looking straight ahead, like he'd seen a ghost and didn't want to see any more. That made two of us.

I turned the ignition key and got us rolling back to town. If the kid was ever going to talk, it surely wasn't gonna be now. I figured I'd give us both a little while to cool off, then maybe ask again tomorrow.

But there was no later. When I got up the next morning and found my way to the alleyway, it was deserted. If the kid's eyes were any indication of his emotions, he probably just took the money and went into hiding. If ten American dollars—a fortune to a kid like that—wasn't enough motivation for him to talk to me, he was clearly scared out of his wits.

I figured Ensenada had already given up whatever secrets it was going to divulge. I went back to my room and packed my stuff, then settled up with the guy at the front desk. Pedro was at his usual post out front, begging again. I slipped him a couple of bucks. Then, when he impulsively wrapped a big hug around my legs, I almost busted out crying. I'd never even thought of having kids before, but that hug tore something open inside of me, and this time it wasn't my ribs. I laid a hand on his shoulder, and when he looked up at me with those big, wet brown eyes and said, "Mi amigo," I thought of Danny so bad I had to force myself to turn away or I might never have left.

Why do we have to leave those we love?

Why do we love those we can never have?

*   *   *

I headed the Ford back north, wondering all the way if the Ensenada trip had amounted to much more than taking one bad beating and making one good friend. It felt good to be on the road again; maybe it was the same thing I'd felt on the trip down, where the brain equates forward motion with forward progress, regardless of the facts. At least I knew now that Lionel Swopes, the big plunger, had taken his final plunge. Not only was he dead, but someone, or someones, had murdered him and disposed of his body. And I knew that someone, maybe the same someone, had not wanted me in Ensenada, or at least wanted me to *think* he didn't want me there. Well, that made it unanimous: Pedro notwithstanding, I didn't want to be in Ensenada either. Oh, and then there was Marie's intelligence report from the "front," which is what the Tam apparently was for Monique Smythe and her cohort. But did her information really amount to anything?

Well, I was bloody but still unbowed. I had a hard head and plenty of bravery, but I was running out of leads. If I couldn't locate the mysterious Arnold Hagemayer or Ernie Finnegan, then who and what was left? I suddenly realized that I'd forgotten to check in on Monique during the trip, as she requested. But somehow after what Marie had told me, it didn't seem that big an omission. I had a feeling that Monique Smythe might not be the poor little thing she portrayed herself to be; maybe she just figured the helpless act was the best way to jerk me around.

The sad thing is, she was probably right.

Chapter Seven

It was good to get back to my own place and lie down on a functional bed with sheets that were reasonably clean and even dry—at least until my next three-alarm nightmare.

Thank God I slept just fine that night and woke up mostly headache-free. I didn't even get beaten up for once. The first thing I did the next morning was to place two calls.

The first was to Doc Grimes.

"Hello? Doctor Grimes office."

"Hi, Katy, it's Cole. Been a while, huh?"

She laughed. "Yeah, I was starting to think you were cured or something."

"No such luck. What do you have for me?"

"This week? Let me see. I can give you today at four . . ."

"I'll take it."

She laughed again. "From that I take it you're not actually cured?"

"I may get pickled from time to time, but I'm definitely not cured."

"Okay then, see you at four."

The next one was no surprise: Bert Fawcett.

"Argyle Investments."

"May I speak to the head Argyle?"

There was a pause. "Is this Cole?"

"None other."

"Would you like to set up an appointment?"

"Honey, whether I'd like to or not, I need to."

"Okay, looks like maybe tomorrow around two could work?"

"Book it."

Good, making those two appointments felt like putting down roots again in good, rich soil. Not like the chalky sand of the cactus patch where Lionel Swopes had been unceremoniously dumped and forgotten. It was funny, I was probably the only soul on earth who'd even given the guy a thought in years. No matter what he did in life, everyone deserves better than that. And that placed Lionel on a par with Danny Trueluck: no living relatives, no sweetheart, no kids, no one but me to mourn his loss, or remember his smiling face and his big heart. That started me feeling sick again, but I forced my thoughts back to the things I had to do.

I drove to the office lot and tossed the keys to George.

"Where ya been, man?"

"Oh, down south, seeking fame and fortune."

"Find any?"

"Nope," I grinned, "guess I didn't drive far enough."

In the office I dialed my service.

"Answer World, Hattie speaking."

"It's Cole Dunbar. Any live ones?"

"Looks like a Mr. Rogers called three times. And let's see, a Miss Smythe, too."

"Did they leave any messages?"

"Nope, just their names."

"Thanks, honey."

Hmm, Monique could wait, but what did Buck Rogers want with me? Checking on what I've turned up so far? Seeing whether I still have any moxie left after the two beatings I'd taken since I saw him? Beatings he might have been behind?

I dialed his number.

"Hello?"

"Buck? Cole Dunbar here. What's up?"

"Where the hell ya been?"

"Nice to hear your voice, too, Johnny."

"Cut the crap; I asked you a question."

"You mean you don't know?"

"Now why in hell would I be asking if I already knew?"

"I was out of town for a few days, on business. Why?"

He said, "We need to talk."

"About?"

"Not on the phone. How about today?"

"Okay then, Pink's at one."

Slam!

I muttered, "Always a pleasure" into the dead receiver.

What the hell was the urgency about? Was he scared? Did he finally want to get on board and actually do his job on the Smythe case? Or just wash the taste of failure out of his mouth, something a bar full of Tail O' the Cock whiskey had been unable to do? Either way, I had a feeling Ernie Finnegan was behind it. Oh well, at worst I'd end up with a great chili dog.

*   *   *

I found a spot in the Pink's lot, then took a seat in the sun at one of the outside tables.

"Hey Cole, long time no see!"

It was Helen, waving at me from the counter.

I waved back. "Been out of town. I'm waiting for someone, but keep a chili dog in your heart for me."

She grinned. "You don't have to tell me that!"

I grabbed the sports section from a *Times* that was floating around. A large, round, beer-drinking first baseman for the Angels named Steve Bilko had been taking LA, and the Pacific Coast League, by storm all season, putting up triple crown numbers day after day, and carrying the whole team on his broad back. There hadn't been this much excitement about the Angels in years, maybe since they took the pennant back in '47. Bilko was the talk of the town, and his exploits took up much of the sports page every day.

"So tell me what you got."

I looked up. Buck Rogers' big body was blocking the sun.

I smiled. "For a minute there, I thought you were Steve Bilko."

"Very funny, kid. Now we talk."

I shook my head. "Wrong; first we order, then we talk. I just spent a whole week on a steady diet of tacos and beans, and right now I need a chili dog in the worst way."

He looked impatient, clearly a guy not used to waiting. "Okay then, order up and get it over with."

I said, "That's no way to talk about a Pink's chili dog." I walked over to the counter and confirmed what Helen already knew.

Buck was sitting there drumming his fingers on the table when I got back. He asked, "So? What do you have?"

I yawned and stretched. "Oh, you mean on the Smythe case?" There are few things more fun than making a guy like that wait.

He growled, "You know damn well I mean the Smythe case."

"Okay then, I just spent a week down in Ensenada, gettin' knocked around for my trouble."

"What the hell were you doin' down there?"

I looked him in the eye. "I thought you might know."

"How the hell would *I* know?"

I was time to level with him. "Listen, right after I talked to you at the Tail O' the Cock, someone got into my place and beat the hell out of me. Then, down in Ensenada, I got more of the same, except this time the guy was even more committed to his work; I was laid up in bed for a whole week. And both times the guy left a sweet little note saying drop the Smythe case, or else." I paused. "Now, considering the timing of the first beating, wouldn't *you* be wondering if Buck Rogers might be mixed up in it somehow?"

He actually raised his right hand and said, "Kid, I swear to you, I got nothin' to do with any of it. Listen, I got as much reason as you to want to see the Smythe case through." He licked his lips. "Maybe more."

I'd never seen him look sincerely upset like this before. I said, "All right Buck, I'm giving you a pass for now, but if I ever hear of you doing anything on this case that isn't absolutely kosher . . ."

"Kid, you don't have to worry about me; look, I know I got a reputation for being hard to handle, but I'm playing this one by the book." He looked down. "I got my reasons." When he looked up he licked his lips again and said, "So, you gonna tell me what you found out down there?"

I thought it over for a minute, then finally decided to trust him, at least as far as I had to. "Okay then, what I found out is that Lionel Swopes was murdered down there and dumped in a sand pit out of town."

Buck's eyes perked up with interest. "Well, that's one down, I guess. And it also confirms that there *was* some funny business going on behind the scenes." He thought for a moment and said, "Maybe it was a falling out among thieves?"

I shrugged. "Your guess is as good as mine. But don't forget, rich gringos, or at least white guys who're thought to be rich, do get killed in Mexico. And from what I hear the guy was a player anyway; he might've made a loan shark mad, or any one of a hundred other possibilities."

Now it was my turn to ask the questions. "Okay Buck, I coughed up what I know; now maybe you have some information for me."

He frowned. "Like for example?"

"Oh, like maybe where the hell Ernie Finnegan's gotten himself to, for starters."

The moment I said the name, I could see something shift in his face. Whatever it was, he composed himself again and said, "How would I know?"

I was getting tired of his act. "Because you were Ernie's fucking partner for years, Buck, and because you know damn well that if you were me, you'd be asking the same exact questions . . ." I paused ". . . and not getting any answers."

His red cop face told me he wasn't used to being put on the defensive. But he clearly wanted something from me, so he had to play nice for now. Besides, I had common sense on my side; anybody working an old case would want to talk to the original investigating officers.

"Honest to God, I don't know where the guy is." He shrugged. "Sure, it's true I was his partner, but he was always kind of a borderline character, and frankly it didn't surprise me that after the Department was through with him, he drifted out of sight. He was that kind of a guy." He looked at me. "Why does it matter so much?"

Helen brought my chili dog and I took a big bite out of it; it really hit the spot. Between bites I said, "You know why: you two were the only Departmental link to the investigation, the only two who were actually there and spent time figuring motivation, opportunity and all that other Dick Tracy crap. I want to know your thoughts, your suspicions, your dead ends. But you haven't really said a usable word, and Ernie Finnegan has disappeared off the face of the earth. Now, how do you think that looks to me?"

His fat face went beet-red again. "I don't give a flying fuck how that looks to you, wise ass. I was there, and I'm telling you, the fuckin' thing was air-tight all the way around the block. Sure, the sale was suspect, the fire was a big red flag, but in the end, there was nothing illegal we could pin on anybody." He leaned forward. "And you know I wanted to, the way the whole damn mess made us look."

I said, "So then why are you here?" I took another big bite. "I know it's not for the chili dogs."

I watched his expression go from rage to frustration to defeat. "All right, look, much as I hate to admit it to a young pup like you, we couldn't crack it, and it galls me from here to Sunday to be made a fool of by some mystery scam artist and his pet pyro, whoever they were." He paused. "Yeah, I know I'm no Sir Galahad anymore; I've been around the block a few too many times for that. But I still have some professional pride left, and this one just sticks in my craw." He shook his head. "As for Ernie Finnegan, I'll even help you find him, if it makes you feel good. But he's too dumb to know anything, and too uninterested, too. Oh, he was pissed off that the case made him look bad, but that's all. He's the type who does the least possible, gets his pension, then gets out."

"Except he didn't *get* his pension, and he was *told* to get out." I finished off the dog and wiped my mouth. "And for that matter, if he's the kind of a guy you say he is, what makes you think he couldn't be dirty?"

His face flashed red again. "Hell, that's the first place the public always goes, isn't it? 'The goddam cops are dirty.' That way they don't have to face the fact that the Department's always understaffed and undertrained, that we're working on a million cases at once, that everything's a goddam priority, and that solving crimes is hard—sometimes impossible."

I pulled out a Camel. Buck grunted "Gimme," and I shook one out for him, then lit us both up.

He took a deep drag, then said, "But like I say, if it makes you feel good, I'll help you find Finny. You won't get anything useful out of him, but I'll help." He looked at me. "Is that what you want?"

I nodded. "Yes. And for the record, it *would* make me feel good." I paused. "And now that we're getting down to brass tacks, what is it that *you* want,

Detective Rogers? Because you don't look like any Salvation Army lady to me."

He nodded. "All right, I want in on whatever you find out—all the way. I want . . ." I couldn't believe it, but he actually teared up. "I want a chance to clear myself."

Maybe he was just a good faker, but those watery blue eyes made me feel like the big blowhard might be worth taking a chance on. "Okay Buck, it's a deal, but that goes both ways; I want in on whatever you found out in the initial investigation, and whatever you find out now. And don't forget, I'm working for my client, not the LAPD, so if I can put a stop to the extortion, maybe I'm satisfied. And if you end up smelling like a rose too, that's just gravy."

He nodded. "I got it." He threw down the lit cigarette and ground it into the asphalt. "Okay, I'll get on the Finnegan thing right now and get back to you in a couple days. We can talk more then." He took out his LAPD business card and wrote something on the back of it. "Here's my private number. I'm alone when I'm at home nowadays, so you can call anytime."

There was something sad about watching him walk away. Was it that such a proud, forceful man had been reduced to humbling himself in front of me? That he was clearly still hurting about the Departmental guff he took about the Smythe case? Or was it the haunted look in his eyes when he said, "I'm alone when I'm at home nowadays"?

Either way, I was glad to have a "real" detective on this case with me, because to be honest, I still didn't feel good enough, professionally or personally, to wrap this thing up on my own.

Speaking of low self-esteem, it was time for my appointment with Doc Grimes.

*   *   *

"Have a seat, Cole, Doc's running just a bit late."

I picked up my usual *New Yorker* and pretended to read. I'd been observing Doc's other patients for a while now and concluded that therapy patients don't actually read the magazines anyway; their minds are so focused on the coming session that they just skim the magazines and try to look stable, like the kind of people who read magazines and *don't* go to therapists. If Doc ever gave his patients a test on our waiting room reading material, we'd all get 'F's.

"C'mon in Cole, you're looking well."

"Shows what you know; I got beat up in Mexico, and my head and ribs have just started speaking to me again."

Doc raised his eyebrows. "Oh my God, what happened?"

I shrugged. "Someone decided I shoulda stood in bed."

"Well, better bed than dead."

I nodded. "That's true; you can come back from the bed."

I spent the next fifteen minutes filling him in on the Smythe case, the search for Swopes and Hagemayer, and everything that happened in Ensenada, including finding the grave and my body's reaction to it. I also told him about Pedro, and how he'd taken such good care of me. And how hard it was for me to leave him.

Doc just nodded and listened quietly until I ran out of words.

Then he turned that damn truth beam of his on me, and I knew we were ready for the second act. "So tell me, how's the inner Cole doing?"

I froze; fear of this moment was exactly why I couldn't focus on the *New Yorker*. I gamely said, "Uh, I'll try." But some backstage Johnny rang down the curtain again and I blanked out.

A couple of silent minutes later Jim said, "Can you tell me what it's like right now?"

I nodded. "Sure. It's like I'm a writer sitting in front of a blank page and coming up empty." I thought for a moment. "I remember my mother sitting there like that a thousand times. Except instead of feeling like a loser like I do, she'd get real mad, then take it out on me."

Jim said, "Okay, but let's get back to you right now. So you say you can't find the words?"

"Hell, I can't even find the music."

He smiled in that long-suffering way of his that was both encouraging and maddening at the same time. "Okay, so let's give it a little while longer. Now try to focus on your feelings, not your thoughts."

"My feeling is that I'm wasting your time."

"Let me be the judge of that, please."

"Now you're mad at me."

"I'm not mad at you, Cole; where'd you get that idea?"

I thought back. "From Mom, I guess; she was always mad at me for everything that didn't go exactly the way she wanted."

"Like you?"

I cringed. "You mean I'm always mad when things don't go my way, too?"

He shook his head. "No, Cole, I mean that you're an example of something that didn't go the way she wanted."

I said, "Oh, well that's a given." I pictured my childhood. "It seemed like I couldn't do anything right, so I just tried to stay out of sight and, you know, kind of bide my time."

"You mean, until you could get away?"

I nodded.

"And is that why you joined the Marines? To run away from home?"

I rubbed my chin. "I don't know. Yeah, maybe. But honestly, the Marines felt more like running *to* home. We were all in it together, we took an oath to do our best, and we took pride in being in it together till . . . you know . . .

death do us part." I felt the tears coming now, images of Danny flooding my mind: boot camp, nights in San Diego, then the final, indelible horror of the mortar shell that erased his wonderful grin forever. I pushed the pictures back and went on. "It was the first time I ever felt proud to be part of a group, and proud of the guys I was with, too. Kind of like walking down the street with a beautiful girl; you feel proud to be with her, proud by association, like 'We're the best, and I'm a part of it'—all the things I never felt about my own so-called family."

I reached for a Kleenex and wiped the tears, then held the wet tissue out to Jim and grinned. "Are you happy now?"

Jim laughed out loud. "Yeah, I'm happy now." Then he turned serious. "Can we talk about something else for a minute?"

I laughed. "Oh, so now *you're* the one deflecting us away from my emotions?"

He was still serious. "No, not really. I just wanted to say I'm concerned that you've been beaten up twice now . . . maybe not by the same guy, but the same guy was probably behind it both times." I could see the concern in his eyes. "How do we know that the next time they're not going to finish the job?"

I sighed. "I've thought about that too. And maybe to someone outside the PI business this is gonna sound ridiculous, but my best life insurance is that I don't know enough for them to kill me yet."

He nodded ironically. "Very reassuring." He paused. "And I'm sure that was very comforting to Swopes and Hagemayer, too, right up to the moment they were killed."

"Wait a minute; you don't know for sure that Hagemayer was killed."

Jim gave a mirthless chuckle. "Right, and I can't prove definitively that there isn't a Santa Claus either, but just the same, I can be pretty sure."

I didn't have a smart-ass rejoinder for that one.

Jim glanced at the clock. "Cole, looks like we're just about out of time for today."

I *did* have a smart-ass rejoinder for that one. "So tell me, Sigmund, what did we learn today?"

Jim Grimes wasn't laughing now. "Well, I don't know what you learned, but what I learned is that when Danny Trueluck was killed, you lost not only your whole family, but your innocence too. And that's a big loss."

I got that sick feeling in the pit of my stomach again. "Jeez Doc, I was just kidding. You didn't have to hit me with a haymaker right at the bell, did you?"

He said, "I'm sorry Cole, but you did ask." He paused. "And I have another one for you, too."

I rolled my eyes. "Lay it on me, Bwana."

"When I asked about your being in danger, did it even occur to you that it was because I *care* about you—a lot?"

I thought it over as I fumbled a cigarette out and held the lighter to it. "To be perfectly honest, Doc, I think I mostly felt guilty for *putting* myself in danger, because it upset *you*." I took a drag on the cigarette and cocked my head at him. "Why, isn't that normal?"

Jim sighed and rolled his eyes. "Mr. Dunbar, offhand I'd say we still have work to do."

Chapter Eight

That night I fought the battle of Okinawa again, in Cinerama. Blood and guts filled the air, a lot of it splattering the survivors, as we took hill after hill straight-on, right in the face of enemy fire. The most nightmarish part was that we had orders not to stop, no matter what, so we had to keep plowing ahead despite horrendous losses, exhaustion, despair and even thirst that parched our throats so bad that after a while we didn't even have enough spit left to form words anymore; we just made these croaking, animal sounds that no one could hear or understand, leaving each of us alone in his private hell.

I fought my way back to wakefulness for what felt like hours, like a man trapped under the frozen surface of a lake searching desperately for a breathing hole. And when I finally popped up out of it, I had the worst headache of all time, a throbbing monster that even those leftover Mexican horse pills couldn't touch. There was nothing to do the rest of the morning but lie there and take it, half-comatose from the pills, yet still in such hammering, head-exploding agony that I half-wished I'd just stayed in the nightmare and died on the battlefield like a man . . . like Danny.

At noon the shrill ringing of the phone shocked me out of the abyss I'd fallen into, each ring piercing my brain like a dentist's drill. I reached over and snatched up the receiver. I didn't give a damn who it was; I just wanted the noise to stop.

I barked, "What the hell do *you* want?"

"Mr. Dunbar? It's, uh, Hattie—you know, from Answer World?"

I forced myself to sit up. "Sorry, I didn't mean to bite your head off. I'm just having a bad day here."

"Yeah, I kind of guessed that. Anyway, I wouldn't have bothered you, but I just thought I should tell you Miss Smythe has been calling for days, and she's rather distressed that you haven't answered her calls for more than a week."

"Oh shit, of course. Okay, I'll get back to her in a few minutes. Thanks for the heads up."

"Hope you feel better, sir."

Hell, it wasn't just about calling Monique; I had to get back to the real world pronto. My little vacation, such as it was, was over. I had jobs to do for my clients and they didn't allow for shell shock, battle fatigue or whatever they were calling it this week. I was now out of my Ensenada morphine, so I did the next best thing: I went to the icebox and pulled out two bottles of Eastside. I snapped the cap off the first one and drank it with one hand, while the other hand rolled the coolness of the other bottle against my aching head. When I finished the first bottle, I uncapped the second one and repeated the whole procedure with the next bottle until the whole six-pack had died in a good cause. Of course, by the time I finished, I was half in the bag from the morphine, the beer and the headache, but at least I didn't want to die anymore.

I took a quick shower, shaved and threw on some clean clothes, then sat down to call Monique. But what was I going to tell her? That I'd seen Lionel Swopes' grave and it made me sick? That she and Uriah Heep were now suspects too? I finally decided to play it by ear, which is a polite way of saying I had no idea what to do.

"Hello?"

"Hi Monique, it's Cole Dunbar."

"Well, it's about time! Do you know I've been calling you for days?"

"I'm sorry about that. But as you know I was in Mexico, and the phone connections with the U.S. aren't . . ."

"Don't give me that eyewash. I want to know what you found out while you were off spending all my goddam money down there!"

Hmm, this wasn't the charm school sophisticate I'd first met at the Tam. "Well, before I get into all that, is there anything you want to tell *me*?"

"Like what? Remember, you're the one playing detective in this little drama of ours; I'm just the helpless victim of a blackmail racket."

Should I press her further? I decided to try. "Is there anyone else who's part of this thing? That is, anyone you know?"

"What the hell do you mean by that?" I'd never heard that tone in her voice before. I didn't like it, and it made me feel like pushing her harder.

"Someone mentioned something about seeing you with a man occasionally—a tall, slim man with spiky hair?"

She exploded. "Who the fuck do you think you are, spying on me like that? How *dare* you question me about my social connections, you little lowlife worm! My personal life is my own affair, and always has been! And by the way, who told you about these imaginary meetings anyway?"

"I'm not at liberty to . . ."

"It's that little redheaded bitch, isn't it? She's had the cow eyes for you ever since that first day. Why that little sneak, I knew from the beginning she was out to sink me. I'll fix her little red wagon . . ."

"Monique, it's not her, I promise you. If you'd think for a minute, you'll realize I didn't even say it took place at the Tam. In my business I know many people around town, who . . ."

"Who spy on your own clients for you? Is that what you've been doing with my money?"

"Miss Smythe, calm down, please. I just asked you a simple question. I'm not implying anything sinister. I merely wanted to know if there's anyone in your life who's following this case, or taking a hand in it, even if it's behind the scenes. This could be very important information for me, even if you think they're totally trustworthy. After all, it's often the close associates of . . ."

"Well screw you and the horse you rode in on, buster!" Now she was yelling. "None of my friends or associates, as you call them, could possibly be involved in any way with a sinister plot like that! I resent your implication, and furthermore, I resent the hell out of you!"

"Miss Smythe, look, I'm sorry if I've . . ."

"You're fired!"

Slam!

Look, I hate being fired as much as the next guy, but at the moment the sound of the slammed phone was my biggest problem. It went off like a depth charge in my eardrums and made my whole head ring with a rolling ice cream headache.

Now I was a castaway, out of pills *and* beer. I had to get creative. I took both ice trays out of the freezer and dumped all the cubes into the biggest bowl I could find. Then I took an ice pick and cracked the cubes into small chips. I filled the rest of the bowl with water and waited a couple of minutes. Then I put my face down into the cold water. I would hold it there until I couldn't feel anything anymore, then pull my face out for a while, then repeat the dunking procedure as many times as I could until the water wasn't cold anymore. It worked, or at least it made all the feeling in my head go away until I didn't even know I *had* a head anymore. I'm not sure that was a major loss.

Then the phone shrilled again and ruined all my hard work.

My first thought: maybe it was Monique, calling to take it all back.

Fat chance.

"Hello?"

"I got somethin' for ya."

"Buck? Is that you?"

"You wanna hear it or not?"

"Tell you what; come to my place on North Highland and bring two cold six-packs of beer; then you can sing to me all night if you want."

"Sing? Beer? What the hell's wrong with you?"

"Just do it." I gave him the address.

He was silent.

"Please?"

"Okay okay, I'm on my way. Any special brand?"

"Yeah, cold."

"That ain't a brand."

"It is tonight."

"Jesus Christ, kid, you have got it bad. Gimme a half hour."

"Right."

I tried to clean up the place a little, between shockwaves of headache. I even straightened up the living room, which in my condition was a heroic gesture. Then I lay down on the couch and turned on the radio. Very low. Thank God it was only Perry Como, the old whisperer himself, crooning *Hello, Young Lovers*. The song certainly didn't apply to me now, now that I'd killed whatever small chance I ever had to make any music with Monique Smythe. But to be honest, her last verbal exhibition had scotched her chances with me anyway. Not that there ever were any such chances. The woman had a mouth on her like a truck driver, and that definitely wasn't my brand.

Knock! Knock!

I eased myself upright, remembering not to try and shake the cobwebs out of my splitting head.

I opened the door. "Buck, c'mon in."

He was standing there holding a brown shopping bag out to me, eyeing me like I had the cooties. I took the bag over to the icebox and unloaded the beer, taking out one for libation and one for first aid.

Buck stood there giving me the fisheye. "You look like hell; what happened?"

I shrugged. "A hard night, with bad dreams and no sleep." I held out a beer to him. "Want one?"

"Naw, I'm not much for beer," he said, still giving me the eye, "especially on the job."

It was a good shot at me, but from his red, bulbous nose and distended gut I was betting he *was* "much" for the hard stuff, off *or* on the job.

I indicated the living room chair to him, then took a seat on the couch and asked, "So, what you got for me?"

"I located Ernie."

"Wow, that was fast!" I hoped he got my "shot" back at him, seeing as how he'd denied all knowledge of his old running mate just yesterday.

He took his time lighting a cigarette, then said, "But see, the thing is, the guy's not in real good shape." He fiddled with the cigarette some more before stabbing it back between thin lips. "In fact, I guess you could say he's kind of down and out."

I angled my head. "You mean, like in a rescue mission?"

He cleared his throat and rubbed his chin, obviously more than a little uncomfortable with this whole conversation. "Well, not even that. It's more like a . . ."

I waited him out, sensing that he was still feeling protective of his old partner. Being a cynical bastard of course, I immediately wondered why, but I wasn't entirely ruling out genuine human feelings either.

". . . I guess you could call it a hobo jungle."

My eyes went wide. "Really? Was it the booze that got him, or what?"

Buck nodded slowly. "Yeah, among other things. But he says he's willing to talk to you." He squirmed in his chair. "Just don't expect too much." He reached up and tapped his head. "He's not all there anymore."

I nodded. "Yeah, I get it." Whether Ernie Finnegan was worth talking to or not, it was still my job to be thorough and see it through, even though, technically, I wasn't even *on* a job anymore. "So, where do we meet?"

He stood up, looking more uncomfortable than ever, his face flushing red like before. "Meet me at noon tomorrow at a place called El Buono Etoile, at Olympic and Western, and I'll take you there."

For an awkward moment we sat there looking at each other. It felt like he wanted something, but if it was company, my head was voting no with every painful throb. Finally, I forced myself to say, "Sure you don't want a beer?"

He shook his big head. "Naw, like I said, I'm not really a beer man."

If that was my cue to offer him a "real" drink, he was out of luck. All I wanted was to lie down and be left alone with cold beer and dark silence. Besides, if he wanted booze and company, society had thoughtfully provided places like the Tail O' the Cock to fulfill the late-night needs of discriminating gentlemen.

He finally stood up. "Okay then, I guess I'll be shoving off."

He'd get no argument from me. I got up to let him out and had that same feeling of sadness again as I watched him walk to his car. But why? Was he actually lonely? Did it hurt him to give up his friend to someone outside their own little world? Or was he afraid that Ernie, in his demented state, might slip up and spill the beans to me about something incriminating that was supposed to be their little secret?

Chapter Nine

As I turned onto Western for the drive to El Buono Etoile, I marveled—in a bad way—that, after all this time on the Smythe case, it was still nothing more than an endless series of loose ends. In my racket, I was used to moral confusion, where sometimes the bad guy hired me to get the good guy; I was even used to doing dirty jobs for people who were operating from raw, twisted emotions—jealousy, resentment, spite—with only the ugliest of reasons to pay me to do what they wanted me to do. But this time everything was up for grabs and all I knew was what showed on the surface: Someone was blackmailing Monique Smythe for money. Period. Did it even have any connection with the odd circumstances surrounding the sale of the building? The burning of the building? The police who did the initial investigation?

Maybe I was just wasting my time, and all it amounted to was that some crumbum sitting at home read in the society column where Monique Smythe, wealthy daughter of a retired accountant, had attended a fancy party, and wham bam, they did a little research on the case and decided they wanted that insurance money for themselves. Was I even the right man for the job? It sure didn't feel like it now. And thinking about Monique reminded me of her outburst last night. Sure, it shocked and disappointed me, but there was more to it than that. Was she upset that somebody had seen her with that man, or was she upset that the somebody was Marie? I was embarrassed to even admit it to myself, but some ridiculous part of me still hoped she saw Marie as a rival . . . for me.

I pulled into the lot behind the little food joint and parked. I rounded the front of the building and looked up at a garish neon sigh that blinked out El Buono Etoile, showcasing some misguided soul's flair for linguistic incest. A smaller sign with chipped and faded paint told me they specialized in tamales, lasagna and chicken fried steak. But that's LA for you; shove all the cultures together, sprinkle some glitter on it, and light it up with neon.

Buck Rogers was just polishing off a tamale when I walked up to him. I grinned. "So this is your Pink's, huh?"

He stuffed the last piece into his mouth. "Order up and let's go."

I ordered a Coke and a tamale to go and said, "Your car or mine?"

He grunted, "I'll drive."

We walked to his two-tone '55 Chevy coupe and I slid into the passenger seat.

He started it up and we took off down Olympic, me balancing the food on my lap as I ate.

"So, where's it at?" I asked, just to break the silence, expecting a Buck Rogers non-answer.

"You'll see."

There it was, right on schedule.

He seemed preoccupied with something, something other than what we were doing at the moment. Finally I asked. "What's on your mind, anyway? You seem like you're a million miles away."

I could see him come back to the present, his sadness palpable. A minute later he said, "Okay then, it's my wife. She left me about a year ago, and I guess I never really saw how much I depended on her. I still don't understand what the hell went wrong; maybe I never will. She said being married to a cop is like being with a husband who's having an affair every day, right out in the open, except the other woman is his job. Christ, you miss a few dinners and before you know it, it's strike three, you're out. I don't know what the hell the woman expected." He turned to me. "Dammit, I have to do my job, don't I?"

I nodded. "Sure you do. But it takes a certain kind of woman to be a cop's wife. Some women just aren't built that way, and sometimes love isn't enough." I sounded wise, but he'd just articulated one of the main reasons I never got heavily involved with women: inevitably their needs end up tearing you in two and before you know it you're guilty, miserable and angry all the time. How could "love" ever last under those circumstances?

Buck just shook his head and looked even sadder.

It's funny, but it made me feel closer to the guy. Whenever I thought about sharing things like that with someone, I felt like I'd be burdening them. But Buck's telling me about his wife didn't feel like a burden at all; it was more like being trusted with something private. Is that what my meeting Ernie Finnegan would be for him, too?

We pulled onto the Harbor Freeway and headed south. Five minutes later he exited the freeway and pulled off to the right, heading into the industrial section of LA, a place where you wouldn't want to get caught alone—or even with a squad of Marines—at night. Shortly after we crossed Alameda Avenue, he pulled up in front of an empty lot with cyclone fencing all around it, topped by forbidding razor wire. It looked and felt like a war zone.

He rammed the gearshift into Park and barked, "Get out."

Trash rattled down the empty sidewalks. The only sign of life was the Mexican gang graffiti scrawled on the sides of the buildings. For maybe the first time since I'd quit the Force, I was glad I was with a cop.

Buck jerked his thumb and said, "This way," as we walked to the other side of the vacant lot and around the corner. Twenty feet later there was a wide opening between two tall warehouses. I followed him into the narrow space and we made our way past a whole series of pitiful hovels that people had fashioned out of blankets, discarded packing boxes and sheets of corrugated metal. Men were lying out in the open on ragged mattresses, newspapers, or right on the pavement, looking half-dazed, some of them nursing green bottles of cheap wine, some just staring blankly into the distance. Women and small children huddled inside the makeshift dwellings, watching us pass with wary eyes, like we were men from Mars.

Buck stopped in front of a shelter covered with a blanket, then turned back to me and pointed. "In here." As I turned, he tapped me on the shoulder, then pulled a screw-top bottle of wine out from under his windbreaker and handed it to me. "Here, this might help."

I took the bottle, then lifted up the black blanket and edged warily into the gloom on the other side. It took my eyes a moment to adjust, but then I made out the barely-recognizable outline of Ernie Finnegan propped up against the building that formed the back wall. His head was lolling a bit, but his eyes were open and watching me. Before I could say anything, he muttered, "Bucky says you want somethin' with me."

I crouched down about five feet in front of him, trying to ignore the rank stench, and said, "Yeah Ernie, I wanted to talk to you about one of your old cases."

He squinted at me. "One of my old cases? What for? That's stuff's all over with now." Then he waved his hand around aimlessly and muttered, "I can't give you nothin', kid; I'm done for."

Moving slowly, I handed him the bottle. "Well, it might be that one of those cases isn't really over yet. It was about a commercial building that burned down under mysterious circumstances. There was some question of arson, but no one ever proved anything. You and Buck worked the case together; the Smythe case."

I could see in his eyes that it registered. He reached out for the bottle, unscrewed the top quickly and took two long slugs. Then he shook his head like a man trying to make something go away. "Well, fuck the Department, and fuck you too, man. You lookin' to cause trouble for me? More trouble? Fuck you!" He took another long slug of wine and glared at me, panting like an animal at bay.

I said, "Ernie, I swear I'm not here to cause you any trouble. And I'm not with the Department either, okay? I'm a friend of Buck's. He told you it's okay to talk to me, didn't he? Well, all I'm asking is anything you might remember about the case; any small detail, anything at all."

He seemed to calm down a little then, keeping at the wine until his eyelids started to droop. I knew this was my last chance before I lost him. I said, "Please, Ernie, was there anything that came up at all, maybe something the Department didn't know?"

No response.

"How about the names Lionel Swopes or Arnold Hagemayer? Do they bring back anything?"

He was fading fast now; I had to try again. "Swopes? Hagemayer? Anything at all?"

He started to sway back and forth. Then, in a little singsong voice he muttered something that sounded like, "Kissy, kissy, kissy."

"What's that, Ernie? Kissy?"

He shook his head and again said, "Kissy, kissy." Then he gathered himself and, with great effort, said, "Ki-*tee*." Then he rocked back and forth again, almost smiling to himself.

"You mean, Kitty?"

He nodded. "Yeah, Ki-tee. Down at the fuzz."

I was stumped. I repeated, "The fuzz?" but it was too late; he was passed out now with the wine bottle clutched to his chest, the last drops spilling onto his shirt. My "interview" was over.

Suddenly the thick reek of cheap wine, urine, feces and body odor became a taste, not a smell, bringing back Okinawa with a sudden rush, as I started feeling queasy again.

Quickly I ducked back under the blanket and came out into the light again, gulping clean air. I was grateful that, unlike Okinawa, when I left this place, it would leave me.

Buck was waiting for me out on the sidewalk. He flicked the remains of his cigarette to the ground and crushed it on the cracked concrete with his heavy shoe. "Whujya get?"

I shook my head. "Not much, probably nothing."

He still looked at me.

"Kissy? Kitty something? The fuzz, or fozz?"

He shook his head. "Beats me; probably just drunken babbling."

I shrugged and lit up a Camel, passing him one for the road, and said, "Yeah, that's what I thought too." I took a deep drag. The smell of burning tobacco was like heaven compared to the foul miasma of Ernie's last stand.

I sighed. "This one's got me beat. I'm no closer to the finish line now than I was weeks ago."

Buck nodded. "That's exactly how we felt on the Smythe case years ago. The whole goddam thing just wouldn't screw together, no matter how you twisted it."

I took a another pull on my cigarette. "Well, you've got company, Buck; now that gorilla's on my back, too."

My body gave an involuntary shudder. "Christ, let's get outta here; this place gives me the willies."

We drove all the way back in dead silence, both staring into blankness, thinking about our failure to move the needle one iota on this hellish case. Of course, technically, I had been fired, so I could've just quit the case cold, but for guys like me and the Johnny Rogers I was just beginning to know, a case wasn't like a shack-up job with some gal, where one day either of you can just turn around and say, "I don't like you so much anymore, I'm leaving." No, for us a job of work was somehow all mixed up with personal responsibility and duty. Even honor, to be corny about it.

Like I told Doc, maybe that's why I loved the Marines so much, why I joined up in the first place: I wanted to be around the best; people who meant it, who weren't there to do the minimum, who took personal pride in a job well done, a job finished. I don't know, maybe Doc would say it all started with a kid who wasn't even able to love his own mother; maybe that was the original sin, the original unfinished job, and I wanted to atone by pledging my best effort, maybe even my life, to seeing a hard job through, to prove to myself that I wasn't a piker, a feather merchant. And maybe, too, that I was finally worthy, finally good enough. I had been hired to do a job and now I had to see it through. Was that the torch Danny handed me as he disintegrated?

Finally, Buck pulled the Chevy up in front of what I now privately called El Bueno Ptomaino and we said goodbye wordlessly, knowing we'd be in touch again soon, because the case wasn't finished.

Or maybe just because we couldn't let it go.

After Buck drove off, I went to the counter, ordered up against my better judgment and polished off another tamale. After all the frustration of the case and all the despair of Ernie's half-life, even a bad tamale and a flat Coke hit the spot.

Sometimes the simplest things make life worth living.

Or at least beguile you into believing again, for a little while.

*   *   *

The LA Angels' management had called me to work security detail for the big game against their bitter crosstown rivals, the Hollywood Stars, the next night. With the whole town atwitter about big Steve Bilko, the Angels' rooters would be there in rabid numbers to cheer him on, which might create trouble with the Stars' fans who'd driven across town to little Wrigley Field, hoping Big Steve would strike out four times. The potential for drunken fisticuffs was obvious. I still owed Marie one, so I called her up to ask if she'd like to come along, and to my surprise she agreed happily, even after I explained that I probably wouldn't be able to spend much time with her during the game. It turned out she was a big Angels' fan herself.

Marie was standing there in front of her apartment waving when I pulled into the driveway. With her white blouse, pink pedal pushers, black flats and an Angels' cap with that flaming red hair spilling out from it, she looked like one of those gorgeous "outdoor" cover girls they pose in front of speedboats and campfires.

She walked over to me and I rolled down my window as she held up a knapsack. "Hi, I brought us some fried chicken and a few other things."

I grinned. "You don't mean you can cook, too?"

She rolled her eyes. "What say we leave the Neanderthal back in his cave for tonight, okay?"

I reached my hand out. "Deal."

She shook my hand, then ran around to the other side and hopped in. "Looks like Dick Drott's going for us tonight; whaddya think?"

I turned around to back out of the driveway. "Gee, I haven't had much time to follow the stats this season, but as I remember he's just a kid, isn't he?"

She said, "Sure, but I think he's destined for the Majors. Yeah, he's young, but he's got *some* curveball." She grinned. "Plus he looks real cute in his uniform, especially from behind."

I laughed. "Hey, knock it off; what do you call the female version of a Neanderthal?"

"There *is* no female version in this car; just a modern, multidimensional woman."

"I'll have to take your word for that. After all, you *are* the brains of this outfit."

She grinned. "Now you're talking sense."

We drove along in silence for a long time. Finally, I turned left into the Wrigley Field parking lot and pulled into an empty space.

Marie turned to me and put her hand on my arm. "It's really eating at you, isn't it?"

I angled my head. "What is?"

"You know what: the Smythe case."

I bit my lip. "I . . . I don't know . . . I mean, I guess so."

"It's pretty obvious, from your dark, brooding silences."

"Aw jeez, I'm sorry, I didn't mean to . . ."

She shook her head. "No, that's not it; I'm just worried about you. I mean, I see that your profession means a lot to you, but you can't let a single case take over your whole life." She smiled. "I mean, you're not even following Steve Bilko and the Angels; that's practically un-American in LA this season!"

I held up my hands. "Okay, I'll try to do better."

Still looking serious, she said, "Maybe we can talk about it later." Then she shrugged nonchalantly and said, "If you want to, that is." I wasn't buying the nonchalance.

This girl was different somehow; I wasn't used to anyone being that interested in me or my work—she'd even called it a profession—except maybe Doc, and I didn't even know how much of his interest was because it was his job. Doc was getting paid; what was Marie's excuse? Feeling awkward, I just said, "Okay, we'll see."

As we waited in line at the turnstile, I debated whether to tell Marie that Monique had fired me, finally nixing the idea because I didn't want to spoil the mood or make her feel responsible in any way. I showed my security pass to the ticket-taker and handed him Marie's ticket. He tore off the stub and I passed it to her as we entered the reserved seat area. She studied the stub for a moment then smiled and waved it at me. "Hey, you did good! The first base line, right where I like to sit!"

I grinned. "Well, I had to pull a few strings, but I guess you'll be worth it."

She gave me a smoldering look. "That remains to be seen."

I walked with her down to her seat and said, "I got you one on the aisle, so I can come visit you later, provided the crowd behaves itself."

She took her seat, then dug a couple of wrapped pieces of fried chicken out of the knapsack, put them in a paper bag and handed it to me. "Here, take these, just so's you don't forget me."

"Thanks," I laughed as I took them, "but I don't think I'll need chicken to remember you."

My station was up in the bleachers, where the serious "fun" usually broke out. When you've worked crowd control for a while, you get to where you can sense the overall mood of a group pretty quickly, that is, whether they're out for blood or fun. This bunch was already pretty rowdy, with Bilko Fever running rampant, but unless something disastrous happened during the game, I had a feeling the next couple of hours would be pretty light duty.

The game started and all was going well, but for the first time in my life, I had a hard time keeping my mind on my job. As I went through the motions of scanning for trouble in the stands, I sifted through all the meager "evidence" I'd gathered on the Smythe case over and over again in my mind, like a down-on-his-luck old sourdough miner desperate to find the nugget that would finally lead him to the mother lode. Why couldn't I crack the code? What was I missing? I ducked out to the concession stand in the middle of a slow inning and got myself a Coke, then sat down on the concrete steps and started in on Marie's fried chicken. It was about the best I'd ever had; at least one of us wasn't an abject failure. As I ate I started going back over it all again: the trip to Ensenada, the gravesite, the strange talk with Ernie Finnegan . . .

"You're out of your fuckin' mind!"

"He's nothin' but a big fat flash in the pan!"

"Bilko's on his way to a goddam PCL Triple Crown, you moron!"

"Yeah? Well Mantle is too, but *he's* doing it with the *big* boys, not some broken-down has-beens and never-will-bes!"

Two drunks a few rows down from me were dancing around each other, both of them getting ready to swing. I sprang to my feet and took the steps two at a time until I got down to their level. I reached in and separated them, inserting my body into the space I created. "Hey boys, you don't really want to do this, do you? Let's all settle down and enjoy the game now. We're here to have fun, not kill each other."

I separated the struggling bodies still further as they kept shouting at each other to save face. As they cooled off, I could see disappointment on the faces of the men in the crowd. A pimple-faced teenage boy shouted out, "Boo! Stand back, bud, and let 'em duke it out!" Everyone laughed. But both combatants were out of steam now. Like with most sports-event scuffles, neither of them really wanted to fight; they'd just gotten in over their heads until there was no manly way to back out of it. That was security's job: giving them a way to retreat with honor.

Finally it was the seventh-inning stretch, and I hotfooted it down to the reserved seats to see how Marie was doing. When I spotted her, she was sharing some chicken with an older lady next to her, both of them gabbing away.

I stood in the aisle and said, "Hey there Red, got another piece for me?"

She turned around and smiled. "Hi, I saw you up there stopping a fight!" She clasped her hands together over her head. "My hero!"

I laughed. "Security's never the hero; the fans up there *wanted* a fight!" I knelt down on the concrete. "But how'd you see me all the way up there?"

She pointed to the powerful binoculars of the woman in the next seat. "I shared the chicken, she shared the binocs."

I said, "Well, at least you were looking at something other than the pitcher's heinie."

She smiled. "Oh? What makes you think I wasn't doing that, too?"

I stood up. "Listen, I gotta get back. I just wanted to check in and see if you were doing all right."

She said, "Thanks," and reached over to squeeze my hand.

For a second there, something inside me wanted to stop running away.

I hurried back to the cheap seats, confused about what I'd felt with Marie. It was great, but it wasn't that same ethereal feeling I'd had with Monique: giddy, almost desperate, and yearning, like reaching for a star. No, this was something different, something new and unfamiliar. I would never say this to Marie because she wouldn't understand how I meant it, but it reminded me of something one of my old buddies in the Marines used to do. He'd pull out a picture of his girl back home and say, "She's like an old shoe; she makes me feel like it's safe to be me."

Danny and I used to wait till he walked away and then repeat it, laughing our heads off.

I wasn't laughing anymore.

The Angels won the game, six to two, with Bilko contributing an RBI double and a run scored, and Dick Drott pitching his fabulous rear end off for eight strong innings to handcuff the Stars. And outside of a couple of minor scuffles, the happy fans behaved themselves. The security detail was expected to linger a while after the game and see that the place emptied out peaceably, then drift outside and keep an eye on the parking lots too. I made my way down to the reserved section, hoping Marie would understand.

As I approached her, sitting there in a sea of empty seats, she pointed to the bleachers and said, "It looked pretty quiet up there, far as I could tell."

I nodded. "Yep, pretty tame, other than those two bums in heat that I had to put the kibosh on." I leaned over toward her and grimaced. "Really sorry, but I gotta hang around for a while here and make sure all goes well."

She shrugged. "Hey, a job's a job, right? Whatever they need, that's what you gotta do." She packed up the knapsack and slung it on her back.

I smiled. "Hey, I like your attitude. Most girls would be moaning and groaning about having to stick around after the game's over."

She shrugged. "Like I said, a job's a job." As we walked together, she slipped her hand into mine. "And for the record," she said as she bumped me with her hip, "I'm *not* most girls."

"Yeah," I grinned, "I'm starting to see that."

On the drive back to Marie's apartment, we made some perfunctory conversation, then she lapsed into a thoughtful silence. After I pulled into her driveway, I turned off the ignition and said, "Hey lady, on the way to the game you accused me of brooding. I could say the same for you on the way back. What's up?"

She looked surprised at first. "You pay attention to things, don't you?"

I shrugged. "Well, I guess you could say that's my business." I reached out for her hand. "But you're more than business to me."

She looked at me. "Am I?" She pulled her hand away and turned away to look out her window. "Because I could have sworn you were spoken for."

Ouch. That hit a nerve, and if she was smart enough to say it, she was smart enough to know it. I tried to think of a response, but nothing came.

Finally, she turned back to me. "Listen Cole, let's just say we had a real nice time tonight and leave it at that." She laid a hand on her door lever.

"Marie, I don't want you to think . . ."

She nodded. "I know. That's my big problem: I think, and it gets me in trouble." She gathered her things, opened the car door and started up the walkway to the building.

I pulled the lever to open my door, but she held up a hand to me. "No, please don't; let's not ruin it."

Shit, in my experience, when a girl says, "Let's not ruin it," it's already ruined. I could see tears in her eyes. All I could think to say was, "I guess I'll be seeing you at the Tam." I regretted saying it as soon as the words came out of my mouth, but what came next was worse.

She turned and shook her head. "I doubt it. I got fired yesterday."

I said, "What?" and started out of the car again, but she held up her hand to me again and said, "Cole, I already told you; no!"

She ran into the building.

My God, how could such a great evening fall off the cliff so suddenly? I felt like I'd never understand women's ways. Why did she act like peaches and cream all night, then suddenly turn and drop an atom bomb on me? Was the drive home some kind of a test? Was I supposed to say something that I didn't?

And for that matter, why did Monique act like she did last night, if she had nothing to hide? And if it was because she liked me, why didn't she show it, instead of firing me?

All I knew was that this was par for the course for me with women. Christ, I was already half crazy with the Smythe case; if this is what being "cared about" by a woman was like, I'd rather sit this dance out.

*   *   *

The next morning, I woke up determined to get my life back to normal, or at least normal for me. After Marie's dramatic walkout and the firing by Monique—of myself *and* Marie—plus drawing a blank all around on the Smythe case, my "old" life was looking better and better by the minute. At least in those days I knew what to do for a client when they hired me: find a missing child; locate a witness who will exonerate the client; prove adultery to get someone out of their marriage. Like tacos and beans, the work was cheap but filling.

I drove to the office, then walked in and took a good look around. This was my world, my office, my domain. Yes, that felt much better. I sat in my chair and put my feet up on the desk.

It was time to go to work. I called the service.

"Mr. Dunbar? We have a couple messages for you."

"Okay, shoot."

"Uh, a Mr. Rogers said to call him, he might be onto something. And yes, there's one from a Miss Smythe, too."

I cringed inside, expecting the worst. "Go ahead, read it: what does it say?"

"It says, 'You're hired again.'"

Shit. I didn't know whether to be happy or sad. Last night it felt like a relief to have a way out of the marathon that was the Smythe case, but now . . . damn, I just didn't know anymore.

Well, since I was in the hunt again, the least I could do was return Buck's call. I dialed his cop number: nothing. His home number: zippo. He was probably out in the field, doing the job the taxpayers were actually paying him to do. I couldn't fault him for that; part of me was starting to wish I had the support of a whole police force again too, not to mention the benefits and the camaraderie. But at the time I'd had good reasons for quitting—I just couldn't remember what they were at the moment.

Did I dare call Marie? Maybe it was too soon. Or maybe I was just chicken.

In any case, if I told myself it was too soon, I wouldn't have to call her now.

I told myself it was too soon.

Okay, I was back on the Smythe case. But what more could I do at the moment? I started pacing the floor.

Ring. Ring.

"Hello?"

"Dunbar? Get your ass downtown, immediately."

"What? Who *is* this?"

"Detective Lieutenant Philip Crosetti. That good enough for ya?"

"What's this all about?"

"It's all about the fact that Johnny Rogers turned up a little dead last night, in the LA River. And what do you know, a little while later we pulled some old stiff out of the river, too. His prints match someone you just might know of."

"Look Crosetti, just tell me already."

"Oh, just a certain party named Arnold Hagemayer. Ever hear of him?"

"Oh shit."

"Oh shit is right, because we're pretty sure you either did it or know plenty about it."

"What the hell would I want to kill Buck Rogers for? Or Hagemayer, for that matter?"

He snorted. "That's exactly what we're gonna find out the second you get here. Now are you comin', or do I need to send a wet nurse down there for you with a baby buggy?"

I fell back into my chair. "I'm on my way."

"You'd better be."

Christ, and I thought this was going to be my get-life-back-to-normal day.

My mind raced: if they really thought they had me made for Buck's murder, or Hagemayer's, they wouldn't be calling me like this to come in . . . would they? That helped, a little. And I had a pretty good idea what it would be like at the station, too: they were going to pound on me until I coughed up every little detail of the Smythe case, then threaten to pull my license for not disclosing it all earlier as "police business." But sweet Jesus, if they tagged me as a cop killer—even if they had to back me into it with planted evidence and bought-and-paid-for testimony—a tough interrogation and losing my PI license would be the least of my problems. Buck Rogers had been the only buffer between me and the department, the only one who could testify that I'd let him in fully on the facts as I knew them. But now he was gone, and I couldn't clear myself unless I was free.

God help me.

Chapter Ten

"Listen guys, if you'd just let me . . ."

"Get in there and shut the hell up." Phil Crosetti shoved me roughly into the bare interrogation room, alone. I knew what was coming, and I felt nauseous. I mentally listed the few things in my favor: they hadn't booked me, so I still had hope on that score; and I was praying that as an ex-cop, I had some benefit of the doubt coming to me; plus for a cop to be killed by a former cop wouldn't be great PR for the department.

After they'd kept me cooling my heels for a good half hour, Phil Crosetti finally bulled his way through the door. "So, you're gonna go through this whole thing for me, step by step." He was at least six three, with the body of a moose and eyes like flat, black stones set into a wide mask of rage. He spun a folding chair around and straddled it.

I said, "That's all I want to do."

"Then shut up and do it, or I'll see to it that you spend a year in jail for parking violations before we even *remember* that you murdered a cop, *and* a civilian."

Standard scare tactics. I breathed a little easier knowing the less they have on you, the more they're forced to rely on boogey man stuff like this. In that instant I made a command decision to stonewall them about the Smythe case as much as I could, praying that, knowing Buck, he hadn't talked to his pals on the force about our work. I had a plan, but I needed to stall. I said, "Okay, what is it you want to know, Phil?"

He yelled, "It's Detective Crosetti to you, rat bait!" I thought he was going to have a stroke.

I shrugged. "Okay then, Detective Crosetti, what would you like to know?"

"The whole story of what you and Rogers were up to."

"What do you mean, 'up to', Detective Crosetti?"

"Don't give me that crap. You were seen with Buck Rogers at the Tail O' the Cock more than once recently."

I put on a loose grin. "Oh that? Yeah, we did meet there a couple of times."

He sneered. "Oh, good. Pals, were you now?"

I shrugged. "Well, we weren't enemies." I deliberately smirked. "Besides, we had something in common."

"See, I knew it; what was it?"

"We both liked to drink."

His veins bulged. "So, *that's* what you're gonna give me, you little prick? I want a statement from you, and I want it now."

"Didn't you forget something, Detective Crosetti?"

He was steaming now. "Yeah, I forgot to knock you from here to Cucamonga and back; but don't worry, it's all coming back to me now."

"No, it's not that; it's something else."

"And what would that be?"

"Am I being charged with a crime? And if so, what?"

"No, not at the moment, but I have a very fertile imagination."

"Well, put it to work finding the real killer then. Buck Rogers was a friend of mine. I mean it. And Hagemeyer was nothing more to me than a person of interest in some long-ago case. And if I'm locked up here, I can't very well help you find out who actually did it."

Crosetti snorted. "Oh, I'm sure the Department would suffer terribly if you weren't involved, asshole." He was on the edge of losing control now. "Where *were* you from two to four this morning, Dunbar?"

"Is that the time of death?"

"I asked you a question!"

"Asleep in bed, just like you, Detective."

"Any way you can prove that?"

I had to stall him. "Look, Crosetti, either charge me or let me go. I've got work to do."

He shook his head in disgust. "Yeah, there might be two less ugly divorces in town because I detained you."

I shrugged. "To each his own."

A pale, thin cop opened the door and nodded to Crosetti. "Better c'mere a minute, Cro."

The big detective stood up and barked at him. "This better be good, MacIntyre." Then he pointed at me. "And you? You just sit tight and think about the whole truth and nothing but. I'll be right back." He went out the door.

Two minutes later he yanked the door open and stood there looking at me in disgust. "All right Romeo, get the hell out of here! But brother, if you *do* happen to stumble over any information, you better let us know right quick." He smirked. "Oh, and you might like to know, I released your name and picture to the morning papers as a possible suspect, so don't leave town!"

I shrugged. "Why would I leave town? I love LA! Fante's my favorite, for God's sake."

As I left the room, I heard Crosetti muttering, "MacIntyre, what the hell's a Fante?"

When I reached the front desk I had the surprise of my life: Marie was standing there.

I angled my head at her. "Did they haul you in too, or are you dating a cop now?"

She looked hurt. "That was nasty."

I sighed. "Sorry, I guess I'm not having a good day."

She said, "Not a very nice way to treat your alibi."

My mouth flew open. "What? You mean you . . ."

She nodded. "Yeah, why do you think they released you?" She wrinkled her delicate nose. "And don't think it didn't tarnish my maidenly reputation, either."

I hugged her. "Oh my God, you're a lifesaver."

The desk sergeant growled, "Hire a hall, you two! Take your lying little tramp and beat it!"

We moved out onto the front steps.

I said, "But how did you know?"

"I saw your picture in the paper, and read that you were the prime suspect. And when I read about the time of the murder . . ." She paused and glared at me. "Of course, for all I know, you probably weren't alone anyway."

I held up my right hand. "I was alone. Believe me, I was alone."

She looked doubtful. "The court will take that under advisement."

I still couldn't believe she had come through for me like this. "Well, c'mon, let's go to my car so I can at least take you out for that nice dinner I promised you."

She shook her head. "No, I think I'll just head on home."

I cocked my head. "But why?"

She just stood there, tapping her foot impatiently. Finally she said, "Well, I guess if that's all you have to say for yourself, then . . ." She turned to go.

I caught her arm. "Marie, please! I'm sorry if I'm being dense, but I just don't understand what all this is about. I guess I hurt you in some way, but I'm damned if I know how. If you'd just tell me what it is, I'll do everything in my power to make it up to you."

She considered that for a moment, then turned again to go.

In desperation, I fell down on my knees on the sidewalk behind her, arms outstretched like Al Jolson, and sang, *I'd walk a million miles for one of your smiles, Marie....eeeee...*

Several pedestrians stopped to gawk.

When Marie turned back and saw me, she couldn't resist smiling. "Get up off your knees, you damn fool; you're embarrassing me."

"I will," I said, still on my knees, "if you'll go to dinner with me."

A lady bystander threw down a candy wrapper and brayed, "Aww honey, that's so romantic; you oughta go out with the poor guy! Besides, he's a real looker!"

Then her male companion fell to his knees like me and held out his hands to Marie. "C'mon, tootsie, give the poor guy a break!"

Marie finally rolled her eyes and said, "Okay, okay then, I'll go to dinner with you, if only to stop this ridiculous nonsense!"

To Marie's mortification, several people applauded as we started walking to my car. I whispered, "Is it really me, or do you just care about pleasing your public?"

She snapped, "Button it, buster; now you're *really* pushing your luck!"

I parked the Ford in the lot at Ninth and Figueroa and we got in line at The Pantry.

Marie whispered. "So, this is your idea of fine dining?"

I grinned. "It sure is, tootsie."

She jabbed me in the ribs. "I told you, don't push it! You're already on thin ice."

I looked at her seriously. "But why? I thought we had a nice time at the game. Were you mad because I couldn't spend more time with you?"

She shook her head. "No, of course not. And we *did* have a good time. It's just that . . . well, I waited all the way home for you to say something, and then when you didn't . . ."

"To say what? That I like you? Of course I like you!"

"You big dope, it's not that! I mean about you-know-who."

This was starting to feel like an Abbott and Costello routine. "What do you mean, I know who? Who the hell is *who*?"

"Little miss stuck-up society queen, that's who. The one who I know called you; the one who got me fired." She looked hurt. "The girl with the platinum key to your heart, anytime she feels like using it." She had tears in her eyes now.

I pulled out my handkerchief and wiped her tears. "Now *you're* being a big dope; she's no competition for you, Marie. Oh, maybe at first I was kind of taken with all the glamor, but she put the final nail in that coffin with our last conversation. And the fact that she got you fired over nothing . . ."

"Nothing? What do you mean nothing? You obviously told her I was the one who tattled to you about her meetings with that guy. And then when you didn't even have the decency to *tell* me about it . . ."

"Whoa there! I certainly did *not* tell her anything of the kind! In fact, I specifically told her it *wasn't* you. And furthermore, I didn't even say the meetings were at the Tam! And I didn't tell you about it because I figured she was just letting off steam and the whole thing would blow over. Frankly, I was a lot more focused on this mysterious Mr. X that she was meeting with, and who he was; if he's the blackmailer, that might mean she's in league with him, and I'd have to rethink this whole case. And as far as you, I thought she was just feeling around in the dark about you, to see how I'd react."

She nodded, her eyes still spitting green fire. "But at the same time, you were kind of flattered that she hated me that much, weren't you?"

I felt my face turn red. "Okay, maybe for a second or two, but . . ."

She was on a roll now. "And maybe the reason you were so focused on Mr. X is because *he* might be your competition for Queenie."

"That's not fair!"

"Are you two baboons gonna argue or eat?"

I turned around. It was Carl, the old headwaiter whom I'd known forever, standing there looking at us. He said, "Oh sorry, Mr. Dunbar, I didn't recognize you."

"Sorry, Carl. We were just having a lively discussion about Al Jolson."

He gave a dubious nod and waved us in. "Right this way, Mr. Dunbar. I already know what you want; we'll be by to take the lady's order in a minute."

"Thanks, Carl."

As I held the chair for her, Marie said, "This seems to be my day for embarrassment: first I confess to a roomful of cops that I was making mad love with you in the middle of the night, then I'm made a fool of in front of a crowd at City Hall, and now the headwaiter at The Pantry bawls us out. I've already struck out three times, and it's only the seventh inning." She smiled. "Maybe when we're finished eating, I could get up and do a kootch dance on top of the table."

I laughed. "Knowing the Pantry crowd, they'd probably throw money. Or maybe French fries."

Fifteen minutes later I was cutting into my T-bone and Marie was placing a tiny forkful of lamb stew into her mouth like she was afraid it was going to explode.

She chewed it tentatively, then nodded in surprise. "Not bad, actually."

I smiled, "See, you can find fine dining in all kinds of places."

"Okay, you're officially off the hook."

I grimaced. "For everything?"

"Well, there's still that matter of your betraying me by holding out on your conversation with Queenie."

Apparently "Queenie" was her new nom de guerre for Monique, since Marie seemed to think they were at war with each other. I said, "I tried to explain all that to you..."

"You've already admitted you were flattered that she hates me."

I shook my head. "No, I only said that for a couple of seconds it went through my mind..."

"And how about not telling me that she was going to have me fired? And, I might add, *after* I jeopardized my job by trying to help you!" She was mad again—not raising her voice, but getting there.

I held up my hands. "Marie, please calm down. This isn't the place to fight about it."

"Then where is?"

I grinned. "Maybe the same place you told the cops you were at two o'clock this morning." I knew right away it was a dumb thing to say. "Marie, I'm sorry. I was an idiot for saying that."

She had tears in her eyes now.

I tried again. "I guess I'm just not very good at arguing."

"What's that supposed to mean?"

"I don't know. It seems like whenever anyone gets mad at me, I try to deflect it, or ignore it, or..."

"But why?"

I shook my head. "I don't know; you'd have to ask my psychiatrist."

Her eyes opened wide. "Your what?"

I put my head down. "Ah hell, I don't want to get into all that stuff. I thought we were supposed to be having a good time."

She said, "You're doing it again."

"Doing what?"

"Deflecting away from what we were talking about."

"Yeah, I guess you're right. I mean, sometimes I don't even know *what* the hell I'm doing."

She was silent a moment, then she said, "Maybe your suggestion wasn't that dumb after all."

I frowned in confusion.

"I mean, maybe we *should* go to your place to discuss this stuff. It's not something to talk about with lots of people around us, and all this clanging and banging."

Oh God, I thought to myself, leave it to me: here I get a wonderful girl to go back to my place with me, but it's only for a discussion of all my failings.

A real smooth operator.

*   *   *

On the drive back to my apartment, Marie snuggled up close to me, practically purring. Now I was more confused than ever; in the restaurant I'd shown myself to be a weakling, if not a neurotic wreck. Christ, I'd even told her I was seeing a psychiatrist. If that's what it took to get a girl to respond to you, I had to rethink this whole woman thing from scratch. Could this be what Doc meant about a new way of being tough? I needed a drink.

I let her in, then went right to the icebox. "I'm having a beer. Want anything?"

"Sure, I'll have some coffee."

"Uh, I don't really drink coffee. It looks like it's either beer or milk."

"Okay then, ice water."

"One water, on the rocks, coming up."

She went and sat on the couch. "Who cleans up around here, Atilla the Hun?"

I laughed. "Well, there is a maid who pushes things around once a week, but I guess she didn't push very well this week."

She shook her head. "Typical male; blame a woman for your own mess."

I put the water glass down on the coffee table. "Guilty as charged, your honor."

She said, "Speaking of honor . . ."

Marie was looking serious again. It would have been easy to "deflect," but I tried not to. "Are we back on Queenie?"

"There you go, blaming the woman again. Much as I loathe her, it wasn't Queenie who withheld important information from me." She looked at me, waiting for something again. The only problem was, I didn't know what.

"I've already explained about that," I shrugged, "I'm not sure what else you need."

"I need you to understand the concept involved."

I was fresh out of concepts. "I don't get what you mean by that."

"Okay then, how about the principle?"

I took a shot in the dark. "You mean loyalty?"

She smiled. "See, you're not entirely hopeless after all. Yes, I mean loyalty. And honesty. If I'm going to be with somebody, I need to know he places the trust we have together above any other concerns."

"You mean you want him to put you on a pedestal?"

She shook her head. "No, I mean I want him to put *us* on a pedestal. Because that's what I'd be offering *him*: everything that's in me, in exchange for everything that's in him. I don't want some pinch hitter; I want . . . well, I want the Steve Bilko of love."

That sounded pretty daunting, but I managed to say, "Does that imply you're thinking of being with me?"

She nodded, slowly. "It's definitely under consideration, but only if we can come to a meeting of the minds about certain things."

"Kind of big on tests, aren't you?"

She laughed. "How do you assess something properly without a test? That's the scientific method in action."

"Do I have to give blood and urine before I can pass?"

She smiled. "No, I'll take your word that you have blood and urine."

I grinned. "Well, there are some *other* bodily fluids we could exchange . . ."

"See, you're doing it again!"

I shook my head. "Uh uh, deflection is not the same thing as seduction; I can prove that in the dictionary."

"That won't be necessary; I concede the point."

I smiled. "Ah, now we're beginning to get somewhere!"

She shook her finger at me. "Ah ah, don't forget your principles!"

I moved next to her on the couch. "Why don't you keep my principles warm while I assess a few things of my own?"

*　　　*　　　*

The next morning I awoke in bed alone. At first I thought I'd only imagined the glories of the night before, but then I heard Marie humming to herself in the kitchen. I looked at the clock: eight thirty. Hardly a fit time to be fully conscious. I traipsed out to the kitchen and said, "Hey, what are you doing up so early?"

"Who, me? I've been up since seven. You didn't have any coffee, so I had to go out and get myself some, and a pot to perk it in."

I came up behind her and put my arms around her waist. "Tell me I didn't just imagine last night."

"Hmm, tell me what you think happened, and I'll tell you whether you imagined it or not." She gave me a bump and grind in a very salacious spot.

I said, "That's okay, I'll just go back to bed and play with my imagination."

She turned. "What time do you usually get up?"

"Oh, ten or so, unless I can sleep late."

"Well, you have something important to do today."

"Such as?"

"Such as talking to me about the Smythe case. According to you, there have already been at least three men killed, and you've been beaten up several times. And I'm assuming someone found out Buck Rogers was working on the case again, and he was killed for it. Now if Buck Rogers was killed, who do you suppose might be next in line?"

I frowned. "Why the sudden concern with the Smythe case?"

"Because I'm *with* you now; remember our discussion about principles?"

I grinned. "Gee, and here I thought you were the type to screw and run."

She lifted the coffee pot. "Watch yourself Dunbar, this stuff is hot!"

I held up my hands. "Okay, I give, but I need another couple hours of sleep in order to function. If you're an early riser, that's fine, but part of the deal with me is that I stay up late and I sleep late; that's just my nature."

"Okay Nature Boy, go get your beauty sleep. But when you do get up, we're going to have a talk."

"Cole, wake up!"

Someone was shaking me. Was I in a fight? Was that why I was gasping for breath?

"Sweetie, it's only a dream!"

Hmm, would a guy I was fighting with be calling me Sweetie?

I opened my eyes. It was Marie. But why would I be fighting with *her*?

"Cole, you were having a nightmare. It's okay, just try and relax now."

She was wiping the sweat off my face. It felt good.

"It was just a bad dream. It's okay, I'm here."

She was right; it *was* okay that she was there. I struggled to sit up and said, "Sorry if I scared you."

She laughed. "I wasn't the one who was scared." She said, "Raise your arms," then pulled my soaked t-shirt off and tossed it in the hamper. Then she said, "Okay, now the bottoms."

I crossed my arms over my chest. "Please madam, I hardly know you!"

"Well, we'll know each other a lot better when you get those pants off. Now strip!"

Still under the sheets, I tugged my pajama bottoms down, then looked her up and down. "How about *your* bottoms? They say turnabout's fair play."

She smiled. "They say a lot of things, but right now you need a hot shower."

She pulled the soaked sheets off of my body and took a good look. "Well, maybe a cold shower."

A half hour later we were both sitting at the kitchen table, Marie with a cup of hot coffee and me with a cold beer and a Camel.

Marie picked up her cup. "All right, so let's talk."

I groaned. "Oh no, is this gonna be about principles again?"

"Nope, we've already covered principles, and I think we're both in agreement now."

"Then what?"

"The Smythe case, from A to Z."

I frowned. "Wait, so you're my gal Friday now?"

"Well, since I'm currently out of work, due to the actions of certain parties to this discussion . . ."

"Okay, I get the picture. So you want to help me solve this thing?"

She had that serious look again. "First of all, I want to keep you alive. Then, if there's any time left over, I'd be glad to help you solve the case too."

I noticed an irresistible spray of freckles across her nose and reached out to touch them. "Are you sure you want to spend our precious time just talking?"

She grinned as she batted my hand away. "Hey, I can wait if you need another cold shower. Or, we could just go ahead and talk now."

I shrugged. "Okay, if that's what you really want."

"Right now it is." She twisted her warm, full mouth into a phony grin. "After all, Queenie's waiting."

I cringed. "You're not going to start all that again, are you?"

"If you start talking right now, I won't."

"Okay, I guess we talk." I paused. "So, what is it you want to know?"

"Everything."

In twenty minutes, I had filled her in on the basics of the case, from the story Monique told me at our first meeting about Swopes and Hagemeyer selling the building cheap, to the suspicious fire and Matthew Smythe's fragile health. Then the threats I'd received, the beatings, my talks with Bert Fawcett, Dick Hartwick and the insurance investigator, my meetings with Buck Rogers, the trip to Ensenada to see the lonely grave of Lionel Swopes, and lastly the story of the visit to Ernie Finnegan's hovel and his incoherent mumbling.

I finished with, "And then I got pulled in for the murders of Buck Rogers and Arnold Hagemayer, and thanks to you, I'm a free man again, and back on the case." I paused. "And then, there was spending the night with you, but I guess you know about all that."

She had questions, lots of them. She was right; she had the mind of a scientist. But when she had finished, she said, "Buck's death is really weighing on you, isn't it?"

An unexpected wave of sadness engulfed me. Marie reached out and rubbed my shoulder. Finally, I said, "Before I came along and dragged him back into this haunted house of a case again, he had left it where it belonged, in the rearview mirror. It was only because of me that he put his life on the line again. And for what? To salvage a thread of pride about a cold case that no other cop could have solved either? And now, I feel like the only thing left to do for the poor guy is to bring this maniac, or maniacs, to justice." I paused. "And even that's looking like a long shot at the moment."

Marie took my hand. "Sounds like you're not just working for Monique Smythe anymore."

We were silent a long time. Then, she took a sip of her coffee and looked at me. "Okay, so first of all, do you think it's important to find out what really happened with the sale of the building, and the fire?"

I sighed. "I've thought about that so much in these past weeks, I can't even tell you. I honestly don't know; it certainly could establish motivation, and every cop knows that when you backtrack on motivation, you usually find the bad guys. Maybe Swopes and Hagemayer had good reason to skip town and sell out fast; maybe the fire was set to destroy evidence; maybe they planned all along to come back later and bleed Smythe dry. But it's just as plausible that someone who discovered the story of the building figured they could just swoop in and squeeze Monique, with the threat of framing her father for the fire—maybe even a friend of hers." I shook my head. "Hell, I could go on and on like that for another fifteen minutes. It makes my head spin."

Marie's green eyes narrowed with intensity. "Just a minute, for me there are two things about this case that stick out like a sore thumb: First, Swopes, Hagemayer and Johnny Rogers are all dead. Why?"

I shrugged. "Because somebody saw them as a threat, or competition."

"Right. So we need to try and connect those three deaths. Second, there was a building that burned down under suspicious circumstances. Was it arson, and if so, why?"

"The cops and Pettibone say no."

"Maybe we could find out for ourselves."

"And just how do you propose to do that?"

"Easy, we obtain the physical evidence, then do our own investigation."

I stood up. "If you're gonna start talking science fiction, I need another beer." I went to the icebox.

She shook her head. "Cole, I'm *not* talking science fiction. Why can't we analyze the data ourselves?"

I opened the beer and sat back down. "Because for one, it's sitting somewhere in a police evidence locker. And for another, we're not arson investigators. And for a third, the people who *are* arson investigators came up dry."

"Maybe they were incompetent, or not thorough enough. Or maybe they just weren't that highly motivated, or didn't have access to the right technology."

I shrugged. "Yeah, and maybe the guys who make atomic bombs should have turned some tiny screw a little more to the right too, but what does that have to do with us?"

"You forget, I'm a chemist; this is what we do!"

"You mean you could look at stuff from a burned building and make sense of it?"

"On the basis of a thorough chemical analysis of the debris for fuels and accelerants, of course."

I was stunned. "Go on."

"All arson investigators have to have some degree of specialized chemical training, but believe me, I have one hell of a lot more of it than most of them do. And now . . ." she leaned over and kissed me, "I have some pretty good motivation of my own." She looked at me. "So, if you can get me that evidence from the fire, I'll try and take care of the chemistry part. And that leaves you free to figure out what three dead men have in common."

I lit another cigarette and said, almost to myself, "People don't murder themselves."

Marie frowned. "What?"

I stood up and started pacing the kitchen. "I said people don't murder themselves. So maybe what the three dead men had in common was information which might be dangerous to a fourth party."

Marie said, "You mean like maybe he was in on it with them?"

I nodded. "Sure. A freelancer wouldn't have had to kill other people; only someone they all knew, or knew about, would need to eliminate them."

"You mean like if the killer came in later and tried to take over the operation?"

"Could be, or if it all started out as a joint operation, but the killer decided later he didn't want to split with the others."

"Wait a minute, are you implying that Buck Rogers was part of the original plot?"

I shook my head. "Naw, I'd stake my reputation on that. I mean sure, it's possible, but for my money he had too much pride in being a cop for that, especially about this case. But maybe he was nosing around and found out something he wasn't supposed to know—something that earned him a bullet in the head."

Marie stood up and stretched. "Okay, I've got to go to class in a while, and I've got a dissertation conference with my adviser, too, so I have to catch my bus." She came over to me and we held each other tight, then kissed. She said, "I wish you luck."

I said, "Thanks for the moral support. It helps. This is the first time in a while this case hasn't felt like a ball and chain."

She laughed and dropped me a curtsy. "That's because you have a *new* ball and chain."

Chapter Eleven

All the way to the office I racked my brain about what happened to Buck Rogers, and why. What could he have found out? It wasn't until I got to the parking lot and handed the keys to George that it occurred to me Buck's death might have absolutely nothing to do with the Smythe case, despite Hagemayer's body turning up at the same time. Career cops make lots of enemies. Jesus, I was so deep in this thing that I'd lost all perspective. Oh, and to be honest I have to admit it also crossed my mind that if Monique ever found out I was seeing Marie, much less working with her on the case, she wouldn't be terribly happy. I mean, she'd already fired me for a whole lot less, plus gotten Marie fired too, on what amounted to a suspicious whim.

It's usually the client who hides information from the PI, not vice versa, but in this case . . .

As I rode the elevator up, I mentally went over what I needed to accomplish that day: Call the service, make appointments with Doc Grimes and Bert Fawcett, feel out Dick Hartwick about his "obtaining" the fire evidence, then start tracking every one of Buck Rogers' last steps. Maybe I could start with the Tail O' the Cock, and if that involved a drink or two in the service of the cause, so much the better.

"Answer World, Sabrina."

"Hi Sabrina, Cole Dunbar here. Got anything for me?"

"Yes, a Miss Smythe called, and she didn't sound very happy."

"Nothin' new about that is there? Is that it?"

"Nope, a Detective Crosetti called too, and he wasn't in no party mood either, hon."

"Lovely. Anything else?"

"There was a strange call from a woman."

"I know a lot of strange women; anyone in particular?"

"The strange part is she wouldn't leave her name. She did leave a number, though."

"Okay, hit me."

Sabrina gave me an Adams number, which could be downtown, though I wasn't sure.

"Thanks, dear."

"Nothin' to it."

Oh no, it hit me that the Adams call was probably some kind of a sales promotion; I'd once made the mistake of ordering a Mission Pak gift basket for somebody, and the damn company had never let me alone since. Their phone number also had an Adams exchange. Their inane jingle blared nonstop from the radio and the TV at holiday time:

Say the magic word, say Mission Pak, and it's on its merry way. No gift so bright, so gay, so bright, give the Mission Pak magic way.

But then that number could also mean new business, or even new dope on the Smythe case too, so I dialed and waited for one ring, then two, three . . .

"What is it?" The voice sounded distraught, but then when women call me, they're often in a crisis.

"Uh, Cole Dunbar Investigations here. Did you wish to speak to me?"

"Oh God, where can we meet?"

"Well, I'm at my office at the moment. What's wrong with that?"

"Because they're probably watching your office."

"You mean the cops?"

She gave a harsh, grating laugh. "Hardly, Mr. Dunbar. Name another place, somewhere out of the way."

"Do you have a car?"

"Yes."

"Okay then, how about Fern Dell, up in Griffith Park, above Los Feliz? If you head north on Vermont, then take a left . . ."

"I know where it is, Mr. Dunbar. My father used to take us . . ."

To my surprise, I heard broken sobbing.

I was sympathetic, but had other things to do. "All right then, four o'clock."

She sniffled, "Four o'clock, okay."

"May I ask your name?"

"I'd . . . rather not say."

"How will I know you?"

"I'll know *you*; I saw your picture in the paper the other day."

Shit, I was becoming the new John Dillinger.

She hung up.

Well, not giving a name wasn't so unusual on a first call; people who are facing divorce or dealing with a partner's amorous adventures are often gun-shy at first.

I called Bert Fawcett and made an appointment for the next day at five, then rang Doc Grimes' office.

"Katy? It's Cole Dunbar. When can the Straw Man come see the Wizard?"

She chuckled. "Hmm, could tomorrow at five work?"

"You managed to find the one time I can't make."

"How about Wednesday at nine?"

"At night?"

"No, in the morning."

"Sorry, I'm booked solid with nightmares at that time of day. Try again—something post meridiem."

"Got it: Thursday at six."

"Evening, right?"

"Yes, Mr. Dunbar, that's in the evening."

"You got a deal."

Good, my two mainstays were on the books. Now it was time for the diciest one: Dick Hartwick.

"Hello, Dick?"

"Speaking. Who's this?"

"Cole Dunbar."

"Oh good, you finally decided to take us up on that dinner invite?"

"Uh, well, maybe, but it's not really about that."

"Cole, are you in trouble again? The fellas told me they hauled you in on that Rogers beef, but a pretty mystery girl sprung you. Christ, Phil Crosetti even had your mug in the morning papers."

"Don't I know it."

"So what time you wanna come over? Say seven or so? Brenda'll be over the moon when I tell her."

I was getting myself in deeper, but if that dinner bought me a trade-off, it was worth it. "Sure, seven sounds fine. Now, could we meet at our old lunch place today?"

"You mean the Copper Kettle?"

"Yeah." I looked at my watch. "Say around two?"

"I'm not much liking the sound of this, Cole. Have you been a bad boy again?"

"No Dick, I swear it; I'm just working a case."

"The same one that put Buck Rogers in the deep freeze?"

"Well maybe, but this is important."

"Okay, a friend in need, etcetera, etcetera, so I'll be there."

"Thanks, pal."

Hell, I didn't want to be a "bad boy" either, but this case was forcing my hand. Under normal circumstances I might have been able to reason with Crosetti and get him to show me the files on the Smythe case, but there was no way LAPD was going to pull the scab off this old, gangrenous wound of a case and condone an outsider digging around at this late date.

I chose the last table at the Copper Kettle, against the back wall. A minute later, Dick walked in.

"Hi, Dick, glad you could come." I gave him a forced smile that needed no explanation.

He looked around carefully for anyone he knew. Then we signaled the waitress and we both ordered a cheeseburger and a Coke.

"Look Cole, I'll do whatever I can for you, but you're not exactly 1-A around these parts now, you know."

I nodded. "Yeah, I got a few hints to that effect from Detective Crosetti while he was turning me on the spit."

Dick smiled. "That guy woke up on the bad side of the bed about twenty years ago and still hasn't gotten over it." He paused. "So what is it that's driving you to meet me in the wee hours of the afternoon like this?"

"It's the Smythe case. And it's Buck Rogers' death, and maybe a couple of others too." I cast around for a way to put it that didn't make me sound like a candidate for physical restraints. Finally, I said, "Okay, it's about the physical evidence of the fire."

"What about it?"

I cleared my throat and looked around. "I, uh, need it."

His eyes flew open. "Do you realize what you're saying? They wouldn't give you access to that stuff even if you had photographic evidence that Chief Parker's a Communist spy who dresses up in women's underwear!"

"Dick, I know, believe me. That's why I . . . uh, we . . ."

He cocked his head. "That's why we what? And who the hell is *we*?"

I pulled out a cigarette and offered him one.

"Cole, you know I don't smoke. Now what is it you're really trying to say?"

I took a deep drag and exhaled. "I need that physical evidence, by hook or crook. I need to know whether it was arson or not. Then I'll have something to go on."

Just then, the waitress arrived with our orders.

After she left, Dick nodded, biting into his burger. "Okay, now I see it all; you're so anxious to get into the Smythe dame's pantaloons that you'd even rob the Los Angeles Police Department to make her happy?"

"Dick, no, it's not that. It's actually . . . well, it involves a different woman."

He started to rise. "Okay this is getting out of hand. I wish you luck with your sexual escapades, but . . ."

I took hold of his arm. "Dick, sit down. At least hear me out, for God's sake. I'm not an idiot."

He reluctantly took his seat again. "Is this new one the pretty little thing they say came in and told Crosetti she was shacked up with you at two in the morning?"

I nodded. "Yes, but she wasn't actually with me."

"Oh, excuse me; then I guess that makes her that pretty little *lying* thing?"

"As it happens, she's a graduate student in chemistry at UCLA, and smart as a whip. She knows the whole Smythe case, and she thinks if she can analyze the fire evidence, she can prove it one way or the other."

He threw his head back. "Oh my God, you're saying some coed chem major you have a crush on is going to find out what LAPD's crime scene investigators *and* the insurance pros couldn't prove?"

"Yes, that's exactly what I'm saying. She has access to tools that those guys didn't."

He snorted. "She sure does: she can bat her eyes and get a grown man to make a damn fool of himself."

Now I was getting annoyed. "Okay Dick, tell you what: I'll bring her to your place tonight for dinner and you and Brenda can meet her and judge for yourselves. If after that, you still think she's a stupid little coed, I'll drop the whole thing. What do you say?"

Dick thought a minute. "Okay, it's a deal, but I still think we both need to get our heads examined."

Little did he know, I was getting mine examined Thursday at six.

As I stood there on the sidewalk, with busy pedestrians surging past me on all sides, and watched Dick walk into the fading afternoon, I couldn't help but envy the way he'd managed to make a go of the Department, get himself a great woman and now two sweet kids. If life were a hockey game, Dick Hartwick would be the goalie, if a baseball game, the catcher—the solid, wise one who doesn't create trouble for himself and keeps everyone else pulling together. Why are some people able to keep things so solid, so normal, while others . . .

But you can't find answers to those questions in a police evidence locker. Oh well, more questions for Doc Grimes. A while ago, Jim had told me he was anxious to try something new on me this time, some kind of drug they used in the war, that might help me pull back the black curtain and access my insides. At first I'd said, "You're serious? You mean there's actually a real truth serum?" But he reassured me, and though it all sounded like voodoo to me, I was sick and tired of going to sleep in Dante's Inferno every night and waking up with a head full of hell, so I figured screw it, what did I have to lose?

*   *   *

It was time to head up to Fern Dell and meet the mystery lady. I hoped it would be quick and easy; this Smythe thing was eating up all my time. I turned north on Vermont, then cut left on Los Feliz and after a while I pulled into the lot and parked. I checked my watch, I was ten minutes early. Good, I could use the time to recover from laying myself bare before Dick Hartwick, with the very real prospect of still more embarrassment tonight. I rolled down my window, fired up a Camel and tried to resist going back over all the loose ends of the case for the umpteenth time. At four I got out of the car and made my way down the path to Fern Dell, a secluded little retreat that's one of the jewels of Griffith Park. I walked down the trail a hundred feet or so and stood facing the parking lot, hoping I was obvious enough to be recognized by someone who'd only seen my "mug shot" in the paper.

"Mr. Dunbar?"

I turned around to see a statuesque woman clad in a Chinese-style red silk wrapper that didn't do much to conceal her voluptuous figure. I said, "Oh, there you are."

"Yes, I've been here for about an hour, just walking around. It reminds me so much of my childhood." She was starting to cry again.

I didn't know what to do. "Uh, maybe we'd better wait until you're a little more . . ."

"No, I'll be all right in a minute. When you mentioned Fern Dell, our meeting almost seemed like it was fated or something."

Uh oh, was she going to be the type who consulted mediums and based her life on her horoscope every day?

"Mr. Dunbar, you can ask me my name now."

I was confused. "Okay, I'll play: what's your name?"

"Hagemayer. Myrtle Hagemayer."

The blood rushed from my face. "Hagemayer, as in . . . Arnold Hagemayer?"

She nodded. "Yes. My professional name is Kitty. Kitty Stacker. I'm a stripper at the Third and Main Follies." It was LA's biggest burlesque house.

I thought back to Ernie Finnegan mumbling, "Kitty . . . Kitty fozz." If she was Kitty, could fozz be the Follies?

She went on. "Maybe I can tell you something about the murder of a cop named Johnny Rogers."

"How did you know Buck Rogers?"

"He contacted me a few days ago. He and Ernie Finnegan used to be regulars at the Follies years ago, when they were partners. Then, the other day when you talked to Ernie and told Buck what he was mumbling, Buck put two and two together and came up with me."

I was confused. "But what does that have to do with his being killed?"

She held up her hands. "I'm getting to that, Mr. Dunbar. Buck knew that Ernie and I used to . . . well, let's just say we were very close at one time, before Ernie got into all that trouble with the Department and . . . slipped. Back when that office building burned, Ernie and Buck were assigned to the case—but I guess you already know that. Of course, I knew my father was one of the former owners who disappeared, along with that louse Lionel Swopes, and I even knew they'd fled to Mexico, but I never let on to anybody. I didn't know if Daddy had done anything wrong or not. He told me he didn't—but I at least owed him my silence.

"Well, one day Ernie came backstage when I was on, and happened to find an old letter in my desk drawer that was addressed to Myrtle Hagemayer. He asked me about it. I gave him some cock and bull story, but Ernie was a cop, and he wouldn't let it go until he finally forced me to admit that I was Arnold Hagemayer's daughter. But I swore him to silence, for the sake of my father. He knew he should tell Buck and the Department about it, but he loved me so much that he . . ."

She broke down again.

I waited, hardly believing my ears.

She struggled to get herself under control for a moment, then went on. "Well, it ate at him something awful. He knew he was cheating the Department of a lead, cheating his partner, cheating himself. But he knew how much it meant to me to keep Daddy out of trouble, not just with the cops but maybe with the underworld too, and so he kept his promise to me. But it added to the problems he already had, and his drinking got out of hand . . . and finally it led to his being put on suspension. And in the end, they just pushed him out."

She started crying again. "I know it wasn't fair of me to do that to him, but I was torn, too."

"Okay, I get all that," I said, "but did you ever hear from your father again?"

She shook her head. "No, and then after a while, I started to hear the rumors that he was dead—him and Swopes too." She paused. "Not just dead, but killed."

I said, "I know Lionel Swopes is dead; I saw his grave in Ensenada. And until your father was found with Buck Rogers, I always figured they gave Arnold Hagemayer the same kind of send-off."

She said, "Me too, up until about a year ago."

That gave me a jolt. "You mean to tell me you saw your father alive again?"

She nodded. "Yes." She started crying.

I waited her out.

She finally went on. "If you'll just listen, I'll explain—at least the part that I know about.

I nodded. "Okay, I'm listening."

"So about a year ago, I was in my dressing room between shows when someone knocked on the door. When I opened it, this funny little man was standing there. He said, 'If you want to see your father again, come with me.' I figured it was some kind of a gag, or shakedown. I told him, 'I have a show to do in two minutes; the band's already started playing my theme song!'" She turned to me. "That's *Lawdy Miss Clawdy* by the way—you know, the one by Lloyd Price? The boys do a real low-down version of it, special for my act.

All the other girls use stuff like *Night Train* and *Harlem Nocturne*, but I like to be a little more original ..."

"That's great, Miss Hagemayer. But can we please get back to your story?"

"Oh, sorry. Well anyway, so I says, 'How do I know you're on the level?' The little man pulled a ruby ring out of his pocket that used to belong to my mother. Well, I almost fainted then and there. So I asked one of the other girls to trade spots with me, and she said okay. He told me to bring cab fare for a long ride, so I did. Then I got dressed and followed the guy out to the street. We got in a taxi and he gave the cabbie an address way out in Gardena somewhere. It was a real long ride, but the cabbie finally pulled up in front of this old, broken-down house and I paid him off.

"The little guy knocked on the front door, and a creepy-looking lady answered it. The little guy said, 'We're here to see George,' and she took us back down a long hallway to the last room on the right. The little guy knocked on the door and a beat-up old man answered it. At first I didn't even recognize him in the dim light, but when the little man handed him the ring and said, 'Here ya go, Arnie,' I think I passed out. When I came to, the old man was holding a cold washcloth to my forehead. He said, 'Myrtle, my dear, it's been so long.' I looked up, still in a daze. 'Are you really Arnold Hagemayer? Is it really you, Daddy?' When he nodded, I almost passed out again."

Kitty struggled for control again, then went on. "I asked him what he was doing back in LA; didn't he know about the suspicious fire and that the cops were looking for him? He laughed then and said, 'Honey, it's not the cops I'm worried about.' He said he'd been on the run all these years: Mexico, Peru, Venezuela. But now he had terminal cancer, and he had to come back and see me at least once, before ..."

She broke down again. I was desperate to hear the rest of her story, but I had to respect her suffering.

"He said he only had a short time to live anyway, so at this point it didn't really matter whether they found him or not. But he wanted to tell me he loved me, and that he was sorry he'd put me through all this misery." She stopped again to gather herself.

"Miss Hagemayer, I don't want to seem rude, but . . ."

She nodded her head. "I know what you want to hear, Mr. Dunbar. And I did ask Daddy if he burned that building down. All he said was, 'All I can tell you is that if someone burned it down deliberately, it wasn't me.' Then he looked at me with great pain in his face and said, 'But Lionel and I did have to get out of town fast; we were afraid for our lives because of some business dealings with organized crime that he'd never bothered to tell me about: loans, big gambling debts and God knows what else, all secured, at least in theory, by our joint business assets, including the building on Wilshire. But as to whether Lionel was actually behind the fire, I really don't know; all I can tell you is that he was a very shady guy who was certainly capable of it.'"

She went on. "But I know that someone else was involved, too. Daddy told me that the last time he talked to Swopes, when Swopes was living somewhere in Mexico, Swopes told him a man was threatening him. Swopes admitted to Daddy later that after the fire happened, blackmailing the Smythes for the insurance money years later had been his plan anyway. But Swopes would never disclose to father whether he'd actually been behind the fire or not, or whether it was even arson at all. But before they left LA, Swopes must have bragged to someone about his plan to frame the Smythes for arson and get the insurance money, because somehow this other man found out about the blackmail scheme and decided to cut himself in on the deal. Then he tracked Swopes down to Ensenada."

At that point Kitty looked at me. "I swear to you, my father knew nothing about the fire, and had nothing to do with Swopes' plan to blackmail the Smythes!"

I nodded. "Okay, I'm still trying to believe you. But I'm also waiting to hear who the man behind the scenes is, and what really happened to Buck Rogers."

She said, "Wait a minute, there's more. So Swopes told Daddy that this man thought Daddy was in on the whole thing too, even after Swopes cleared him. Swopes had even agreed to cut the guy in on the deal for half, but the guy insisted he had to make sure that Daddy would agree to it too."

I said, "But you said your father wasn't in on the blackmail plot."

She nodded. "That's right, he wasn't, and Swopes *told* the guy that, but this fella didn't believe him. That's why Swopes called father to warn him. And that's the last thing Daddy ever heard from Lionel Swopes. It's pretty obvious now that this man decided to take over the whole operation himself by eliminating Lionel Swopes and any possible partners. And that meant Daddy would be the next to go. So, when he heard Swopes had been murdered, he went on the run again."

"And then?"

"And then, a year ago, when he found out he had cancer, he decided to come back to LA, despite the danger, to see me one last time." She sighed. "Except someone who was helping to hide him must have sold him out to the killer, who demanded a meeting with Daddy. So Daddy did meet with the guy and tried to convince him that he'd had no part in the arson and no intention of blackmailing anybody, that he was dying and wanted nothing more than to be left alone. But just to make sure of that, the guy told him, 'Don't think I don't know about Kitty Stacker being your daughter; the Follies used to be on my beat.' And that's when Daddy knew he had to meet with me immediately, so he had me brought to the house in Glendora."

My ears perked up. "Beat? You mean this guy was a cop?"

She shrugged. "I suppose so, but I really have no idea. The only cops I ever knew personally at the Follies were Buck and Ernie, but cops were always coming by to watch the shows. All I know is what my father told me, which I just repeated to you, verbatim. And that was the last time I ever saw Daddy. We said our last goodbyes and he told me he would have to go on the run again, and not to try and contact him. That was about a year ago, and it's the last I ever heard of him until I read in the newspapers about his death. I guess he must have stayed around LA because he was sick, so whoever killed him must have tracked him down somewhere here in town."

I said, "Hmm, a year ago was just about the time someone started blackmailing the Smythes." I looked at her. "But didn't your father tell you anything at all about this mystery man? A name, a description, anything?"

She shook her head. "I asked him of course, but he said what I didn't know couldn't hurt me. And he probably figured that after he was dead, whether from the cancer or murder, I'd be safe anyway."

"But what about Buck Rogers?"

She sighed again. "Okay, so a few days ago Buck called me at home. He was real nice, said he wanted to talk to me about something important. Well, we used to be friends, so I told him he could come by my dressing room after the ten o'clock show."

"And?"

"And he did. At first he was real sweet, said he missed me and all. We talked about old times. But then he told me Ernie Finnegan had mentioned my name in conjunction with the Smythe case, and he wanted to know why. Well, I figured Daddy was already in enough trouble with the guy who killed Swopes; why would I want to sic a cop on him, too? But you know Johnny Rogers: he kept pushing me and pushing me. Finally I admitted I was Arnold Hagemayer's daughter, and told him about the cab ride to Glendora and all the stuff I just told you.

"Well, he jumped up and said, 'Give me that address, right now!' Of course I knew the address didn't matter anymore, but if you knew Johnny Rogers, you knew how bull-headed he could be. So I finally wrote down the address and he rushed out of there like a house afire." She was crying again. "And that's the last I heard from Buck either, until I read in the paper that the police found those two bodies."

By the time she finished, I was feeling the strain; to come so close to the answers and be left holding the bag was sheer torture. Reflexively I said, "Where's the house? Someone who rented that house knows who the killer is and where to find him, or they couldn't have contacted him when your father came to town."

She shook her head again. "No, no, that's what I tried to tell Johnny too, but he wouldn't listen; the first thing I did a year ago was to go back to that house. It was empty then and it's empty now. Whoever was there is long gone."

She was right of, course; there was nothing more to say or do. We walked together in silence back down to the parking lot. I saw her to her car, then wrote my home number on the back of one of my cards and handed it to her. "Miss Hagemayer, if you hear anything, anything at all, please call me immediately, day or night. But also, I'm a little concerned for you. It sounds like this guy's been watching you; that's probably how he knew you'd been back in contact with Buck Rogers."

She shrugged. "If he was, he probably isn't any more. The only connections I had to this case were father and Johnny Rogers, and now they're both in the . . . the morgue." She teared up again. "And from what I hear, poor Ernie Finnegan is all but dead, too."

Her eyes were red now, tears streaking her mascara. Suddenly she reached out the car window and gripped my arm. "Mr. Dunbar, please find this horrible man and avenge my father's death! But be careful; if he *is* still watching, he might know that I met with you now."

I nodded dumbly, feeling helpless, like I was letting everyone down. But by now that feeling wasn't unusual; I'd been marinating in it since the day I first signed on to work for Monique Smythe. It was as if all my nightmares of helpless desperation had started bleeding into my real life.

After Kitty left, I sat in my car thinking. This guy, whoever he was, must have been keeping tabs on her. Then, when Buck Rogers showed up, he realized Buck was working the old case again, and he saw a way to kill two birds with one stone, and maybe even confuse things further by blaming the killing of one of them on the other one. Or on me. Either way, it turned suspicion away from himself.

Very neat.

*   *   *

I called the Chemistry Department at UCLA and asked for Marie. I waited a couple of minutes.

"Yes?"

It was her. I said, "Hi, it's the man in the wet sheets."

She laughed. "Listen, I'd rather be in wet sheets with you than dry ones with . . ."

"Steve Bilko?"

"Hmm, did you have to make it so hard?"

"I thought that was *my* line."

"I'll take a pass on that one. I assume you called for some less intimate reason?"

"Yes, I made a dinner date for us tonight, and I'm hoping you can make it."

"The Pantry again?"

"Nope, my old cop friend Dick Hartwick's house. He, uh, wants to meet you."

"Something tells me you're leaving something out."

"You're right; I'll explain later."

"Guess I should get back to my place then, and make myself look decent?"

"It wouldn't hurt, but your looks aren't really the main event."

"Is this about the case, by any chance?"

"Bullseye. How about we meet at your place around six, and all will be revealed? I have lots to tell."

"Sold."

I drove back to my apartment, grabbed a beer and prepared myself to make the two calls I was dreading.

I dialed Monique first.

"Yes?"

"Monique? It's Cole Dunbar. You rang?"

"Oh, I was just on my way out to an auction. Can't this wait?"

"Monique, you called *me*, remember?"

"Oh, that's right. I just wanted to let you know that I made the next payment of one thousand dollars. Is there anything going on with the case? They haven't asked for more yet, but I'm expecting it very soon." She paused. "I did read about John Rogers' death in the paper. And Hagemayer's too. I even saw a picture of you, which was very disturbing. Are you following up on all that? I hope you know what you're doing, but you sure couldn't prove it from your results so far!"

What should I tell her? I finally just said, "I'm well aware of those deaths, and yes, I'm following up on them intensively, hoping it might lead us in the right direction. But so far. nothing substantive."

"All right. Well, I've gotta fly to a charity event, so tata."

That was relatively painless. One down, one to go. I drained the beer and dialed Crosetti's number.

"Detective Crosetti, please."

I waited.

"Crosetti here. Whaddya want?"

"It's Cole Dunbar, returning your call."

"I thought you might like to hear the latest on the Rogers case."

"Do you have any leads?"

"That would be confidential information as far as you're concerned . . . but I guess it wouldn't hurt to tell you that the murder weapon we found in the wash, about a hundred feet from Hagemayer's body, wasn't your gun. So I guess it wasn't you after all. Just thought you might like to know you're no longer our prime suspect."

"Gee, that's a big relief, Phil; thanks for letting me know I'm not the murderer." I paused. "Did you get a make on the weapon, or any fingerprints?"

"Not that it's any of your business, but . . ."

"But what?"

"Well, I probably shouldn't be tellin' you this, but the weapon we found in the wash was Buck Rogers' service revolver. And it matches the bullets found in him and Hagemayer. So for the moment it's lookin' like Buck shot Hagemayer, then turned the gun on himself. This is off the record, of course, but I hear the guy was pretty depressed about his marriage blowin' up. And don't ask me for more than that; it's an ongoing investigation that's strictly police business."

"Okay then, thanks at least for letting me know I'm not the murderer."

"Listen buster, I'm still not convinced you aren't involved in some way, so don't leave town."

"Hey man, don't you remember Fante?"

We hung up, and for an instant I smiled, picturing Crosetti's face. But the smile soon faded; if I'd been there to answer when Buck Rogers called me, he might not be dead now. I didn't believe for a second that Buck shot Hagemayer, unless . . . no, it couldn't be possible, could it, that Buck was in on the arson job or the blackmail scheme somehow and needed to eliminate Hagemayer, then killed himself because he couldn't live with a life that now included murder, a painful divorce and God knows what else?

My intuition told me it was much more likely that both jobs were done by the killer cop behind the scenes, maybe hoping to throw a monkey wrench into the whole case and divert suspicion from himself while eliminating the competition and muddying the waters.

And Arnold Hagemayer?

He wasn't just some broken-down old bum to me now.

Or even a disappeared suspect.

It was looking more and more like the poor guy was just an unfortunate dupe whose whole life had been hijacked by Lionel Swopes' crazy schemes and expensive habits, and then ended by a sick killer who couldn't even wait for cancer to do the job.

But more than that, I now knew that Hagemayer had been somebody's Daddy.

Somewhere, the mystery killer was out there chuckling to himself, thinking he now had everything in place for his final move.

And I was the only one between him and the goal line.

Chapter Twelve

As I pulled up in front of Marie's apartment building, it hit me that I really had no right to use her as the stakes in my gamble to get Dick Hartwick to help me out on the arson investigation. I was hoping she wouldn't see it that way, but if this turned out to be another "test" that I failed, chances were pretty good that I'd soon be facing the little redhead's Irish temper again.

I knocked, preparing myself for the worst.

She opened the door, looking radiant. "Hi there. Looks like we're going to have to get you your own key to the place pretty soon."

My body relaxed a bit. "Sounds good."

When I came into the living room she backed away from me and turned around, looking like a vision.

I gulped. Her gorgeous red hair was up, and she had on a pink and gray print dress with a full skirt and petticoats under it, complemented by pink high heels.

She twirled around again. "So, do I pass muster?"

I'd never really seen her dressed like this, and she took my breath away. "I don't know what to say, Marie; you're stunning."

She came over and kissed me. "Thanks, want a beer?" and when I nodded she went out to the kitchen to get it, leaving me alone with my thoughts.

I wondered how I could have missed seeing her true beauty before. Was it because I had Monique Smythe in my eyes? But seeing her now like this made Monique seem like a distant memory of tinsel and bangles and bright shiny beads; to my way of thinking, Monique was now El Buono Etoile and Marie was The Pantry. Oops, I knew better than to try that line on Marie, or I'd be in big trouble again; I was already tempting fate by putting her in the crosshairs tonight with the Hartwicks.

She was laughing to herself as she brought back the beer and set it down on the coffee table, still looking like a fairy princess. I sat there looking at her and tried to tell myself I was worthy of a magnificent woman like this, but it was a hard sell. Another fragment from Fante raced through my mind:

Her beauty was too much . . . she was so much more beautiful than I, deeper rooted than I. She made me a stranger unto myself, she was all of those calm nights and tall eucalyptus trees, the desert stars, that land and sky, that fog outside . . .

More raw material for Jim Grimes and I to muck around in.

She blushed. "Cole, you're staring."

"Sorry, I can't help it."

She laughed again. "Wow, after that buildup, I guess I have nowhere to go but down." Then she sat on the chair opposite the couch and said, "So, what was it you wanted to tell me?"

Shoot, at this point *I* had no place to go but down, either. But at least she had to know what she was up against tonight at the Hartwicks, even if it did tick her off again.

I took a big gulp of the cold beer and cleared my throat. "Well, it's like this: as you know, I need that police evidence on the Smythe fire, and my friend in the Department would have to have a damn good reason to go in and get it for me. So I told him about you, but frankly . . ."

Her eyes had that fiery look again. "But frankly what?"

I cleared my throat again. "Okay, remember, I didn't say this, but well, in his words, he thinks you're just a pretty UCLA coed who's turned my head."

"And what did you say to that?" Uh oh, she was revving up again.

"I told him you were a brilliant doctoral student in chemistry who knows a lot more than any arson cop, and probably has access to more advanced facilities, too."

That seemed to mollify her a bit. "And so you offered to trot out the pretty little filly and let him examine my hocks and withers first hand . . . sort of like a livestock auction?"

I stood up. "Marie, you know that's not what I . . ."

She smiled. "I know, I know, I'm just teasing you." She paused. "But if that's what he wants, sure, I can put on a good show for him."

I said, "Him and his wife Brenda, too."

She nodded thoughtfully. "Ahh, in that case it'll be the wife who makes the final decision. And he'll have to clear it with her anyway, since he'd be risking his job, right?"

I nodded.

She went and brought out her coat and I stood and helped her on with it. As she slipped her arms into it, she said, "All right then, let's go find out exactly how much this filly *is* worth at auction."

*   *   *

Dick Hartwick had the dream setup every normal guy was supposed to want in those days: a nice wife, two sweet kids, a ranch house in the Valley with a well-manicured front lawn and a patio out back where he could barbecue steaks for company.

We rang the bell and waited.

Brenda opened the door. "Hello Cole, I don't even *know* how long it's been. C'mon in."

I stepped forward. "Brenda Hartwick, I'd like you to meet Marie O'Malley." *Your guinea pig for tonight.*

Brenda looked at Marie, then turned back to me. "What a lovely girl!" Then to Marie, "I'm very glad to meet you, dear." She held out her hand. "Let me take your coats. Why don't you two both go back and say hello to Dick." She smiled. "He's been back there fussing with that barbecue for so long, you'd think it was Fort Knox. Besides, I have a lot to do in the kitchen."

We crossed the living room and went through the open sliding glass doors to the patio.

Dick looked up from the barbecue. "Well hello, Mr. Dunbar, long time no see."

I shook his hand, then swept my arm toward Marie. "Dick Hartwick, Marie O'Malley."

I could see Dick's eyes widen at her beauty, and immediately knew Marie was right; Brenda would be the toughest nut to crack tonight.

Dick said, "Well, well, Cole said you were pretty, but I wasn't expecting Miss America."

Marie's pale skin blushed winningly at the compliment. She said, "Thank you, you certainly have a lovely house, Mr. Hartwick."

"Please, call me Dick."

She bowed her head demurely. "Okay then, Dick." She waited quietly while Dick and I exchanged a few pleasantries, then waved her hand up toward the house and said, "Say, you know what, I'm gonna leave you two fellas here to catch up, and go see if Brenda needs any help with dinner or the kids." As she walked away, I could see Dick's eyes following her.

He turned back to me and said, "Well, I have to admit, you know how to pick 'em, sport; she certainly gets top marks in looks and deportment."

I smiled. "Believe me, that's not all she gets 'A's in, Dick."

We were off to a good start.

The dinner went like a charm. Marie made friends with Brenda while helping her prepare the meal. She was even a smash with the kids, Madeline and little Dickie.

Finally, Brenda went to put the kids down, and Marie and I exchanged glances; I knew the "filly," as she'd called herself, was leading at the far turn, but now that she was heading into the homestretch, she was on her own.

We were all sitting at the table having a glass of wine when Dick started it, trying to sound casual. "So Marie, I hear you're tops in chemistry, and Cole says you might have a way to look at the evidence on the Smythe fire that the Department and the insurance people might have missed."

She nodded. "Well, it's not that I'm any smarter than they are necessarily; it's more about having access to much better analytical tools."

Dick turned his head. "What do you mean by tools?"

"Well, gas chromatography, for one. It's a pioneering technology that gives you the ability to separate different components out in the debris sample, thus identifying key fuels and accelerants."

I saw Brenda kind of gasp and cut her eyes to Dick. Then Dick pushed on. "So, how does this gas, uh . . ."

Marie smiled. "Chromatography."

". . . chromatography thing work?"

If the filly had a closing spurt in her, now was her time to turn it on.

She nodded, then began. "Well, here's a simple way to explain it. GC relies on the differing affinities of vapor components for surfaces. In a gas chromatograph, a mixture is first vaporized and picked up by an inert gas. This carrier gas is then pushed into a tube or 'column.' Due to their different chemical properties, some compounds interact with the solid surfaces more strongly than others and are slowed in their race through the column. At the end of the column is a specialized detector that produces a signal as each compound exits the column, with the signal intensity corresponding roughly to the relative amount of each component. Plotting the signal on graph paper gives a peak for each component in the mix. A given sample will always produce the same pattern of peaks, or 'chromatogram,' when run through the column under the same conditions." She smiled and shrugged. "So, in very basic terms, that's about it."

Dick laughed out loud. "Er, you say that's the *simple* explanation?"

Marie looked flustered and began again. "Well, as I say, the outcome really depends upon a number of . . ."

Brenda held up her hand and smiled. "Dear, it would be useless to try and explain it to us any further." She looked at Dick and then Marie. "Marie, I'd say at this point we're both convinced you're the real McCoy. The only thing left now is for Dick and I to talk it all over tonight and decide if he's willing to do whatever it takes to get you the information you need." She looked over at me. "And on the record, Cole, I'd say you got yourself a wonderful girl."

"Yep: brains and beauty . . ." I pointed to myself and grimaced ". . . along with the beast."

We gabbed a bit more, but we all knew the "festivities" were over. About ten minutes later I stood and said, "Well, you guys have been wonderful hosts, but I think we're gonna have to hit the trail."

We said our goodbyes. Brenda said, "Please come back soon." Then she took Marie's arm. "And I do mean both of you."

We rode together in silence for a couple of minutes. Then I said, "Whew, that was an 'A' plus performance if ever I saw one."

Marie nodded. "Thanks, but to tell you the truth, after I talked to Brenda for a few minutes in the kitchen, I really wasn't even trying anymore; she's such a sweetheart, I knew I just had to be myself."

I laughed. "Maybe we could set up a transfusion sometime; I could use a little of your attitude."

She slid over next to me and I put my arm around her. She said, "Cole Dunbar, don't you know by now that you're good enough?" She grinned. "You're even good enough for me!"

*   *   *

I lay awake until the early hours of the morning, turning things over and over in my mind while Marie slept peacefully beside me. The whole case had moved way beyond being just another job at this point. Sure, I wanted to find the blackmailer—who I now knew was also a multiple murderer—for Monique. But it was more than that now. I was taking the baton from Ernie, the cop who'd been virtually destroyed by the case, and Buck, the cop who'd given his life, and maybe his marriage, for it. And now there was also an unspoken promise to Kitty Stacker to avenge the murder of her blameless father.

And lastly, I felt a need, even if an irrational one, to prove myself to Marie. Well maybe not to Marie herself, but to feel worthy of her and her love. And somehow it involved Danny too: something about atonement for the sin of losing him, of letting him down, and justifying the fact that I had lived on. I knew it was crazy, but also I felt like Danny couldn't come home until I'd redeemed myself. Christ, my brain was starting to feel like the "stack," that monstrous four-level freeway interchange that opened a few years ago.

Before, when I'd been focused on Monique, it was all about not being worthy of her station in life, her social connections, her fancy friends and their upscale haunts. But now with Marie, the whole mental chess game had switched around; it was more about living up to her character, her goodness, her . . . principles.

Is this what I did: find each person's strongest quality and then compare myself to it unfavorably? For that matter, what were *my* strongest qualities, if any? A proclivity for lost causes? A tendency to throw good emotional investment after bad? A loyalty to the lost?

I knew I'd be seeing Doc Grimes tomorrow; maybe he'd be able to straighten me out with some of that truth juice of his.

*   *   *

When I woke up late the next morning, Marie had already left to teach her undergrad chem class at UCLA. I took a shower and shaved, trying to think of a plan that was better than just following my nose, which is what I usually did. The only thing I felt sure of was backtracking on Buck Rogers' movements and contacts for the last hours of his life. I was also well aware that now, with Buck dead, I would soon have to report everything—or *most* everything—I knew to the LAPD. But if I wanted to retain my independence and my case for the moment, the time wasn't right for that yet, nor did I trust Crosetti and his pals to handle it properly anyway. Since I was going to be on Ventura Boulevard anyway later for my meeting with Bert Fawcett, it made sense to hit the Tail O' the Cock before seeing him, and ask the staff there if they might have heard or seen anything concerning Buck in his last days of life.

I decided to swing by El Bueno Etoile for a tamale to go—kind of a bizarre homage to Buck, I suppose—then head to the office to take care of all the bills and paperwork that had piled up while I'd been out playing tag with a homicide-happy monster.

It felt better than I expected to be back in my old familiar office chair again as I finished off the tamale and drank my Coke. Then it was time to get down to business.

"Answer World, Stella."

"Hi Stella, Cole Dunbar here. What's the haps?"

"Not much, but I did take one for you about an hour ago."

"Shoot."

"A Mr. Hartwick called. Call him back. Want the number?"

"Nope, got it. You're the best."

"Don't I know it."

I dialed Dick's cop number, feeling a lot more anxious than I expected to.

"Yeah?"

"Dick? It's Cole."

I heard a deep sigh, and almost stopped breathing.

Finally, he said, "All right, we talked it over."

"And?"

"It's a go." He was whispering now. "Though I think I'm half-crazy, and my common sense is fighting back at me like Carmen Basilio."

"Well, just pretend you're Sugar Ray Robinson!"

"Pretending won't keep me out of jail."

"Well, at least I'll be there in the cell to keep you company."

"That's a great comfort, pal."

We were silent for a moment before he said, "I'll be in touch. Bye."

After a couple hours in the office I had things in order, or as close to order as they ever got, given my aversion to paperwork. Then it was time to head to the Valley. I decided to stop first at UCLA and give Marie the good word, then take Beverly Glen over the hill.

I asked directions to the Chem Department and was told to go to Young Hall. There I was informed that Miss O'Malley was teaching a class nearby. I found the room, opened the door quietly and sat down at the back of the class.

There she was in a dark business suit, red hair tucked up in a bun, in front of probably fifty earnest kids, talking rapidly and pointing to a sliding chalkboard filled with strange squiggles and symbols. She was saying lots of ten-dollar words, but whether she was speaking English or not was strictly six to five and pick 'em.

Finally, she said, "Okay, that's all for today. For next week, read chapters ten and twelve and be prepared to discuss acids, bases and pH." Just then she saw me smiling at her from the back row.

I walked up the aisle to her and smiled. "I brought an apple for teacher."

She turned to me and smiled. "You mean he's willing to do it?"

I nodded. "Yep, after that bravura performance of yours, what else could he say?"

We hugged each other and jumped around together. Then she grabbed her purse. "Where did you park? I'll walk with you."

I shook my head. "Jeez, I don't know; somewhere in the next county, I think. This place goes on forever, like a French country estate or something."

She laughed. "I know, it can be kind of daunting at first."

We started walking.

I said, "Speaking of daunting, what was all that stuff you were talking about in class?"

"Oh, just basic intro to chemistry stuff."

"That's just the *introduction*? In that case, I'm glad I dropped out of school in the eleventh grade to join the Marines; drill instructors are hard to understand, but that stuff you were saying was downright . . ."

"Unintelligible?"

I nodded. "Yeah, what you just said."

She smiled. "C'mon, you're not as unschooled as you pretend to be. Anyone who loves Fante can't be that limited."

"So you heard that stuff at the police station?"

She nodded. "I was in the next room humiliating myself to spring you, remember?"

I said, "But how do *you* know about Fante?"

"Why wouldn't I? I'm a native Angelina, and I even know how to read."

We continued walking in silence until we reached the Ford, parked in front of a long row of sun-dappled eucalyptus. Then we kissed and I got in the car. I leaned out and asked, "So I guess the next step is hoping your professor's willing to ask his former student back east if he'll do him a favor, right?"

She nodded. "Yeah, the hard part is that it's not part of my research, and he knows it, so it really amounts to using his lab to do a personal favor for a friend of mine."

We both held up crossed fingers. I said, "Okay, I'm off to the Valley to do some more digging on Buck Rogers."

She cradled my face in her small hand. "Be careful."

"Workin' on it, prof."

Chapter Thirteen

The drive through Beverly Glen gave me time to think—maybe too much time, as my mind flitted wildly from topic to topic. What if Dick and Marie went to all this trouble and the sample only confirmed what LAPD and the insurance man had already said? On the other hand, if there really was no arson, that would clear both Hagemayer and Swopes, and Monique Smythe could tell the blackmailer to go pound sand, at least if he was convinced we were prepared to release the results publicly, which we certainly weren't at this time. What if the mystery man was still watching Kitty when she met with me in Griffith Park? Could I be the one he killed next? Maybe, but to be honest, I wasn't any closer to identifying him than I was when I first met Monique Smythe, and he must know that. Scaring me away with a beating once in a while made sense; killing me, not so much. Plus, now that he'd liquidated Swopes, Hagemayer and Rogers, all of the original stakeholders in the Smythe case except Matthew Smythe were gone, and the killer had the field to himself. Is that why he'd waited so long to put the big bite on Monique and go for the rest of the money? Was the rest of her fortune now due and payable?

The Valley was hot as hell. A solid wall of heat hits you as soon as you crest Mulholland Drive, and things only get worse as you weave your way down to the valley floor. By the time I found a parking space, my shirt was glued to my back and I was sliding around on the seat covers.

My mood only got worse after the Tail O' the Cock turned out to be a bust. Firstly, the cops had already been there, and, true to the breed, had not exactly handled the employees with kid gloves, so they were already in a surly mood.

For another thing, Nick, the regular bartender, had quit and moved back home to Connecticut. And the one waitress who admitted to remembering Buck at all called him, "That fat cop who was always either sad or angry." (Actually, not a bad characterization.) She had a few more mundane things to say about him: he seemed to be a decent guy, no flirting, decent tipper, liked to eat. And she had no memory of his meeting anyone in particular there, including me.

Then it was on to Argyle Investments. If Bert Fawcett turned out to be a bust too, at least I'd be getting disappointed in air conditioned splendor.

"Hi Norma, please tell the grand vizier I'm here."

She rose and salaamed to me, then pushed a button somewhere on her desk. "I've let him know you're here. It won't be long."

I pretended to be interested in a *Fortune* magazine article about plastics while I tried to organize the facts of the Smythe case in my mind for Bert as if I were sitting for my orals in crime-fighting. Ironic, because if Bert Fawcett were handing out doctorates in anything it would be in *committing* crimes. Non-violent ones, of course.

"Hey kiddo, so good to see you!"

Bert put his arm around me, guiding me back toward his office.

He sat on his throne and began. "So, it's been a while. I trust you've been propitiously occupied in the interim?"

He offered me one of those expensive Cuban stogies again, and this time I took it. He took his guillotine cutter and snipped off the cap in one clean stroke, then chuckled, "How's that for the perfect briss?"

I said, "Don't tell me you're Jewish?"

He held out his hands. "Hey, a name like Fawcett works better in the confidence game, but I take a lot of pride in my lineage: Rothstein, Lansky, Siegel—all of them my illustrious forbears."

I cocked my head. "So, what's your real name?"

He looked around comically, then said, "Well, it's a trade secret, but since you're like a son to me . . ." He leaned over to me. "It's Cohen."

"Cohen? Bertram Cohen?"

He smiled and leaned over again. "Now mind you, this is all off the record, but my real name is Barney Cohen."

I laughed, then nodded. "Yeah, you'd better stick with Bert Fawcett."

We enjoyed our cigars in silence for a minute or so, then he said, "Well my boy, I suspect that my genealogy isn't what you really came here for, so let's get down to it."

I spent most of the next half hour telling him the whole story of the Smythe investigation, including Buck, the Ensenada trip, Marie, Detective Crosetti, Kitty Hagemayer and her father, right up to gas chromatography and the possible theft of official police evidence. He mostly sat there, nodding with his patented poker face, though I did catch him smiling when I talked about Marie.

When I had finished, all he said was, "So why'd you go to the Tail O' the Cock?"

"Well, I felt like I had to check out anything I could find out about Buck Rogers' last days."

"But we both know already who killed him; at least the man, if not his exact identity."

"I guess that's true, but if there's anything more I can . . ."

"Kid, this has become more than a case for you, hasn't it?" He looked at me carefully. "It's become a debt of honor, hasn't it?"

I nodded in resignation. "You always could see through me."

He stood up and put his hand on my shoulder. "Cole, I know you feel like you haven't done enough, that you've failed in some way, because it's your nature to see things that way. But the truth is, you've done a hell of a job on this thing. You may even be on the verge of cracking the case wide open."

I shrugged. "I seriously doubt that."

"See what I mean? You always downgrade yourself, even though nobody I know could have done a better job of peeling back the layers of this crazy onion. Try and believe in yourself a little bit, man." He sat back down. "And that brings up something else: you're breathing down the neck of a very clever, very vicious man, and now that you may be all that stands between him and hundreds of thousands of dollars, you might be the next man up on his punch list: pun intended."

I shook my head. "Maybe, but I don't think so. He couldn't know anything about our obtaining the arson evidence, or the lab tests we're planning. And the only people who could finger him are now dead. Plus, he knows I never talked to Hagemayer at all, and Buck Rogers didn't really know any more than I did."

Bert nodded. "Just the same, you watch yourself, son. A man who's killed at least three times and had enough chutzpah to burn down a six-story office building is not going to quail at removing one more obstacle in his path."

"Okay Bert, I hear what you're saying." I smiled. "But it sounds like you've got kind of a personal stake in this whole thing, too."

He laughed. "I do, kiddo: you!"

It was time to change the subject. "Is there anything else you think I should keep in mind? Have I missed anything big?"

He shook his head. "Nope, I'd say you've got it pretty well covered. Now, it all depends on getting that sample tested, and what you do with the results. So, it looks like it's all up to the professors now." He paused. "And by the way, this Marie? She sounds like a champ. Well, please keep me apprised of any new developments," he grinned, "romantically, pedantically, or otherwise." He looked at his Rolex. "Now, there's an important call I've gotta take, but I hope to hear from you soon."

I got up and we shook hands again. Then I headed for the door. As I opened it, he said, "Watch yourself, kid. If I ever hear that you took a slug in the back, I'm gonna be very angry with you. Now, don't you forget that!"

I turned back and said, "Yes, sir."

Walking to my car, I was embarrassed; I hadn't said "Yes, sir" to anyone since the LAPD, and before that, the Marines. And I never had a father to say it to. So why had it come out my mouth in Bert's office?

It guess it felt strange to be cared about.

But good.

*   *   *

As I drove back across the canyon, I realized Bert was right: backtracking on Buck's movements was probably a waste of time, but sometimes you do what you do because you have to do something, even if it only amounts to chasing your own tail. The man was dead, and I knew, roughly, who did it; finding out exactly how Buck walked his last mile would just be an exercise in futility now. Besides, the cops would be all over that case now, seeing as how he was one of their own.

The cooler air on the city side of the hills was a blessing, though a temp in the high eighties with heavy smog was no picnic either. I searched my brain for any angle on the Smythe case I might have missed, but came up empty. Well, I started out on this case with just a pretty client and a nice retainer; now I at least had a fuzzy outline of who was behind the whole thing. But unfortunately, they don't convict fuzzy outlines.

One thing I did know: if and when I ever did catch up with this monster, it wasn't just gonna be, "Now you knock off bothering Monique Smythe, please." No, with multiple homicides on his lengthy resume, especially that of a peace officer, if I did my job right they'd be reserving a private chamber for the guy at San Quentin.

It's true that I wasn't a cop anymore, but on this case I was determined to be the closest thing to it.

*   *   *

Marie and I had arranged to meet at her place in Westwood for dinner around seven. That gave me about a half hour's leeway, so I wandered around Westwood Village for a while, feeling useless—a detective who at the moment had nothing to detect. I was thinking of buying a bottle of wine for dinner, but on impulse I stopped into a little florist shop and browsed around for a minute or two.

"May I help you, sir?" An older woman with a nice smile stood there next to me, gesturing around the store with her hand.

I shrugged. "I don't know. What would be good for a dinner date with a lady?"

"What kind of a lady?"

"A *real* lady."

She smiled. "In that case, you can't go wrong with roses; they're classic."

"So is she."

She walked over and picked out a beautiful arrangement of red roses. "These ought to do the trick, son. Any woman would be flattered to receive these."

I laughed. "Even from a guy like me?"

She tweaked my cheek. "Especially from a guy like you, you handsome devil, you."

I turned as red as the roses and muttered, "Guess I'll have to take your word on that, ma'am. Ring me up, please."

I drove down Le Conte and parked in front of Marie's apartment house, then took the flowers and walked up her front steps, feeling awkward. I hadn't really courted a woman in years; in fact it took my feelings about Marie to remind me that I hadn't actually cared about much of anything, or anyone, in years. Okinawa taught me that the cover charge you pay for caring is too steep for the show you get inside. Suddenly my hands were shaking. Beads of sweat broke out on my forehead. I felt clammy, dizzy . . .

"Are you okay?"

Marie had come out the door and was leading me up to her apartment by the arm.

I forced myself to snap out of it. "What are you doing out here? I didn't even ring."

"I was looking for you out the window, silly."

I made it to the couch and collapsed.

She pointed to the flowers. "Are those for me?"

"Uh, yeah. Here." I handed her the green wrapper that held the roses and half-fainted onto the couch, thinking: *Some Romeo. Some handsome devil.*

The next thing I knew, she was leaning over me, looking worried. "Can I get you anything?"

"Uh yeah, if you've got anything in a whiskey and soda, size large, I'll try it on."

"Let me go check."

My head was still swimming. My God, what brought this on? I hadn't had one of these shaking fits in years. *I* was supposed to be the detective around here, but this particular mystery was out of my league.

"Here, try this."

"Thanks." I took the glass, then gulped it down and almost gagged. "My God, what *is* this stuff?"

She grimaced. "Celery tonic; they say it's good for you."

"Good for you? Good for a lube job, maybe." I handed her the glass. "Please, take this away. Haven't you got a *real* drink somewhere?"

"Sorry, I'm not much of drinker." She looked hurt.

"Jeez, I'm sorry, Marie. I'm not exactly at my best right now." I struggled to get up. "Maybe I should just go . . ."

She gently pushed me back down. "No, of course not. I can see you're having some kind of trouble. Isn't there anything I can do besides bringing you a drink?" She got up and said, "Hang on a minute," and went into another room.

She came back with a wet towel and smoothed it over my forehead and face. It felt good until it reminded me of Kitty's story about her father doing this for her at his "safe house."

I tried to sit up again. "Look, are you sure I shouldn't just leave? I mean, before I ruined it, this was supposed to be a romantic evening, with roses, a nice meal . . ."

"You haven't ruined anything. It's still going to be a romantic evening, with roses and a nice meal." She had an impish smile on her face now. "And maybe even a special dessert."

She was smiling at me, her eyes dancing.

Finally I said, "Okay, I give up; what is it: strawberry shortcake?"

She said, "We got it!" with her green eyes sparkling.

My thoughts raced, but I came up blank. "Huh? Got what?"

She stood up and twirled around, clapping her hands. "The Perkin-Elmer Vapor Fractometer, of course!"

'You mean the machine that . . .'

"Yes!" She was still dancing around the room. "And he told my professor he'd run anything we send him, as soon as he receives it!"

That was almost as good as a large whiskey and soda. After another ten minutes or so, I had recovered enough to get up.

Marie pulled me toward the table. "C'mon, before everything's all dried up."

I took a seat and she went back out to the kitchen. She came back holding two big plates, and set one of them down in front of me, loaded with a big T-bone, a baked potato, and asparagus in some kind of fancy sauce. "Now, if that's not better than The Pantry, I'll eat this tablecloth . . . and there's no line here, either!"

She sat down next to me. "Go ahead, start."

I took a few bites. "Marie, the tablecloth is definitely safe."

She jumped up. "Oh, I almost forgot!" She went over and got the roses, then put them in a blue glass vase and set the vase down on the table. "Now, we're dining at the Rose Room. Bon appetit!"

I pointed to her. "I remember *Rose Room*: Benny Goodman, right?"

She nodded. "Yep, and Charlie Christian. I have a record of it. Say, we should dance later."

"I'm not much of a dancer."

"You will be tonight; we have something to celebrate!"

An hour later we had cleared the table and washed the dishes. As we sat together in the living room I smoked a cigarette and started feeling more like myself.

My mind drifted back to the case. I said, "So, if this guy says it's not arson, what happens to the case?"

Marie patted my knee. "Then you tell Monique not to pay this guy another cent, and it's case dismissed—or at least your part of it."

I shook my head. "But we can't go public with those results; we're not even supposed to *have* the evidence."

She thought a minute. "Isn't it possible the Department would be happy to have their initial findings verified, and all doubt removed?"

I nodded thoughtfully. "Could be, I suppose. Guess we'll have to cross that bridge when we come to it, *if* we come to it. Of course, the Department must never find out that Dick was in on it."

Marie said, "And if it *is* arson?"

"Then we work it like an arson case."

She looked at me. "You're the former cop; what does an arson case look like?"

I shrugged. "Heck, I was just a prowl car stiff. That stuff's for the real detectives, like that guy Crosetti."

"So what are you, a *fake* detective?"

I nodded. "In a way, yeah. Real police detective work was above my level."

She went over and shuffled through her record collection, then picked one out and put it on the turntable. She turned off most of the lights and came over to me again. "C'mon, that's enough shop talk; we both need a night off—just dinner, dancing, and us."

She held her arms out, already moving to the beat.

I said, "Are you sure? I might be kind of hard on your feet."

"I'll take that chance, mister."

While it's true that I'm not much of a dancer, Marie was light as a feather and easy to lead.

I don't really know how much time went by; we floated along as one in the near-dark and it felt like we were in our own little world, oblivious to time and care.

What I remember distinctly is that at one point she put her head close to me and whispered, "Cole, it feels like we were made for each other; it always has, at least for me, ever since the first time I saw you in the restaurant that day. Even then, before I knew you, it hurt that you were with another woman. I wanted to be your only one. Please, tell me you feel the same."

I could feel her hot tears on my cheek. I knew what she wanted to hear, but there weren't any words for the million crazy-mixed-up things I was feeling. I just kissed her long and hard, afraid she would ask me to talk, afraid of caring again, afraid she was above my station in life, afraid of plummeting back into the black pit I lived in at the VA hospital after the war, the pit it took me years to climb back out of, like a damaged creature without a mother, struggling to give birth to itself. I had no words to offer her.

After I don't know how long, she went and put on one last record, then came back into my arms and said, "*I Want a Sunday Kind of Love*. It's my favorite song. For me, it says it all." She paused. "Do you understand what I'm saying?"

I shrugged. "Well, I know the song, but I'm not positive."

She said, "For all I'm willing and able to give the right guy, I would never settle for less, even if it meant being alone for a lifetime."

The music started and we began moving together. I recognized the intro right away. I knew what was coming next; the words of a loving woman who wants a loving man:

> *I want a Sunday kind of love,*
>
> *A love to last past Saturday night,*
>
> *And I'd like to know it's more than love at first sight.*
>
> *I want a Sunday kind of love.*

We danced together without a word, and I felt the old panic rising in me. Could I offer anyone a love like that? Marie deserved the best, someone like the men I saw at the Chem Department: bright, normal, on their way to all the good things in life. Could I even offer her a life like Dick Hartwick's: a house, kids, a barbecue in the backyard with nice neighbors? I was a loner, an alley cat who'd found a way to scratch around on the outskirts of society. I never even felt close to another human being until I got to the Marine Corps, and look how *that* turned out. Marie was stable, beautiful, brilliant . . . what could I do for a girl like that except drag her down? I had no right to do that to her, to lie and say I would be there for her "past Saturday night," like in the song, when I had never really been there for anyone, and never expected anyone to be there for me, either.

The song ended, and we stopped moving. I could feel her body tense, as I waited there like a sheep in the slaughtering pen for the words I knew were coming.

"Cole, what's wrong?"

"Look, I don't know. Maybe it's what happened earlier. Those things are hard to shake off."

"You mean when you passed out?"

"Yeah."

"Honey, is it something from the war? You can talk to me about anything, you know."

Oh sure, I could talk your ear off about flying body parts, and how a mortar hit reduces a human being—even the best of them—to a fine red spray. I'm a real expert on that stuff, probably the only thing I actually am a real expert on.

I shook my head. "I just . . . I think I need to be alone for a while . . . too many things going on in my head."

"Is this why you have those horrible nightmares?"

"Marie, stop digging into my life! I don't know what to tell you. I don't even know what to tell myself!"

She looked horrified now.

I thought about Rick in *Casablanca*, saying bitterly, "Now go into your wow finish." Okay, I would: "You want a regular guy, someone who has a lot more to give you than I can. I don't know what you see in me, but whatever it is, I don't think it's actually in me."

Her eyes were wide now. "Cole, why are you talking like this? There isn't anything we can't . . ."

I grabbed my coat and opened the front door. I knew I had to say something, but I couldn't look at her.

All that came out was, "Some other time. We'll deal with this some other time!"

I fled down the walkway and drove off.

*   *   *

It was a huge relief to get back to my own place, where no one wanted anything from me, expected anything I couldn't give. I knew shame was coming at some point, but for now, relief suited me just fine. I grabbed a six-pack out of the icebox, then stripped off my pants, shirt, shoes and socks, turned out the lights and fell into bed. I lit a cigarette and lay there trying to settle down, keeping up a steady chant in my brain: *I don't know; I don't wanna know. I don't know; I don't wanna know.* And for some reason, my brain kept throwing back a twisted picture of Bert Fawcett saying, "Good job, kiddo, you sure put a quick end to that romance. And it's a damn shame, too, because she was a real champ."

I didn't want to think anything, I didn't want to know anything. I just wanted reality to stop. Finally I got up and turned on the TV; if there was any hope of mindless distraction, that was it. I turned the channel selector, first trying the big network channels, hoping for something engaging. Nothing doing. Then I gave up and tried the cheesy local stations, 5, 11 and 13, flipping past Dick Lane hysterically screaming, "Whoa, Nellie!" as he emceed the mayhem on *Roller Derby*, and then that blowhard George Putnam intoning the late news like it was the *Sermon on the Mount*. Then, on channel 13, I caught the start of an old movie I'd never seen: *The Dark Corner*, starring Mark Stevens and Lucille Ball. Wait a minute, Lucille Ball, from *I Love Lucy*, in a real drama?

Oh well, it was a perfect night for the surreal. I opened another beer and settled down on the couch to watch. Oh no, it was about a private eye. And he and his secretary are solving an impossible case together. And they're going to end up falling in love. I tried to hang in there, but when the private eye said, *I feel all dead inside. I'm backed up in a dark corner, and I don't know who's hitting me*, it was too close for comfort, and I turned it off.

The phone started ringing. I knew who it was of course, but I had nothing to say to her right now, at least nothing that wouldn't make things worse. Why talk to her when either way was an impossible choice: either I lie to her, or break her heart? I tried jamming one of the sofa cushions down over the phone, but it didn't help much. Each ring felt like my conscience yelling at me, *You did it! You did it! You know you did it!*

Finally the ringing stopped. I prayed she wouldn't come over and knock on the door now. Or worse yet, come at seven a.m., bringing piping hot coffee.

I flopped down on the bed. I really was bone-tired now: tired of impossible choices, unsolvable crimes and my own unexplainable problems. Was all this sturm und drang really just about my fear of getting closer to Marie? And why was I too personally invested in solving the Smythe case, like it was the make-or-break of my whole professional career . . . and maybe even my own value as a person?

I had another beer, then another, then killed the whole six-pack, chain smoking Camels until they tasted like the outhouse floor. Two things kept spinning around in my mind like a worn-out record. Side A was: "You idiot, if it's *not* arson, how are you going to tell anyone, since it's based on stolen material?" Side B: "You idiot, if it *is* arson, how are you going to tell anyone, since it's based on stolen material!"

Who needs nightmares when you've got my brain?

*   *   *

I came to at two thirty the next afternoon. That was good, because I had an appointment later with Doc Grimes, and I felt like a car that was 200,000 miles overdue for an oil change. It hurt to move, but I managed to pee and brush the things that live under the rocks out of my mouth, all while successfully warding off cogent thought.

And then, as they say in the movies, it all came back to me. Oh shit, did I really say that stuff to Marie? Oh no, did I really have another one of those fainting spells? Oh God, did I really screw up the best chance I'll probably ever have for a decent relationship? I don't want to go all dramatic and say I felt like a Jekyll and Hyde, but when you can't trust your own brain to conduct the business of life, it's not a good sign.

My appointment with Jim Grimes was at six. That meant I had to tread water for three hours before I could try and grab a lifeline from his passing ship. I took a hot shower and threw on some clean chinos and a long-sleeved shirt. At least it wasn't a felony in the city and county of Los Angeles to try and pass for a human being; plenty of movie producers I'd done security work for were getting away with it every day.

I decided to drive west on Santa Monica toward the beach, hoping to escape the heat and maybe catch a breath of smog-free salt air. When I hit Pacific Coast Highway I made a right and pulled up into an empty parking space, then grabbed a blanket out of the trunk and clambered down to relax on the sand. I sat there watching the gray clouds at play, shifting shapes and swapping places with each other. I was glad they were having a good time, because down here on earth a monster was prowling the city, and I might be on his menu.

It was low tide. The reek of the seaweed and festering crud left behind by the retreating water was bad enough, but a moment later I noticed something worse, something acrid and foul that permeated the air. Then I saw it, lying there about ten feet above the rim of wet sand; the putrefying remains of a sea lion. The stench was terrific.

Christ, no wonder the tide ran away.

I tried to stand up but doubled over, gagging; the smell of rotting flesh never really leaves you once you've lived in it for months. Finally I stood up and made for the Ford.

So much for my make-out session with Mother Nature.

I drove back down Santa Monica with the wind in my face, and after a while the smell left me and I realized I was hungry. I had to smile: is this what Doc Grimes meant by resilience?

"Hi, Cole." Helen waved at me as I parked the Ford in front of Pink's. At least someone still liked me. I went up toward the counter and said, "You know what I want." *Yeah, gimme a different life story—one with a little luck in it.*

She waved back. "Comin' right up!"

I went to one of the tables outside and lit a cigarette, trying to think of what I was going to tell Doc Grimes. I stared out at the cars passing by and wished I could meet with him a few times a week, like those rich folks he did *real* analysis with.

"Here you go, sir."

I looked up in shock: it was Marie, bringing my order.

I could feel myself blush redder than her hair. "What, uh, are *you* doing here?"

She sat down. "I work here. I *am* a working girl, you know, and as it happens I lost my last job recently. I figured you owed me, so I came here, told them I was a good friend of Cole Dunbar's, and voila." She paused. "And what are *you* doing here?"

My throat went dry. I barely had enough spit to talk. "I'm, uh, waiting for, uh, an appointment."

"With your psychiatrist?"

Damn. "How did you know *that*?"

She gestured to the counter. "Helen told me." She gave a wry smile. "You see, here at Pink's, we don't keep secrets from each other. You might remember that." She stood up. "Now, I have work to do." She walked away, while Helen stood there grinning at me from the counter.

I knew Marie well enough to know that when she was chipper like this, there was a Mount Vesuvius underneath it all.

So much for treading water.

Shit, now even Pink's, my one safe spot, was enemy territory. I finished my dog, cleared the table and headed for the Ford. Regardless of how explosive Marie was now, I needed to contact Dick and tell him the "caper" was a go.

I drove to the office and dialed the service.

"Answer World, Thelma."

"Thelma? What happened to Hattie and Stella?"

"Oh, they quit."

"What about Sabrina?"

"Ditto."

"Any particular reason?"

"I'm not at liberty to divulge that information, sir. Now, *whom* are you, and what do you want?"

Hmm, apparently at Answer World we *do* keep secrets from each other. "Uh, yeah, this is Cole Dunbar, of Dunbar Investigations."

"Let's see, Mr. Doober. Oh yes, it looks like you do have a few here. Would you like to hear them?"

"I hope my messages aren't a secret, too. Sure, go ahead and divulge that information to me, if you would."

She gave me a couple of brief messages from potential new clients, both of them women. Sounded like husband trouble, but you never know.

"What's the next one, Thelma?"

"I suppose it's okay to give it to you."

"Thelma, give it to me, whether you feel it's okay or not."

"You should do something about your attitude, Mr. Doober; I'm telling you this for your own good."

"Thanks for the tip, but I've already talked to doctors about it."

She said, "I guess it didn't take," and snorted with laughter.

"May I have it now?"

"Say pretty please."

"Thelma, just give me the goddam message."

"Well, if you're gonna be that way about it . . . okay, it's from a Dick." She snorted a couple of times again. "Dick Hardwig, or something? That's a funny name."

"It's Hartwick. Go on."

"Oh, so you know him, then?"

"The message, please."

"Okay then, it says, 'Waiting for your response.'"

"That's it?"

"I gave you the message he left, Mr. Doober. Now do you want me to make up something more?"

"No, Thelma, that'll be all."

"You have yourself a dandy day now, Mr. Doober."

"This has been a real good start. Goodbye, Velma."

Hmm, with Thelma on the loose, I had a pretty good idea why Hattie and the others had quit.

It sounded like Dick was getting nervous. Well, he had every right. I decided it might be better not to call him at the Department. I dialed the Hartwicks' home number.

"Hello?"

"Hello, Brenda? It's Cole Dunbar."

Her momentary silence felt damning.

"Look, Brenda, I'm sorry to be putting you guys in this situation, but . . ."

"Cole dear, you know we talked about it and decided together that if it was that important to you . . ."

Oof, that landed like a guilt bomb to the gut. Not that she intended it that way; Brenda wasn't like that. But after seeing Marie at Pink's, I was about as primed for guilt as a fox with a chicken-feather mustache. "So, the deal's on, Brenda. Please tell Dick that for me."

"Sure. And I hope it helps you, Cole. You know how much we value your friendship."

Ow. "Look, Brenda, if you guys aren't positive that . . ."

"No, we made a decision, and we stick by our decisions. I'm sure it'll all turn out just fine."

"I, uh, hope so too. Bye, Brenda."

"Goodbye, Cole."

It was now official: I had put a good friend in a compromising position. It was hard to resist twisting the knife on myself by tallying up all the people who'd already been hurt, or worse, while I caromed off the walls trying to solve this case. Maybe I should have told Monique at the beginning to just hand over all the money to the blackmailer and have done with it. It might have saved a few lives, and in the case of Dick Hartwick, a career too. Even Marie had lost her job, thanks to me, and maybe her heart too, courtesy of same. How many more dominos had to fall before this thing was over? And me? Why was I the one who always lived, when people all around me, better people than I, were being struck down? Why couldn't that mortar have hit me instead of Danny? Maybe God intended it for me, but He just had bad aim that day.

I still had about an hour or so before I could head over to Doc Grimes' office. I wasn't back to normal exactly, but the chili dog and the drive to and from the beach at least helped me feel like I wasn't treading water anymore. I really hoped Doc was in good form, because I was a walking diagnostic manual today.

The office phone rang. I half-decided to let it ring through to Answer World, but on impulse I grabbed it. "Hello?"

"It's me."

It was Marie. I was never so glad to hear anyone's voice, surprising even myself. "Marie, I'm so glad you called. I don't even know how to start to explain . . ."

"Sorry, I know I was kind of a snot at Pink's."

"Marie, you'd be perfectly justified if you never even spoke to me again. I, uh, I acted pretty badly last night, and . . . well, please try and be patient with me. I'm not used to human beings yet."

I heard her laugh. "Well, if you *do* go to jail, at least I have a job now, so I can support us . . . maybe even sneak a chili dog into your cell once in a while."

God, it was good to hear her talk like this. "Look, I'm so sorry I involved you in this whole thing."

"You mean your life, or the Smythe case?"

Now I laughed. "Both, I guess. They're both an endless chain of unsolvable problems."

She said, "I think it's 'insoluble.'"

"No, I think insoluble's for salt and sugar, isn't it?"

"Wait a minute, who's the chemistry brain here?"

"Sorry, I wasn't thinking."

"Okay, I gotta go. I just wanted to connect with you."

"Consider it done. And thanks."

"You're welcome. See you later at my place?"

"'You bet, unless my psychiatrist has me committed today."

"Hmm, commitment always seems to be your problem, doesn't it?"

"No excuse, sir."

I remembered my mother reading a Charles Dickens book to me once at bedtime which had the phrase, "Recalled to life" in it, describing one character's liberation from prison and another's spiritual awakening through love. Well Chuck got that one right; talking with Marie lifted a huge load off my shoulders. I was still a mess, but at least I was a lesser mess. It dawned on me that if you're all over the place emotionally, it makes it hard to evaluate the things that are happening to you and the people you interact with. Without a stable observation point, it's almost impossible to make any long-term commitments or promises about the future. It would be like the weatherman taking two recent temperature readings, one of twenty degrees and another of ninety, and then saying with utter conviction, "The temperature is fifty-five degrees." In my inner life, there were lots of twenties and quite a few nineties, but not much in between. How could I give Marie a Sunday kind of love when I couldn't even tell who I was going to be on Monday or Tuesday? I wondered if Doc Grimes would understand this problem, and I resolved to ask him about it when I came in today.

I hated to admit it, even to myself, but I realized these things bothered me a lot more now that Marie was in the picture than they did when Monique was on my mind. I think Monique and I both knew we were grasshoppers, people who lived for the day, then hopped off to the next food source. Plans were short-term and changeable, the cast of characters filled with temps and walk-ons, and commitment not something you ever really expected to give or get, but just a word you threw out there in order to mollify or cajole, as the case may be.

I suppose it all came from life with my mother: On the rare occasions when I asked her for help, she would give me an answer off the top of her head. Then if I came back later and said it didn't work, she'd just say, "Sorry, one to a customer." Or, if she promised to take me somewhere special on a Saturday and I asked her that morning when we were leaving, she'd think nothing of saying, "Oh, it's off. Something else came up." And if I asked, "What?" she'd say, "I don't know yet; ask me later."

What a contrast to life in the Marines. In the Corps, commitment was real, a way of life and a matter of honor and duty, not something you weaseled out of, or a flag you waved while the officers were watching, then dropped as soon as they were out of sight.

So the fact that Marines kept their promises was a totally new experience for me. And I wanted to be around guys like that forever.

But of course all that came to a screeching halt with the death of Danny Trueluck.

*   *   *

"Cole, good to see you again."

"You too, Katy. I hope Doc's wise and wonderful today."

"You mean you're not just here on a social call?"

"Not even a little."

"Well, it shouldn't be long."

"Okay, I'll just sit and read my *New Yorker*. I've been reading the damn thing so long, I oughta be getting royalties."

I was deep into fake-reading an article on making the perfect martini when Doc poked his head out the door and smiled. "So, we meet again."

I set down the magazine and shook my head. "Go ahead and smile, Jim; it may be your last one for a while."

"Uh oh, sounds serious."

In fact, Jim's face did look serious. "Okay Cole, as we discussed earlier, we're going to try something new today, something that may help you pull back that black curtain." He paused. "Now, I don't feel comfortable doing this unless you're all in, Cole."

I nodded. "I'm in, Doc." I gave him a grim smile. "Guess it's gonna take a jackhammer to break through that wall of cement in my brain. I'm scared, but I trust you. And besides," I continued, thinking of last night with Marie, "I can't go on like this."

Doc nodded. "You see, for some reason you tend to see attention as a demand, rather than a gift. And I'm hoping this agent I'm injecting might help you bypass those defenses, so we both can get some more insight into the root causes of it all."

I frowned. "What do you mean by a demand and a gift?"

"Well, people wanting to help you, and you letting them in, is what I'm talking about. As soon as someone focuses on you, even with genuinely good intentions, your black curtain comes down. Your defenses tell you, mistakenly, that the attention is a danger, an intrusion and a demand, rather than a gift, given freely. So you end up isolated and alone, at least psychologically, unable to avail yourself of the meaningfulness of love, or even help." He gave me a friendly nod. "So why don't you just lie back and we'll begin."

A moment later he was standing over me with a loaded hypo in his hand. He began to roll up my right sleeve. "I've titrated the dose pretty carefully for your body mass, and if anything, I've erred on the safe side. So we'll start with this, then adjust as necessary."

I felt the prick on my upper arm, then after a while something in me seemed to float away to a better place. I remember thinking, "That's the first decent breath I've taken in months."

Then I heard Doc's voice, calm and steady. "Cole, everything's going fine. We're not going for world's records here; today is just a preliminary exploration of how you respond to the drug. How are you feeling right now?"

It took my mouth and tongue a while to agree about how to form words. When they finally figured it out, I said, "I feel relaxed. It's good."

"Fine, fine. Now we're just going to try a little regression, for starters. Do you know what I mean by that?"

My head felt like a balloon, but I was able to nod, slowly. "Yes, going back . . . the past."

"Right. Now can you take me back to when you first joined the Marines?"

I took another one of those delicious, deep breaths. "Okay, I was underage, and I needed my mother's signature to . . ."

"To enlist?"

"Yes, to enlist."

"And then?"

"And then I brought her the paper. She had to sign it. I thought she would get, you know . . ."

"Upset?"

"Yes, but she was busy writing. She was writing a screenplay. She was always busy writing a screenplay."

Jim said, "Too busy to sign the paper?"

I was starting to get agitated.

Jim said, "Cole, it's all right, we don't have to go on right now. Just take your time and we'll come back to it whenever you're ready."

"I am . . . I'm ready now, I think."

"Okay, so you had to get your mother's signature?"

"Yes, and . . . and it was hard to get her attention. It was . . . always hard to get her attention."

"And how did you do it?"

"I yelled at her. I said, 'Mom, this is important to me!' And then she stopped writing and turned her head around to look at me. That was my chance, so

I put the paper in front of her and said, 'Ma, you need to sign this, so I can get in the Marines.'"

"And what did she do then?"

Part of me wanted to stop, but I made myself go on. "Well, I've never told anybody this before, but the first thing you should know is that she was a hard core radical in the Thirties, maybe even a Communist. So when I told her about joining up, she shouted, 'You want to join the Marines? I can't believe a son of mine could be that stupid, giving your life for a country that doesn't even take care of its own! But hell, go ahead and make a fool of yourself, for all I care.' So she signed it and then . . . she just went back to writing."

I'm pretty sure a long time went by after that part of the session, but I can't remember it. The next thing I recall Doc saying was, "You've done a good job today, Cole. You're doing fine. Now you just rest here for a while. When you leave, you'll find that the things we talked about here today will feel more real to you; you'll be able to remember them, and feel them, but you won't have to wall them off. Okay?"

I nodded. "Okay."

And that was all I remembered until he said, "Okay, we can stop whenever you're ready, Cole."

I yawned and stretched. "How'd I do?"

"Fine, you did great. Let's plan on meeting again next week. Just call me as soon as you know your schedule, and we'll fit you in somewhere."

I nodded. I was a little confused when we said goodbye to each other, because I thought I saw tears in his eyes. But then I couldn't be sure. Besides, I was still pretty loopy from the drugs.

I walked out of the room, went down in the elevator, got in my car and headed down Olympic, growing more angry by the minute, but not knowing why. But when one of those fancy little Corvettes cut in front of me and I tried to chase him down and ram him, I figured I'd better get myself off the road.

I pulled up in front of the darkest bar I could find, one that suited my mood. Two stiff bourbons later, some fat doofus at the other end of the bar started playing *Ain't That a Shame* on the jukebox. I don't know why, but that song set off all my anger again. I felt like the words were mocking me. And that fucking Pat Boone and his smooth voice too, that big white phony who'd made a whole career out of spinning race music into cotton candy and making millions from it. It was disgusting. Finally I went over to the jukebox and pulled the plug. Dammit, *someone* had to do it.

Then the big lug who'd put on the song picked up his beer and stumbled over to me at the other end of the bar. I could feel his bulk lurking just behind me, but I tried to ignore him. I boxed light-heavy in the Corps, and had even held my own against semi-pros in a few smokers after the war. Sure I was mad, but I didn't want to hurt anyone. But when he yelled, "And just what the hell do you think *you're* doing? Hey, I'm talkin' to . . ."

He palmed my shoulder and spun my stool around to face him. The instant I saw him cock his fist, I beat him to the punch, nailing him right on the button. He went down hard. Then I stood over him and emptied the rest of his beer on his head, saying, "Ain't that a shame?"

The barkeep made a quick move toward the phone.

I said, "Don't worry, I'm going." I threw a couple of bucks on the bar. "Here's a refill for his beer. And for the love of God, you need a better brand of music in this dump."

As I got into the Ford, I noticed my hands were shaking. Okay, I thought, maybe Jim's right and I *am* angry. Could this be related to what I'd said in the session about my mother? How could something that happened a couple of lifetimes ago still make me this mad? It didn't make any sense. I drove home, still seething. What was happening to me? Damn, what was *in* that stuff Doc shot me up with?

By the time I got home I still felt shaky but I had calmed down a bit and felt more like myself. As I opened the front door the phone was ringing. I went over and grabbed it. "Yeah?"

"Uh, it's Jim Grimes. I just wanted to . . ."

"Look Doc, I'm sorry I upset you, okay? Can't you just let it go?"

"Cole, I'm not calling for an apology. Besides, I don't even know what you're apologizing about. I just wanted to see if you're all right."

I found myself laughing. "Well, I did kind of bust up a bar on my way home, but yeah, I guess I'm basically all right."

"Do you think it was a reaction to the drugs?"

"Jeez I don't know. All I know is I was mad as a hatter after I walked out of your place."

He said, "Well, people can have strong emotional reactions to . . ."

I found myself blurting, "Wait a minute, don't hang up. There's a lot more to this thing than I thought, isn't there? I mean, it goes back even *before* the war, doesn't it?"

"Yes."

"And you'll help me make sense of it all? You're not just going to sit there crying?"

"Cole, I wasn't crying, and even if I was, it wouldn't be something you *did* to me. Yeah, maybe you saw some tears in my eyes, but that's because I care about you."

"I guess I'm not used to that shit."

"Well *get* used to that shit, Mac, because I intend to keep on caring about you."

Then the black curtain came down. "I . . . I gotta go."

"You sure you're okay?"

"Sure."

"Call me and we'll set something up."

"Will do."

Part of me wanted to see Marie, but a bigger part felt wrung out by what happened at Doc's, and afterwards at the bar. I had nothing to give anyone tonight, and it would be crazy to try. Damn, I knew I should call Marie to try and explain, but how could she understand what I couldn't even explain to myself? But after my last performance at her place, I owed it to her to at least make the attempt.

I forced myself to dial her number.

"Where are you?"

"I'm at home. Marie, I just don't think I can make it tonight."

There was a silence—the kind that doesn't bring puppies and lilacs to mind.

I said, "Did you hear me?"

"Yes, I heard you. Don't you have anything else to say for yourself?"

"Look, this is hard for me, but I'll try. You know I went to see my psychiatrist tonight, right?"

"Yes."

"Well, a lot of things happened."

"What kind of things? You realized you don't really care for me after all?"

"No, no, nothing like that. Things that have to do with my background, and ... why I'm the way I am."

"And what way *are* you?"

"I'm not sure I can put it into words. It's just that ... well, I guess I have trouble with people, with connection."

"People? People like me?"

"Maybe especially you, because of ... how much you matter."

"So because I matter, you can't see me tonight?" Her voice wasn't unfriendly yet, but it was in the neighborhood.

"No, Marie, because you *do* matter, and maybe even more because I matter to *you*, it's hard for me."

"It's hard for you that I care about you?"

"I know that sounds ridiculous, but yes, something like that. Something about a gift and a demand."

"A gift and a demand? What's that supposed to mean?"

"I'm not exactly sure right now; that's what I'm supposed to be working on."

She was silent for a while. Then she said "Okay, okay, if you need some time to yourself, I understand. I guess everything happened pretty fast for us; it's kind of thrown me for a loop too."

"Thanks for understanding. I know I acted like a jerk the other night. I've just gotta get myself straightened out. The Doc is helping me."

"Can't I help too?"

"I don't know. Maybe. But that would be a whole new world for me, and it's just a little . . ."

"Overwhelming?"

"Yeah, like I can't tell if people are hurting or helping me sometimes."

"So you'll be in touch soon?"

"Yes, of course."

"Okay then, I guess I'll see you whenever you drop in for a chili dog . . . or a refresher on pH values."

I could picture her smile. It helped. "It's a date. Bye."

"Bye."

Good, I had another night to myself. At least when you're alone, you can't let anyone down. I grabbed a beer from the icebox and turned on the TV, flipping channels until I finally found *Dragnet*. I lay down on the couch, pulled out a cigarette, and watched Jack Webb put on a neat, tidy tutorial on proper investigative procedure, solving the crime and tying it up with a bow by the end of the program. It was hard not to laugh at the difference between what the actors on the show depicted and real police work, like watching someone give a lecture about the parts of the brain, then handing you a scalpel and saying, "Now you can do brain surgery, too!"

Jack Webb: another guy who grew up in the rundown neighborhood of Bunker Hill, like me, and probably rode Angels Flight down the hill to school, just as I did. Our place was a second floor flat in one of those rambling, crumbling old Victorians that was on its last legs by the Thirties. The Hill was a ubiquitous character in Fante's books; he once described homes like ours as "frame houses reeking with murder stories." Soul murder, maybe; the area was aptly-named, because our apartment really was a bunker for Mom, a place where she could hide out from the real world and make up her own, typing away from morning to night. Sometimes I wondered if we only lived there so she could feel closer to Fante.

But in *Dragnet* the world was fair. It made sense. I don't know, maybe *Dragnet* is what it's really like for people like Dick Hartwick, going through the proper motions and getting the proper results. For me cop work was always a jungle of procedures that made no sense, and time-consuming, unnecessary paper-work. Plus, working with cops who were either doing the absolute minimum, or flat-out on the take. And ultimately you had to make so many concessions to the "real world" that it made a joke of the justice system. How were people like Dick able to navigate all that and still keep their integrity and self-respect? And now I'd even put *him* in jeopardy.

The phone rang. Oh no. I really wasn't ready to go another ten rounds with Marie, if she'd gotten herself all revved up again. I already felt bad about how I acted at her place, and now I'd ditched her again. And what's worse, I had no way of knowing whether I'd do the same thing to her tomorrow, the day after that, or forever. I sure wasn't the Steve Bilko of love; I couldn't even make the love team as a batboy.

It rang and rang until the damn thing finally gave up. I had another beer, another cigarette and another TV show until I passed out on the couch.

That night I had the mother of all nightmares. I can't remember all of it, thank God, but I know that at one point my mother was sitting on top of me, writing, and each time she finished a page she'd reach down and stuff it down my throat. I couldn't breathe, but she didn't care. She made me eat every page of it, like those parents who force their kids to eat their vegetables. Later, in part two, I was back on Okinawa. I saw a Japanese artillery shell arcing down at my men in slow motion. I had time to warn them, except I was paralyzed: I couldn't move, I couldn't talk. Then, just as the shell was going to land I woke up, my throat aching from silent screams.

I swam my way up from the depths and rolled out of bed. It was two in the morning. I peeled off my clammy pajamas and hit the shower, trying to wash the dream stink off my body. My mind was another matter. Christ, managing my mental problems was starting to feel like a full-time job. How was I supposed to go out into a tough world and track down bad guys for my clients too?

*　　　*　　　*

The phone was at it again. I jerked awake and looked at the clock: four thirty a.m. Nobody ever called me—or anyone—at home this early. But then it might be an emergency. I forced myself to get up and cradled the receiver.

"Yeah?"

"So, you finally made it home."

It was Dick Hartwick. He was the kind of guy who'd think it was inconceivable to be at home and not answer your phone, so I didn't bother to rebut the implied accusation in his words.

"Dick, what's up?"

"I, uh, just wanted to tell you I got it."

"The evidence?"

"Yeah." He paused. "I want this stuff out of here as soon as possible. Tonight."

"All right, give me fifteen minutes."

"Okay."

Click.

Damn, now I felt worse than ever about dragging him into this thing. I threw some water on my face, brushed my teeth and pulled on some clean clothes.

The streets were eerily empty in the gray gloom of pre-dawn, the only time traffic in LA isn't a real bitch. I drove up Highland to the Hollywood Freeway, trying to push away all my guilt about Dick and use the time to concentrate harder on any angle I might have overlooked on the Smythe case: the sale of the building, the disappearance of the sellers, the possible culpability of Matthew Smythe or his daughter, the circumstances of the fire, the involvement of Rogers and Finnegan, the insurance company, the grave in Mexico, the bodies of Buck and Hagemayer, Kitty's story . . .

What was I missing? . . . What was I missing? . . . What was I missing?

Finally I stood at Dick's front door. I rang the bell.

He instantly jerked the door open and handed me the package, saying nothing.

"Hi Dick, I just wanted to let you know, I really appreciate . . ."

"Here, just take it and go."

Ugh. "Okay, I'm off. Say hi to . . ."

Slam.

Well, if I ever had any doubts about feeling bad for dragging Dick into this mess, that door slam put an end to my speculations.

And if I ever had any doubts about Jim Grimes' theories that I took relationships as a demand, that drive home down the dark, deserted streets dispelled those, too. I could feel everyone's expectations pressing down on me like a ten-ton weight. They were all counting on me: Monique and her father to get this murderous bloodsucker off their backs; Marie, hoping for a normal future with a regular guy. I even felt like Bert was holding his breath, waiting for me to take a wrong step and disappoint him. And then there was my mother, and her effect on me. Can you try your best at parenting and still do a piss-poor job of it? She always seemed bitterly disappointed that she never really made it as a major screenwriter; disappointed in men, disappointed in America, disappointed in the whole world, I guess. I always figured I was just another insignificant part of that disappointment, that it didn't really affect me personally, once I got away. But now, after that last session, that idea seemed pretty naive.

The murky light of dawn still hadn't peeled the shadows from the empty streets as I drove home. Like the sleeping city, I was in darkness too, with nothing left by the time I got home. I jammed the evidence package under the bed and pulled the covers over my head, praying that I'd already made enough sacrificial offerings to the god of nightmares for one night.

Chapter Fourteen

The phone was bleating again.

Jesus, didn't I just go through all this a minute ago?

I opened my eyes. It was light. Oh no, time had done it to me again: why did tomorrows always arrive too soon? Christ, the days kept coming at me like Pancho Gonzales' big, booming serves. From somewhere I heard that hellish advertising jingle:

Say the magic word, say Mission Pak and it's on its merry way!

Was it part of a bad dream? Oh shit, I'd forgotten to turn off the TV when I went to bed. I lurched out of bed and staggered to the living room.

Give us the address, we do the rest. To find your nearest Mission Pak store, call
. . .

Yeah, yeah, I knew the number. Now if you could only order a Mission Pak basket of beer and cigarettes, I might actually *dial* Adams 2-4184. I snapped off the TV, eliminating the phone's only competition.

I lifted the receiver, if only to make it stop. "Yeah?"

"It's Marie."

"Oh, hi Marie. What time is it anyway?"

"It's nearly noon, Cole. Don't tell me you were still in bed?"

Let the disappoinments begin!

"Uh no, not really. I was just kind of noodling around, getting ready for the day."

She said, "I just wanted to touch base. That last conversation ended kind of awkwardly."

Let the apologies begin!

"Yeah, sorry about that."

"No, it was both of us."

"That's nice of you, but . . ."

"You sound tired."

"I was up all night with a sick friend."

"Oh really, who?"

"Me."

"Cole, you're not making any sense. Listen, maybe you need some coffee."

"No, I'm fine, really. Say Marie, there's something I have to show you."

"Okay, I get off at three today. Wanna meet at my place?"

"You have your car at work?"

"No, Helen gave me a ride here."

"Okay, I'll come by and pick you up at three."

"One pup, coming up!"

We hung up. My God, Marie sounded fine again. How could she have so much . . . what was that word Jim used again? Resilience. How could she have so much resilience, when for me, each day started out even more deeply in debt than the last one; life felt like serial usury.

I managed to steal a couple more hours of jagged sleep, then got up and drove down La Brea to Pink's. I found a space in the lot then got into a line of about twenty people, mostly working men from the looks of them. Hmm, maybe they were all coming to see that new redheaded waitress. Why should she choose me when just about any one of those guys would be thrilled to accept her love without running for their lives?

Just then Helen leaned over the counter and gestured to me. "Hi Cole, she's working in the back." She winked. "And I already know your order."

I got out of line and went around back, where Marie was bent over, busily washing out a big bucket with a hose.

I came up behind her quietly. "You've really got a *much* better behind than Dick Drott!"

She jumped a mile. "Oh, you startled me!"

"You mean because I like your bustle?"

She grinned. "Well, maybe that too, but I wasn't expecting you so soon."

I put my arms around her. "Well, maybe I couldn't wait."

She smiled. "Hmm, now you're sounding like my Cole again." She reached up to give me a kiss, then added, "Why don't you go around front and find a table; I'll be right out." She bent down again to finish her job.

Helen called my order and when I went up to the counter to get it, she said, "Hey, thanks for the referral, Cole; that gal of yours is some worker! And she's supposed to be a hot shot scientist too? Woowee, you better snap that one up, toot sweet!"

I nodded my agreement and tried to push away the resultant guilt as I sat down at an empty table and started in on my dog.

"To what do I owe the honor?"

Marie sat down and looked at me questioningly as she swept a thick lock of red hair off her glowing face, then rested her chin on her hands. She'd never looked so gorgeous.

I asked. "The honor of what?"

"The good mood, of course. It has been a while, you know."

I tried gamely to force a smile. "Yeah, well lately my moods have been like a bus stop: if you don't like this one, there'll be another one along in a minute, going somewhere totally unpredictable." I motioned to the line of men at the counter. "You know, I was just thinking, any one of the guys in that line would be thrilled to have a girl like you. And they wouldn't run screaming into the woods, either."

"But I don't want them. I want you."

"I can't understand why, since I seem to be an unsolvable crossword puzzle."

"Insoluble."

I had to laugh. "Are we gonna go through that again?"

"No, just admit that I'm right and we'll move on."

I bowed my head. "Okay, you're right: I'm insoluble. But why wouldn't you want a guy who dissolves more easily?"

She grinned. "Look, you can't explain love. It isn't logical like science. It's something you either feel or you don't. It's a . . ."

"Gift?"

Her green eyes twinkled. "Yes, now you're starting to get it. That's a beautiful way to put it." She paused. "Say, isn't that the word you used the other night? I remember, you said gift and . . ."

"Demand."

"Yes, demand. What was all that about, anyway?"

"It's just something Doc Grimes said in my last therapy session."

"So that's your psychiatrist?"

"Uh huh. He claims that I see love, caring and even attention as demands. So then it all becomes overwhelming and I . . ."

"Run out of apartments?"

I nodded.

Marie looked thoughtful. "Good, at least that gives me something to go on. The other night at my place when you ran out, I was afraid it was because you didn't feel anything for me." Her eyes were etched with tears now. "And that's what really hurt. But your being afraid . . . that, I can deal with." She reached over and took my hand. "Cole, if you do love me, I have all the patience in the world for you. Just talk to me and let me know what you need."

Now I had to fight hard to keep the black curtain from coming down. "Marie, all I can do is try. This is all new to me: talking to the other person, asking for what I need, even *knowing* what I need. I've always been a loner I guess, even more than I realized, until the other day with Doc Grimes. I think my childhood was a lot weirder than I realized, too."

Marie held my hand to her lips. "Cole, I want to hear about it, all of it."

I felt panicky. "Can we go now?"

She looked concerned. "Sure, just let me get my things. Wait for me in the car. I'll be there in a minute."

I waved goodbye to Helen and slid in behind the wheel. I needed some noise to block out the curtain, so I turned the key and switched on the radio:

The wayward wind is a restless wind, a restless wind that yearns to wander. And he was born the next of kin, the next of kin, to the wayward wind. Though he tried his best to settle down, I'm now alone with a broken heart.

Hmm, would that be Marie's future with me? I listened as Gogi Grant wailed on about having her heart broken by a man who's incapable of giving back what she's offering him. Well at least that meant I wasn't the only unsolvable—no, insoluble—man on earth.

Marie scooted over next to me. "Okay, let's go." When she heard the song, she reached over and snapped off the radio. "I think we can do without that."

I headed out on La Brea and in a few minutes we were cruising west on Sunset. I asked her about her day and she rattled on about how nice Helen was, how Jerry Lewis had come by from Paramount for lunch, how the Angels were leading the pennant race, and other news from the normal world.

I deliberately hadn't said a word about the fire evidence I'd gotten from Dick, which I had locked safely in the trunk. Even if I couldn't provide what she needed emotionally, at least I had something special to show her later.

We pulled up in front of her building on Le Conte. It was a sweet little two-story place, done up in fake Spanish, with pink walls and crimson bougainvillea flanking the front door like a welcome home. I went around and opened the car door for her. But as we made our way up the front steps, I started experiencing that faint feeling again.

Fortunately, the plan I had for presenting the evidence to her would give me some breathing room. I said, "Oh, sorry, I forgot something in the car. You go on in and I'll be back in a minute."

Marie let herself in to the building and I went back out to the car and unlocked the trunk. I had placed the evidence packet inside an ordinary shopping bag, so it just looked like groceries as I carried it in.

Marie looked at me from the kitchen. "Oh, did you bring us something for dinner?"

I shook my head. "No, not exactly." I sat down on the living room couch with the bag next to me and waited.

She came into the living room. "I got some beer," she grinned, handing me an open bottle, "in case you ever came back."

She sat down in the chair across from me. "So, what do you want to do tonight?"

I said, "I brought you a present."

She furrowed her brow. "But it isn't my birthday or anything. Gee, you don't even *know* my birthday!"

"Nope."

Marie tilted her head. "Wait a minute, what are you sitting there looking so smug about?"

I lifted up the bag. "Trick or treat."

She shrugged as I shoved the bag across the coffee table.

Then she looked in the bag and saw the sealed cardbox box inside, with an ID tag affixed to it. "Oh my God, you got it! Did Dick have any trouble getting it?"

"I don't know; he wasn't in a very expansive mood when he demanded that I come by his house in the dead of night to take it from him."

She looked over at me. "Oh no, I hope this doesn't affect your friendship with Dick and Brenda; they're such wonderful people."

I sighed. "Amen to that."

Marie took the box out and set it on the coffee table. "Hmm, so how do we handle this? I suppose we have to be very careful so no one knows we ever had it, right?"

I shook my head. "I've thought about this a lot. I don't think there's any way I can ultimately hide what we're doing, because no matter how the results come out, we're going to want the cops as our allies. All I can do up front is shield you and your colleagues from the whole thing by insisting that none of you had any idea what it was about. As far as you or your associates know, all they're doing is carrying out an assessment of a blind sample from a confidential private fire investigation, which at this point it literally is. That way, I take all the heat."

She looked panicky. "But how are you ever going to get the cops as your allies?"

"I don't know; one step at a time."

"Couldn't you try and talk to them now, before we take the next step?"

"No, they'd never go for it; for one thing, it would make them look bad."

"Then what's the plan for later?"

"Marie, I already said I don't know." I stood and raised my arms. "I don't *know!!*"

She was shocked for a moment, but maybe she was getting used to my outbursts, because she got herself under control and said, "And what about Dick? Will he be vulnerable in all this?" I shook my head again. "Nope. I'll say I hired a professional thief to do the job, then refuse to divulge the person's name. Believe me, they'll buy it; Crosetti would like nothing more than to pin something like this on me, and prove it was all my doing." I paused. "But all that comes later. Right now we just need to get those results. If it is arson, it'll at least give us another important link in the chain of evidence that I can backtrack on."

She reached out and stroked my face. "Sorry if I pushed you. I know you've been under terrible pressure. I just panicked for a minute there. But you've had this on your shoulders for a long time now, all alone."

I shook my head. "No, I'm the one who should be sorry for snapping at you like that."

The rest of the night was kind of a make-up session for what I had done the last time. After I told her about the session with Doc, Marie asked me a million questions about my childhood and my life before the war. She was the first person, other than Jim, I'd ever really told about my mother and her strange ways . . . ways that always seemed normal to me before that last session with Jim. I guess it took that pentothal "jackhammer" to jolt me out of protecting her, or maybe protecting myself from the truth. We must have talked for hours. Finally, I told her all about Danny, and the time I spent in the VA hospital after the war, fighting for my sanity and trying to forgive myself for still being alive.

At the end I said, "Look, the gist of it is that, even if it's illogical, I can't forgive myself for losing Danny, for not protecting him, for being alive while he's dead. I didn't complete my job, which was to bring everyone back alive, especially Danny. I got to come home to Los Angeles, but Danny had to stay behind, in the *real* city of the angels. And so I feel like he'll never be free until

I redeem myself, whatever that means. Maybe that's why this damn Smythe case has been eating me up; somehow, I think maybe if I nail this guy, I'll be off the hook for the Trueluck job."

Marie's emerald eyes were flashing now. "The Trueluck job? Oh my God, listen to yourself: you make Danny's death sound like you committed a homicide! Now Cole, you listen to me, I think you've got it all backwards; if Danny *is* stuck in time or space, I think it's because he sees that *you're* not fully alive yet, still not ready to accept *yourself*, never mind love or help. If Danny can't let go, it's because he sees you still being alone, still holding yourself back from showing who you really are. You're afraid of love because you think you won't be able to give anything back, but Cole, love isn't like buying a rug, where you receive something and then owe somebody in exchange for it; it's more like making a commitment to show the other person who you really are, and the only 'exchange' is that *you'll* be interested in who *they* are, and gentle when they show it to you."

I didn't know what to say to that. To me, it was even more Greek than those crazy symbols she wrote on the chalkboard that day in her chem class. Of course I could never say this to Marie, but truthfully what she'd said made me feel not only guilty for being alive, but that now it was *my* own failings that were keeping Danny stuck in time. I knew she'd said it with good intentions, to take some pressure off of me, but honestly, the whole thing made me feel like a submarine that's gone too far below its crush depth, with massive forces closing in on all sides. Still, there was nothing I could say or do about it now, especially after I'd upset her with my performance the other night . . .nothing I could do but just shut up, grab another beer and try to fight off the black curtain.

Fortunately, Marie got up and put on some records again, so I didn't have to talk anymore. I was finally able to relax a little as we danced there together in the dark, the way it should have been that first time. Holding her slim waist helped center me, and after a while, the blackness seemed to recede and I was able to be there with her, together in the moment. I think we both needed that—a way to reclaim something beautiful that almost slipped away. And this time when she leaned over and whispered in my ear, she only said, "Cole, please don't give up. You can't deny the bad things that happened to you, but with enough love, I know we can make a good life together."

Was it true? I knew it was for her. But me? Other than Danny, I'd never even imagined another person having a starring role in my life story. But at least for tonight, I was willing to let the dancing and the darkness blur the line between past, present and future, and carry me away like a sweet dream.

That night, we made love in Marie's bed for the first time, and put the perfect coda on a perfect night. And afterwards was the first time I could remember when drifting off to sleep felt like being escorted by angels.

*   *   *

"I don't know!"

"Cole, wake up!"

"I don't know!"

"Cole, you're having a nightmare!"

I opened my eyes, gasping for breath. But instead of a court martial, there was Marie, looking at me with terror in her eyes.

"It's all right, Cole, you were just having a bad dream."

The dream still felt more real than real life. "I have to defend myself." The words came in ragged bunches. "They say I . . . stood there and let him die . . . to save my own life."

Marie was smoothing my moist forehead with her cool hand now. "It's not true, Cole. You had nothing to do with his death. You were an innocent bystander."

"Tell that to them!"

"To who?"

"I don't know, the accusers."

"The accusers are in your own mind."

"Sometimes I can't tell."

"Maybe that's a way I could help you sometimes; be a voice from outside."

"I don't know."

"Oh no, are we back to 'I don't know' again?" She looked worried.

I finally smiled. "Calm down, it wasn't that kind of 'I don't know'; this one was a *regular* 'I don't know.'"

Marie shook her head and laughed. "Looks like I'm going to need an advanced degree in Cole Dunbar, too."

I grimaced. "Yeah, except this degree you only get in the school of hard knocks."

She murmured, "Or maybe by running a midnight rescue mission," but her eyes were closing.

I got up to get the Camels I'd left in the living room. When I got back to the bed I checked the clock: four thirty. This was the second night in a row that four thirty and I had hooked up, and we still hadn't even been properly introduced.

I turned back to Marie, but she was already somewhere peaceful, far beyond me and my problems.

Asleep or awake, I wished there was such a place for me.

*   *   *

When I woke up at one the next afternoon, it was raining hard. It was cozy lying there in soft sheets that still smelled like Marie. I got up to get a beer and saw that the evidence package was gone. I knew Marie had classes to teach this morning and a meeting set up with her adviser; she'd probably give him the stuff then. I hoped she remembered what I told her to tell them, that it was a private fire investigation; it was the only way I could figure to keep them, and her, out of harm's way later.

I smoked a leisurely cigarette while looking out the window at the driving rain, then took a shower and shaved from the travel kit I'd brought in hopes of getting lucky. Well, that's not really accurate; more in hopes of not destroying the evening this time, which I almost did anyway by making Marie run a midnight rescue mission, as she'd called it.

I got myself looking passable and went out to the living room to call my service. Halfway through dialing, it hit me that Thelma might pick up, so I was already preparing myself for the onslaught as it rang.

"Answer World, Hattie."

"Praise the Lord!"

"Excuse me, sir? This wouldn't be Mr. Dunbar, by any chance?"

"Who else?"

"What's with the holy roller talk?"

"Well, not to cast aspersions, but I was expecting Thelma."

She gave a hearty laugh. "That offspring of an unwed mother is long gone, Mr. D."

"What happened, if I'm not being too nosy?"

"No, it isn't too nosy. After a few days of her, all the other girls ganged up and just about rioted, that's all, and management had to can her fat ass quick or lose the whole staff. Pardon my French."

"Well, I hope she's gone on to better things."

"Well I don't, and I don't mind sayin' it, one little bit."

"Okay then, congratulations all around. And if I'm not being too nosy again, do I have any messages?"

"Yeah, let me look. One from a Miss Smythe, no message, and two more, from those same two ladies who called the other day? Remember them?"

"Oh no, I forgot to call them back."

"Need the numbers again?"

"No, I wrote 'em down in my book right here. I'll give them both a call now. Thanks, Hattie, and welcome back."

"Sure, Mr. D, you always were one of the nicer ones."

Well, the fact is, I did have a detective agency to run, and no matter how the Smythe saga ultimately played out, the agency needed to keep churning out business if I wanted to keep myself in chili dogs and T-bones. Besides, there wasn't much I could do on the Smythe job at the moment anyway, other than wait for the results and maybe send up a prayer or two to the patron saint of gas chromatography.

I dialed the numbers I had written in my book and came up with this:

Mrs. Lucy LeVoi had a problem: her husband Martin had left on a business trip to Palm Springs with his secretary four days ago, and she hadn't heard from him since. Would it be possible for me to run down there and check out the situation? Not that she doubted his fidelity for a moment, mind you, but something might have happened to him on the way. After all, he was a diabetic and his car had two worn tires. She didn't know where he was staying, but hoped I could figure it out. I took a good physical description of him from her: mid-forties, tall and overweight, with thick black hair, slicked straight back with lots of Wildroot. And then the secretary, a short, squat, thirtyish gal with dishwater-blonde hair, "All fuzzy, you know, like a sheep or something?" She also had a wandering eye on her right side. For Lucy's sake, I hoped that wasn't her husband's problem too. I told her I'd make a few calls and get back to her on Tuesday with any information I could dig up.

Marilyn Marson had a problem too, but hers wasn't man trouble. She ran a good-sized stationery store, and a woman claiming to be an elementary school principal had ordered five hundred dollars' worth of children's arts and crafts supplies, from construction paper to crayons to glue to fingerpaints to scissors to water colors. On credit. Only now it was four unpaid weeks later, and there didn't seem to be a school named Ethan Allen Elementary anywhere, much less a principal named Evelyn Porter. Was there anything I could do about it? Yes, I told her, skip-tracing is part of being a PI. I asked her where she found my name. She said an employee gave her the name and even my business card, and said I came highly recommended. After taking down every bit of information Miss Marson could give me about this Evelyn Porter, I told her I'd get right on it and get back to her Tuesday with any information I could dig up.

It felt good to be "just" a private investigator again for a while, doing regular PI things that didn't involve murder, bodily harm or hundreds of thousands of dollars. In fact, it even occurred to me that after the work day was over, maybe Marie and I could actually go out together tonight, maybe for dinner and a movie. I couldn't even remember the last time I took a girl out on an honest-to-God date. I had been living like a hermit for so long that my social graces—or what passed for them—had atrophied. The only events I'd even attended for years were when I was working security, and that's a far cry from being there as a civilian.

I got down to the office and rummaged around in the file cabinet until I found the number for Harold Barnes, the doorman at one of the swankier hotels in Palm Springs. I had gotten to know Harold on a previous case down there, working for a defense attorney, tracking down alibi witnesses in a murder case.

"Hello, Harold? Cole Dunbar. Remember me?"

There was a momentary pause. "Oh yeah, mister private eye, right?"

"You got it. Listen Harold, I've got a question for you. Are you game?"

"You got questions, I got answers, Mr. D."

"What are the places in town where an out-of-town businessman would be likely to go for a few-day shackup job? You know, cheap but not so ratty that it would offend the young lady involved, if you know what I mean?"

I heard a chuckle. "Sure boss, I know what you mean all right. Hmm, lemme see . . ."

He named three motels, two of them in town, one on the outskirts.

"Thanks, Harold. There's a twenty on its way to you."

"Oh, you don't have to do that, Mister D. But then, it's welcome just the same."

I called the first two places, asking for a Martin LeVoi, maybe traveling with a young blonde?

Nothing.

Then I phoned the Desert Star.

"Star, Manny speaking. Whaddya want?"

"Well I'll tell ya, Manny, have you got a Martin LeVoi registered there, lots of greasy, black hair, maybe traveling with a shortish blonde?"

"Nope. Oh, wait a minute. You must mean Mr. Smith, that fat guy who's with the gal with a weird eye?"

"You're singin' my tune, Manny."

"What about him?"

"Could you ring his room for me, please?"

"Well, I'm pretty busy . . ."

"A sawbuck for your pains?"

"Done. Hang on."

I heard the buzz. Then, "Yes?"

I said, "Mr. Smith?"

"Uh, yeah. What about it?"

"Or more accurately, Mr. Martin LeVoi?"

"Who is this?"

"Let's not worry about that; what you *do* need to worry about is getting you and your little friend out of there pronto, plus what you're going to tell Lucy when you get home."

Dead silence.

"I *have* got the right Martin LeVoi, haven't I? The one who's shacked up with Liddle Lamzy Divey?"

"Knock it off, I get the message."

"That's a good boy, Marty. Now get in your car and head home; that oughta give you plenty of time to think of a good story that doesn't hurt your wife, because if you don't, Little Bo Peep is gonna have a weird eye on *both* sides of her face. You dig?"

"I dig."

"Better hurry, I'll be clocking you."

"Yes, sir."

On the LeVoi job, I would hold off calling my client until Tuesday. Hopefully by then nature would have taken its course and the whole thing would be papered over between them. I don't go out of my way to cause trouble; if I can solve the problem quick and quiet, so much the better. Men make mistakes; if Mr. LeVoi had any sense, he'd watch his ways from now on and no one would be the wiser. I put two tens in the mail to Harold. As for Manny, he could go spin on his thumb.

Okay, that was one down, one to go.

The Marson case was a little different. I'd start with the m.o., and maybe if I got lucky I wouldn't have to do much work. I grabbed the Yellow Pages, looked up the big art supply houses in town and started calling around, asking if a woman calling herself Evelyn Porter of a certain physical description had made any large purchases, then skipped out on the bill. I racked up four "No, not to my knowledge" before I called the Flax art supplies store in Westwood Village and heard, "Yes, as a matter of fact. But how do *you* know about it?"

"I represent a client who's been victimized in the same exact way. I wonder if perhaps we could work together on this troubling situation?"

"Well, it is somewhat unusual, but seeing as this woman appears to be a repeat offender, I suppose . . ."

"Good, good. Now, can you tell me anything about her or her behavior that stood out in any way?"

"I did not service that purchase. Let me get Gail for you."

I waited.

"Gail here, what can I do for you?"

"You recently waited on a woman calling herself Evelyn Porter, who made a rather large purchase?"

"I did."

"Please tell me what she said and did."

"Well, let's see, she said she was the principal of an elementary school, and the school board wouldn't authorize the purchase of new art supplies, so she had to buy them with her own funds."

"Did she name the school?"

"Uh, let me think . . ."

"Could it have been Ethan Allen Elementary?"

"Yes, that's it!"

"Now can you tell me anything, anything at all, about her manner or behavior, her belongings—anything that might help me identify her?"

"I don't think so."

"Think hard, Gail, this is important."

"Well, I did notice one thing, although I don't think . . ."

"And what was that, Gail?"

"Well, she was pretty nondescript, but there was one thing: she kept looking over her shoulder, out to the front of the store, where a man was parked with a truck. After she bought the goods, the man came in and helped her carry the merchandise out to the truck."

"Can you tell me about the man, or the truck?"

"Hmm, the man was kind of short, with dark, close-cropped hair. He had on a blue work shirt, rolled up at the sleeves."

"Anything else? It could be very important."

"Hmm, let's see. Yes, he had a very bad complexion. Like maybe old acne scars or something?"

"Did you hear the lady call him anything?"

"Uh, no."

"And the truck?"

"It was the kind with the metal, uh . . ."

"Box?"

"Yes. And they loaded all the stuff into the back. But he also had things in there like a gardener might have. You know, like a power mower, a rake, that sort of thing."

"Do you remember the color?"

"Uh, that was kind of nondescript too, I guess. Like maybe it used to be white or off-white, but it was so beat-up . . ."

"Good, that's very helpful. Now, how did the lady pay?"

"Well, she said she didn't have any checks on her, so we opened an account for her."

"Like a charge account?"

"No, just a one-time deal where we mail out a bill and then you send us a check."

"Or not."

"Yeah, I guess so, in this case."

"Do you still have that paperwork?"

"Well sure, I assume Mr. Weinberg, the man you talked to before, would have it filed somewhere in the back. You want me to ask him?"

"No, I'll come by later and take a look myself."

"I'm sorry, but is that all? Because I do have customers . . ."

"Yes, that's all. You've been very helpful, Gail."

It was already three thirty and I was getting hungry. I drove over to Pink's and pulled into the lot. I had to smile at myself: when I first saw Marie there, it felt like an invasion of privacy; but now, with Marie off teaching, the place didn't feel right *without* her. I sat down at an outdoor table and got Helen's attention. She nodded, then turned behind her to call out my order while I tried to keep my mind on the Marson case.

Why would anyone come up with a scheme to steal large amounts of children's art supplies? It didn't make any sense unless they were wired into a connection where they could dump it all cheap and still make a killing. Or had plans for it themselves. Maybe someone who ran a nursery school, or a private school? Someone who used to be a school teacher, but got fired? A disgruntled teacher might feel the world owed her something. After all, the lady had mentioned the school board in a negative light. And what about the gardener angle? A school gardener maybe, and the two of them met up when they worked at the same school, then things went wrong and they came up with this plan together?

Helen brought my chili dog and said, "Speaking of dogs, you are one lucky one yourself, Cole."

"And why's that?"

She laughed. "Come on, you're with a gal like Marie, and you have to ask me that? Brilliant, pretty, nice. I mean, what more could a guy want?"

Maybe the ability to have a girl like that without becoming a basket case?

I nodded my acknowledgment and she walked away. It was second nature to nod and smile to everyone and let them think whatever they wanted about me and my life. What was that stuff Doc Grimes was saying about "we"? Something about using other people to help you deal with your own problems? Did that mean I was supposed to tell people like Helen what I was really thinking? About Marie? That made no sense to me. For one thing, that was private information. As my mother always said, "We don't air our dirty laundry in public!" And for another, why burden someone like Helen with my problems? She's gotta have plenty of her own; why bring any more trouble into her life, or anyone else's?

I finally got my mind back on the case at hand. Would it be a waste of time to check out new nursery schools or private schools? If so, in what area? LA is a big, spread-out city, covering nearly five hundred square miles and extending almost fifty miles, north to south. It's an easy place to hide. I suppose I could keep calling art supply houses, in the hopes that someone, somewhere would remember more identifying material. At least the paperwork on the account that "Evelyn Porter" opened would give me a handwriting sample to go on. I decided to swing by Westwood Village and see what they had.

Besides, the Flax art supply store was practically down the street from UCLA, so I figured I could drop in and see if Marie had run into any problems in giving the fire evidence to her professor. Then maybe we could talk about actually having a real date that evening. I found myself looking forward to the prospect of going out together, like regular people.

The store manager showed me the receipt and the paperwork on the account opening. I noticed the address "Evelyn Porter" gave was on Longmyre Street, in Sherman Oaks. I'd never heard of the street, but that didn't mean much; I hadn't worked the Valley for years, and the post-war building boom was still going great guns out there. The manager was a little reluctant to let me take the paperwork with me, but when I explained that the handwriting might be vital evidence in connecting the Flax scam with all the others, he readily agreed.

Once I finished at the store, I planned to drive to the lot nearest the chem building, but I couldn't be positive Marie was even there. So just to make sure, I walked to a pay phone, dialed the department and asked for her.

"Hello?"

"Marie O'Malley, please."

"One moment, sir, I'll get her."

"Hello? Marie O'Malley here."

"Marie, it's Cole. I'm just down the street from you on a case. Mind if I come by and see you?"

"Uh, it's probably not a good idea right now. Why don't we just meet at my place? Say around seven or so?"

Suddenly a pang of something hit me hard. Jealousy? Insecurity? Paranoia? "Okay, if that's the way you want it."

"Now don't be like that, Cole. It's just that, you know . . ."

". . . it would be better if I stayed away. Yeah, I get the message, loud and clear."

"Listen sweetie, I'm sorry, but I'm right in the middle of something here, so I'll see you at home later, okay?"

"Sure thing."

This whole "we" thing was starting to smell like three-day-old fish. If this is how it felt to care or let someone in, I could easily skip the whole Cole Dunbar reclamation project. I hopped in my car and headed home. I really didn't feel like seeing Marie now; I'd think up a good excuse later. She had her own life to live, and so did I; I'd try harder to remember that in the future.

I got home around seven, grabbed a beer and lay down on the couch to catch the Angels' game on TV. The phone rang. The sadistic instrument was doing its best "guilty conscience" ring: shrill and piercing. Sorry, Mr. Bell, but I'm taking the night off from guilt, so you can ring your little heart out, but the doctor's not in tonight. Besides, Steve Bilko was up; nobody should have to answer the phone during one of his at bats.

It started ringing again. And again. And again. I finally heaved myself up and got it.

"Yeah?"

"I'd say, 'Where are you?' but I guess the answer's pretty obvious." Marie was still in her pre-anger mode.

"And?"

She said, "What's wrong? Why are you there instead of here?"

"Because I live here."

Long silence. "And I live *here*, which is where we agreed to meet tonight."

"I just didn't feel like it."

"You mean because I wasn't able to see you at school?"

"No, I just don't feel like being social tonight."

"Social? You call seeing me a social obligation?"

"I don't know; I guess tonight it feels like it."

She was silent. Finally I said, "Look, do we have to argue about this? Let's just go to our separate corners and . . ."

"Separate corners? This isn't a prizefight!"

Damn, I was in for it now. "I know that, Marie, I was just . . ."

"It hurt your feelings when I didn't want you to come see me at school. I don't understand why you can't just come right out and admit it!"

"Okay then, if that's what it takes, I admit it. Now can I go?"

She slammed the phone down.

Okay, okay, I deserved that. I knew it. I just didn't have any experience talking to people about personal things, even if it involved them. Where I grew up you didn't resolve things; they just passed. Was there a school I could go to where they teach Remedial Human Relations or something? I suppose Doc would say therapy is that school, but right now all I wanted was to see if Bilko could handle Bob Purkey's knuckler.

Like me, he struck out.

I went out to the ice box and got the six-pack, smoking a steady stream of Camels as I let the hum and buzz of the ballgame lull my stirred-up insides. Maybe it was better not to care, or maybe to care only about inconsequential things, like whether Bilko could launch another tape measure home run, which he eventually did. Or whether the Angels would lose to the Stars, which they eventually did. I lay there in a daze and thought back to what Helen said about how lucky I was to have Marie. Does anyone really ever *have* anyone else? And what if what you *can* have of someone brings you pain? I knew I'd overreacted to Marie's not wanting me to come see her at school; I knew it was crazy to think she had another boyfriend, or just didn't care enough to make the time. But what choice did I have? My body just punched out a response and there it was, like it or not. I didn't want to live on a roller coaster like that, even if the operator of the ride was a wonderful girl like Marie.

I finally rolled into bed in a sweaty jumble of emotions and abandoned myself to the cruelties of the night. I didn't need Paul Revere to tell me the nightmares were coming. Maybe I was only so-so as a private eye, and probably a bust as a lover too, but I was definitely the Steve Bilko of nightmares.

Chapter Fifteen

The next day arrived in dream segments. At four a.m. it was Danny again, except that this time, instead of a mortar round, a body was hurtling through the air directly at him, as if shot out of a cannon. Just as the body was about to hit him, I recognized it as the blonde girl Danny loved that night in San Diego. Except she was dead. Danny saw it too, but he held out his arms to her anyway. Just before the impact, I jerked awake.

Then, around seven, it was Marie's turn in hell. I was walking alone in the woods when suddenly I turned around and saw that she was being hanged by the neck from a big oak tree. I rushed over to release her, but couldn't reach high enough. So I ran and got a box to stand on, but it still wasn't quite high enough. I raced for another box, frantically stacking it on top of the first one. Finally I was high enough to reach the noose and set her free, but by this time her tongue was lolling out of her mouth and she was dead. A big group of crows perched in a tree nearby was cawing at me in mockery. I tried to throw rocks at them, but no matter how hard I threw them, they always fell just short, and the crows cawed with laughter at my puny efforts.

I tried to get back to sleep, but when sleep is more dangerous than being awake, it's hard, maybe even foolish, to surrender to it. At long last, around ten I fell into a kind of writhing, comatose state that was closer to a prolonged seizure than sleep.

Around noon I finally thrashed up to wakefulness. I got up and dragged myself into the shower. For most people, sleep is supposed to be about rest and release, but this morning, waking up was the real relief. The hot, enveloping cascade pouring down on my body was like holy water, christening me back into the real world, washing away the tangled webs of the endless night, where nothing was what it appeared to be and the demons called the shots. The soap and hot water were wonderfully real and solid—just what the doctor ordered.

The day's agenda loomed in front of me as I sat at the kitchen table having my morning beer and cigarette. Somehow I had to find a way to reach out to Marie. Is that what the dream meant: freeing her from the slow "twisting in the wind" that being in a relationship with Cole Dunbar amounted to? Was it kinder to let her go instead of keeping her in the noose?

I bit the bullet and finally called Monique, but when I told her there was no substantive progress to report at this time, all I got was an earful of what a no-good, useless fool I was. Jeez, I already knew *that*.

With nothing more I could do now on the Smythe job, I needed to follow up on the art supplies case, either by means, motive, appearance, or something I hadn't thought of yet.

Hell, at the moment, it seemed like everything that mattered in life was "something I hadn't thought of yet."

*   *   *

I got to my office around two and called the service.

"Answer World, Sabrina."

"Bless you for not being Thelma."

She chuckled. "Mr. Dunbar?"

"Guilty as charged."

"Oh yes, I do have one for you. Hang on."

I waited.

"It's from a Miss O'Malley."

I could hear the smile in her voice; it was clear the girls at the service had been gabbing about my checkered love life.

"Go on."

"She says, 'No word yet. It's taking a little longer than expected.'"

"Is that it?"

"Yep."

"Thanks, Sabrina."

Hmm, so Marie left a message with the service instead of calling me at home, and was now billing herself as "Miss O'Malley."

Ouch. On second thought, maybe I was wrong and waking life *is* harder than sleep. But did that mean I was off the hook in terms of calling her today? All my instincts told me to flee, but I figured, better to face the music sooner than later. The worst she could do was hang up. I dialed her home number. *Ring, ring, ring* . . . nothing. Was she home, but figured if it was me, I could just twist in the wind? Well, a guy could circle the drain forever trying to figure out a woman's mind, so I thought I'd better hedge my bet and try her at school too.

"Chemistry Department."

"Marie O'Malley, please."

"Whom shall I say is calling?"

"Cole Dunbar."

"Just a moment, I'll check."

A minute went by, then two.

"Sir? She's out for the day. May I take a message?"

"No, I guess not. Just tell her I called."

Whew, so now I could check that off: I'd done my duty, and it was on record. My guess was that Marie was there all right, but she was going to make me sweat it out for a while. Hell, I couldn't blame her. But I have to admit, while half of me was sweating it out, the other half was relieved. Not that I didn't want to put things to rights with her—if that was even possible at this point—but in the world of caring and relationships I felt like I was so far behind the eight-ball that it was just a matter of time before I alienated Marie or anyone else I happened to career past, like a brakeless car speeding down an icy mountain road.

Now it was time to get on with my professional life, the one part of it I hadn't managed to destroy yet. Not that the Smythe squeal wasn't the main event, but I had already cast my line out on the arson angle, and there was nothing to do at the moment but wait and see.

In the meantime my bank account was beckoning me with shriveled fingers. The first thing I did was to call Frank Spitz, one of my old cop cronies whose beat included Sherman Oaks. I asked for him and a minute later he answered. "Spitz here, what can I do for you?"

"Hey Frankie, it's Cole Dunbar."

"Cole, I hear you went private."

"Yeah, but then I was always kinda private, wasn't I?"

He laughed. "A couple of the guys said they seen ya down at the Cock a while ago. What's doin'?"

"Oh, it's just that I had to meet Johnny Rogers about a small matter, and that used to be his hangout."

"Yeah, I heard old Buck came to a bad end not long ago."

"I heard that too, Frankie. But that's not what's on my mind today."

"Shoot."

"I'm trying to run down an address out in Sherman Oaks, possibly a phony: Longmyre Street?" I spelled it out for him and gave him the street number.

He said, "Not in this lifetime, Cole; you're right, it's strictly phonus balonus."

"I was afraid of that. Well, thanks a bunch, gotta run now."

"Come by and see the old gang sometime, wouldya?"

"Will do, Spitzer. Say hi for me."

It seemed the elusive Evelyn Porter was running true to form.

Suddenly I got a flash: if they hit the Westwood Flax, why not their big flag-ship store downtown?

I grabbed the Yellow Pages and got the number, then dialed.

"Flax Art Supplies."

"Hello? May I speak to the manager, please?"

"Are you sure I can't help you, sir?"

"Quite sure; this is a criminal investigation."

"Oh, sorry. Just a moment, I'll transfer you."

After some beeps I heard, "Manager's office. May I help you?"

"Yes, I'd like to speak to the manager, please."

"What is this in reference to, sir?"

"A large-scale robbery ring that may have affected your store already."

"Oh I see. Just a moment."

Another click. "Mr. Butler speaking; may I help you?"

"Yes, this is Cole Dunbar, of Dunbar Investigations. I'm investigating a series of robberies of art supply houses. I have reason to believe your store might be affected."

I heard a loud sigh, then silence.

"Does the name Evelyn Porter mean anything to you?"

Another sigh. "I'm afraid it does, to the tune of fourteen hundred dollars."

"I thought so."

"But why are you calling us about this?"

"I'm a private investigator who's been hired by the owner of a stationery store in the Valley who was victimized by these people, same as you. Plus, the Westwood Flax is in the same boat too, I'm afraid."

"Oh no. What is it you want of us?"

"Mr. Butler, if I could just speak to the salesperson who handled the transaction, it might help a great deal."

"Well, as a matter of fact, since it was such a large transaction, I was called in personally to handle it."

"Good. Now, can you tell me anything that you remember about the woman— her appearance, her manner, or anyone else who may have been with her?"

After a moment's thought, he said, "Let's see, she was about fifty, medium height, dark hair, worn in a bun, dark eyes. She said she was a school principal and that's pretty much what she looked like: conservative dress, nothing that stands out particularly. She had a . . . what do you call those things women wear? It had an oval gem on it, maybe an opal or something?"

"A stickpin?"

"Yes, a stickpin in the lapel of her blouse, with a roundish gemstone of some kind on it. I'm pretty sure it was an opal. Does that help?"

"You're doing fine. Now was there anything else you can remember?"

"No, not at the moment. But I suppose you could ask Roberto, too."

"Who's Roberto?"

"Our stockboy and delivery boy, who loaded up all the merchandise on the dolly for her and pushed it out to her car, or whatever she was driving."

"May I speak to Roberto then?"

"It's his day off. He'll be back tomorrow at eight thirty."

"Is he reliable?"

"Like a twenty-one-jewel Swiss watch."

"You wouldn't happen to have his home number, would you?"

"Well, it's somewhat irregular . . ."

"I know, but this is urgent. We don't want these people to continue cheating honest merchants one minute more than . . ."

"Hang on."

A minute later he came back and gave me a Sunset number.

"Thank you very much, sir, I appreciate your time. Oh, one more thing; do you have a record of the billing address she gave you?"

"Hang on, just let me just check here . . ."

Sure enough, he gave me that same phony Longmyre number.

"Thank you for your time, Mr. Butler, you've been very helpful."

"Please let me know what you find out, Mr. Dunbar."

"That I will. Goodbye."

Sunset. As I remembered from old cases, the SU exchange was somewhere out in the Valley.

I dialed and waited while it rang.

"Sí?"

"Roberto Lopez?"

Silence. Then, "Sí, what you want, señor?"

"The manager at Flax, Mr. Butler, gave me your number. I believe you helped a Mrs. Porter out to her car with a large amount of merchandise the other day?"

"Sí. But who are *you*, señor?"

"My name is Cole Dunbar. I'm a private investigator who is looking into a series of fraudulent purchases by this woman, and I was wondering if you could tell me anything about her, anything at all."

"Well, she looked like a regular white woman; you know, like normal."

Uh oh, this was going to be harder than I thought.

Suddenly he added. "Oh, and then there was the truck."

"What about the truck?"

"Well, you don't see too many of those around anymore."

"What do you mean?"

"It was a real old Studebaker, a '38 I think, cuz my brother used to have one just like it. You know, like a gardener's truck or something, with the real big thing in front?"

"What do you mean?"

"You know, the metal thing on the front of the hood."

"The grille?"

"Sí, one of those real big grilles."

"Anything else about it?"

"It was all smashed up on the sides. You know, dented in? But the sides were high all around. You know, metal?"

"Like enclosed?"

"Sí."

"Okay. Go on."

"Well, that's all I can remember. I brought the stuff out, and the guy helped me . . ."

"What guy?"

"Oh, the man that was there with the lady; the sailor guy."

"Why do you call him that?"

"Well, it was hot, loading all that stuff, so he took off his shirt and he had one of those . . . you know . . . the picture on his body . . ."

"Tattoo?"

"Sí, a tattoo. You know, like a sailor man. I see when he bend over to load the truck. On his back."

"And what was the picture on his back?"

"That pirate thing, like uh . . . the bones . . ."

"A skull and crossbones?"

"Sí! The head with the bones thing across it. Like a pirate."

"Do you remember if the lady said his name?"

"Hmm, no, I don't hear no name."

"What about his face?"

"Lots of those . . ."

"Acne scars?"

"Yes, those pits."

"Did you happen to notice the license plate number on the rear of the truck?"

"No, I'm too busy loading." He paused. "No wait, I remember part of license, because . . ."

"Because what?"

"Because it was funny, señor; the first three letters were STU, same like Studebaker, you know?"

"Well thanks, Roberto, you've been a big help."

"Por nada."

Okay, so what did I have? A fiftyish, normal-looking white lady with an opal stickpin, a banged-up white '38 Studey pickup with a high, enclosed metal box, and a man with bad acne and a skull and crossbones on his back. Where to next? The tattoo parlors downtown? The docks at San Pedro? My friend at the DMV? Legitimate elementary schools, that might unknowingly buy things on the cheap from a fence who hustled art supplies? I pictured an old lady school administrator slinking along dark streets to meet her connection at midnight in a dark alley, as he opened up his overcoat to display his wares: "Whaddya need tonight, honey? I got erasers, fingerpaints, tempera and construction paper galore, in red, pink, yellow and orange. I got it all, toots, and for peanuts."

I got in my car and shook out a Camel, trying to sort out everything I'd just heard. But it was hard to keep my mind on business, because I knew it was time to quit running from Marie and face the music, no matter how painful the conversation promised to be, and it promised to be like taking a non-stop pounding from a tough opponent in the last round of a title fight.

That's when I remembered I had an appointment with Doc Grimes later that day; whew, that felt like an oasis. Maybe he could help me figure out what to tell Marie, how to explain to her what I didn't know myself. But that was just for starters: I still had to call back Monique, and I had a multiple homicide case to solve. Then it hit me that maybe I was avoiding both Marie and Monique because I was afraid the lab results would be negative, leaving me sitting there in the corner with a dunce cap on my head, after all these weeks of supposedly "professional" work. Jesus, had I just thrown myself whole hog into this art supplies thing in order to ignore my failure on the Smythe job? I sat there in the car, starting to feel panic welling up in me like the old days at the VA hospital, when my sleep and waking overlapped into a huge, nightmare ocean, so that no matter how far I swam in any direction, I got farther from land.

*　　*　　*

"Hello, Cole, good to see you."

"Hi, Katy, likewise."

"Doctor should be out in just a few minutes."

"Guess he's still putting the icing on his previous victim?"

She smiled indulgently. "Well, something like that."

My old friend *The New Yorker* saw me through the wait and kept my mind off the panic gurgling around inside.

"Cole, c'mon in."

Doc Grimes swept his arm toward the office with the old familiar gesture that was somehow comforting.

I took a seat on the leather recliner.

Jim leaned forward, looking at me with friendly concern. "So, how's it been going?"

That did it; the cork popped out of the bottle and my anxiety fizzled out of it as I sat there gasping for air, my eyes rolling like a panicky horse.

Jim's eyes widened. "Cole, what's wrong? I haven't seen you like this since . . ."

I finally found my voice. "I know, since the bad old days."

"But what's brought all this on?"

"I don't know, it just feels like everything's piling up on me at once."

Doc nodded in slow comprehension. "Okay, let's just try and take a step back from all this and catch our breath for a minute. Just lean back in the chair and concentrate on being here with me, right this minute. I'm not expecting anything from you, so there's nothing you need to do right. You're not going to disappoint anyone here. Okay?"

I eased the recliner back, then quickly brought it back up. "Nope, leaning back feels too vulnerable, too easy to . . ."

"Hurt?"

I checked inside. "I'd say it's closer to 'attack.'"

"Okay, I get it, so right now you're too close to the vulnerability to tolerate leaning back. So just stay upright and see if you can get yourself here, in this exact moment, with me, with no demands, no expectations . . ."

"Except to get better."

He turned his head at me. "Are you saying that I expect you to get better, and therefore it's your job to fulfill that expectation?"

I nodded. "Yeah, sure; isn't that how it works?"

He shook his head. "Oh Cole, can't you see how distorted that viewpoint is? You've come to me for help; *I'm* the one who's supposed to meet *your* expectations for help, not vice versa."

I closed my eyes, starting to get a lulu of a headache, and said, "Stop confusing me. You asked me how I felt and I told you; if you don't like the answer I gave you, I'm very sorry."

Jim sighed. "Cole, take another deep breath. I can see that you're feeling snowed under with other people's expectations, or demands, as you experience them." He hesitated for a moment, then went on. "Where would you like to be right now?"

"In a bar, getting drunk."

"Okay," he nodded, "I get it, that's one way to handle it. But think back to a moment in your life where you felt peaceful; which one would you like to escape to right now?"

I didn't want the thought that kept coming. I kept pushing it away, but it kept knocking on the door, and wouldn't go away.

Doc's voice said, "What are you thinking about, right now?"

"Okay, goddam it, I'll tell you, but I think it's the wrong one."

"What do you mean, the wrong one?"

"It's not what you want to hear."

"Cole, it's not about what *I* want; it's about what comes up for *you*."

"Okay then, it's my mother reading to me at night, when I was a kid."

"And what was she reading?"

"That passage from John Fante, the one I told you about before."

"That's funny, I remember you mentioning Fante, but I don't recall you quoting a specific passage before."

"Then you weren't listening."

"Cole, I recall that conversation pretty well, and I know you didn't tell me the exact words." He paused. "But either way, would you be willing to tell me now?"

"Are you going to listen this time?" I was being a jerk, but I was enjoying myself.

He gave me his best patient smile. "Yes: you'll talk, and I'll listen."

I sighed dramatically, maybe to be annoying. "Okay then, if I have to. The passage goes like this:

*Los Angeles, give me some of you! Come to me the way I came to you, my feet
over your streets, you pretty town I loved you so much, you sad flower in the
sand, you pretty town!"*

Suddenly I felt like a raw nerve-ending, waiting to be criticized, analyzed,
poked at. I'd said too much, exposed too much. Tears weren't there yet, but
they were somewhere close.

"That's very beautiful language, Cole, poetic and elegant." He paused. "It must
have touched something in you very deeply, and maybe in your mother, too.
Could that shared experience be why it meant so much to you?"

There it was, the poking, the prodding. I cringed inside. "Okay, so I *told* you,
dammit. Now can't we just move on?"

"Why would you want to move on from something so beautiful?"

"Look," I held my hands out to him, "I did what you wanted; isn't there such
a thing as King's X in therapy?"

"You mean a space where you're safe from expectations?"

I nodded, knowing I was disappointing him yet again, but wanting to get
away from being picked apart like a soft-shell crab.

"Cole, I'm not trying to hurt you. Is it too demanding for me to wonder what
there was in that passage that you responded to?" Jim paused, his kind face
contradicting my insides. "Couldn't it just be that I'm interested in knowing
you, not trying to judge you?"

I nodded, finally beginning to calm down a little. "I suppose so, but it just
feels unusual, uncomfortable. I don't know, attention always feels . . ."

"Like a demand?"

"Yeah, like: 'What do you want of me *now*?'"

Doc nodded. "And if attention feels uncomfortable, love must feel like incoming artillery."

I returned his nod. "Now you're getting the picture; love is the ulti-
mate demand."

"Cole, if you're willing to go back to that passage from Fante for a minute, I'd really appreciate it." His voice was kind, soothing, not the pitiless harpy my insides were telling me he was.

"Okay, what do you want to know?"

"It's not what *I* want to know; it's what I want *both* of us to find out about you, together."

I gave him a sarcastic smirk. "All right then, have it your way."

That one was so blatant it made us both smile.

Jim went on. "So what is there in that passage you quoted that was really meaningful to you? What is the emotional heart of it?"

I had to fight to get inside without feeling I was on the grill at a weenie roast. But I stayed with it until I got there. "It's the part about LA being a sad flower in the sand, I think."

"And why was that so powerful?"

"I guess because Fante was . . . well, maybe revealing something about himself."

He nodded. "And what about you and your mother?"

Now my insides were really fighting back, a civil war in full swing. But once again I shoved it away and tried to dig deep. "Maybe it's that *she* felt like a sad flower in the sand, too. And maybe . . ."

"Go on Cole. Please."

"And maybe because that's something we had in common, that sadness, that feeling of not . . ."

"Not what?"

"I don't know. Not . . . being good enough, I guess, or maybe just not being enough, period."

"Do you think it's possible that you felt that the sadness was your bond with her, that only if you felt that sadness too, that sense of not being enough, would you still be connected to her?"

"Christ, are we back to her being a bad mother again?"

"Cole, that's not what I'm saying. But sometimes a child can feel a bond, a connection, with a parent that's based on a shared emotional experience that becomes like a family coat of arms, so that in order to be part of the family, you have to feel that way about yourself, and about life, too. And if you don't, you not only feel cut off from your parent, but even disloyal." He paused, then continued. "Especially being the only child of a single mother, in which case that mother is your entire family system."

I threw up my hands. "I don't know, Doc, you're getting too fancy for me now, with all these theories." I paused. "Are you saying that if someone is feeling sad or bad about themselves, it might not be their actual emotional reality but sort of a . . ."

He nodded. "A defense? A family obligation? Yes, that's what I'm saying."

"But Jim, that's crazy. If all that stuff is true, then how do you know when your feelings are real, as opposed to a defense, or some kind of cockamamie misplaced loyalty?"

"That's one of the reasons there's therapy, Cole, to sort the wheat from the chaff."

I snapped, "That's good, because for a minute there, I thought the purpose was to take the only good thing I have left from my mother and throw it in the garbage."

I could see Jim's face twitch in response, and even thought I saw his eyes well up again. I shook my head. "Sorry, Jim, that was ugly. I don't know why I said it."

"That's okay, Cole, it's important for you to express yourself freely in here," he winced, "even if it *is* a bit hard on the receiving end sometimes." He thought a moment then added, "Is that how your mother used to talk?"

"What do you mean?"

"You know, barking like that when she was mad?"

I nodded slowly. "As a matter of fact, yes. I always had to be on the alert in case something I said set her off."

That's exactly what I did to Marie that night on the phone when I said, "Now can I go?"

After a while I said, "Why is it that I spend my whole life solving other people's mysteries when I can't even solve my own?"

Jim ran his hands through his hair. "Because you know all about fulfilling other people's needs; what you *don't* know about is letting them help you fulfill *yours*."

"Shouldn't each person handle that stuff on his own?"

He shook his head. "Nope, people need more than achievements, more than objects, more than money, more than a job well done. They need important things from other people: help, caring, understanding, love."

I snapped back. "You mean devastation, pain, disappointment and loss? Because that's what letting other people in always leads to."

Doc thought awhile. "Well Cole, that's kind of a tricky subject, because when you're harboring a lot of hurt, pain and disappointment down deep inside you from childhood, and you let someone in, some of that old pain does get triggered, and you assume it's all because of the new relationship, when in fact a lot of times it's just that old pain surfacing, longing to be heard and understood by someone else."

I closed my eyes, thinking of that phone call I had with Marie in Westwood, the one where she said she wasn't able to see me. "So you mean when you care about someone and hurtful things happen, you might have exaggerated feelings that aren't all from that moment?"

He nodded again. "Exactly. And once you understand that they might be exaggerated because of feelings from your own past, you have more control over the situation, because it not only gives you some insight into your past, it helps you sort out how much of it is actually due to what's happening now.

Plus, you can talk to the other person about the feelings as *feelings*, instead of just yelling at them, or running away."

Wow, he just described exactly what I had done that day. I was starting to see things a little more clearly: by running away, I not only cheated myself out of any possible kindness from Marie, but cheated her out of knowing what was really going on with me, too, and the closeness that talking together might have created.

And now that he'd helped me to stop defending my mother so vehemently, I could finally see how meager, how withholding her parenting really was. Had *I* been a sad flower too, trying to grow in sand?

I guess all of that qualified as "insight," as Doc would put it, but hell, now that the world of emotions and relationships was getting more complicated, dealing with it all felt like being forced to write a long term paper for a class you hate.

*   *   *

That night I stayed up late, trying to piece together everything Doc had said, and wondering if I would ever be part of the normal world again. And if I ever had been. Ideas flooded my mind, like a Pandora's Box suddenly opening up. Why did the loss of Danny hit me so hard? For some reason, I'd never really asked myself that question. Could the powerlessness and guilt I felt about Danny somehow be connected with how I could never ease my mother's sadness and anger? Then again, Doc seemed to be implying that Danny was so important to me because whatever I got from my mother was so inconstant and meager that I could never rely on it long enough to establish myself firmly; then when I joined the Marines and found Danny and the other guys, maybe they became the northern star I didn't even know I was seeking, the new hope for belonging and believing.

But after the chaos of Okinawa, and then seeing Danny vaporized right in front of me like that, it felt like a slap in the face, a wake-up call, and I returned to Plan A: I would never have anybody, and maybe didn't deserve to anyway. And besides, caring just sets you up for loss, so take care of your own business. And as for the rest of society's expectations, just fake it. Were those the lessons I learned in childhood?

When I went over to get a beer and light a cigarette, something came back to me, a snatch of a quote from Proust that my mother used to read me, something about loss. My face turned to look at the books sitting on my shelf, the ones my mother left me when she died, the ones I'd scorned, never touching or even looking at, except Fante's *Ask the Dust*, since she died. Her only legacy to me, I suppose. I went over and ran my hand over the titles until I found the one I was looking for, and turned the pages until I found it:

People do not die for us immediately, but remain bathed in a sort of aura of life which bears no relation to true immortality but through which they continue to occupy our thoughts in the same way as when they were alive. It is as though they were traveling abroad.

Yeah, that made sense. For me, Danny didn't really die; he just went away for a while on a long trip. It was really not that different than if he'd moved somewhere far away; the relationship was still there, the thoughts were still there, the caring.

And maybe the same was true for my mother too. Why, in all this time, had I never even looked at the books she left me—the best part of her, and the best part of us? Was it a way of punishing her for not being enough? For leaving with the job of raising me undone? For leaving, period?

Of course, being an old socialist, she had no use for organized religion of any stripe, but now that I thought about it, I suppose the ritual of the nightly readings was our own version of church. Maybe it wasn't what most people would call spiritual, but for me the experience of lying there in the dark and listening to the scripture of Dickens or Fante came close to being holy.

Maybe people aren't good enough; they fail, they drop the ball. And mother was certainly no exception. But maybe if I took what I could get, accepted the things she *did* have to offer, I could at least inherit the legacy she *was* capable of leaving me.

I went over to the shelf and picked out *Ask the Dust* again, the Fante book she loved the best, the one about LA, and read long into the night, smiling occasionally at the parts she delighted in, parts she would return to over and over, loving Fante's choices and the flow of his language. In fact, looking back, it struck me that maybe reading Fante's words over and over was the closest she ever came to real intimacy with a man.

Or with me.

As I read, the words were like a transfusion from a lifeblood that I'd lost, a recoupling with a past I gave up voluntarily, maybe for spite. It didn't bring her back, or Danny either, but it did bring back some of me.

And when my head finally hit the pillow, I had the strangest feeling of release, like I could finally let go of waiting for miracles that would never happen, and maybe didn't *need* to happen. Instead of waiting for miracles, with my eyes focused on some vague tomorrow, maybe I could appreciate some of the miracles that were happening today, right in front of my eyes.

That night I slept like a rock.

Chapter Sixteen

Emotional growth is all well and good, and so is a good night's sleep, but they only go so far; no matter how good a job Doc Grimes was doing on me, it was time for me to practice my *own* profession—and at a much higher level than I'd managed so far. No matter what I thought of Monique Smythe, she and her father had been waiting a long time for results, not speculation, which is about all I'd given them so far. And now it wasn't just some penny ante black-mailer trying to bleed her of her inheritance, but a known multiple murderer who ruthlessly eliminated all possible competition and was undoubtedly rubbing his hands together with glee, just waiting to grab the pot of gold.

The first thing I did was phone Marie at UCLA, trying like the coward I was to avoid anything personal. Fortunately, she was too busy to call me on it, but she told me that nope, there was still no word on the arson analysis. Damn, all this waiting was starting to feel like sitting in a movie theater during a climactic chase scene, then suddenly having the film break while you sit there in a frenzy of anticipation.

Well, there was nothing to do with my unwanted "free time" but keep going on the Marson case, although right now even the theft of thousands of dollars in school supplies was looking pretty tame. But I dutifully followed through, calling in a favor from Eddie Sachs, a guy at DMV who'd helped me out from time to time in exchange for my smoothing a few things over with his bookies. I gave him what I could: '38 Studey pickup, maybe white, license STU-something. He said he'd do what he could, but don't expect miracles.

Miracles? At this point, I'd settle for a Camel and a chili dog, although Pink's itself wasn't always a haven anymore, not with Marie working there now. I finally made it down to the office and called the answering service, both hoping and not hoping for new business. I needn't have worried; Sabrina told me there was nothing on the griddle for me anyway.

I was just about to leave the office when the phone rang. It was Eddie Sachs.

"Cole? It's Eddie, over at DMV?"

"Wow, that was fast."

"Yeah well, I think I got something for ya: it's registered to an Alice Jeans, at 11126 Emelita, over in North Hollywood."

"Thanks a bunch, Eddie."

"Anytime, slugger."

I grabbed a Valley directory and found the Jeans listing right away. So far, so good. I was pretty sure the car was stolen, but it was just possible I could shake something out of this Jeans dame. I dialed.

"Hello?"

"Alice Jeans?"

"Uh, yes. What is this about?"

"Do you own a 1938 Studebaker pickup, ma'am?"

She was silent a moment. Then, "Yes, I do . . . or rather, I did. Why?"

"Look, I'm a private investigator working a case, and I have reason to believe the vehicle was used in a series of crimes involving fraudulent purchases."

"Goodness, you don't suspect me . . ."

"No ma'am, not at all. I was just backtracking on the registration, and came up with you. Now, could you tell me, when was the last time you saw the car, ma'am?"

"Oh, let's see, several weeks ago. My son Billy was using it all summer, doing some gardening and yardwork for folks in the neighborhood. And then one morning, when he went out to go to a job, it was just gone." She paused. "My father left it to me when he died; it was pretty beat up, but it was perfect for Billy, and he loved being able to make some money of his own." She paused. "Are you sure we're not in some kind of trouble? I promise you, sir, the truck just disappeared . . ."

"No, you're fine. I figured it was stolen, but I have to cover all possibilities. You understand that, don't you, ma'am?"

"You mean like Jack Webb?"

I laughed. "Yeah, something like that. Like I say, I figured the vehicle was stolen, but just wanted to confirm it with you. Sorry to have bothered you."

"Well, I wish you the best of luck. Sorry I couldn't have been more help. And if you do locate it, please call us, won't you? Billy's pretty upset about losing his gardening truck."

"That I will, ma'am. You have a good day."

Too bad, but at least it felt like the kernels were starting to pop on the case, and something is always better than nothing. Now if the Smythe case would only get hot . . .

The phone rang again.

"Yeah? Dunbar speaking."

"Señor Dunbar? I seen it again—you know, that truck?"

"Roberto?"

"Yes."

"You mean the Studebaker?"

"Sí."

"The boss send me to another store, because they run out of some supplies, and there she is, that truck, driving right in front of me. So I follow it."

"Where is the truck now?"

"I follow it for a few miles to this little alley off Alvarado. He park down at the . . . the, how you say . . . street of death?"

"You mean dead end?"

"Sí, dead end. Palm Alley, it says."

"Did you see the driver?"

"No, not when I'm following it. But when I was running to the phone booth I look back and see a man walk out of that alley, real fast."

"Was it the sailor man?"

"No, for sure not him. He was wearing a raincoat and a hat, but I could see he was tall and real skinny."

Hmm, I could just picture the spiky hair under that hat.

"Thanks, Roberto, there's a twenty with your name on it."

"Oh, muchas gracias, señor."

I reached into my lower desk drawer and pulled out my gun and shoulder holster, then strapped it on and headed for the door.

Wow, an embarrassment of riches; clues were suddenly coming in bunches.

I hurried down to the lot and signaled George to get the Ford out of hock. I could see it sitting there in the back row. Weaving through a sea of parked cars, tires squealing, he pulled it up to the front, then got out and waved me in. "Keys are in the ignition, Mr. D."

As I slid in and rolled down the window. George leaned in, whispering dramatically. "Workin' on somethin' big, Mr. D?"

I gave him a wink. "The biggest."

He shook his head in admiration. "Jeez, some guys have all the luck. And other guys spend their whole lives just movin' oversize tin cans around an asphalt chess board all day long."

I started the car, then turned to him with a grin. "Anytime you want to apprentice in the peeper racket, I'm game."

George scratched his chin. "I may just do that, Mr. D. One of these days, I may just do that."

Suddenly dark, puffy clouds rolled in from nowhere, blocking the sunlight. We both looked up and George said, "Hey, Mr. D, lemme help you with that ragtop. Looks like you're gonna need it."

"Thanks, George, you might be right."

He reached back and shoved the top up and then forward, over my head. I fastened the locking pin on my side, then he ran around to dog it down on the right side too. He nodded. "All set."

I returned his gesture and headed out onto Sunset just as fat raindrops started plopping onto the canvas top one by one at first, the sound gradually morphing into a rolling staccato as the storm got going good.

I twisted the wiper knob to High, then yanked the wheel hard left to rocket past two old biddies in an ancient Cadillac, sitting there at a dead stop in the middle of the right lane, both looking up in amazement as if they'd never been briefed on the concept of rain before.

I tried to hurry despite the rain, and in no time I was tearing along the Hollywood Freeway, passing cars right and left. I had to find that truck before it was moved again. By the time I got to the alleyway Roberto described, the rain was really pummeling the ragtop and I could barely see to drive, even with the wipers slapping themselves silly

I parked across Alvarado and tried to peer through the torrent to eyeball the truck. There was a vehicle parked down there at the end all right, but it was too dark and rainy to identify it. I zipped up my light jacket all the way and grabbed the flat cap I always keep in the car, more for disguise than for weather, because neither one was going to do me much good in this downpour. I felt for the comforting bulge of the .38 under my jacket and readied my senses for anything out of the ordinary.

The alley was already ankle-deep in water, so staying dry was out of the question after the first few steps. I sloshed forward, shielding my eyes the best I could against the wind-lashed barrage. Now I could see the vehicle more clearly; yes, it was an old Studebaker pickup truck, with the high metal enclosure all the way around and a license plate starting with STU. Eureka! I pulled my gun out and took the last few steps to the truck, then leaned over the back gate to check out the bed. With a jolt I saw the body of a woman, face-down. Conservatively dressed, dark hair in a bun. A normal-looking, fiftyish white woman.

My God, was I looking at Evelyn Porter?

"Drop it, Dunbar!"

I spun around. Phil Crosetti was standing there in the rain, with MacIntyre and another one of his goons beside him. Three drawn guns were covering me. I dropped the .38 and put my hands in the air. "Listen, Crosetti, I've got nothing to do with this."

"Shut up, Dunbar. This time you really hung yourself, but good. Walk this way, and enjoy it, because they might be your last free steps."

"I'm telling you, Crosetti, I just got here!"

He gave me his best sneer. "Thank God there are still some decent citizens in this town."

"Huh? What's that supposed to mean?"

"It means that someone who still cares about law and order tipped us that you'd return to the scene of your crime to dispose of the body." He chuckled to himself. "All we had to do was stake out the alley and wait for you to put your fat head right in the noose." He gestured to one of the cops. "Go get his gun, but be careful, it'll be Exhibit A."

I shook my head. "Exhibit A my ass; I haven't even fired the thing in years!"

He sneered again. "We'll see about that, peeper." Then he motioned me out of the alley with the gun, toward his black and white, which was now blocking the alley entrance. "Get in there, Dunbar, you're going downtown. And this time there'll be no pretty little bimbo to lie for you; you were caught dead to rights."

I sloshed back down the alley and got into the back seat of the police car. "I don't need an alibi; I wasn't here whenever this thing happened, and I just got here now. Hell, you just *saw* me drive up!"

Crosetti barked, "Shut up!" then leaned into the front seat and palmed the microphone to request the evidence team and a meat wagon. He yelled out to the cop holding my gun. "You two stand right there and hold onto that thing until the evidence guys get here, while I give this scum a police escort downtown."

The cops who stood there getting soaked nodded their miserable assent.

All the way downtown Crosetti taunted me, crowing that he'd finally nabbed me for the lowlife he always knew I was. Whenever I tried to interject a word, he'd yell, "Can it!" For the moment there was nothing I could do but huddle there in my sopping-wet clothes and take it.

As soon as we got to the station, Crosetti threw me into my old pal the interrogation room again, where I waited in handcuffs, wet and shivering, for almost an hour.

When he finally came swaggering back in, he was just about drooling with delight. "This time, we throw away the key, you phony gumshoe."

Now I was getting mad. "Listen, you idiot, what are you going to charge me with: being present at the scene of a crime, *after* it was committed? Is that a felony in this state? Hey, I've got an idea: maybe you can arrest a few of the other people who happened to pass by that truck in the alley too; with a little luck, you could have the gas chamber booked solid for years with innocent passersby. You might even make Captain someday."

He slammed his fist down on the wooden table. "I told you to shut up, and this time you're *gonna* shut up! Because we got the goods on you, you little weasel. We've got the murder weapon, and you know how we got it? We took it off *you*, just about an hour ago."

"What do you mean, you took it off me? All you took off me was my office .38."

"Exactly. And it just so happens that your office .38 has one bullet missing from the chamber, the one we found in the dead lady, the one that just happened to match your gun exactly."

My jaw dropped. "Oh my God, I've been set up!"

Crosetti walked over and patted my shoulder condescendingly. "Sure, sure, honey, that's what they all say. Now tell the officer why you killed the nice lady."

"Phil, I didn't kill anyone! I haven't even fired that gun in years! Okay, now I'm starting to get the picture: someone went to an awful lot of trouble to set me up. They must have broken into my office, stole my gun, shot that woman, then returned the gun to the office." I paused, looking at Crosetti. "Then he called in an anonymous tip, didn't he?"

Crosetti was shaking his head mockingly. "Go ahead, lie your fool head off, but it'll go better for you if you make a clean breast of it now; we're gonna nail ya either way."

I was talking out loud now, more to myself than Crosetti. "Son of a bitch; he deliberately let Roberto tail him, just to set me up for murder. God damn, the whole Evelyn Porter thing has been nothing but a red herring, from beginning to end. The whole thing was only a set-up to frame me for murder and get me out of his hair, so he could operate on the Smythes in peace. He's getting me out of the way, just like he did all the others, tying up his loose ends."

Crosetti was confused now. "Look, you idiot, what are you babbling about? Do you realize you're in for murder? Because if you're trying to cop an insanity plea, I'll . . ."

I yelled, "Shut up, I'm thinking!"

Crosetti went wild. He ripped the door open and yelled, "Book this bum for murder and lock him up! If he thinks he's gonna convince us he's out of his mind, then he's . . . he's out of his goddam mind!"

In the cell I had plenty of time to think. The killer had set me up good; yes, they had the murder weapon, and yes, it was mine. But that didn't mean I was the one who fired it. I needed a lawyer to demand a paraffin test that would show I hadn't fired that gun, or any weapon, recently. They also had no motive; after all, why would a private dick who was actively working a case shoot and kill his own suspect, just when he thought he was close to solving the case? But there was something else: the guy behind all this had made a bad mistake; by framing me, he'd brought himself out in the open. After all, it was obvious now that the tattooed man with the pitted face had been tailing me for some time, that he knew my movements and what I'd been working on. Why go to all that trouble unless there was something bigger at stake than classroom supplies? Much bigger.

Like, say, $300,000.

The next day I called Bert Fawcett from jail and explained the whole thing to him. I could almost see him on the other end of the phone, shaking his head at the stupidity of the cops. He said not to worry, he'd call Milton Latimer, a personal friend of his and one of the best criminal defense attorneys in town, and get him on the case right away. That helped. But there was something else. The creep who'd tried to frame me had accomplished at least one of his apparent aims; my being locked up in jail severely curtailed my ability to investigate anything beyond my steel bars.

Marie showed up the following day for "visiting hours," holding up a newspaper that sported the bold headline:

LOCAL SLEUTH HELD IN MURDER

Great, I could just imagine Monique's reaction to that. Not to mention all my possible future clients. Marie sat down on the bench and said, "Now, we don't have a lot of time, so first let me tell you the news; we got the lab results back, and it *was* arson after all."

I licked my lips. "Well, I guess that could be bad news for the Smythes in the short run, but we've got to find a way to use it to our advantage."

Marie nodded. "That's exactly what I was thinking. Now listen; the materials analyst said the reason the cops and the insurance investigators weren't able to call it arson was because they were probably using the steam distillation method. But the stuff the arsonist used was water soluble, so it would have shown up as a negative on their tests. The good news is that it looks like the arsonist used butyl alcohol, an odorless solvent."

I looked at her. "And the bad?"

She shrugged. "Sorry, Cole, but it would have been easily obtainable in town." She touched my arm. "So it looks like for all my brilliant help, you're still up against a brick wall."

"Wait a minute, I'm not so certain of that. Now that we know it was arson, maybe we could spread a little nectar around; you know, for the hummingbirds?"

Marie gave me a quizzical look, then reached out and touched my arm. "Do you have any idea who might have set you up like this?"

I nodded. "I sure do. It's the same guy who hired the arsonist. The same guy who killed all those people. The same one who's been blackmailing Monique. I can feel it."

"Cole, you're kidding!"

"No, it's no joke; believe me, it all adds up." I told her the whole story of the school supplies investigation and the man with the skull and crossbones on his back. Then I said, "He lured me into this murder rap by setting up a bogus case to hogtie me while he goes in for the kill. I haven't heard from Monique Smythe since I've been in here, but I'd stake my license that as soon as I was locked up, he pounced on her with a demand for the big money."

Marie was stunned. "Very clever guy. And now that it really *is* arson, the best way to counteract his threat to smear Mr. Smythe is for us to prove who *really* did it."

She went on. "What did you mean before, about the nectar?"

I thought a minute. "Just that maybe we can set a little trap of our own."

Marie cocked her head. "What do you mean?"

"By getting word out that we're looking for someone who can pull off a real slick arson job, using methods that'd pass muster by the cops and the insurance men; after all, they still don't have access to that crazy machine the professor used, right?"

"But who could get the word out to those kind of people?"

I smiled. "I just happen to have a friend who's very well connected. Leave it to me. As soon as I have any leads, I'll let you know."

Suddenly Marie got a funny look on her face. Her whole mood changed. "So what's been going on with Queenie lately?"

"What do you mean?"

"You know what I mean. I know you're a sucker for that lady-in-distress routine, and she's got a patent on that act."

"Marie, I already told you, there's nothing going on there but a normal business relationship."

"Relationship? That's a funny word to call business."

"Well, I do feel kind of sorry for her. After all, she's been under a lot of pressure."

"Oh, I get it now: when it's Queenie, a relationship is a gift, but when it's me, it's a demand."

She was on full boil now.

"Please, Marie, I've already got my hands full here . . ."

Her pale face turned a blotchy red. "I'm sorry to make so many demands on you . . ." she was crying now ". . . especially when you already have your hands full with Monique and the terrible pressure the poor thing's under."

And with that, she turned and left.

Whew, Marie O'Malley was one lady who didn't need butyl alcohol to start a fire. Someday maybe I would understand what I'd said or done that set her off, but at the moment I was in jail for murder.

*   *   *

My high-powered lawyer did get the cops to perform the paraffin test on my hand. Of course it turned out negative, indicating that I hadn't fired a gun lately. And when I told the cops the full story of the fraudulent purchase case, and everyone involved, including Roberto, backed up my story right down the line, it got pretty hard for them to keep holding me. Finally, with a lot of help from Mr. Latimer—some of it political pressure bought and paid for by Bert Fawcett in smoke-filled back rooms—I was released.

Of course Phil Crosetti was hopping mad, trying to figure how I'd beaten the paraffin test, and enraged that I'd now embarrassed him twice in a row.

"Dunbar, I'm gonna get you, if it's the last thing I ever do!"

"Lieutenant, if you'd ever put half the energy you spend framing the wrong people into catching the *right* ones, you might actually *make* Captain someday."

My snotty demeanor aside, it was terrifying to see how easily someone could be set up for a murder rap and shoved into that chamber they keep filled with high-test up at Quentin.

The first thing I did was to call my service.

"Answer World, Hattie."

"Hi Hattie, it's Cole Dunbar."

"Oh, Mr. D, I'd ask you where you've been keeping yourself, but it's been in the headlines every day. I feel so terrible for you."

"Thanks, Hattie. What you got?"

"Only about a thousand messages from Monique Smythe, each one madder than the last."

I cringed. "I guess she reads the papers too."

Hattie said, "Anyway, please call her as soon as possible."

"Will do. Anything else?"

There were no other client messages—understandably, I suppose, given my latest job references—but she did give me several personal messages, all from friends like Dick and Brenda, offering to help in any way they could. It made me feel a little less alone.

It was time to buckle up and face Monique, in all her angry hauteur. Well, I had to do it sometime. I dialed the number and waited.

"Smythe residence."

"Monique Smythe, please."

"Just a moment. May I say who's calling?"

"Cole Dunbar."

"Oh. Oh my God. Just a moment, sir."

Ten seconds later, I heard this: "Do you know how many goddam times I've tried to reach you?"

I muttered, "Not exactly, but I know it was a lot. You do know they don't let you have a private phone line in a jail cell, right?"

"Listen mister, a long time ago I hired you to get this blackmailing creep off my back. And now, after you've consistently failed to do so, he calls me and makes the final demand, while you sit in jail on a goddam murder charge!"

"I know, and I'm sorry. How did the demand come?"

"Who the hell cares how it came: they've got father!"

"Oh Christ, so they've gone that far?"

"Hell yes, they've gone that far! Now, what are you going to *do* about it?"

"What does he want?"

"I'm to airmail several packages of cash, totaling three hundred thousand dollars in unmarked bills, to an address in Kuching."

"Where?"

"Kuching."

"Where the hell is that?"

"Sarawak. I had to look it up."

"You mean like Borneo or something?"

"Yes."

"And what about your father?"

"The man says once he gets notification that the packages have arrived, he'll release father, alive and unharmed."

"It sounds to me like if you ever want to see your father alive again, we're going to have to find this guy *before* you send the money."

"Maybe, but if I don't pay it, he won't release him."

"Monique, I don't believe he'll ever release your father alive, whether you pay the money or not. This guy's already killed multiple times; he has nothing to lose by . . . well, you know what I mean."

"What about the money?"

"Stall him for as long as you can. Tell him you're having trouble getting that much money together, that you're going to have to sell a lot of different stocks and bonds that are kind of difficult to unload—you know, things that will take some time. Tell him you demand to speak to your father once a day until you can get the money ready; that might at least keep your father alive a while longer. We're going to need all the time we can get to do what we have to do."

"What do you mean, what you have to do? It's been precious little so far. How do I know you'll get any better results now?"

"Because we have several promising avenues we're working on now. There are things I can't tell you right now; you're going to have to trust me just a little longer, Monique."

"What do you mean, 'we'? Is that little redheaded backstabber part of this?"

"There are several colleagues who are helping me on this. I'll be in touch as soon as I know anything."

"Okay, damn you, but I don't like this one bit."

"Oh, Monique, can I ask you one thing?"

She sighed dramatically. "Go ahead."

"Does a skull and crossbones tattooed on a man's back mean anything to you?"

"Mister Dunbar, I don't know who you're used to socializing with, but I don't hang around much in sailors' bars."

"Is that a no?"

"It's a most definitive no."

"Thank you. I'll be in touch."

"You mean if you're not in jail?"

"Good bye, Monique."

And this was the "relationship" Marie was so jealous of?

I thought back over the whole Marson case. How did the killer know Marilyn Marson would call me? I remembered she'd said that an employee had recommended me. That person must have been a plant. I had to get the name.

"Hello? How may I help you?"

"Is this Marilyn Marson?"

"Is that you, Mr. Dunbar?"

"Yes. I have one question for you: who was the employee who recommended me? Remember, you said he even had my business card?"

"Let me think. It was Emile something . . . oh I remember now. Costa. Emile Costa. And it's a funny thing about that; he left the next day and we haven't seen him since."

"Hmm, probably an alias, but I'll check it out. Any chance you could give me a physical description, or an address?"

"I don't remember much; after all, he was only here a few days. But he was extremely thin, had kind of strange eyes, and his hair . . ."

"Stiff and bristly, by any chance?"

"Yes, you've got it exactly; how did you know that?"

"Oh, I'm a good guesser. And the address?" I had a pretty good guess about that, too.

"Give me just a moment to check his employee card here. Let me see, yes, it's 29222 Longmyre, in Sherman Oaks."

Bingo.

"Thank you very much, Miss Marson."

"I was frightened and upset for you when I saw your picture in the paper, Mr. Dunbar," she said, "May I assume that everything turned out well?"

"Yes. I was framed for murder by the same person who stole your merchandise and planted Emile Costa in your store, Miss Marson. I think the whole thing was just a red herring, to get me busy on something other than the main case I've been working on."

"I guess that means I won't be getting my money back then?"

"Unfortunately I doubt that you will, but I'll keep you informed."

"Oh my. Well, best of luck, for your sake as well as mine."

"Thank you, I appreciate it."

I left a message with Dick Hartwick, asking him to run down the name Emile Costa. I couldn't imagine a guy using his right name on a job like that, but I had to cover every possibility. So Marie was right all along about that creep, huddling in the corner booth with his "friend" Monique to keep tabs on her—and my—activities.

I dialed Monique, dreading having to ask her about her Tam playmate.

"Yes?"

"Monique?"

"What do you want now?"

"Remember the gentleman I asked you about before? The skinny one with the bristly hair?"

"How dare you? I already told you . . ."

"Well, I was right; he's in on the blackmail case."

That shut her up for a moment.

She began. "But . . . "

"What did he say his name was?"

"Thomas Christopherson. But surely there must be some mistake. He's a prominent investment banker in Baltimore."

"Well, Mr. Christopherson, or Mr. Costa, or whatever he's calling himself at the moment, is a cheap hood, hired to spy on you and keep tabs on your state of mind, and the state of my investigation. And I'd bet my life the closest he's ever gotten to Baltimore is Wilshire Boulevard."

"Oh my God, you mean I actually might have undermined my own case?"

"That doesn't matter right now, Monique. But tell me, did you ever go to his place? Is there anything he ever said or did that might help me find him now?"

"I . . . well, come to think of it, he never really did say anything personal about himself or his private life. He was a . . . a very good listener. We mostly talked about the blackmail situation, and Daddy."

"Such as where the rest home is, your father's medical condition, and how much it's costing you?"

"Well, yes." She sounded defeated.

"And how terrified you are about his being accused of arson?"

"Oh God, I'm such a fool."

"Don't blame yourself; you couldn't have known. After all, I'm a professional investigator and they managed to get me thrown in jail for murder. So they're obviously very slick and dangerous. But in the future . . ."

"I know, trust no one. Cole, I . . . I'm so sorry."

"We all make mistakes, Monique. Now just remember, stall him on the money for as long as you can, and demand to talk to your father daily. And stay in touch if anything happens."

"Got it. Goodbye, Cole."

As soon as I hung up with Monique, I left a message with Dick Hartwick, asking him to add the name Thomas Christopherson to the Emile Costa query.

My next call was to Bert Fawcett. After thanking him profusely for getting me a great lawyer, I explained my plan: to put out a false feeler to the underworld about needing a very slick arson job, maybe using advanced, untraceable materials, for which the client was willing to pay beaucoup. Then we'd see what kind of creatures rose to the bait. Maybe even whisper that the buyer might pay a big bonus for a torch with expertise in undetectible solvents.

Bert agreed, happily; it was just his kind of play. I also asked him if he'd ever heard of a guy in the con game named Emile Costa, or Thomas Christopherson, or a tall, skinny guy with weird eyes and spiky hair?

No, he hadn't, but he'd ask around.

With Monique stalling the blackmailer for a few days and Bert Fawcett gleefully trawling for a high-class torch, there wasn't much for me to do but haunt the sailors' bars in San Pedro and Long Beach, an assignment I was eminently qualified for, having spent several months of my teens keeping places like that in business.

Several hours later, I had drunk enough beer to sink a battleship, but although I finally ran out of bars and sobriety, I still came up dry on identifying the suspect. My fellow barmates had seen guys with ships on their chests, anchors on their biceps and hearts in all kinds of places. Even one with an octopus on his stomach.

But where was the man with the skull and crossbones on his back, acne on his face, and blood on his hands?

Chapter Seventeen

In all decency, I couldn't avoid Marie forever, especially since she'd gone out on a limb to help me with the investigation. I still didn't understand what she'd been so mad about at the jail, but whatever it was, I had to go see her now. Although, to be brutally honest, I also had an ulterior motive for going to see her at work: after days of eating jail food on a murder charge, what I really *could* kill for was a chili dog.

As I pulled up and parked, I saw her behind the counter, looking like a field of poppies. I walked up to the counter and got in line, determined to see how far I could push my glib act.

"Hi, beautiful. What do you have for me today?"

She didn't even make eye contact.

So much for glib. "Look Marie, I'm sorry . . ."

"Sorry isn't on the menu, sir. Please make a selection from what's available."

I could see it was useless to try and get beyond the deep freeze at the moment. "Okay then, I'll have a chili dog and a Coke."

"All right, sir." She looked past me. "Next!"

I took a seat at one of the outside tables, fired up a Camel and waited for my own personal Armageddon to begin. Why wasn't I able to be close to Marie without screwing it up? It sounded so simple on paper. In the Marines, someone said, "Battle Plan A: execute!" and you did it, no matter what the consequences. You took the objective, or you died trying. Why wasn't real life like that?

"Here you go, sir: one arsenic dog, with a side of crow."

I looked up at Marie's stony face. "That isn't what I ordered."

"But it's what you're getting." She turned to go. "Now, will there be anything else?"

I knew Marie must have asked Helen to man the counter so she could come out and bring the food to me, so maybe I had my foot in the door. "Please Marie, stay for just a minute."

She turned back to me. "For a minute? Oh yes, that's all you're capable of tolerating, if I remember correctly." She walked back to my table. "Okay then, I guess I can stand it for that long." She gave me a fake smile. "And speaking of your personal life, how's the Queen Bee, if I may butt into your private affairs for a few seconds?"

What was I missing here? "Marie, did somebody tell you something about me and Monique?"

Something passed over her face as she thought about it. "I don't want to get anyone in trouble."

"Like who, for example?"

"Okay, well one of the girls at your service told me Monique was calling you at all hours, and that the two of you were thick as thieves."

Inside, I was steaming about Answer World, but I played it cool. "Of *course* she's been calling me! What would you expect? The killer kidnapped her father a few days ago and is demanding every cent she's got in the world to release him. And I, who's supposed to be helping her, was sitting there in jail! Of *course* she was desperate to talk to me!" I thought for a moment, then I had it. "Wait a minute: the girl who told you all this; was her name Thelma, by any chance?"

Marie licked her lips. "Why? Does it matter?"

"It sure does; she just got fired for being a loudmouthed troublemaker and driving the other girls crazy."

She winced. "Oops, I guess you're not the only one who sometimes has rocks in his head. Oh God, I'm so sorry I said that stuff to you. I feel like such an idiot."

"Marie, that aside, forget your suspicions, will you? Monique's a client and nothing more." I hesitated a second, but decided to go on. "And if it still matters to you, I think I worked some things out in my last session with Doc Grimes, before . . ."

She smiled, despite herself. "Before you became Public Enemy Number One?"

I nodded.

She put her hand on mine. "I've gotta get back to the counter, but maybe we can talk more about these latest developments some other time."

I shrugged. "Latest developments?"

She laughed. "In *you*, silly!"

As I drove back to the office, I racked my brain for more ideas on the Smythe case. I hoped that having Monique demand to talk to the old man every day would buy us some time, but I also knew that Matthew Smythe's already tenuous hold on life was probably ebbing away by the second; the guy could easily die just from the stress of being held captive, whether the blackmailer wanted him to or not.

I called Answer World and got Hattie.

"Mister D? I got one here from a Bert something—he wouldn't give his last name."

"Okay, give me the one from Bert something."

"He just says, 'Call me immediately.'"

"Bless you, dear. Say, Hattie, by the way, are you aware that Thelma upset my girlfriend by implying that there was something . . ."

"I'm sorry, Mr. Dunbar. She called us afterwards, and was even *bragging* about it after she got fired."

"Bragging? In what way?"

"It seems that when she read you were in jail, she called Marie and told her there was another woman in your life named Monique, and that you two were very close and calling each other all the time. The idiot actually thought she was doing a public service. Now do you see why we all quit when she was hired? The woman is sick in the head."

I was dumbfounded. "I don't even know what to say to that, Hattie. But thanks for letting me know."

"No problem, Mister D. So are you out of jail for good now?"

"Thanks for asking, Hattie, but I gotta go."

"I just wanted you to know, we're all praying for you."

"Hattie, you're a doll. Talk to you later."

I dialed Bert Fawcett, desperate for any kind of break in the case.

"Argyle Investments."

"It's Cole Dunbar, please put me through to Mr. Fawcett, right away."

"Oh yes, he said you were top priority. Hang on."

Me, top priority? Now that was a new wrinkle.

"Cole?"

"Yes, Bert."

"I think I might have something for you. Got a pencil handy?"

I yanked out my desk drawer and grabbed a pencil. "I do now: shoot."

"There's this guy, Eugenio Impresa. The number is Angelus 4-2121. Got that?"

"Got it. That Angelus exchange, that's East LA, right?"

"I wouldn't know, I'm not a detective."

"Okay thanks. Anything else you got on this guy?"

"They say he's the torch's torch. Guarantees his work is untraceable, uses all the latest stuff, one step ahead of the experts. A genius, pricey as hell, only touches the big jobs."

"Like a six-story office building on Wilshire?"

"Could be. Oh, and when my guy whispered about undetectible solvents, his eyes almost bugged out of his head."

"Great work, Bert!"

"And one more thing; if he asks, Mr. Jonas sent you."

"Okay. Thank you, Mr. Jonas."

"Ciao."

Finally, something to go on. But I had to be careful with this bird; the first thing I had to do was con him along far enough to get something on him, something I could force his hand with later. I thought a minute, then I had it: I'd tell him I was a cripple and could only make the arrangements on the phone, couldn't meet him in person. I'd get him to talk, and record the whole conversation. Was it legal? Could a recorded phone conversation hold up in court? Who cares, as long as I could put the fear of God into the guy and get him to spill what he knew about the Smythe job, *if* he was involved in the Smythe job, which was admittedly a long shot.

But then, long shots were the only horses running on this track today.

*   *   *

I unscrewed the cap on the phone receiver and put a tap on my own phone, leading to a wire recorder. First I turned on the recorder and said, "This is Cole Dunbar, private investigator, making this recording on behalf of my client, Miss Monique Smythe, on this tenth day of September, 1956." I played it back: perfect. Okay, all was ready. I started the recorder again, took a deep breath and dialed AN 4-2121. It rang once, twice.

"What you want?"

"Is this Mr. Impresa?"

"Maybe. Why does it matter?"

"I may have a job for you, Eugenio. A big job."

"What kinda job?"

"The kind that needs the best guy in town, who gets paid like it."

"Oh yeah? Who sent you?"

"Mr. Jonas."

He was silent a moment. Then, "Okay then, suppose I *am* this Eugenio Impresa; what's this all about?"

"There's an office building downtown that's lived too long. And I'm hoping ten grand might help give it a decent sendoff."

"Okay, I might be interested, depending."

Now it was time to get tough. "But none of this nickel-and-dime soaking a pile of rags in kerosene then lighting it, Eugenio. This has gotta be top quality work, strictly untraceable."

"Hey, don't insult me, pendejo. My work is high-class, professional. I use materials and methods that fool the cops, the insurance dicks, everyone. Workmanship guaranteed."

"Wait a minute, you mean, if they call it arson, you don't get paid?"

"No. You pay me to do the job. Then if it's called arson, you get your money back."

"How do I know you'll pay me back?"

"I never failed yet. Besides, if I fail and don't pay you back, my reputation's shot, right? And in my business, reputation is everything. That's why you called me tonight, ain't it?"

"That's right; they say you're the best."

"I *am* the best!"

"Okay, do we have a deal then? For ten big ones, you torch the building I name?"

"What building?"

"I'll tell you later. It's on Wilshire. Six stories."

"Ha! I already fried one like that a few years ago—piece of cake."

"You don't mean the Smythe job, do you? That one was sheer genius!"

"Genius is right. I see you appreciate the work of a master."

"I'm thrilled to do business with a real pro, Mr. Impresa. Now where can I send my man with your money?"

"What man?"

"Look, I already told you, I can't get around anymore. Arthritis has cut the legs out from under me. So I've got a valet; he's my arms and legs, does all my confidential work. His name is Walter Emmerich. Okay?"

"Hmm, okay, I guess." He gave me an address on Soto Street in East LA. "Have him here tomorrow at twelve."

"Midnight?"

"Yes, midnight. I don't like to take no chances. It's a warehouse. Tell him to come around to the back. And tell him to come alone, or it's no deal."

"He'll be there, Mr. Impresa."

We hung up.

I leaned over and played back the conversation on the recorder. I smiled—it was all there, every lovely, self-incriminating syllable of it. I quickly made two copies and started getting things ready for tomorrow night. This might be the only break I'd ever get in this case; I was going to have to give the performance of my life.

I was meeting a career criminal alone, in back of a warehouse in a tough section of LA in the middle of the night.

What could go wrong?

Chapter Eighteen

For some extra life insurance, I drove to Bert Fawcett's office and explained the whole layout to him, then left a copy of the wire recording with him. I debated leaving one with Dick Hartwick too, but I'd involved him too much already. In case I turned up missing, Bert would at least have something to bargain with. And if I happened to be found floating facedown in MacArthur Park Lake, he could always turn the recording over to the police and help them solve the Smythe arson case, a kidnapping and maybe a few murders too.

Including mine.

Then I called Marie. This was the hardest call. I didn't want to worry her, but at least I wanted to leave things on good terms, if I hadn't already screwed it up too badly for that.

"Hi Marie."

She said, "It's good to hear your voice. I still feel terrible about what happened. But what's that old song: *What can I say after I say I'm sorry?* Besides, you know I could never really stay mad at you, much less hate you, don't you?"

"Marie, it's okay, really. There's something I need to tell you."

"Cole, what is it?"

"I just wanted to tell you that I love you."

"Now you really *are* playing hard to hate!"

I was out of words.

She said, "Are you still there? This isn't another Cole Dunbar hit-and-run operation, where you sound promising, then disappear, is it?"

"Look, just give me twenty-four hours to take care of some important business; then I'm all yours to do with as you will."

"What do you mean, twenty-four hours? Cole, there's something serious-sounding about all this. What are you up to, anyway?"

Damn, I knew she'd see through me and force the issue like this; that's why I was reluctant to call her in the first place. Now what could I say? "Marie, yes, there's something serious going on that I have to take care of. After that, I won't disappear anymore; I promise."

"Cole, are you saying you're up to something dangerous? Because if you are . . ."

"Marie, I'm taking all possible precautions . . ."

"Precautions? Then it *is* dangerous!"

"Look, I was just trying to spare you . . ."

"Spare me? That's all you ever do! I don't *want* to be spared, darn you, I want to be *included*! If this isn't a true partnership, then it's nothing!"

Part of me wanted to hang up on her and run away so bad I could almost feel my hand pulling the receiver down. I already had all I could manage just preparing for the meeting with Impresa. Now Marie wanted to know all about it. Did I have the right to burden her with all this, even if keeping quiet about it might hurt her too?

"Cole, okay, I understand, you don't want to upset me with whatever this thing is. And I admire you for that, in a way. But it's not just your choice anymore; *I'm* entitled to know about your problems too, otherwise, we're just two ships passing in the night. I'm not a child like your mother was. I'm a grown woman who wants to share your troubles with you. If this were reversed, wouldn't you want me to tell you?"

She had me there. "Yeah, I guess so."

"You guess so?"

"Okay then, yes, I would."

"So would you please come over here and tell me what's going on?"

I was still fighting a civil war inside, but I knew what Doc Grimes would say: you've got to start allowing other people in, allowing them to care for you. "Okay, I'll be there in half an hour."

"Thank you."

Dammit, now I felt like I was committed to dumping my problems on an innocent bystander. Of course, according to Doc, feelings don't always represent reality. And even I had to smile when I imagined how Marie would react to the word bystander.

Actually, my talk with Marie that night didn't go too badly. I filled her in on all the latest about Monique and the kidnapper's demands, including the crazy Sarawak mail drop. She even understood what I was trying to accomplish with the meeting with Impresa, and why I needed to give it a try right now, before it was too late for Matthew Smythe. But of course she was worried about the danger to me.

"Why not call Dick Hartwick at least? He could park nearby and provide some backup if things got rough."

I shook my head. "Marie, I've involved him way too much in this thing already. He could lose his job if the police ever found out about his stealing from the evidence locker, and now you want me to involve him further? I just can't do it to him. Besides, if Impresa even suspects anyone else is out there, I'll lose my only chance to solve this thing in time to save Matthew Smythe and nail the killer."

"How about *another* private eye, then? You must have colleagues whom you trust."

"That's an idea, but it would queer the whole deal if Impresa had a man out there watching the street and my guy was spotted. Nope, I can't take that chance. I have to go it alone. And don't forget, I'm not threatening the guy's life, I'm just asking him for some information."

"Yes, with the threat of criminal exposure hanging over him."

"That's up to him. I don't want to use what I have against him; it's only there for leverage. Besides, don't forget the duplicate recording I left with Bert Fawcett; Impresa would be a fool to risk that evidence coming out if he roughed me up. Or killed me."

Marie covered her ears. "Cole, don't even say that!"

"See, that's why I didn't want to tell you all this. What good does it do for you to sit up and worry all night?"

"So that I can be *with* you, even if it's just in spirit; *that's* what good it does! Can't you see that?"

I shrugged. "I guess I'm starting to. I admit it does feel good to have your support." I couldn't resist adding. "As long as you're sure I'm not burdening you."

Marie laughed. "Would you stop with that stuff already? Love is *not* a burden!"

That was still news to me, but I had other things on my mind as I drove to the office late the next afternoon. While I didn't really think Impresa would kill me, I wasn't naive enough to go to the meeting unarmed. Of course I'd wear my shoulder holster with the .38 I'd finally gotten back from Crosetti. Impresa would be a fool not to frisk me when I came in, but the .38 would just be there for show. I had an ankle holster in my desk drawer that I'd once used while investigating a crooked poker ring when I was a cop. I rooted around in the drawer and pulled out the holster and the small Beretta that went with it. As I cleaned and oiled it, I tried to reassure myself: this guy was no armed robbery thug; he was an arsonist—in his mind, an artist—who'd probably never even owned a gun.

Then there was the problem of the wire recorder. How was I going to lug that big thing into the meeting without scaring the guy half to death? Let's see, I could put it in a suitcase and tell him the suitcase was a way to carry stacks of cash inconspicuously. That should at least get me in the door, if luck was with me.

I drove to a local steakhouse for a late dinner, appreciating the dark lighting and soft music. I tried not to think of it as The Last Supper, but I suppose that's the price of an active imagination.

I got home around ten and called the service, hoping to hear from Dick about Emile Costa or Thomas Christopherson. There was a message from him, but it just said he hadn't turned up a thing on either name. Damn.

I grabbed an Eastside and put on the ballgame, just in time to see Steve Bilko drive in three runs with a booming double. He was a lock for the PCL Triple Crown, and his bat had carried the Angels to such a big lead that they'd already clinched the pennant, even though the season wasn't over. Everyone was wondering how the guy could still be in the minors.

The phone rang. I turned down the TV volume and picked up.

"Hello?"

"How's my boy?"

"Excuse me, who is this?"

"Bert Fawcett. Don't you recognize my voice?"

"Uh, I guess it's that you've never called me at home before. But it's good to hear from you. What's up?"

"Oh nothing. I just wanted to wish you luck tonight and tell you to, you know, watch your tuches in the clinches."

Son of a gun, the guy was actually worried about me! What was this, a conspiracy to force me to accept everyone's caring? "Thanks a lot, Bert, I really appreciate it."

He went on. "Please let me know as soon as you get out of there, any time of the night—my service can always take a message. And don't take any chances, son."

I remembered Humphrey Bogart in a movie saying, "I get paid to take chances," but this was no movie. "Okay Bert, you got it. I'll let you know when I'm in the clear."

We hung up. That tug-of-war was still raging inside me. I wasn't used to mattering to people. Service, danger, sacrifice, loyalty, commitment: all these things I knew well. But being on the receiving end of caring was strictly terra incognita. When all a flower has ever known is sand, even good earth is suspect.

*   *   *

It was eleven twenty, time to get rolling. I checked my weapons and ammo for the hundredth time and picked up the battered suitcase that would carry the wire recorder into battle. At least it would be a cinch to drive to East LA this late, with no traffic jams, no horns blaring. To my surprise, it was starting to rain a little, so I tugged the top up.

I started the Ford and clicked on the radio. Of course it was *All Shook Up*, by the latest heartthrob, Elvis: score one for Mr. Presley. I took it slow, knowing I had plenty of time. On the way there I reviewed my whole game plan again, as I'd always done before going into any military operation. I tried to tell myself that, as far as Impresa knew, this was just another job, maybe bigger than most, maybe even something to be excited about. This was how he made his living, and he took pride in his skills. That meant landing my business would be a coup for him, maybe a whole year's work; my "valet" was only there in my stead to make a final decision about whether to drop ten thousand bucks on him or not. In other words, Impresa had to impress *me*. That helped some.

As I hit Soto, the rain turned serious, just like the day Crosetti busted me for murder. But I like the rain; it always provides good cover for an assault.

It was hard to see, but there was only one large warehouse in the neighborhood, so I made a left into its wide driveway and pulled into the back lot to park. If this wasn't it, I was at least close. Peering through the downpour, I could see a dim light under a big aluminum sliding door.

I pulled on my flat cap and white nylon jacket.

I grabbed the suitcase.

This was it.

I walked out into the pounding rain and half-trotted to the back door. I knocked on it hard, three times, and waited.

"Who is it?"

It was Impresa's voice. Jeez, was he really going to do it this way, while I stood out here in the rain?

"It's me, Walt Emmerich, dammit. Christ, let me in already, I'm gettin' soaked out here!" Sometimes the best defense is a good offense.

The heavy door slid open a fraction. He said, "What are you *doing* here?"

Now I was getting mad. "What, you really want me to yell it out loud, in the open air like this? Who the fuck do you *think* I am, the Fuller Brush man?"

"Okay, okay." He slid the door open wide enough for me to squeeze through.

He was a round guy, maybe five five and flabby, with eyes like little black beads and a pencil mustache. He pointed to the suitcase. "What's that for?"

"How would *you* carry ten thousand in cash on a rainy night—in your underwear?"

Again he said "Okay, okay." Then he looked me up and down and said, "You packin'?"

"What do *you* think, carryin' this kind of dough around in a suitcase in a crummy neighborhood like this?"

He crooked his finger at me. "Shell out." I showily unbuckled my shoulder holster and set it down on the workbench in front of me, then said, "What about you?"

He licked his lips hesitantly, then nodded again in that resigned way of his and reached behind his back for the .38 automatic that was jammed into his belt. He placed it on the workbench next to mine.

He said, "Now we talk."

It was time. I said, "No, Eugenio, now we listen."

His eyebrows went up. "What do you mean, listen?" His eyes cut to his automatic. I reached over and removed the magazine, then tossed the gun to the floor.

"What I mean is that we're going to listen to something first; then we're going to have a man to man discussion. But first comes the listening." I opened the suitcase and took the wire recorder out of it. I plugged it into the outlet I spied when I first walked in.

Now he was getting nervous. "What do you think you're doing? You came here to talk business."

"We *are* going to talk business, Mr. Impresa, but first we listen." I started the playback, and soon we heard . . . *This is Cole Dunbar, private investigator, making this recording on behalf of my client, Miss Monique Smythe . . .*

At the name Smythe, Impresa turned purple. He started to fidget and looked around like a cornered badger, his nostrils flaring.

I said, "Keep listening, Eugenio, here comes the good part," as the recording of what amounted to a confession played out.

"Stop it! Stop it! That's enough!" he yelled, holding his hands over his face in defeat. "What the fuck do you want of me? I didn't do nothin'."

"Mr. Impresa, I don't want you, and I don't want to hurt you. If you give me the information I need, you're in the clear."

He staggered backwards, shaking his head. "What is it you want? I didn't do nothin'!"

I stepped forward, towering over him. "As a matter of fact, you *did* do somethin', Mister Impresa. A few years ago, you torched a six-story office building on Wilshire. All I want is the man who hired you for the job. But I don't want him for arson; since that time he's murdered several people associated with that event, some of them innocent, and he might not be done yet. He's also blackmailing Monique Smythe with the threat of killing her old man, whom he has now kidnapped. So you see, arson's the least of it, Mr. Impresa."

His beady eyes were pinwheeling now. He was still looking around frantically.

Suddenly he made a lunge for my shoulder holster. I reached out and cuffed him hard across his ear, then yanked his arm away from the gun and pinned it behind his back.

"I don't want to have to teach you manners, Eugenio, but if I have to, I will."

His whole body slumped in defeat. "Okay, okay, what you want?"

"I already told you; I want the name of the man who hired you for the Smythe job—the dark-haired man with the tattoos and the bad skin."

I could see his face jerk in recognition. "Oh, you mean that little newspaper creep? He ain't the one that hired me."

"What do you mean, the little newspaper creep? Tell me the whole story."

Impresa said, "Look, you win okay? Can't we sit down somewheres? I ain't feelin' so hot."

I saw a couple of folding chairs propped against the wall. I pointed. "Bring those over here and we'll sit."

He did as I asked, then flopped his sweaty body gratefully onto the seat and began.

"Okay first of all, the guy who hired me was this Swopes fella: Lionel Swopes."

I said, "Just Swopes?"

He nodded. "Yeah, just Swopes." He paused. "At first."

"What do you mean, at first?"

"Well, he paid me five thousand for the job. And man, it was a work of art." His eyes were misty with pride now. "You see, it takes a real pro to fool the arson guys, and I was so far ahead of them experts . . ."

I nodded. "Yeah, I know: butyl alcohol."

He was stunned. "How do you know about that? *No one* knows about that!"

I smiled. "They got fancy machines nowadays that know all about that. But go on with your story."

His professional pride still hurt, he blinked a few times before he got his con-centration back. "So this Swopes guy, he comes in with the final payment . . ."

"You mean he didn't pay you everything up front?"

He shook his head. "Nah, he said he needed to wait till the sale went through, then he'd get the rest of the money. I knew that was a lie, because of course they got the money from the sale *before* the fire. But some guys are funny that way, so I let it go, hoping he'd treat me right. So we set up a meet for a couple days after the fire."

The rain was pounding on the tin roof so hard now that it was getting hard to hear each other talk. I said, "Go on Eugenio, but speak up, please."

He nodded, warming to his task. He was clearly a guy who liked doing a good job of whatever he was assigned. "So this Swopes guy, he comes in later for the payoff, and with him is this other guy—you know, the one you was askin' about, the little guy with the bad skin."

"Did you happen to catch his name?"

He held up his hand. "Hey, just a minute. I'm telling this story; I gotta tell it my own way."

I had to smile to myself; in his own way, Impresa was a perfectionist. "Sure, go on, Eugenio, tell it your own way."

He sighed. "Okay, now like I started to say, this Swopes guy, he come in for the final payment, and this little fella's with him. A little scary guy, dark, eyes like a wolf or somethin'. And it was pretty clear the little guy was in charge now. Swopes wouldn't say a fuckin' word without checking with him. Swopes tells me, 'This is Leonard Malinsky, the reporter, Eugenio. A very big man on the newspaper. He writes that daily entertainment column, *Town Beat*.' So I nod, 'Sure, I know that column.' I stuck out my hand to shake his hand but Jesus, the guy just took off talking and didn't stop for the next half hour. I never seen a guy could talk like that. Like a machine gun, he talked. You know what I mean?"

"Talking?" I said. "Talking about what?"

"Oh, all about how he got screwed over by the newspaper. How he was hot on the arson story, the Smythe story. It was gonna be his story, make him a big man with the newspaper, make him famous. No more *Town Beat*, see? Now he was gonna be a star reporter. Then suddenly the publisher tells him to knock it off, kill the story, because it made the cops look bad or somethin'. He already knew that Smythe didn't do it, and from his contacts around town, he had a pretty good idea who did, but the paper wouldn't let him go any further with it, wouldn't print it. Christ, I never seen a guy so goddam mad when he told me that stuff. So he figures, screw 'em all, I'll track down the guy that did it and cut myself in on the deal. Why settle for a couple of lousy headlines when I could deal myself in on a three hundred thousand dollar pot? So he dug around a little more, found Swopes and cut himself in for half the split.

"Then he starts laughin' at Swopes, right in front of me, laughing at him for shootin' his mouth off around town about his blackmail plans, because that's how Malinsky tracked him down. Called him an idiot and a bungler, saying the guy gambled and whored himself into big trouble with the LA mob, owed hundreds of thousands to loan sharks, and that's why he had to cash out of the Wilshire building for peanuts, to get some quick traveling money so he could duck the mob, blow town and lam to Mexico, dragging his innocent partner along with him. You see, all his mob loans were backed up by their joint business assets, including the Wilshire building. So he sold the building out from under the mob before they could force him to sign it over to them, then had me do a real high-end torch job to make sure it wasn't called arson, so the Smythes would be sure and get the insurance money later. So it had to be foolproof; that's why he hired me. It was like Swopes was just letting this Smythe fella hold the money for a few years, until he could come back later when the heat died down and force Smythe to cough it all up."

Impresa seemed to come out of a dream at that point. He turned back to me and shrugged. "And that's it, they paid me, took off and I never seen 'em no more." He cocked his head at me. "Is that what you're all hot and bothered about?"

I nodded, thinking out loud. "So the asset represented by that building was like a hot potato: you throw it to someone else when it's too hot to handle, then come back later when it's cooled off, and force the other guy to give it back to you. Very clever." For a long time the rain was the only one doing any talking, while I stood there trying to cram all the details into my head, figuring the angles.

Impresa just sat there looking nervous for a while, wiping his sweaty face and neck with a white handkerchief. Finally, he said, "So I gave you what you asked for, didn't I? You gonna let me go now? You ain't after me no more, right? I got a wife and kids waitin' for me at home, mister."

I wasn't quite done yet. "This Malinsky guy sure talked a lot; he must have felt safe saying all that stuff, for some reason."

Eugenio shrugged. "Sure he felt safe; he didn't *hire* the torch job, he didn't *do* the torch job. He just came in later to pick up all the marbles. He knows Swopes and me ain't never gonna say nothin', because we're in it a lot deeper than him."

I said, more to myself than him. "But now he's in it up to his neck; the guy has murdered at least four times to get the whole pot for himself."

Impresa held up his hands and shut his eyes. "Hey mister, please don't tell me no more; I don't wanna know from nothin'. I was outta this thing years ago. Hey, I'm an *artist*, not some dime-a-dance head whacker. Just gimme my gun back and I'll drive home in the rain and forget tonight ever happened." He held out his hands, pleading. "How 'bout it, fella? Be a square John, why don't ya? I ain't no bad guy, I just make an honest livin'." A urine stain was spreading slowly over his khakis. "If they ever find out I told you all this, I'm a dead man. I saw Malinsky's eyes, mister. I may be a criminal, but I'm a nice guy. This Malinsky, he ain't a nice man; there's something bad wrong with him. Now, please let me go!"

I walked over and strapped on my gun, then kicked Impresa's .38 over to him across the concrete floor and tossed the magazine onto the workbench. "You can forget tonight, buster, but I can't, until my job's done. I don't want to hurt you, so go on, get out of here and drive home to your wife and kids. I only wish I could do the same."

Where did that last sentence come from? It was all news to me.

But more important, I finally had a name to work with: Leonard Malinsky.

*   *   *

Mr. Malinsky had been a busy little man these past few years. And now I knew why Arnold Hagemayer told Kitty that Malinsky said, "the Follies used to be on my beat." He wasn't a cop at all: the Follies had been on his beat as the entertainment columnist for the paper. But now he was on *my* beat; I was going to put on a full-court press for this creep, and with any luck, he'd be the one doing all the suffering for once. I just hoped it would be in time to save Matthew Smythe.

I drove home and called Marie. She'd been waiting up and sounded exhausted. I told her I was fine, that we'd talk soon, then let her finally get some sleep. Then I left a message with Bert's service, saying I was okay. I would call him tomorrow about hunting down Leonard Malinsky.

For the first time in weeks, I felt like I'd actually accomplished something.

Chapter Nineteen

The first order of business early the next morning was to call Monique. Finally, I had something solid to show for all my work. I made the effort to get up early and after a shower and shave, I settled down on the couch and pulled the phone over to me. I dialed her number.

"Hello?"

"Monique? It's Cole Dunbar."

"Well, it's about time! For all we know, father might be dead by now!"

"I'm well aware of that; I'm sweating it out almost as much as you are. That's why I'm calling to tell you what I found out last night."

"What, how many hot dogs you can eat in one sitting?"

"Look Monique, I'm serious. I found out who's been behind this whole thing—the blackmail, the murders, all of it."

She was silent. "Oh, I'm sorry I was mean to you then. Who is this horrible man?"

"He's a former newspaper columnist named Leonard Malinsky."

"Malinsky? You mean that little guy who used to write *Town Beat*? He used to cover all the society functions."

"Yes, that's the guy. It's a long story, but I just wanted to let you know before I go to war against him. In order to save your father, I've gotta throw a net over the whole town until this creep is found. Oh, and it's time to let the police in on this whole thing now; we'll need a lot more manpower if we're going to catch up with this guy before it's too late."

Monique said, "I understand. I suppose there's no way to avoid the publicity of such an undertaking?"

"Monique, publicity is not your biggest problem now. Oh, and I wanted to tell you, your father definitely had *no* part in burning down that building. And it *was* arson by the way, very sophisticated arson."

"Thank you, Cole, that's a huge relief; I knew all along that Daddy could never do a thing like that."

I said, "Have you spoken to the blackmailer again?"

"Yes, and I handled it exactly as you suggested: I told him I'm having a great deal of trouble liquidating my assets and getting the cash package together, so it's going to take a little time, but that I'm doing it as quickly as I can. It was easy to sound terrified, because I am. And he agreed to let me speak to father once a day until he gets the signal that the packages have arrived."

"And have you spoken directly to your father?"

"Yes, once a day, but he's only allowed to say a few words. Then someone hangs up."

"All right, keep stalling and I'll try and get the whole town in on this manhunt."

Monique said, "Please keep me informed about what's happening. And Cole, hurry!"

"Will do. Now make sure when you're talking to Malinsky that you don't let on that we're aware of his identity."

"Okay, sure."

"And don't tell any friends!"

"I've learned my lesson."

"Goodbye."

I had told her the truth about calling in the cops. I even had the germ of an idea about how to keep the Department happy in the long run. What I *didn't* tell her was that I had access to another agency at least as powerful as the police: Bert Fawcett and the LA underworld.

*　　　*　　　*

I knew I wasn't Phil Crosetti's favorite person, but I had no idea how enraged he'd be when I poked my head into the Homicide squadroom that morning.

"Run this bum out of here, I don't want to see his ugly mug one more second!"

"Phil, try to calm yourself. If you'll just hear me out . . ."

"Hear you out? I'd sooner stick my hand in a nest of rattlesnakes!"

"Okay then, if you really insist, I suppose I could try and take it up with the Chief directly. Honestly, I'd much rather you get the credit for solving a case involving kidnapping, blackmail, arson and multiple homicides." I picked up my coat. "But if you feel that strongly about it, I'll accede to your wishes." I started to walk out of the room.

I hadn't gone two steps when he grabbed my elbow. "Now wait a goddam minute willya; what kind of tricks are you up to now?"

I shrugged. "Nothing. It just happens that I need police help, a lot of it, on a case I haven't been able to crack on my own." I looked him in the eye. "Phil, I'm serious, this is life and death, and every minute counts. It involves Buck Rogers' murder and a lot more besides. Now, are you at least willing to hear me out? I swear to you this is on the up and up. We don't have much time."

He sighed. "Okay, but if this turns out to be . . ."

"It won't, and if we can pull it off, the Department's going to come out smelling like a rose. It might even mean a promotion for you from a grateful Chief."

"God damn you, get in my office and tell me about this, but make it quick."

Fifteen minutes later I had laid out the whole trail of breadcrumbs for him, including Lionel Swopes' underworld debts and his desperate need to skip town, the quick sale of the building to Smythe, the arson job, Mexico, Melinsky's undoubted murders of Swopes, Hagemayer and Rogers, the blackmail scheme, the sacrifice of the so-called Evelyn Porter to create a red herring, the kidnapping of Matthew Smythe and the final blow-off demand for three hundred grand. I told him all about Kitty Stacker, the Follies, Buck Rogers and Ernie Finnegan, the attempt by the Department to squash the story about their failure in the Smythe arson investigation, and how a desperate and angry Leonard Malinsky had muscled in on the whole operation, killing as he went, like a tattooed bowling ball knocking down every pin in his path.

And then I told him that I'd hired a guy to "borrow" the Smythe arson package from the police evidence locker.

Of course Crosetti blew his cork at that point. "By God, Dunbar, you should have told the Department about this from the very beginning! This is police business if I've ever heard of it. Fer chrissakes, stealing files from a goddam police evidence locker? What the hell did you think you were doing, going around concealing evidence right and left, like a squirrel hiding nuts?"

I put a hand on his shoulder. "Steady now, Cro. Picture this: we catch this monster, free Mr. Smythe and solve a major arson and blackmail case, as well as the brutal murders of at least four people, including a cop. Then we announce, jointly, that the Department was working with me the whole time, reaching out to the scientific community to use pioneering technology that no other police force in the country has even *heard* of."

I looked at him. "Got that picture?"

He was still sputtering, but I knew I had him now. He stormed over to the coatrack and threw on his sport coat, carefully buttoning the middle button. "C'mon, damn you, we gotta see the Chief."

I reached for his collar. "Here, let me fix your tie first, Captain."

* * *

The Chief raised the riot act at first. Hell, I would have too. But being the consummate political animal that he was, it didn't take him long to see the wisdom of a strategy that would finally clear the Department of incompetence in the Smythe arson case and give LA's finest lots of public credit for helping nab a blackmailer, kidnapper and murderer of at least four, including a cop. Especially since I had already done most of the spadework. All the Chief had to do was agree to immediately release every available man on a city-wide manhunt for Leonard Malinsky, and then later, if we were successful, go along with the fiction that the Department had cooperated fully with the investigation all the way, and had the wisdom and foresight to utilize the finest technology in the world to bring this fiend to justice. Oh sure, he foamed at the mouth when I told him I'd hired someone to steal the Smythe arson file from his precious evidence locker, but when I explained that overlooking a few unorthodox things here and there was justified by the solemn debt we owed the memory of Detective Rogers and all the fine work he had done on this case, he agreed, reluctantly, that the ends justified the means and that there was enough glory to go around.

The meeting ended with the Chief banging his fist on his desk, visions of political capital dancing in his head. "By God, Crosetti, I'm depending on you! You get a whole army of men out there. We're gonna find this guy, and we're gonna find him soon! Now beat it, you two, I've got a manicure at one."

I spent another hour giving Crosetti and his men everything I could possibly think of about the case and about Leonard Malinsky. I agreed to keep them abreast of everything I did.

Well, maybe not everything.

*   *   *

This time I didn't even bother to call for an appointment; Bert would have to *make* the time.

I drove to the Valley like a maniac, parked on Ventura, rode the elevator up and burst into the Argyle office, out of breath.

"Katy, I have to see Bert immed . . ."

She swept her arm to the rear. "Go right in Cole, he's been waiting for you."

"What? How could he possibly . . ?"

Bert stood up as I rushed in. "Cole, so glad to see you. I know our boys in blue are blanketing the city, looking for Mr. Malinsky even as we speak. But . . ." he rolled the cigar around in his fingers, "perhaps you've come to talk about something else?"

I was stunned. "Uh, well no. I mean, how could you already . . ."

He smiled and took a luxurious puff. "Son, if I didn't have my own people in the bowels of the Department, I'd be out of business in a heartbeat." He motioned me to the plush recliner. "Please, have a seat and tell me what I can do for you."

I was still standing there in shock. "Wait, you mean you already know the whole story of the school supplies con, Evelyn Porter's death, the tattoo, the fact that he used to write *Town Beat* . . ?"

He nodded. "Sure, I get my stories hot off the press."

I finally sat down and adjusted the chair to an upright position. "Well, here's the thing: I figure that your people could probably find this bird a lot faster than a whole army of clumsy beat cops. Are you willing to . . ."

He nodded. "I already have, kiddo. I put the word out to the guys on the street as soon as I heard, about an hour ago."

I just sat there, open-mouthed.

He rolled his cigar around for a moment, then added, "And by the way, I threw in a little enticement of my own, just to keep it interesting for some of the fellas who get bored easy."

I angled my head. "What do you mean, 'enticement'?"

Bert leaned back in his chair. "Oh, just a small emolument of five thousand dollars to the boy who comes up with a legit lead on Mr. Malinsky, with an addditional five if Matthew Smythe is found alive."

I had to hold back the tears that came to my eyes; this business of being cared about was starting to wear on me. I finally managed to say, "Thanks, Bert, you didn't have to do that."

He nodded. "Exactly. That's why I did it; that's one way to tell love from duty."

Christ, what's a guy supposed to say to that? What do you do when the biggest mobster in town starts talking about love? This was a job for Doc Grimes. Doc was right; love and caring still felt like incoming rounds. But any kind of emotional reckoning would have to wait; I had too much to do now.

I stood up awkwardly and stuck out my hand, feeling like an elementary school kid talking to the principal. "Dammit, Bert, I don't know what to say; you've got me all mixed up now. But I appreciate the hell out of everything you've done. And please call me the moment you hear anything."

He gave me a mischievous beam like he was enjoying my awkwardness, then put his arm around my shoulders. "Sure thing, son."

They say an army travels on its stomach, and for tonight's operation, that applied to this Marine, too. I needed the kind of food that sticks to your ribs, so I swung over to Pink's and grabbed a couple of dogs, a large order of fries and a large Coke, to go. I knew Marie was off that day, teaching a chem class at UCLA. Helen was sweet and tried to be friendly, but I was much too preoccupied to do justice to the conversation.

Then I drove to the office, picking up a couple of six-packs of Eastside and a carton of Camels on my way—necessary supplies for a long siege. I always kept a cot in the office, with a few blankets and some bedding, in case I needed to bunk in overnight. The office was going to be my command post for the duration of the search for Malinsky, a place where anyone could reach me immediately. The next few days were going to mean the success or the failure of everything I'd done all summer long.

I polished off one of the chili dogs and the fries, washed it all down with the Coke, and kept the other dog in reserve in case I was up late on the job, or on nightmare duty. I propped my feet up on the desk, lit a Camel and cracked a beer as I sat and swiveled in the chair, staring out the blinds at the night lights of the boulevard. A light wind was stirring, which normally might have relaxed me, but my mind was spinning like a top: What else could I do? What had I missed? Why had it taken this long? Losing Malinsky at this late date would be like fighting a giant marlin for hours, then having him throw the hook just as you set the gaff.

The phone jingled to life.

"Hello?"

"Hi, it's me. How you holdin' up?" It was Marie. Her voice was a balm.

"I'm bunking in at the office for the duration, sweating it out. I've got the cops and the underworld blanketing the whole town. But other than that, I'm fresh out of brilliant ideas."

"Honey, don't forget, you actually identified the guy. You're close; give yourself some credit for how much you *have* done."

"Marie, the detective business is like a ball game: you either win or lose; the fact that you only lost by one run doesn't matter."

She said, "Speaking of which, the Angels lost tonight, but the season's over; they took the pennant by sixteen games and Bilko hit fifty-five homers. The whole town's celebrating."

"I wish that could matter more to me right now but . . ."

"Well, I love you. Does *that* matter?"

"I'm, uh, trying to let it. Does *that* matter?"

She laughed. "Do you need me to come down there and share the vigil with you?"

I took a deep breath and tried to act normal. "Not right now I think, but I appreciate the gesture."

She laughed again, this time with a tincture of hurt mixed in. "Spoken like a diplomat. But I guess this whole love thing is still hard for you, so I'll give you a pass."

"Thanks. Sorry, but I should probably keep this line clear tonight, in case of any urgent calls."

"Now *that* sounds like you!" She paused. "Okay, I'll let you go. But you know, it's funny, there's only one word in this whole investigation that keeps sticking out like a sore thumb."

"What do you mean?"

"Kuching. Why Kuching? As a scientist, you learn that if something doesn't fit, you work backwards step by step until you find out why it *does* fit." She paused before adding. "Just a thought."

We said our goodbyes and hung up.

She was right. Instead of throwing Kuching out because it was so crazy, maybe I needed to figure out why it *wasn't* so crazy.

I heard the patter of raindrops start hitting the pavement below my office. I turned out the office lights, went over to the window and pulled up the blinds. Sure enough, it was raining—raining hard, something dry old LA can always use. I breathed in the sweet smell of the wet sidewalks below me and thought again of Fante's love letter to Los Angeles, the "sad flower in the sand." Was it possible for me to let Marie's love in, to let her rain trickle down and nourish me, or was I always doomed to see the caring of others as an obligation, a demand, glancing off my back in sheets like run-off racing down a storm drain?

The phone jangled again.

"Dunbar Investigations."

"We got nothin' on your guy so far. But dammit, this city is one *big* sonuvabitch."

It was Crosetti. "Okay Cro, thanks for letting me know. I got a big fat zero so far on my end, too. I been sitting here racking my brain for hours to come up with new leads but . . . say, have your guys questioned the girls at the Follies?"

"Hours ago. Grilled every girl, all the employees, the works. Sure, all the old-timers remember Malinsky from his *Town Beat* days, but nothin' since. And no one there knew him personally—where he lived, his friends, nothing. Same with the newspaper people: everybody knew him, but no one really *knew* him."

I said, "Makes sense. Creeps like that live a shell of a life, looking normal on the outside. But no one really gets in." *Did that describe me, too?*

"Okay," Crosetti's weary voice droned, "keep in touch."

*　　*　　*

Ten o'clock. Eleven. Twelve. I rode out the hours, my only company the steady drumbeat of the rain on darkened streets. The ashtray gradually filled up with a caravan of Camels, and I'd gone though one of the six-packs already. I knew I needed to knock off soon or I was going to pass out. I had that same feeling I'd experienced in Doc's office that day, like I was stripping the gears in my brain, trying to reach beyond my capacity. Real life was starting to resemble all those nightmares, where it was desperately important for me to do something, but I couldn't do it. Maybe I just wasn't good enough to crack this case. I tried to tell myself, *Hell, you've got the whole damn town out there looking for the guy; what more can you do?* But it still wasn't enough. There was something I must be missing.

Kuching. Sarawak. Kuching. Sarawak. It kept dive-bombing my mind like a mosquito that won't leave you alone. Sarawak. It was crazy, the one thing that didn't belong in this case. Maybe Marie was right: why Sarawak, unless . . .

Wait a minute; I remembered Peter Woolton, an Australian I'd met in the islands during the war. He was a coast watcher, one of those crazy-brave guys who hid out in the hills alone and played hide and seek with the Japanese on isolated islands, relaying crucial information about enemy troop movements to the Allies by radio. After the war Peter married an American girl and moved to LA. They'd relocated to Victorville a couple of years ago. We used to get together sometimes, but I hadn't seen him in years. He always said he'd been a "trader" before the war, all over Asia, and I never understood exactly what he meant by that. But if anyone could help me make the jagged pieces of this thing fit, it might be him.

It was way past a "decent hour" to call anyone, but this wasn't a decent emergency. I got his number from Information and dialed it.

It rang at least ten times.

"Hello?"

"Peter?"

"The same".

"It's Cole Dunbar."

"What's on your plate at this ungodly hour, cobber?"

"It's kind of a crisis situation, about a case I'm working on. Someone's life depends on it tonight, and you're the only person I know who might help me."

"I'm no detective, boyo. What could *I* do?"

"Sorry, I know it's a longshot, but do you know anything about Sarawak?"

He laughed out loud. "Sarawak, you say? You are talking about the North Borneo Sarawak, right?"

"Yes, that Sarawak. Specifically, Kuching."

"Righto, that's the capital city. I still know a few blokes there."

I sent up a silent prayer. "This may sound crazy, but does a skull and crossbones tattooed across someone's back mean anything to you?"

He was silent a minute. "You mean the CSR?"

"The what?"

"The CSR: the China Sea Raiders, they called themselves, and a more murderous lot of cutthroats there never was. They were a bloodthirsty gang of pirates, had a few local boys with 'em, but made up mostly of deserters from the U.S. military, that preyed on shipping—both Allied and Jap—in the South

China Sea and the Malacca Straits during the war, then disposed of the loot on the Kuching black market. That tattoo you mentioned was their insignia, a rite of passage, if you will." He paused. "But why are you asking about those bastards now?"

"Because the murderer who's behind this whole thing has that tattoo on his back, and he's demanding that a three hundred thousand dollar blackmail payoff be sent to an address in Kuching."

"Hmm, he must still have an old confederate there who's willing to receive the money, then forward it to him once he can flee the U.S. and hide out somewhere in Asia."

I said, "Yes, and 'somewhere in Asia' is an awful big place to hide."

"There are hundreds of islands he could use as hideouts. Crikey, I did it all through the whole bloody war and the Japs never *did* find me, even though I was a top priority for their whole command structure."

I had an idea. "Hmm, do you suppose your friends in Kuching could find Malinsky's guy and force him to tell anything he knows about where Malinsky is hiding in LA?"

"Malinsky? Is that the guy's name?"

"Yes, Leonard Malinsky. What do you think?"

He laughed out loud. "Are you kidding? Hell, for fifty quid those crazy fools would start a bloody revolution!"

I added. "And of course, once they talk to this guy they'll have to hold him somewhere till this whole thing is over. Malinsky can't know we're on his trail."

"Got it. Like I said, that would just make it more fun for these characters; I tell you, the things they did in the war just beggar description. It'd be small potatoes for this lot."

I gave him the address in Kuching that Malinsky had given Monique.

"Don't worry," Peter said, "I'll get right on it." He chuckled to himself, then added. "Dunbar me boy, I haven't felt this stimulated since the good old days!"

"Thanks Peter, you're a lifesaver."

Sure, it was a crazy-ass longshot, but I had to feel that I'd done every single thing I could think of.

I turned on the radio; anything for a moment's diversion. A girl was singing,

They call me a dreamer, well maybe I am,

But I know that I'm burning to see

Those far away places, with the strange-sounding names,

Calling, calling me.

I thought, no thanks honey; I've already seen those faraway places with the strange-sounding names, and you can keep 'em. And they're not calling me; they're screaming in my ear, night after night.

I called the service one last time, just to be sure: nothing.

I regarded the long husk of ash that dangled precariously on the tip of my Camel, already a good inch or so, and growing longer with every drag I took. How long until it fell off? How long until Matthew Smythe's life was snuffed out?

I knocked off the ash, hard, then ground out the butt and dropped it on the mound that already overflowed the glass ashtray.

It was time for me to knock off too, or I'd be as useless as cigarette ash tomorrow.

When I finally abandoned myself to the whims of the night, the clock read four twenty-five.

Chapter Twenty

The phone was ringing.

I was lying on the floor next to the cot, the blanket twisted all around me, my clothes a sodden mess. Ah yes, now I remembered: it was that recurrent nightmare about the guy who is bound hand and foot, then thrown off a pier.

I untangled myself and struggled up. "Yeah?"

"It's Crosetti. You need to come down here immediately."

Ugh. "Where are you?"

"Queen of Angels. Quick."

"Okay, I'm on my way."

I splashed some water on my face, yanked on pants and a shirt, stuffed a pack of Camels into my chest pocket and tore down the stairs to the parking lot.

"Pretty day, ain't it?" George was in a good mood. "Always is after a nice rain."

"Sorry George, no time to talk. Bring it around pronto, willya?"

I lit my cigarette and inhaled, officially starting the day. Why would Crosetti be at a hospital?

The Ford screeched to a stop. "Here ya go, Mr. D." George looked worried now. "Hope everything turns out all right."

"Thanks, George."

I raced down Sunset, heading for Echo Park. I'd often lost track of the days of the week during the past weeks—or was it years—of working the Smythe case, but today's traffic was too light to be anything but a Sunday, so I made good time, weaving in and out of the few cars I encountered. My brain careened frantically from guess to guess. Who is it? Malinsky? Matthew Smythe? Oh my God: Marie?

I pulled into the hospital lot, jumped out and crossed the lot at a dead run.

"I'm here to meet Officer Crosetti, please. It's a police investigation."

"Yes, sir, that'd be room 408." The receptionist pointed. "Elevator's just to your right."

I told the operator my floor and sweated out the ride, getting another Camel going for moral support.

"Four." The operator stood and opened the door for me.

I saw the sign for 400-420 and trotted down the black linoleum to the right.

Here it was. A surly cop stood outside.

"Cole Dunbar, for Lieutanent Crosetti."

He looked me up and down, and not with delight. "Oh yeah, I seen your picture in the papers: you're the private dick." He jerked his thumb back. "Go on in then."

A group of men was huddled around a bed. Crosetti saw me and crooked his finger. "It's Eugenio Impresa, or what's left of him. He's been in and out of delirium. He told us that Malinsky made him talk about spilling to you. But after that, nothing. He says stuff here and there, but nothin' that makes any sense. I was hoping you could coax something useful out of him, or help make sense of his mumbling."

I stepped up to the bedside and flinched involuntarily. The poor guy's face was a mangled mass of cuts and bruises. He had what looked to be cigarette burns all up and down his arms. His breathing was just a series of jagged gasps. The man had not only been beaten within an inch of his life, but tortured slowly for a long time, and probably left for dead. Or even worse, left alive to suffer.

I took his hand. His eyelids were fluttering, but I had to do what I could before it was too late. "Eugenio, it's Cole Dunbar. I'm so sorry this happened to you."

I had to push him before his own black curtain came down. "Please, tell us what you know, everything you can remember."

The seconds ticked by. I figured him for a lost cause. Suddenly, he gripped my arm and a disembodied voice came out of his mouth. "Mister Cole, I tell you whole thing. Four years ago, a man come to me, want me to do a job on Wilshire, a big six-story job . . ."

Crosetti motioned his steno man over. "Get this, Nolan, every goddam word!" The guy stepped over next to me and began scribbling.

Eugenio told the same basic story he had outlined to me, but in much more detail. Somehow, even on the brink of death, he was able to detail the whole arson job, describing Swopes' hiring him, the materials he used, and how Malinsky had muscled his way into Swopes' plan after the fire. Apparently Malinsky had talked his head off even while torturing Impresa, telling him all about Mexico and how he'd paid two locals a hundred bucks each to kill Swopes and dump his body, then how he'd personally taken care of Hagemayer. He told Impresa that after killing Hagemayer with Buck Rogers' gun, killing became fun, a game, so it was a real joy to kill Buck too, then dump him and Hagemayer in the LA River together, enjoying in advance all the confusion it would cause. Oh, and setting me up for a murder charge too; he got a big kick out of that one. And the so-called Evelyn Porter? She'd only been a pawn in his scheme to frame me, a bit player, so killing her was just a minor detail in his grand plan. And finally about how Matthew Smythe was going to be the next man up on the chopping block, his usefulness at an end as soon as Malinsky got the blackmail money and prepared to skip the country.

After Impresa had made the supreme effort to tell his story, it was clear his tortured body was leaking life quickly. I'd held his hand through the whole recital. I hated to do it, but I had one more thing to ask him. I bent over him and asked softly, "Eugenio, where is Malinsky? How can we find him?"

He shook his head back and forth slowly. "He never tell me nothing about where he . . ." His body jerked in pain. Then, with one final effort, he clutched the sleeve of my jacket and whispered, "He's not a nice . . ."

Eugenio's eyes closed, finally beyond torture.

Crosetti nodded to me. "Well, if a case can be wrapped up—all but finding the perp, this is such a case."

I said, "I suppose you're right, but a man's life is still hanging in the balance. Sorry, but I've gotta go now; I have people I have to check in with." Crosetti nodded again, eyeing me suspiciously. "You just make sure you check in with me every step of the way, gumshoe; there ain't no freelancers on this case anymore."

I mumbled, "Got it," and loped down the hall. In no time I was in my car and heading down Sunset to the office in a big hurry.

"Answer World, Hattie."

"What you got for me, Hattie?"

"Oh, Mr. Dunbar, there was a call from a Mr. Woolton. Funny accent. Urgent, he says. Wants you to call him back, soon as possible. Also a Miss Smythe, sounding pretty worried. You want those numbers?"

"No, Hattie, I've got 'em, thanks."

I dialed Pete Woolton; every nerve in my body screaming for answers.

"Cole?"

"Yes. You have something for me?"

"Well, they had to give this bloke a pretty hard time to get anything out of him; he won't be having any good days for a long time. Hope that was all right."

I made myself sound calm. "No problem there. What did he spill?"

"He says this guy Malinsky's holed up with this Smythe fellow in some cheap hotel in downtown LA."

"The name, Pete, the name?"

"Oh, let's see . . . the State."

"Peter, you're a godsend. Okay, gotta go now."

"Good hunting, sport."

My first call, of course, was to Crosetti. He said he would dispatch the closest black and whites to the State immediately, and they'd button the place up good and tight until he and his men could get there and take over.

I grabbed an Eastside for the road and hightailed it out of the office.

I couldn't miss this one.

*   *   *

When I arrived, the hotel was surrounded by flashing red lights. Cops were four-deep around the front door, with lots more milling around. I even saw a KTLA news van parked across the street.

A chunky, red-faced cop with a wispy mustache and an officious manner seemed to be in charge of the front door.

"Cole Dunbar to see Lieutenant Crosetti." I flashed my license.

"No one goes in or out, buster."

"I'm a major part of this investigation, buster; check with Lieutenant Crosetti."

He jammed his nightstick between us. "The Lieutenant's a little busy right now, mister. You ain't special, you gotta wait your turn, just like *everybody* else."

Just then Crosetti's lapdog, MacIntyre, walked up behind us. "He's okay, O'Keefe, let him through."

The fat cop flushed even redder and stepped aside grudgingly to let us pass.

We rushed to the elevator. MacIntyre said, "He's on the fifth floor, 505. From what I hear, he's armed and dangerous."

I nodded. "Do tell."

The elevator doors opened and we jumped inside. I jabbed Five. The shuddering ride took forever, but when the door finally opened I saw a uniformed cop sprawled on the floor in front of 505, with only a pool of his own blood for company. Crosetti and several of his men were standing on either side of the door, guns drawn.

I approached Crosetti, whispering, "What happened?"

"We cleared all the rooms on this floor. Then I had a cop knock on Malinsky's door, on a ruse to get him to open up. But when the officer said he had a telegram for 505, the bastard plugged him right through the door."

The cop next to us muttered, "Dead as a mackerel."

Crosetti whirled on him. "That'll be enough of that!"

"Sorry, Lieutenant."

I said, "Tell me, Crosetti, Room 505 faces the street, doesn't it?"

He shrugged. "Yeah, I guess it does."

"So then the occupants of Room 505 had a clear view of the street when all your prowl cars pulled up with their flashing lights, and a sea of cops spilled out of 'em?"

Crosetti snarled, "Look, when you have a chance to apprehend a major criminal, you can't always wait for perfect circumstances!"

Suddenly we heard, "I'm coming out with the old man, but only when all you cops are out of here! One funny move and he's a dead man! You got five minutes to clear the area or I kill him anyway!"

I nodded. "Yeah, I figure the only prayer Malinsky's got left is to use the old man as a shield." I looked at Crosetti. "Well Phil, it's your show; how do you want to handle it?"

He motioned to his men and yelled, "You men clear the hallway. Everyone back down to the sidewalk!" Crosetti turned to me and whispered. "We gotta let him think he's got a clear field. I've got sharpshooters stationed in the upper floors across the street anyway; the bastard doesn't have a prayer in the Bible."

I laid a hand on his shoulder, then pointed down the hallway toward the elevator and whispered. "Look, what if I ducked into one of the empty rooms on this side, one he has to pass on his way to the elevator or the stairway? Then, after he passes me, I jump out and take him from behind, before he can react? It could be our only chance to take him, or Smythe, alive."

Crosetti shrugged. "What's the difference, dead or alive?"

"Listen Cro, I understand this guy; if he can't escape on his own terms, he'll want to go out in a blaze of glory, and he'd relish taking Smythe down with him. Can't you see, what would really kill him would be if we took him alive, made him stand trial in the face of public humiliation, then finally put him to death, all on *our* terms."

Crosetti's face fell. "Damn you, this is a police operation now. Why don't you let the experts handle it?"

"Because it's been my show for months now, Crosetti, and you know it. I deserve this chance." I looked him in the eye. "Phil, I *need* this."

He licked his lips. "Damn you, Dunbar, if the Chief finds out I let a private . . ."

I grabbed his hand and shook it. "You won't regret it, I promise."

I tiptoed down the hallway and quietly opened the door to 501. It was the last room before Malinsky and Smythe would hit the elevator or the stairway. I entered the room, nodded to Crosetti, then cracked the door just enough so I could see a flash of movement when they went by. They'd be crossing my field of vision from right to left.

Crosetti waited a moment, then yelled through the door. "Okay Malinsky, this is Lieutenant Crosetti. I'm the last man out. When I go downstairs, you'll be alone on this floor. You hear me?"

"Yeah, I hear ya. Get moving. And no tricks, or the geezer's a dead man!"

I could hear Crosetti taking the stairs two at a time.

Then all was quiet.

I didn't move a muscle. Should I carry my .38? No, too unwieldy for hand to hand combat. I unbuckled it and placed it quietly on the floor; I wanted this guy alive, and I'd need both hands to do it. Besides, once I separated him from his own gun, I could always use it on him later. It felt like the moment before an assault on Okinawa: the metallic taste in your mouth, the jumpy muscles, trying hard to suppress the terror. *This is your chance to make up for Danny.*

Now I could hear raspy breathing. I didn't know if it was Malinsky or Matthew Smythe, but it was clearly audible. Then a voice croaked, "You're hurting me!" and I didn't have to guess who that was.

I focused on the crack in the door fiercely. Suddenly there it was, the flash of two bodies going past the opening.

I eased the door open, gathered myself, then leaped onto Malinsky's back from behind, ripping him away from Smythe and wrestling him down. His gun clattered to the floor and spun away down the bare wood in a blur of silver. As we grappled together he fastened on my ear and almost bit it off, scratching and kicking in a frenzy. He was smaller than me but wiry, and supercharged with the high-voltage power of a madman.

Finally I got him pinned to the floor. I grabbed him by the collar and yanked him to his feet. "Stand up, you little shit. It's good to finally see you as you really are—a little nothing, a pathetic loser. You thought you could just kill your way to three hundred thousand dollars? Well, guess again."

I looked over to Mr. Smythe, looking pale and wan. I nodded toward the elevator. "Please get in the elevator and go down Mr. Smythe. Your daughter's been waiting a long time for this moment." The old man entered the empty car and the door closed.

But Malinsky was talking now. Even as I kept a choke hold on his thrashing body, he sneered, "It took you long enough to find me, you two-bit keyhole-peeper." He cackled. "I outsmarted you—you and the stupid cops, at every turn. And by the way, did you enjoy all the nice beatings I bought for you?"

I said, "You creep, taking lives means nothing to you, does it?"

He was still cackling. "Once I killed Swopes, I saw how easy it was to make things right in life. Instead of sitting back like a little mouse, praying for the breaks, I realized I could make my *own* breaks: bing bang boom."

"Is that what you call murder, you little bastard? Bing bang boom?"

Suddenly with a violent twist, he wrenched free and launched himself at his gun, lying there on the floor six feet away.

I dove after him and grabbed his feet, then braced myself and whipped his body around like a discus thrower, until his head was facing the elevator. Then I yanked him to his feet again, still thrashing and spitting out words as fast as he could talk. When he tried to lunge at me again I drew back and nailed him with the most satisfying Sunday punch of my life.

Malinsky slumped to the floor, out cold. I'd waited months to hang that one on him. His big mouth was finally shut, his bloody killing spree over. I knew it wouldn't bring back the dead, but it felt awful good.

Somewhere, Danny Trueluck was smiling.

Bing bang boom.

Chapter Twenty-One

It was time to meet the press. It was several weeks later; Malinsky was behind bars, the DA was hot to trot for the prosecution, and the Chief had played up the case big in the papers, angling to squeeze all the publicity he could for the Department (and Himself) out of it. In accordance, he had called a massive press conference to tell the story of the case. It was come one, come all, with Lieutenant (soon to be Captain) Crosetti and the Homicide Squad front and center, of course. The Smythes were invited to tell their breathless tale of blackmail and kidnapping, not to mention that the Department was taking the opportunity, at long last, to publicly give Matthew Smythe a clean bill of health as far as any suspicion of arson. Kitty Stacker was brought in to make an appearance as the bereaved daughter of poor, guiltless Arnold Hagemayer. Even Buck Rogers' ex-wife agreed to appear on the dais too, to attest to her former husband's courageous pursuit of the fiend.

And lastly, Cole Dunbar, the intrepid private eye who'd helped the LAPD crack the case, and Marie O'Malley, the girl scientist with both brains and beauty, were also on hand to add a little color to the reporters' stories.

Oh, and Leonard Malinsky even had a new name—cooked up behind the scenes by the Chief's publicity men, of course. Since Malinsky had written the *Town Beat* column, he was now dubbed, "The Newspaper Killer."

The Chief, speaking from notes prepared by his staff, talked at length about the case: the terror and tragedy the Smythes had endured, the murders that kept piling up, the advanced technological assistance that he'd personally authorized (he stumbled over the words gas chromatography several times), and the final citywide manhunt that had resulted in the capture of the Newspaper Killer and the safe return of Matthew Smythe to the bosom of his family.

I have to give the Chief his due, he was a powerful speaker. As I stood up front with the other principals, I watched the reporters writing furiously on their pads, gasping in horror, and even weeping as the Chief detailed the litany of atrocities that Leonard Malinsky left in his wake.

My favorite part was when the Chief said, "In her desperation, Miss Smythe finally turned to Mr. Cole Dunbar, one of our most capable local private investigators. But despite doing a fine job of assembling some preliminary building blocks, Mr. Dunbar finally had to concede that such a challenging case cried out for the vast resources and unparalleled expertise of one of the greatest law enforcement organizations in this nation: the Los Angeles Police Department!"

On cue, the audience rose for a standing ovation, as the Chief beamed and waved in papal benediction.

I took my bows and played the game. I was gracious in giving Crosetti and the Chief the majority of the credit. I waved, smiled and posed for endless group photos of my "good side": my left ear was still heavily bandaged from the twenty stitches it took to reattach it. I was glad to get some of the credit, but in my innermost thoughts I knew that some of the real heroes of the case, though they weren't present, were right there with me in spirit: Pete Woolton, the Aussie with persuasive friends in low places; Eugenio Impresa, the artisan of arson, who gave his life because he'd talked to me; Dick and Brenda, who were willing to risk his career to help a friend; Doc Grimes, who taught me things I was just beginning to understand; and little Pedro, the Mexican niño who nursed me so lovingly for a week, then steered me to the back-alley irregulars and ultimately Lionel Swopes' lonely grave. And of course Bert Fawcett, the tough mobster with a heart of gold who was the closest I was ever to come to a father figure.

When the formal ceremony was over, it was time for all of us to mingle with the reporters, helping them get the "personal angle" on the case. A small knot of them gathered around me and Marie, jockeying for position. One of them called out, "So, what did you think when Monique Smythe first came in to your office?" Then another one jumped in. "Hey Dunbar, when did you know it was gonna be too big for you?"

I smiled to myself, but gave safe and careful answers, going along with the Chief's slant that after some preliminary detective work, I handed the ball off to Lieutenant Crosetti, whose men ran it in for the touchdown. After all, I didn't need the credit; ever since the Malinsky arrest hit the papers, my office phone had been ringing off the hook. Hattie and Stella kidded me that my calls were monopolizing their whole day, but their kidding was on the square.

A woman reporter looked Marie up and down, then yelled out. "I hear you were a big help, honey. They tell me you work over at Pink's. So I guess you mostly kept the buns warm for him, huh?"

Before I could stop her, the Irish anger rose in Marie's cheeks and she snapped, "Well actually, I was the one who realized that advanced analysis by gas chromatography and mass spectrometry might pinpoint the accelerant in the Smythe arson case. Which it *did*." She planted her hands on her hips. "Does that answer your question, *honey*?"

After that, it seemed to me the reporters gave her a wide berth.

Finally all the interviews were over and the camera guys had shot every pose they could think up. Everyone involved in the case was invited to a special fancy-dress, sit-down dinner hosted by the Chief at the Cocoanut Grove at eight o'clock that night.

I spent the rest of the day in the office, fielding calls from potential clients. I don't know which was worse, being an unknown like I was before, or what I was now, the famous miracle-worker who'd helped nab the Newspaper Killer. My new callers all assumed that good results were a foregone conclusion. The newspaper that was delivered to my office that day even carried a big picture of me with the caption:

NEWSPAPER KILLER GUMSHOE TO ATTEND SWANK COPFEST

I finally had to knock off around five, if I was going to have time for the final fitting of my tux at Mister Gino's, the formalwear place a couple of doors down Sunset, and then pick up Marie in time for the dinner. I walked down the street and opened the door to the shop.

"Mister Dunbar? I am Gino, the proprietor." He said, "Permit me," and took off my sport coat. "You famous man now; I personally give you a nice fitting, an *expert* fitting. You gonna wow the girls wherever you go in this clothes, *anywhere* else!"

And with that, Gino and his two assistants swarmed over me, trying on this and measuring that while clucking and muttering to each other in Italian the whole time. Within an hour I'd been fitted for the tux, shoes and socks, a white shirt and tie. The whole thing took a lot longer than I expected.

Finally, Gino walked me over to the multiple mirrors for the unveiling, sweeping his arm to say, "Ecco qui!"

Of course I didn't say it, but to me, I looked like what they used to call Dewey in the '48 election: "The little man on the wedding cake."

I thanked Gino profusely and carried my old things back to the lot.

"George, please bring my car around, would you?"

He stood back, looking at me for a second. "Wow, Mr. D. you're a real knock-out, you are."

I laughed. "I know, I'm gonna wow the girls wherever I go in this clothes."

By the time I got the Ford rolling, it was already six forty-five.

I weaved through heavy traffic as fast as I could and finally pulled into Marie's driveway close to seven thirty. As I walked up the front pathway I hoped she wouldn't be mad; but then I remembered that guests are expected to be "fashionably late" for formal affairs.

I rang the bell.

The woman who opened the door was spectacular.

She stepped back into the light of the living room and turned around in her stunning evening gown. "You like?"

I said, "Like? Are you sure you're even a real woman? You sure you don't come from some other planet, where they've perfected a species of aliens that are beyond beautiful?"

She laughed. "Nope, just shanty Irish, through and through."

I took her arm. "Wow, even Gino never heard of *you*!"

"Who?"

"Oh sorry, nobody."

I went around and opened the car door for her, then got in behind the wheel and we were off.

On the way, she said, "I hope you appreciate that I'm missing *The Enchanted Cottage* on TV tonight to attend this Hail to the Chief clambake."

I nodded. "I know, sorry."

After a while, she looked over at my outfit and put her hand on my leg. "By the way, you're a pretty nifty alien yourself."

Somehow, I felt her touch in a different way, like I'd reoccupied my own body.

The dinner turned out to be another public coronation for the Chief, as he sat there preening at the head table, surrounded by higher-ups in city and state government, the DA, connected fat cats and society royalty. I guess I'd been right about being fashionably late, because people were still drifting in long after we'd been seated.

At one point Marie nudged me and pointed discreetly. "Well, wouldya look what the cat drug in!"

It was Monique Smythe, in a clingy, gold lamé gown, smothered in jewels, making a grand entrance, with all eyes on her.

Marie's eyes crinkled. "Sure you wouldn't rather be with Queenie?"

I smiled. "Positive, and let this be the last of that particular line of questioning, counselor."

She turned to me with a Cheshire cat smile. "We'll discuss it in chambers."

Unfortunately for me, the issue wasn't quite resolved yet. Monique swept over to me, making sure all eyes were following her, then stood there in front of me and threw her arms out dramatically, forcing me to rise and embrace her as she cooed loudly, "Thank you, thank you, thank you, Mr. Dunbar, for all you did for father and me. You'll be in my prayers, always and forever."

My God, how could I ever have been attracted to such a . . .

I disentangled myself from her as quickly as possible. "You're very welcome, Miss Smythe. I only did my job."

There was a smattering of mandatory applause from the surrounding guests as Marie kicked me, hard, under the table.

The dinner was a huge success, at least for the Chief. He stood and gave another speech, once again limning the greatness of the LAPD, the need for more funding and public support for his glorious crusade against the "undermining elements" in society, by which I assume he meant the Communists hiding under every bed, and maybe the non-whites bent on infiltrating our pure neighborhoods.

Afterwards, the Chief and his assistants formed a kind of reception line at the head table, with the Chief at the very end, so that everyone would have a chance to shuffle by one at a time and personally greet and thank him. I had only met him that one time, when Phil Crosetti and I went in and laid the bombshell on him.

As honored guests, Marie and I were ushered close to the head of the line, and after a while we worked our way up to the Deputy Chief.

I put out my hand. "Hello, sir, I'm Cole Dunbar. Pleased to meet you." I gestured to Marie. "And this is Marie. She has helped me in so many ways."

He nodded to us. "Very pleased to meet you both."

Marie dug me in the ribs and whispered, "*That's* all you have to say about me, that I was daddy's little helper? You're *kidding*!"

Oops. Next up was the Chief. I put my hand out again. "Hello, Chief. Cole Dunbar, as you may remember. Pleased to see you again, under better cir-cumstances. You certainly gave a fine speech at the press conference today."

The Chief smiled. "You have to remember son, in life everything is the story; the man who controls the story is the winner."

I put my arm around Marie. "And this, sir, is Professor Marie O'Malley, the esteemed chemist who was my associate and scientific adviser throughout the entire investigation." I smiled. "And someday, if I'm lucky, maybe even my wife."

I felt her body give a little judder.

The Chief regarded her. "Well, Miss O'Malley, I was told you were quite a remarkable woman, and you certainly live up to your rave notices."

*   *   *

On the spur of the moment, Marie and I decided to take a stroll before driving home. We'd grown a lot closer in the last weeks as I gradually got used to her caring, and we didn't really need words anymore to feel connected. Besides, I knew she was thinking about what I'd said to the Chief. I also knew that, as a scientist, she wouldn't say anything until she'd thought it all out.

As we walked along hand in hand, I felt a chilly tingle in the air. The stubborn heat of that year's endless summer was finally loosening its grip on the big city, and some of the more precocious leaves were even starting to turn. There was a bright half moon above the trees, but I was looking somewhere beyond the trees, beyond the moon, beyond battlefields, beyond time and space, and suddenly I knew that, like the characters in that Dickens book Mom used to read me, I too was being recalled to life.

I pulled out a Camel and fired it up, but after one drag I tossed it; I wanted to breathe fresh air for a change. I was noticing things again, as if my senses had been restored to me and were open for business again. I heard the songbirds broadcasting their twilight wrap-up in the trees above us, and watched some windblown trash dancing a jagged conga down the sidewalk. Was it just my imagination, or was the world saying welcome back?

A small knot of teenage boys was roughhousing with each other on the grass in the middle of a grove of giant eucalyptus, and the rising breeze sliced the sharp tang of camphor through the night air. One of the boys stood up as we passed, smiling at the overdressed couple out for an evening stroll. God, he looked an awful lot like Danny. We nodded to each other. Suddenly another line from *Ask the Dust* sprang to my mind, bringing a quiet smile with it:

Are the dead restored? The books say no, the night shouts yes!

Marie had been quiet, deep in thought, as we walked along. But at that moment she squeezed my hand and said, "You know, with a little seasoning in the minors, you just might turn out to be the Steve Bilko of love after all."

*   *   *

Danny Trueluck used to say his name would bring him good fortune. Doc Grimes says life moves on and you move on with it. The Chief says the one who tells the story is the winner. And people in LA will bend your ear with all kinds of legends about the hunt for the Newspaper Killer.

Well, I suppose there's some truth in all of it, but this is *my* story of what happened in that long summer of '56, the year the Angels won the pennant, arson hit the headlines, and Danny Trueluck and I finally came home.

So I guess that makes me the winner.